For my husband Geoffrey

BOUNDARIES

A LOVE STORY

CHRISTINE Z. MASON

BOUNDARIES: A LOVE STORY

This is a work of fiction. Names, characters, places and incidents are the products of the author's imagination or are used fictitiously. Any resemblance to actual events, locales, or persons, living or dead, is entirely coincidental.

Published in the United States and meets CPSIA requirements.

PPB ISBN: 978-1-61170-167-8
Library of Congress Control Number: 2013948344

FIRST PAPERBACK EDITION

To purchase additional copies of this book to go:

amazon.com
barnesandnoble.com
www.rp-author.com/cmason

Everything is for you: my daily prayer,
And the thrilling fever of the insomniac,
And the blue fire of my eyes,
And my poems, that white flock.

—Anna Akhmatova

(Excerpt, ["I don't know if you're living or dead—"]
The Complete Poems of Anna Akhmatova, 1989)

PART ONE

PINE TREE ISLAND

CAPE COD

SUMMER 1980

1

Afraid she'd been forgotten, Kaia Matheson stepped onto the dock and searched for the boat that was supposed to take her across the channel to Pine Tree Island. Though it was early July on the Cape, the air was cold and damp, and she shivered, hugging her arms in the buffeting wind. Bulging, steel-gray clouds hung in the sky, casting shadows over the choppy waves. She could barely make out the island, obscured in the distance by a white haze.

During the long taxi ride from the Boston airport to the Cape Cod dock, she'd pictured her mother waiting for her, but when the driver had finally pulled into the gravel lot, no one was there, and it caused an ache in the pit of her stomach; the only car in the lot was a rusted old Saab. Kaia had asked the taxi driver to wait for her until someone came to take her across the channel—he'd snorted in exasperation before turning off the engine.

Now, shifting from one foot to the other to warm herself, she wished she'd worn jeans instead of shorts for the plane trip. Luckily she was wearing her denim jacket. At last she spotted a small boat bucking against the waves, its male occupant rowing in the direction of the dock, and as the boat came closer, she saw that the man appeared to be using his entire strength against the water's pull. There was a quality of fierceness, an emphatic determination in his rowing, that made her recognize her cousin, Mark Karadonis.

When he glanced in her direction, she waved, and he continued to lever his upper body resolutely against the waves. She hadn't seen him in eight years; he would be twenty-two now, a grown man, she realized nervously, and more or less a stranger to her.

She jogged back to the taxi and paid the driver. He drove off, the tires flinging gravel behind the car, as if in reproach. Returning to the dock, Kaia watched as Mark rowed toward her, and her disappointment at not seeing her mother fell away. When the boat pulled alongside the dock, he stood up, appearing flushed and exhilarated, and grabbed onto a post. Despite the gloom of the afternoon, he was wearing dark shades. A slight growth of beard shadowed the lower half of his face. It amazed her, how tall he was—six feet at least—and massive in the shoulders. When she'd last seen him, he was fourteen and she was eight; she remembered him as rather wild and disobedient—often getting into trouble with his dad—and she'd admired the way Mark seemed to get away with so much.

"There's a stiff southwesterly," he said, without any preliminaries, staring at her through his dark glasses.

He was a man, she would learn, who didn't put much stock in preliminaries. She hesitated a moment, thinking he might offer a hand, but he merely motioned for her to come down, as if he expected a teenage girl to know everything about boats and how to board them. But she sensed a certain restraint in the way he simply watched her, his arms tensed at his sides, as if ready to assist if needed, and this pleased her.

Kaia tossed her duffel bag to him and peered into the algae-green seawater. She stepped gingerly into the boat, causing it to rock unnervingly. Mark reached out and clasped his fingers firmly around her upper arm until she was steady on her feet. He stepped back and did a quick scan of her from her bare legs upward, stopping for a second at her midriff, which was partially exposed beneath her halter top. She buttoned her jacket, her fingers trembling, then looked up to study his face, his expression hard to read behind the sunglasses. His arms and legs were padded with muscle, his legs sunburnt; he didn't appear to be the slightest bit cold in his tank top and cut-offs—he was probably used to the cool summer weather here.

She sat down, and he took a seat on the opposite bench. As he pushed off from the dock, she wondered why he wasn't using the outboard motor; but she didn't ask, afraid to expose her ignorance.

"California tan," he commented, flashing a grin at her. "New denims, too," he added, indicating with a nod her shorts and jacket.

Embarrassed by his scrutiny, she turned her head to the side as the boat moved out onto the waves. "I'm naturally dark," was all she could think to say.

It would have been easier if her father had flown here with her; she wouldn't have been so anxious, waiting alone at the dock. Of course he hadn't been invited, because of the divorce. She'd promised to call him when she arrived at Logan Airport but had forgotten in her frantic search for a taxi. And there would be no phone at the cottage on Pine Tree. She would have to send him a postcard later—otherwise he would be upset about not hearing from her.

Glancing at her cousin, she was sorry she couldn't see his eyes behind the shades. Her mother had once remarked that Mark's eyes were as blue as glaciers, exactly like Kaia's. People always noticed Kaia's eye color, apparently her one remarkable feature.

"I guess you were the only one who was available to row over to get me." She cocked her head, trying for a disdainful look, but a gust of wind blew her long hair into a tangle over her face, spoiling the intended effect. She wished she were more in control, the way Mark was, pulling the oars through the water with such sturdy competence.

"My father's out boating with my buddy, Monty, so I was the only one around. I don't mind, though. I like to be out on the water when it's like this."

She silently watched him row for a few minutes, then said, "I heard you graduated from Boston University."

"Yep. Monty and I are both headed for law school in the fall."

"Dad said you'll be in Berkeley, going to Boalt."

"Right. But for now I'm just trying to enjoy the summer while I can. I'm not looking forward to the grind of studying again." He was quiet for a minute, then broke into a grin. "Last time I saw you, your dad was giving you a spanking."

"Oh, my God." It was the summer the Karadonises had come to Berkeley, when she was eight. Her uncle and her father had been lounging on the deck that day, drinking beer and smoking, and Kaia had grabbed her dad's cigarette pack from his hand and run into the yard with it. Her father had yelled at Mark, who was up in the tree house, to go get her. Mark, a lanky teenager then, had jumped down and begun chasing Kaia through the high grass. When he caught her, he half-dragged, half-carried her over to the deck while she screamed and struggled. Her father reached for her, pried the cigarette pack from her fist, swung her over his knees and slapped her bottom hard a few times while Mark and his father watched.

"I thought I could make Dad quit smoking," she said, trying for a sardonic tone. "They must have been drunk. It was awful." Where had her mother and aunt been? They'd never once come outside, hadn't been around when the men got boisterous. After the humiliation of the spanking, Kaia had been wary, though intrigued, whenever the men were out on the deck; she always sensed she was in for something when she got too close. She'd been drawn to them out of curiosity, she supposed . . . or was it just boredom? At least her father hadn't spanked her in front of the relatives again.

"Don't worry," Mark said now, barely suppressing a grin. "We won't try anything like that here. As long as you behave."

"That's not funny, Mark. I'm sixteen, you know."

She leaned over the side and dragged her fingers through the slick saltwater. Where had he learned to tease like that? He didn't have any brothers or sisters. It was the only thing the two of them had in common—their lack of siblings—except, of course, that their mothers were sisters.

"Where's my mother, by the way?" she asked, making her hand resist the pull of the water.

"Back at the house with Elisa, drinking iced tea on the porch."

Kaia lifted her hand from the water and shook it off. She wondered why he'd referred to his mother as Elisa. "Why didn't my mom come with you?" she asked.

"Jean doesn't like boating."

"I suppose that's true. She likes tennis and golf. Better for business."

Mark kept his eyes on her, no doubt catching the bitterness in her tone. He looked away and maneuvered the boat over a large swell, then once they were in a calmer stretch of water, he glanced at her and said, "You haven't seen your mom in a while, have you?"

Startled by his bluntness, Kaia glanced down, focusing on his hands as he rowed; they were an older person's hands, thick and wide with prominent veins. Still avoiding his gaze, she raised her eyes to the brown tufts of hair sprouting from beneath his tank top. She wasn't willing to admit it had been six months since she'd seen her mother—as if that were her own fault.

It was sickening, how swiftly her mother had managed to get a divorce, then relocate to Manhattan—a move she'd claimed would "present more opportunities," whatever that meant. Kaia recalled her mother standing at the curb beside the taxicab, briefcase in hand, waving good-bye. Her mother had promised to keep in close contact, but of course it hadn't turned out that way. There had been the sporadic phone calls, and then finally in June her mom had mentioned she was spending a couple of weeks at Cape Cod and didn't suppose Kaia could fly out on her own.

Kaia remembered how quickly she'd jumped at the offhand invitation—how pitiful. Now she wondered what she could have done to be more exciting, engaging enough to keep her mother's interest. Even with her father around, their house felt rather empty. What would have made her mother stay?

Kaia wondered, too, what could possibly make her return.

Once they'd docked at Pine Tree, Kaia tramped up the weather-beaten boardwalk while Mark strode on ahead, carrying her duffel bag. He had an athletic walk, and his back and shoulders were broad and solid. As they passed fields of marsh grasses, blown into whorls and scattered with orange wildflowers, an updraft of misty air gusted against Kaia's legs and neck. The air felt deliciously moist on her skin, and was milder here than on the channel.

She hurried to catch up with Mark at a fork in the walkway. An enormous brown house sat amongst the trees in the distance, a white boat cocked against its side. "Where's the cottage?" she asked.

"You're looking at it."

"You're kidding. You call that a cottage?"

"I never kid." He placed his hand on her back, startling her with its welcome warmth and heaviness.

She squinted up at him. "Thanks for coming to get me."

He nodded and motioned for her to go on ahead.

When the boardwalk ended, they hiked up a dirt path, passing an orchard of dwarf apple trees and a garden of corn and vegetables, then they stopped to watch the crows circling over the garden. Kaia wanted to stay here with Mark for a few more moments, inhaling the grass-scented breeze, but he turned and started up the path again.

Soon she caught the sound of women's voices carrying over the field, and spotted her mother and Elisa sitting on the porch, as if they'd been painted into a picture of the old, shingled house.

Suddenly her mother stood up and came forward. "Kaia!" she shouted in her contralto voice, then walked down a few steps.

"Hi, Mom," Kaia called as she approached. She climbed up the stairs to receive her mother's quick hug and peck on the cheek, and caught her familiar fragrance, like spice cake. Her mother's hair was brown and shorter now, feathered around her face—much more chic than her previous frosted-blond look. She wore a gray, button-up blouse, a white skirt and a paisley scarf—rather conservative for a vacation, Kaia thought.

"How was your trip, sweetheart?" her mother asked as they climbed the steps together, with Mark coming up behind them.

"All right."

At the top of the stairs, her mother looked her up and down. "You're taller," she said in an approving tone.

Was that all she could say? "I don't think so," Kaia mumbled. How could she possibly have grown much in the half-year since her mother had left? And what was so great about being big, anyway? Her mother and aunt were both quite tall—five-foot-nine, admittedly more imposing than Kaia's five-foot-three. Their height was the main thing that made the two women appear at all like sisters.

Elisa strolled over with her arms outstretched and hugged Kaia, holding her in a firm embrace for several seconds. Kaia had forgotten how comforting it felt to have her aunt's arms around her. Up close Elisa looked anemically pale, but her long, curly hair was a vibrant red, in startling contrast to her face. She wore a flowing lime-green dress.

"I haven't seen you since when?" Elisa asked in her lovely mellifluous voice. "Christmas, three years ago?"

Kaia nodded. For reasons she never understood, her mother had usually made her trips to see the Karadonises at their home in Maine during the school year, when Kaia and her father couldn't accompany her. The Christmas Kaia and her parents had all flown East was the only time the two families had been together for the holidays, except that Mark had been off skiing in Vermont.

Her cousin now leaned with his forearm propped against a post, exposing his bushy underarm hair, and pointed to Kaia's duffel bag, which sat on the porch. "Where should I put that?" he asked his mother.

"Kaia can have the room next to Jean's. Would you take it upstairs, please, darling?"

"Sure," he said and winked at Kaia as he turned toward the house.

"Mark's friend Monty is here, by the way," her mother said. "He's out fishing with your Uncle Nico. You'll get to meet him later."

"Great." Kaia turned to her aunt. "Could I go inside and take a look around?"

"Of course, my dear." Elisa came over and placed her cool hands on Kaia's cheeks, kissing her on the forehead. "It's your home, too. I'm just so glad you're here."

"Thanks, Elisa."

Following her mother into the house, Kaia stepped into the ample front room, taking in the smell of leather and old wood. They stood together while Kaia surveyed the room. A sofa and several armchairs encircled a rock fireplace, and the burnished mahogany floor gave an ancient, rich feel to the room; it was a room made for drinking tea and reading. There was nothing at all synthetic here. No television set, of course, since there was no electricity, so no one would be watching the stock market report every night. Kaia imagined having little chats with her mother in front of the fireplace, a fire burning in the evenings.

"So this is the summer cottage," she said.

"Yes, Nico's family has owned it forever."

"I take it you've been here before."

"A few times, over the years," her mother said.

"It's so beautiful here. I had no idea." Kaia was curious about the trips her mother had taken to the island, but this wasn't the time to ask. "How's Manhattan, Mom?"

"Fabulous. You'll have to come visit." Her mother stepped closer to Kaia and placed her arm stiffly around her shoulders.

"Do you miss Berkeley?"

"I'm doing all right." Her mother's voice had a clipped edge to it, as if she thought Kaia was leading up to something.

In fact she *was* leading up to something, like when in the hell was her mother going to visit her in Berkeley? But now her mom had dropped her arm and was easing away, obviously finished with tedious questions. Kaia wondered why she had missed her mother so much. Her mom had never been around much, at least during the last few years. Since she'd become a realtor, she was always out showing properties, closing deals, celebrating a big sale. Whatever you did, the important thing was to maintain contacts—her mother's manifesto. How ironic.

"You'll find your room upstairs; Mark can show you where it is," her mother said. "Nico and Monty will be coming back in the boat soon. I'll go out to watch for them."

Kaia headed up the stairs. On the second floor, she strolled down the hallway, peering through several open doorways until she found the bedroom with her duffel bag on the floor. Entering the room, she took in the narrow bed and antique writing table. She liked the room's spareness, and, stepping to the window, was struck by the expansive view of the ocean with its muted teals and grays. The island seemed like a place Thoreau would have loved; she thought he'd even spent time at Cape Cod—he must have liked its peaceful landscape and isolation.

Thinking she had heard a creaking outside the room, she strode into the hallway and again searched the upper floor. But unless Mark was behind one of the closed doors, he was not around. Disappointed, she headed for the bathroom at the end of the hall to freshen up, before going down to join the others.

2

Mark scraped the ashes from the grill and loaded it with charcoal, then started up the fire. Grabbing a Schlitz, his third since he'd come out to the front lawn, he told himself he'd have to take it easy; he didn't want to sport a paunch like his father. He hadn't lifted weights since training for wrestling matches last spring.

He got a good fire going, then gazed out over the channel. His father and Monty should be coming in soon, hopefully with a catch they could grill. From time to time, his mother strolled down from the house with Jean, the two women carrying plates, baskets of bread and side dishes to the picnic table on the lawn. Over the past few days he'd seen his mother throw herself frantically into her constant food preparation, but she seemed calmer this afternoon, less submerged in her various sanity-saving chores. At least she wasn't drinking as much. Why they kept booze in the house he never understood. Something to do with the family's mindless New England traditionalism, maybe—maintaining the selection of brandies and liqueurs in the rear parlor, the display of glistening bottleware a fixture of the Karadonis summer-cottage lifestyle.

This morning when his mother had suggested they put on a barbecue to celebrate Kaia's arrival, Mark hadn't cared one way or another; his mother was always suggesting they celebrate every conceivable thing. He'd just wanted to be on his own, take in the fresh air and enjoy being outdoors. But after retrieving Kaia at the dock, he'd surprised himself with his enthusiasm for the idea of a family barbecue. His first impression, having not seen his cousin in so many years, was that she'd certainly grown up, but didn't seem very sure of herself. He pictured the way she looked on the boat with her brown hair flying around in the wind. There was a slight gap between her two front teeth that showed when she smiled. He wondered if she had any idea how smooth her skin looked, or how beautiful she was, with her unusually pretty face and curvy body.

Mark was glad he hadn't brought Barb Scott with him to the island. Earlier in the summer she'd asked him in her usual direct way if she could come with him, but he'd felt uncomfortable with the idea and had said no. She was a tall, big-boned girl with a flat-cheeked face and assertive green eyes, and had some heft to her that felt good in bed. She was always drinking milk. She was calm and steady, which was what he needed—someone uncomplicated, as different from his mother as possible. But since graduation, she'd been living back home in Chicago and he'd come to realize that he didn't miss seeing her.

Elisa came down again from the house carrying a platter laden with ears of corn and set it next to the grill. Raising her hand to shade her eyes, she looked out toward the water, her red hair scattering over her shoulders in the breeze. Even standing next to him, his mother seemed alone in her thoughts.

"Oh good, there's the boat," she said softly.

Mark spotted their nineteen-foot Lightning as it veered into the wind, its sails luffing. He threw the corn on the grill and poked at the glowing coals.

By the time Nico and Monty had tied up the boat, Elisa was down at the dock, exclaiming about the string of fish Nico was holding up. Monty came up the dock carrying his gear bag and rod. He looked almost comical with his long, pale legs, bony knees and bushy hair.

"What did you catch?" Mark shouted.

"Stripers!" Monty yelled back.

Glamour fish, Mark thought. Lucky. Guys around here stayed up nights trying to catch them. At least his father and Monty had something to show for being out on the water all day.

Mark heard a rustling in the grass, and Kaia appeared next to him. She wasn't wearing her jacket, and he couldn't help noticing her tropical fragrance and the way her belly sloped into her shorts, as well as the fact that her breasts were half-exposed in her skimpy top. Maybe she was naturally dark, as she'd said, or maybe she was tan from lying around in the California sun in a bikini. Jesus, he had to stop thinking like that. But why did girls dress that way and make themselves smell so good if they didn't want you to notice them? Groaning quietly, he fingered the guitar pick in his pocket, then squeezed it hard. This was just his innocent little cousin, he reminded himself.

Kaia peered up at him, smiling.

He tipped his head toward Monty. "That's my buddy."

Monty dropped his gear on the ground and came over. Bending toward Kaia—he was six-foot-five—he grinned and extended his hand.

"Hello, I'm Monty," he said.

Smiling back at him, she shook his hand. "Hi Monty. I'm Kaia."

"So I gathered. I hear you flew by yourself from California."

"Yep, I did."

"She's sixteen," Mark said. "Girls do that, they fly in airplanes by themselves now. We even let them vote later on."

Monty laughed, showing his large, crooked teeth. "Right."

Kaia had started shivering a bit; she had goose bumps on her arms. "Mark came to get me in his rowboat," she said.

"*Did* he." Monty glanced at Mark, raising his eyebrows. "What a cutie your cousin is."

"Monty thinks he's the expert on these things," Mark said to Kaia, who was blushing. "In this case, though, he's got a point."

She turned toward the dock, hooking her thumbs into the rear pockets of her shorts. More than cute, Mark thought, and Monty had better keep his eyes and hands off.

"The coals are ready," Mark yelled to his father, who was strolling up the dock with Elisa on his arm, her long dress flapping in the wind.

Kaia glanced at Mark. "Your parents look good together," she said quietly.

Mark liked her familiarity; she didn't seem as shy now. She probably saw his parents as a happy couple, walking arm-in-arm together. But she didn't know about his parents' screaming matches, or about Elisa sneaking a drink or two in spite of what it did to her, especially mixed with her medication. All of which sometimes made Mark wish he'd stayed in Boston.

"Hey, looks like a decent catch," he shouted to his father.

"Wait until you taste them," Nico yelled back, and Elisa lifted her head, laughing.

"Time to throw them suckers on the fire," Mark said.

He and Monty took the metallic-skinned fish from Nico and hauled them over to the cleaning stand. Mark glanced over as his father gave Kaia a hug, lifting her off the ground while she linked her arms around his neck and kissed him on the cheek. Lucky bastard, Mark thought.

"You should have gone fishing with us," Monty said to Mark. "It was great."

Nico came over to them, with Kaia beside him. "Mark has already caught his limit," he said.

"I don't really care about legal limits," Mark said.

"You should, if you don't want to be cited," his father said.

"To hell with that. You catch as much as you plan to eat. Makes it simple." Mark grabbed one of the fish, preparing to clean it, taking pleasure in the feel of the cold, scaly skin and the pungent smell of the striper.

"Some laws are there for a reason," Monty said, grinning as if he'd said something profound.

Mark grunted. Monty always liked to discuss the legality of a situation, especially since they'd both decided to go to law school.

"Monty," Mark said, "why don't you just shut up and help me clean the goddamned fish." He was used to sparring with Monty, and usually tolerated his excessive enthusiasm pretty well, but felt a little annoyed for some reason. Mark at times imagined tossing him onto the wrestling mat and pinning him down, just to wipe that toothy grin from his face.

⁂

Kaia turned and sprinted up the path to the cottage to change clothes. It was past six o'clock, and the sky was clouding up again, a robust breeze chilling her bare arms and legs. Up in her room, she shut the door and leaned her head back against it, catching her breath, then rummaged around in her duffel bag until she found the burgundy sweater her mother had left behind in Berkeley. She pulled it on, slipped into a pair of jeans, and ran downstairs, stopping in front of the mirror in the foyer to smooth down her wild mass of hair.

The front door flew open suddenly and her uncle came up behind her.

"What do you see in there, Kaia?" he asked, smiling.

She met his eyes in the mirror, then whirled around to face him. "Just me."

He laid a hand on her shoulder. "Come and talk to me. I haven't seen you in so long."

She allowed herself to be steered into the front room, where he gently nudged her into an armchair. He crossed over to a table set with a crystal decanter and glasses, poured out a drink, then, hesitating for just a second, poured some of the liquor into another glass. He came over and offered her a goblet.

"A little cognac, Kaia? You're old enough—seventeen this November, right?" He stood there, staring down at her.

Surprised that he knew when her birthday was, she met his eyes before accepting the bulbous glass. "Sure. Dad lets me have wine with dinner." But she was also aware that cognac was quite different from a glass of wine with dinner.

Nico sat down and drank from his snifter. He was a handsome man, with aqua-blue eyes that contrasted with his swarthy face and dark hair, his features striking, like a movie star. He didn't much resemble Mark, who had a more rugged face, although the two men had the same eye color, similar to Kaia's—she'd forgotten that about her uncle. He wasn't even a blood relative of hers; he was just married to Aunt Elisa.

He asked her about her flight, and about her studies, then said, "Couldn't you stay longer than ten days? Elisa and I plan to be here until early August."

"I have to be back by the twenty-third, for Dad's birthday."

"What a shame." Nico stroked his black moustache with his fingers.

The cognac atomized in her nostrils and stung her throat as she sipped. "Maybe I'll visit Mom at Thanksgiving," she said. "Or Christmas." Why shouldn't she? Now that she'd traveled on her own, it would be easier to convince her father to let her fly to the East Coast again.

"That would be great. Your mother will be up to visit us in Bangor during the holidays, I'm sure. We'll just make her take some time off from that job of hers." He chuckled irrelevantly and settled back in his chair, laying a hand over his slight mound of a belly.

It seemed forced, his jolliness. He was a realtor, like her mother, and realtors tended to be outgoing and cheerful, often in an artificial way. Kaia took another sip from her glass. It felt worldly, drinking the pruny-tasting liqueur with her uncle. He stared at her, his head tilted to the side.

"Such a pretty girl," he mused. "A petite version of your mother, but not a clone by any means. Those crystal-blue eyes, lovely. They're not like hers, are they?"

Kaia shrugged. "I don't think I look at all like her."

"There's something about your features. You have her fine cheekbones, the wavy brown hair. And that nose of yours—" He leaned forward and touched the tip of it with his finger.

"I don't know about that," she said, recoiling. She set down her glass. "Maybe we should see if the food's ready. I'm hungry."

"Whatever you like." He drained his glass and stood up.

At the front door, Nico came close behind her and placed his hand on her upper back. She caught a whiff of his breath, which was as sharp as turpentine, like her father's when he drank brandy in the evenings. Hers probably smelled like that, too. She stepped outside, relieved to be breathing the sea air again, and headed with her uncle toward the picnic area.

3

Mark grabbed a steaming ear of corn from the platter and burned his fingers, dropping it onto his plate. He glanced up to see his mother bowing her head and crossing herself.

"Elisa," his father said, "even Catholics don't have to say grace at a barbecue."

She turned to Nico, seated at her side. "How would you know?"

"Mom can do whatever the hell she likes," Mark said. He hated the way his father always poked fun at her.

Nico sneered at Mark and bit into a roll.

Elisa leaned across the table toward Monty. "I recently converted to Catholicism and have just started crossing myself at the table, and now it seems automatic."

"We all know about this, Elisa," Nico said.

"Jesus, Dad, so what?" Mark said. "Let it go."

Nico frowned at Mark, then turned to Elisa. "You know I'm just teasing." He placed his arm around her shoulders, and she smiled at him.

Jean filled her wine glass to the brim with Chablis, then turned to Monty, who was next to her, and splashed some wine into his glass. Turning to her right, she filled Mark's glass, pouring fast, like a bartender. She set the bottle down with a ringing knock in front of Nico.

"Women pour so well," Mark commented in a bright tone.

Jean glared at him.

"What would you like to drink, Kaia?" Elisa asked. "There's limeade—"

"Who else wants wine?" Nico interrupted. "Kaia?" He reached across Elisa for Kaia's tumbler and poured out a couple of inches of the Chablis with a deft motion of his wrist, then filled his own glass.

"I suppose Kaia can have a little," Jean said belatedly. She swung her glass forward, and the others raised theirs as well. "To friends and family!"

They all drank to that, Elisa with her glass of limeade.

"Actually, I haven't heard much about your conversion," Monty said to Elisa. "When did you decide to do this?"

She smiled and helped herself to some scalloped potatoes. "I spent a week last March at a resort in Zijuatenejo with my friend Julia, who was going for the spiritual retreat, and of course we wanted to take advantage of the amenities at the spa."

"Ah, yes, the amenities," Nico said. "The Mexican masseur, the crisp, white sheets on the massage table, margaritas in the afternoon . . ."

"Nico! Let me finish. I did end up attending a few seminars, just out of curiosity."

He laughed. "Or was it the handsome young padre with the pitch-black eyes?"

"Stop it," Elisa said, "or I'm not going to tell you anything anymore." She turned to Monty. "Anyway, there was this lovely Jesuit priest—they're the most intellectual of all the priests in the various divisions of the Church—"

"Sects," Nico said, and took a long drink from his glass.

"Come on, Dad, let Mom talk," Mark said.

"Branches," Elisa said, flicking a glance at Nico. "There's not so much to tell, actually. I had some very moving discussions with Father Velasquez, and experienced what it was to feel faith, rather than just talk about it, the way we did when we were growing up."

"You were Protestant then?" Monty asked.

"We were Methodists," Jean interjected. "Of course nothing like the Catholics. We missed out on all the ritual and drama, and the costumes."

Elisa stared across the table at Jean. "There's a lot more to it than that."

"Sure there is," Nico said, grinning. "Like the folderol about birth control, divorce, masturbation—"

"Don't talk that way, Nico," Elisa said. "You don't take anything the least bit seriously."

"And there's the bonus of Confession," he went on, looking around the table. "Sin all you want and get absolution. Too bad you can't just buy indulgences anymore. Of course Elisa doesn't sin."

She frowned and brushed at him with her napkin.

"It's true," Nico said. "Elisa never thinks a sinful thought."

"I do, too. I have plenty to confess, don't you worry."

Nico gaped at her in mock astonishment. "Ho, ho!"

Mark studied his mother, who was flushing. He wished they would get off this subject; she was obviously getting upset.

There was silence, then Elisa turned to Kaia, seated next to her. "And what religion are you, sweetheart?"

"I'm a transcendentalist, I guess. I've been reading *Walden*. I love the idea of living in a cabin in the woods like Thoreau did."

"Sounds good to me," Mark said. "Who needs electricity and hot water, anyway?" He stood and opened another bottle of wine. As he bent over the table, he caught a whiff of coconut oil coming off of Kaia, the same scent he'd noticed when she'd first stepped onto his boat.

He refilled the glasses, including Kaia's, and raised his own. "To Catholicism, transcendentalism, and all other such beliefs, however you may feel about any of them."

Kaia smiled and lifted her glass, then took a sip, her eyes focused on his. He sat down, smiling back at her.

Elisa put her arm around Kaia. "I hear you're a ballerina."

Kaia shrugged—a slight, self-effacing gesture. "I dance."

"We'd all love to see you dance in your little tutu," Monty said, grinning.

"Gee, too bad I didn't think to bring it," Kaia said. She glanced at Mark, then looked away, and back again. Her face was a bit ruddy, and a sun-bleached strand of hair had fallen forward, curling around her cheek.

"Yes, isn't it too bad," Mark said in a low voice.

Then he winked at her, and she self-consciously raised her hand to the side of her neck, once again holding his gaze. It gave him a feeling of satisfaction out of all proportion to anything, as if they'd somehow formed an alliance against the others, and he felt a kind of elation he knew wasn't just from the wine.

4

An hour later, enormous lavender clouds moved in overhead, and a strong chilly wind came up suddenly, then rain came sluicing down. They gathered up the dishes and ran laughing to the cottage, and Kaia went upstairs to take a shower. When she returned to her room, she saw that someone had come in and lit an oil lamp on the desk, and she wondered who it was. By the time she'd finished unpacking, rain was battering the roof more fiercely, accompanied by thunderclaps that made the house vibrate. She peered through the window, but it was too dark to see anything clearly through the wet glass; there was only the reflection of her face and the lamp flickering behind her.

Walking down the hallway, she noticed that several bedroom doors were shut, yet it was barely nine o'clock. She went downstairs and didn't see anyone in the living room, so she stepped outside onto the front porch, where she was met by a blast of cold, wet air. Lanterns still burned in the front room, casting erratic shadows onto the porch. A crack of lightning split the sky, followed seconds later by the resounding rumble of thunder, and hail peppered the roof like bits of shattered glass. Kaia turned and saw her mother sitting immobile on a chair at the far end of the porch, gazing toward the sound. As Kaia sat down next to her, another bolt of lightning, ragged as a coastline on a map, electrified the dark sky. A bellow of thunder followed on its heels.

"Thrilling, isn't it?" her mother said.

Kaia nodded and reached for her hand, and it felt good when her mother squeezed hers back. She studied her mother's face in profile—her classic nose and strong jaw, her wavy hair expertly cut, so that even tousled in the wind it looked stylish.

"I brought your *Ms.* magazines, Mom. They're still in my bag."

"I should have the address changed. I hope you're enjoying them. I haven't had time to do much reading lately, anyway."

"I did read a couple of articles."

As the hail subsided, they sat listening to the numbing drone of the rain. A flash of lightning and a thunderclap once again startled Kaia.

After catching her breath, she said, "Do you remember, Mom, the week before you moved to New York, when we were sitting in The Raven, drinking coffee? There was a thunderstorm that afternoon, too."

Her mother nodded. "I think so."

"While you were reading the *Chron*, I was watching the people at the other tables, and I wondered why they all seemed so happy, talking and laughing together."

Her mother let go with a heavy sigh. "What's wrong, Kaia?" It sounded like something she was forced to ask out of politeness.

"Mom, you're asking me what's wrong?"

Her mother tapped with her nails on the wooden armrest. "Maybe a counselor would help. I'll talk to your father."

"I don't need a counselor." Kaia's throat clamped down, and she could hardly speak. "I just want to know why you left me in Berkeley. And why you haven't visited me all this time."

"It wasn't about leaving you, Kaia." Her mother reached out and stroked her cheek with the back of her hand.

Kaia pulled away. "But you did leave me."

"No, it wasn't that at all—it was your father and I. You know that, Kaia. Things were unbearable in ways you don't understand. I stuck it out for your sake as long as I could. It was simply an untenable situation."

Her mother turned and gazed over the water again, as if considering the terrible force that had whisked her out of California. Her thoughts had clearly shifted to some other place, New York probably, with its subway trains, its museums, its "movers and shakers"—as her mother referred to the business types she admired so much—and her extravagant Manhattan apartment. There was something vacant in the way she stared without reaction at the next crack of lightning that lit up the sky, the stark image of her face imprinted on Kaia's mind like patterns on a shroud. Obviously her mother was focused now on a new, exhilarating future, not the reminders of her past.

"What about me, Mom? Why didn't you even ask if I wanted to move to New York with you?"

Her mother moved her head slowly toward Kaia as though her attention had been called back against her will. "You wouldn't have wanted to leave your school, your friends. And there would have been a huge custody battle. Your father never would have let go of you."

"But you would have won a custody fight, Mom. You're the mother. Mothers always win. And you know how Dad gets, especially when he's drinking. You could have brought that up."

Her mother shook her head. "It wouldn't have worked out for so many reasons. But I've really missed you, Kaia. I wish I could have taken more time off this summer and had you stay with me in New York, but the workload has been incredible. I've been working sixty, seventy hours a week." She reached over and patted Kaia's hand. "Please be patient."

Kaia inhaled deeply, her eyes moistening. "You're always so busy, Mother."

"You'll understand when you have a career, and then you have a child—although, as you know, a lot of women are opting out of marriage and children, so they can devote themselves to their profession."

"You sound like Gloria Steinem. No children for Gloria."

Her mother pursed her lips and glanced away.

Kaia sometimes wondered why her mother had chosen to have a child, especially in 1963, when people were building bomb shelters. And it wasn't such a great day for Kaia to be born, as it turned out—November 22, the day JFK was shot. Kaia had read that in the Sixties women were seriously rebelling against the domination of men and the supposed enslavement of motherhood. But Kaia knew she would have children, and she would give them everything. She would never leave them.

"I want things back they way they were, Mom." Kaia thought of the occasional tennis game, the Sunday mornings when her mother would lie around in her pajamas reading the paper, the times they would go jogging in Tilden Park. And the way her mother had served as a kind of buffer between Kaia and her controlling father.

Her mother shook her head again, staring impassively at the sky in the midst of another lightning strike.

"Dad's been drinking way too much, you know," Kaia said, ashamed of the tears leaking down her face.

"More than before?"

Kaia nodded, recalling how her father would get drunk and then angry with her for some stupid thing. In their struggles, her father always came out the victor, one way or another. Since boarding the plane in San Francisco, she'd felt relieved to be away from him. He was often gruff with her, yet always hovering about, wanting too much from her, especially since her mother had left. Slipping away from his grasp had felt like a refreshing plunge into the Pacific.

"That's what I'm telling you, Mom. Why didn't you do anything—"

The screen door squeaked open, and her mother glanced up. As Kaia turned to look, Mark stepped out onto the porch. He stood there in his bare feet, blue jeans and sweatshirt, staring at them.

"What's happening?" he asked.

Kaia quickly swiped at her eyes with her fingertips. "We were just talking."

"I'm going down to the beach." Mark paused, looking at Kaia. "Want to come?"

"It's raining and there's a goddamned thunderstorm out there," her mother said. She leaned forward, frowning at Mark, who simply stood there in masterful contemplation of the two of them. Kaia would always remember it that way, her mother in her black cashmere sweater, trying to stare him down on the windy porch.

Mark took his eyes from Kaia to search over the channel. "It's letting up a bit now," he said. "The storm's moving into the mainland."

Kaia stood up. She was going to get nothing further from her mother.

"I'll get my jacket," she said.

When Kaia returned to the porch, her mother had vanished, and Mark stood facing the water, his hands shoved into his jeans pockets. He swung around and smiled at her. She came up beside him, and when he placed his arm around her shoulders, pulling her toward him, she felt a rush of pleasure that remained even after he let go.

As they strolled onto the beach, Kaia peered up at Mark's determined face; she was afraid he'd seen her tears and felt sorry for her. She tipped her head down into the damp wind—oddly, it was warmer now than it had been earlier in the evening. She liked the gritty feel of the sand sifting into her sandals and between her toes.

A bolt of lightning cracked the sky, and several seconds later a thunderclap followed, making her jump.

Mark stopped and cupped her shoulder with his hand. "Are you okay? You want to go back?"

"No. I love storms like this."

"So do I. The lightning is miles away now. You don't have to worry."

Mark seemed mellower now, out on the beach with her. It seemed understood between them what they both liked—the gentle lashing of the rain on their faces as they sauntered along, the electric flashes and reverberating thunder in the distance, the pungent scent of wet pine trees. The rain soaked the clumps of marsh grass and endless stretch of sand, rendering everything a soft, dark blur.

They walked in silence, keeping an easy pace. Then, as they approached some boulders that jutted into the lapping waves, Mark loped over to the sandy area behind the rocks. He leaned back against one of the boulders, his face skyward. When Kaia came up to him, he turned to meet her eyes, then grabbed her by the waist and lifted her onto the rock.

"Hey!" she shrieked, laughing.

"I thought you looked like a girl who would enjoy sitting on a rock in the rain." He rested his hands on her knees.

She laughed again and tilted her head back, feeling the drops soaking her hair and sliding down her face. Then she reached her arms out to catch the rain and started to teeter to the side. Mark moved his hands up, pressing down on her thighs to steady her.

Enjoying his firm grip, she peered into his face. "I do. I love it."

And then he did something that would later seem remarkable, but at that moment felt natural, out in the night air—he bent forward and pressed his lips against her knee. After a long moment, he raised his head and took a deep breath of the damp, savory air between them.

5

The next morning the house was eerily quiet when Kaia arose. She found her mother's room empty and the other rooms, too, but the beds were neatly made, as if a maid had come while Kaia slept. Chilled by the vacancy upstairs, she took a book and went down to the kitchen, where she found Elisa scrubbing the counter.

"Where is everyone?" Kaia asked.

Her aunt shrugged and offered a vague smile. Then she said, "Oh, I remember now. The boys went on a hike around the island."

Kaia wondered why they hadn't awakened her and taken her with them. Maybe they thought she was too young to hang around with them. But why had Mark just disappeared like that, especially after last night, when he'd seemed to seek out her company? And she couldn't erase the feel of him kissing her knee through her rain-dampened jeans.

When she asked about her mother's whereabouts, Elisa said she thought she'd gone out. Something in Elisa's wistful tone made Kaia refrain from asking for more details; surely her mom would return soon, anyway.

Kaia helped herself to a muffin and tea and retreated to the front room, curling up on the sofa with her copy of *Les Misérables*. She kept thinking about Mark, though, and couldn't concentrate on the French.

She finally heard her mother's voice outside and went to greet her. It turned out that her mother had walked with Nico to a neighboring cottage to make a phone call. When her mother suggested they all go to the beach before lunch, Kaia put on a sweatshirt and went down with the three grownups. The air was cool, and her mother was the only one to brave the water, while Kaia and her aunt and uncle sat on the shore. If only Mark and Monty had stayed around, it would have been so much more fun. What happened last night had seemed so utterly unexpected. Recalling the thrill of him lifting her onto the rock and the gentle pressure of his lips on her knee, the same excitement she'd felt then kept washing over her.

When the two guys finally returned to the cottage around noon, laughing and red-faced, Kaia was instantly cheered. During their picnic lunch, Kaia sought Mark's eyes across the table, but he just gave a quick smile and glanced away. Maybe he regretted going out into the storm with her—she had made too much of it in her imagination, lying awake in bed last night. She'd never been out with a man on the beach at night before, and had never known anyone like Mark. Even though he was her cousin, what was wrong with thinking about him, as long as no one knew? But what was *he* thinking or feeling now, and what had been in his mind last night?

After they'd all finished eating and the table was cleared, Kaia's mother marched away with Nico, announcing that they were going for a hike, and indicating by her emphatic tone that no one should even think about tagging along. Why was her mother so driven, always striding off somewhere? Even now, on their vacation. And why with Nico?

Aunt Elisa had retreated to the cottage for a "lie-down," and Kaia still felt groggy from jet lag and could relate to her aunt's unwillingness, or inability, to keep up with everyone. But Elisa had seemed almost frail as she floated away, like an invalid trying to muster her strength, an empty bread basket dangling from her hand.

In the past when Kaia's mother had gone to Maine, she would refer to Elisa's condition in vague terms, saying that Elisa was overstressed, or having a rough period in her life. Kaia had spent the past six months in a morose state herself after her mother had left; she hadn't been willing to talk about it with anyone, even with her friend Sigourney.

Kaia watched now as her mother and uncle cut across the grassy slope in the distance and then headed up the shore at a vigorous pace, carrying backpacks. As Kaia strolled toward the beach, she could see them wading through the thick chartreuse grasses, then climbing up the dunes toward the scrubby area of pitch pines in the distance. Beyond that, Nico had mentioned, there were meadows where you could pick blueberries. That might explain the backpacks. But why hadn't they invited anyone to go with them? It seemed a little strange.

A brown marsh hawk with enormous wings swooped so closely overhead that Kaia could see its black eyes and long, curved beak, and it frightened her. She followed the bird's flight until it was out of sight, the sky a bleached blue. When she turned to search again for her mother and Nico, they had disappeared into the pines.

Monty had taken his fishing gear out to the dock, and Kaia watched as he tossed a line out onto the water. Then she spotted Mark sitting bare-chested on the beach, playing his guitar. She ambled down and threw herself onto the coarse sand a few feet away from him. Mark glanced at her and smiled, but kept playing a Neil Young tune she recognized. Then he switched to a Latin tune, sensual and rhythmic, a looping melody that reminded her of river water rushing over rocks. He glanced over at her and started playing *The Girl from Ipanema*, and hummed the tune from deep inside his chest.

Finally he rested his arm on the guitar. "Kaia. Funny your mama would name you that."

"Why is it funny?"

"Because it was my grandmother's name. You were named after my dad's mother."

"You're kidding," Kaia said. "Mom never told me that."

"I'm a completely serious kind of guy," he said with a half-smile, then played a few more chords.

"My mom told me my name was Norwegian for earth or something."

"Earth goddess, no doubt—that fits." He smiled. "Kaia," he repeated.

She loved the way he spoke her name, more softly this time, and with his eyes on her.

"Kaia Svendsen was my grandmother's name," he went on. "Then she married a Greek named Loukas Karadonis. Supposedly he was following a family tradition of marrying beautiful, blue-eyed women. In fact I think she was Norwegian."

"Why would my mom name me after her?"

"Maybe your mother met her on one of those trips to Bangor. She probably just liked the name."

"I was never allowed to go with Mom to Maine. I couldn't miss school—that was usually the reason she wouldn't let me go back East with her."

"Back East? That's where we are, sweetness, right here in the East."

He was teasing her again, as if she were a little kid, and it gave her a tight feeling in her stomach.

He squinted at her, then played a few chords on the guitar. "She went back East, to see her sis, to see if anything could be amiss," he sang to the tune of *Blue Tail Fly*.

Kaia laughed, and he switched into a fast bossa nova tune. She lay back and closed her eyes, taking in the sand's heat as it seeped into her muscles and bones. She wondered if music and human voices had physical properties that could become part of a person. It felt like that—as if Mark's voice and the guitar music were soaking into her body along with the warmth of the sand.

After a while, Mark stopped playing. "Nod if you can hear me," he said.

Shading her eyes with her hand, she peered up at him. He was smiling, his face relaxed. His eyes were a clear blue against his reddish-brown skin.

"I'm awake," she said.

"Watch out, you'll get burned." His eyes skimmed the length of her, and a shiver ran through her.

She was wearing shorts and a tank top but wasn't worried, since she rarely burned. "I'll be okay."

He set his guitar in its case and then looked out toward the ocean. He sat cross-legged on the sand in his cut-offs, his hands resting on his knees, his back straight, his face serene, like a guru. Lying this close to him, she caught a whiff of his salty skin. He seemed to fully absorb the glow of the sun and the sand, as if there were no boundary between him and his surroundings.

She sat up and said, "I guess your parents made you come here."

"Not really. I wanted a little relaxation before starting law school. I actually wanted to take more time off, maybe do some farming up at our cabin in Beaulieu. A whole year, snow and all. That would have been great. But dad insisted I start law school right away."

"Too bad."

"Anyway, I like being here on the beach, or out on the water. There's nothing I like better."

"So you'll be in Berkeley in September."

"Yep, figured it would be good to get as far away from Maine as possible." He looked at her and smiled. "And maybe I'll see a little more of you."

"That'd be cool." It would be more than cool, actually.

He rested his eyes on her face and leaned slightly toward her, and she had the feeling he was about to reach over and touch her. She held her breath, realizing how much she wanted him to do that.

"Anyway," he said, "I like it when I can get away from the others—the old folks are getting on my nerves."

"Mom and Elisa are really different, aren't they? Your mom's kind of dreamy sometimes, and other times she seems sort of excitable. She's not down-to-earth like my mother."

He winced, glancing away, then turned back to her. "My mother's manic-depressive, you know."

She paused, taking this in. "No, I didn't. God, that sounds serious. When did that start?"

"It was a long time ago." Mark briefly studied Kaia's face. "You knew my mom lost a baby, didn't you?"

"Yes. That was before you were born, right?"

"Yeah, a crib death, here on Pine Tree. My dad and your mom were supposed to be watching the baby. Her name was April. She was only a couple months old."

Kaia gasped. "Really? My mom never said she was there when it happened."

Mark blew out a long breath. "I guess it was right after that when my mother started having serious problems—the hospitalizations and all."

"Hospitalizations?"

"There have been a few over the years." Mark frowned. "Once she actually tried to kill herself."

"Oh my God."

"That was a few years ago. You were probably too young to know about it. She's doing better now, taking her medication. But there are too many people here now—it's too much stimulation for her. Her mania usually builds up gradually, over a few days, especially when she drinks."

Kaia hadn't noticed anything unusual, except for last night when she'd come in from her walk on the beach and had run into Elisa upstairs. Her aunt had kissed her effusively on her cheeks, and Kaia had detected the perfumy odor of brandy on her.

"It must be really hard for you, Mark." Without thinking, she touched his hand, and he enfolded her hand in his, squeezing it firmly, his grasp strong and warm, making her heartbeat pick up.

A moment later he let go and stared over the sound again. "It's all right, Kaia. I've lived with it. It's something that can't be fixed. I love my mother, but it's frustrating to see what she's going through. My dad's no help, that's for sure. And this religious conversion of hers—it's just another way for her to fool herself into thinking she's all right."

"Maybe she needs it."

"Maybe she does," he said in a conclusive tone. "Anyway, when I'm in Berkeley, I won't have to be part of this whole scene anymore." He reached over and clasped her shin with his hand, then pressed down lightly as he got to his feet. He peered down at her, then turned toward the dock. "Think I'll do a little fishing. Looks like Monty-boy could use some help."

He picked up his guitar case and made his way across the sand. Kaia watched until he reached the pier and took up a fishing rod next to Monty. Didn't Mark see how much she wanted him to stay here on the beach with her? Unreasonably disappointed, she wondered if her walk with Mark in the lightning storm was merely a random incident, not to be repeated, something utterly insignificant to him. She was clearly too young and dull to keep him interested. He probably had girlfriends, and a car he drove them around in, maybe a Dodge Challenger, something cool and irresistible. But she actually hoped he wasn't that kind of guy. He'd mentioned having a motorcycle, and Monty had driven them to the Cape in what Mark had referred to as a junk heap of a car. So maybe Mark had no car, and no girlfriend. But none of that mattered, of course, since he was her cousin, and much older.

She stared at a skiff tied to a pole in the shallow inlet, and at the glassy green sea beyond, sparkling in the blaze of the afternoon. Turning back to the sandy beach, she saw that people had gathered some distance away. Two teenage girls in bikinis had hopped onto two boys' shoulders and started pushing at each other and screaming. The boys' heads were barely visible, buried in the girls' stomachs and thighs. Several other boys stood and watched, as if they were dying to have the girls' legs wrapped around their own necks, the girls' bellies pressing against their heads.

If only she and Mark could be out there with them.

6

Hiking with Jean along the grassy slope, Nico glanced back from time to time toward the cottage. Then he spotted Kaia standing on a knoll, gazing toward the channel, and he thought of calling out to her, to invite her along on the walk. He wouldn't mind having his niece's company, but he didn't think Jean would like it—she seemed to hoard her opportunities to be alone with him, as if she felt entitled to his time.

When he glimpsed back again, Kaia was staring in his direction, and he waved at her. He imagined her eyes narrowing in accusation, but of course that was absurd—she couldn't possibly know anything. Without any sign of acknowledgment, she turned back toward the beach, where Mark sat on the sand, playing his guitar and singing. The melody sounded faint over the crashing of the surf—it was that Neil Young song Mark liked to play.

Jean strode on ahead, and Nico sprinted to catch up with her.

"I wonder what else Mark is going to do this summer besides play his guitar," he said when he reached her.

"Maybe he'll see that girlfriend of his."

"He wasn't exactly forthcoming when I asked about her. I told him he could bring her here, but he didn't want to."

"Too bad," Jean said. "I would have liked to meet her."

Turning back one last time toward the beach, Nico saw Kaia strolling toward Mark, her tumbledown hair blowing flagrantly in the breeze. She was such a sultry beauty and moved so gracefully. He often found himself stealing glances at her, intrigued. She had caught him studying her face this morning, when they were sitting on the beach, and she'd thrown him a reproachful look, as if she'd felt invaded.

Jean veered to the right and marched up the path that led over the hill. Dropping back, Nico admired her strong legs and firm, trim body. He recalled the way she'd looked this morning running toward the water with such exuberance. Elisa and Kaia had been sitting on either side of him, the three of them watching Jean plunge into the waves. Fifteen minutes later Jean emerged from the ocean, loped over to them and stood rubbing her hair with a towel, drops of saltwater coursing down her thighs. When he glanced up at her, she smiled directly at him. There was something in Jean—her drive, her enthusiasm—that always affected him. She was in such a positive mood this morning and for once hadn't carped at Elisa for wearing her violet peasant dress down to the beach instead of "proper beach attire." Nico couldn't imagine his wife wearing a red bathing suit like Jean's and diving into the ocean; that was something that would never happen.

"You seemed more relaxed with Elisa today," he said when he came up next to Jean again.

"She's been calmer, so it's been easier to be around her. I just wish she wouldn't go on about things the way she does."

"She can't help it, as you know."

"It appeals to some people, I guess, the way she puts her feelings on display. I remember how Dad would pick her up when she was small and swing her around, and Elisa would scream with the thrill of it. She had that silly, almost hysterical feminine side he always indulged."

"He never picked you up like that?"

"Never. I was the brainy one. Once when I was nine he took me to his bank and explained everything about how the bank operated and how people applied for loans and invested their money. I think he was hoping I'd be a banker like himself. But Elisa was the one with all the feminine lovability. She still takes it for granted that people will love her, and they always do."

"I'm sure your father loved you just as much," he said, resting his hand briefly on Jean's shoulder as they walked. Maybe that was what she had always needed from him, Nico considered—to feel womanly, and lovable. He was sure he'd given her at least that much. But what about David? Sometimes Nico wondered why her ex-husband hadn't been able to give her what she needed.

They climbed uphill for a while until Nico was breathing hard and sweating profusely and had to take off his sweater. He stowed it in his backpack on top of the wine bottle. Jean was perspiring, too, the back of her shirt wet, and he caught her sweet, pungent scent. She smiled at him with a familiar, knowing look.

When they reached a glen they'd discovered on a previous trek, they found a shady area under some pines and spread out a blanket. Nico opened the bottle of wine and poured some into paper cups. They offered each other their habitual, unspoken toast.

Jean took a drink, leaning back on one arm with her legs extended—a tennis player's legs, tanned to chestnut and prominently muscled. Nico admired the way she worked so hard at keeping fit—the way she went at everything.

"Kaia seems to like Mark a lot," he said.

"They barely know each other."

Nico drank some wine and stared over the meadow. "I guess Mark will see David and Kaia occasionally in Berkeley."

"I'm sure David will see him at the law school, anyway."

"How are Kaia and David getting along these days?"

Jean sighed. "I don't know. She said he's still drinking a lot. She was so mopey before I left Berkeley. I just hope things will get easier for her as time goes on."

"What did you expect? Maybe it wasn't the best time for you to leave Berkeley."

Jean frowned, then took a round of Gouda and a steak knife from her pack. She sliced the cheese into rough hunks on a paper plate. "Kaia will be all right. Even though she and David argue sometimes, he adores her. She and David are alike in some ways—they just love reading and going to foreign movies. Kaia reads David's *New Yorker* every week, and they sometimes talk about the articles."

Nico bit into the cheese, even though he wasn't hungry. "Well, that's something, then, I guess." Jean seemed awfully cavalier about leaving Kaia completely in David's custody, with only visitation rights for herself. "What about his drinking?"

"I'll talk to him about it. I'm sure he won't listen to me, though." Jean nibbled on a piece of the Gouda.

"That can't be good for a young girl to be forced to deal with on her own."

"David's been drinking too much for a long time," Jean said, rather curtly. "But as I said, I'll see what I can do."

At this stage of Kaia's life, she really needed a mother to talk to, Nico felt. Since his niece had arrived yesterday, he'd been shocked at how much she'd changed; she'd become a young woman, and he'd felt awkward relating to her. Watching her, it was as if he were learning a new language that only Kaia spoke with her face and body. He pictured her in her maroon sweater, peering into the hallway mirror yesterday afternoon; he remembered thinking she's not at all like Mark. But why should they be alike? Aside from the blue eyes and brown hair, there didn't seem to be that much familial resemblance.

"You think Kaia's basically like David, then?" he asked.

"In some ways. It's natural, with him being around more—the academic life, you know. They didn't fight as much once I'd decided to leave. David didn't seem as angry and frustrated once things were settled between us—at least toward the end."

"The end," Nico repeated, thinking of the divorce Jean had plunged into with such unseemly gusto.

"Yes," she said, with an edge of irritation in her voice. "The end. And to get there and come out here I had to give up everything—Kaia, my colleagues, my old job. I miss all of that, you know."

Nico's stomach tightened like a fist. It was Jean's idea, after all, to move out here, mainly to be closer to him, she'd said, but he certainly hadn't encouraged it. Anyway, Jean should be glad for some change in her life—living in New York, a high-paying job—except for seeing less of Kaia, of course. He took a long drink of the Cabernet, which tasted slightly sour. He peered into his cup. Things seemed so complicated these days, with Jean's divorce and her heavy reliance on him; it sometimes felt hard to make some of the simplest decisions, let alone the more difficult ones.

He glanced at her. "Did you ever really love David?" He'd surprised himself with the question, but he often wondered why Jean had married him.

She drew in her chin. "Of course." She blew out a short breath. "But things changed after Kaia was born. Our focus was on her, and we didn't spend much time with each other. All through her childhood, he took Kaia everywhere, paid her lots of attention. Even the spankings were a form of attention, I suppose, a way to control her, keep her obedient, close to him. She was so sweet and adoring when she was little. I remember that first ballet performance of hers, when she was eight. David was nearly in a dream afterwards, completely enraptured."

"I can imagine."

"He absolutely loved her, still does—though in a different way now."

"What do you mean?" Nico finished his wine and refilled their cups.

"Just—in a different way than most fathers. She's everything to him, even though they fight at times. He worships her."

"Don't most fathers adore their daughters?" He thought of his own baby daughter who'd died; he'd certainly adored her. But he didn't want to get into that—it was much too painful.

"I don't know, but he seems besotted with Kaia, these past few years especially." She took a sip of her wine. "The same way my father was besotted with Elisa."

Nico shook his head. "Really, Jean, I'm sure it's not as unusual as you make it sound." Jean stared at him, as if she thought he was being obtuse.

"Anyway," he said, "when did you know it was over with David?"

Jean sighed and looked out over the meadow. "It was last September, I guess. After Santa Fe. David seemed a little suspicious about that weekend, but he had no idea I was with you."

It made Nico squeamish, recalling their stolen weekend, even though he'd enjoyed it at the time. Three days at a realtors' convention, eating enchiladas and painfully spicy chili, drinking margaritas by the pitcherful, browsing through shops and galleries. It was the kind of weekend that would have been impossible with Elisa; it would have been too much for her, too stimulating. And even then, Jean had been making plans to find a job in commercial real estate on the East Coast.

"Remember the cowboy hats?" she asked.

Nico rolled his eyes. "Oh, yes." He remembered boarding the plane for Dallas, where they were to catch their connecting flights home; the agent had informed them they had too many carry-ons, including the cowboy hats in their large boxes. Nico had bought the hats for Mark and himself as a joke. Nico simply took the two tall hats out of their boxes and defiantly placed them onto his head, one on top of the other, and discarded the boxes. The agent threw his hands up and waved them on through. Once they'd settled into their seats, the two of them had burst out laughing—Nico knew he looked ridiculous with the two hats on his head.

"Remember the stewardess coming over, wanting to know what our story was?" Jean asked.

"Yep, sure do," Nico chuckled, picturing the raven-haired young woman.

"What *is* our story, anyway?"

He shrugged and took a bite of the cheese, then washed it down with some wine.

"I thought we were going to talk to Elisa while we're here," Jean said, watching him closely.

He shook his head slowly, wiping his mouth with a napkin. "What you and I may have discussed over margaritas back in September doesn't really make much sense at the moment. You can see how Elisa is now—pretty damn shaky. The Lithium doesn't work that consistently, as I'm sure you're aware."

"She's as well as she's ever going to be."

"You don't see her on a day-to-day basis. She's been drinking again. She could turn suicidal in the blink of an eye."

"Not the suicide threat again," Jean said, with a touch of bitterness. "And she *could* just stop drinking, you know."

"You really have no sympathy for her, do you?"

"Of course I do." Jean frowned. "She's my sister, for Christ's sake. But we can't let her condition dictate our lives."

Nico thought of Santa Fe, when Jean seemed to be trying to prove something—how perfect the two of them were together, how their children were finally old enough to weather a divorce, how Elisa could somehow survive on her own.

"Elisa clearly cannot manage by herself," he said, "and I don't want to talk about this during my vacation." He was not prepared to brazen through with anything that would rupture their lives at this point. He still loved Elisa, but they rarely made love, and that was very difficult for him. And Jean was strong in so many ways, a refreshing contrast with her sister. But since Jean had moved East, she'd insinuated herself into a more prominent place in his life, coming up to Bangor to visit him whenever they could spend a few hours together—every couple of weeks lately. There was so much he was forced to keep from Elisa now. And recently Jean had managed to find a real estate deal they could work on together, so they would have a reason to talk on the phone about finding a buyer.

"Fine," Jean said. "Another time."

They were both silent for a while, then he asked, "Do you think Kaia will be all right, then?"

"She can take care of herself. She's a big girl now."

"Then you're not having Kaia come to Manhattan this summer?"

"I'm extremely busy at work right now. It was hard enough taking time off to come here."

"That's too bad." It really was too bad—Kaia left behind in Berkeley with her bristly, alcoholic father.

"I feel terrible about not seeing her these past few months." Jean took a long drink of her wine. "But we don't need to talk about Kaia right now, do we?"

"I suppose not," he mumbled.

Jean set her cup down and leaned over to kiss him, her lips lingering on his. He kissed her back, letting himself relax into it. He was feeling the wine and the heat of the afternoon, and caught her delicious, spicy scent. After a minute, he lay down and pulled her on top of him, feeling her smooth legs against his.

She got up on her knees, straddling him, pulled her polo shirt over her head, then undid her bra and tossed it onto the grass. After all this time he still became aroused at the mere sight of her full, white breasts, and loved to sink his hands and face into them. She unzipped his pants, and once her lips grazed him and she took him in her mouth, he forgot about everything else, it felt so electrifyingly good. And then she was astride him, a woman who would give him everything—if only in the hope of having him all to herself.

*

Sensing a shadow over her face, Kaia opened her eyes to see a cloud like a purple bruise in the sky, and realized she'd dozed off to the drone of the waves. Still dreamy, she shut her eyes again and imagined she heard her mother's voice, calling her from a distance. For a few moments she lay on the baking-hot sand listening to the screech of plovers flying overhead, the same gray birds she'd seen that morning pecking at ropes of seaweed. A faint image of her mother bathing her as a child came to mind, and she dozed off again to a half-dream of fragrant soap and mist and warm water, her mother's jasmine scent and hazel eyes, her mother's voice singing. That was what love was, Kaia felt, her mother singing to her at night, tucking her in and reading to her as a child.

Now she heard her mother's voice again, mixed with Nico's laughter. Kaia sat up, her face and arms roasted from the sun, her ankle itching sharply from a sand fly bite. She shook the sand out of her hair and brushed it from her legs, then took off running across the beach and through the grass toward her mother and uncle. When she joined them at the path leading up to the house, her mother appeared softer, as if seen through a lens that was out of focus. Kaia recalled her mother at lunch, eating with such relish, and occasionally throwing her head back, laughing. Some of the recent tension in her mother was gone—maybe it was the hike; her mother always seemed to need physical activity.

But when her mother put her arm around her shoulders, it seemed like an artificial, token gesture, and Kaia couldn't help sensing some disturbance in the atmosphere, something odd. Maybe it was simply the odor of wine on her mother's breath.

7

Happy to be out of the house the following afternoon, Kaia went for a stroll on the beach by herself. It had been overcast all day, the house dim, the sky mottled with charcoal-gray clouds, and her mother and aunt were occupied with chores. The men had gone fishing, and she was hoping to catch sight of their boat out on the water. At first a hesitant scattering of fat drops began to make indentations in the sand, then the sky let loose with an impressive downpour. Soon her hair, sweatshirt and jeans were soaked, and the muddy sand coated her bare feet. She wondered if it was dangerous for the men to be out in a motorboat in the heavy rain.

Returning to the cottage, she went upstairs to steep herself in a hot bath. Afterwards, on the way to her room, she caught the smell of garlic and spices and heard the clanging of pots and pans in the kitchen. She imagined finding Mark in the living room, greeting her with his smiling, glistening face, his hair disheveled from the storm.

It was dusk and still raining when she went downstairs. She found the front room dark and vacant, though the dining area was lit with several oil lamps that had been set on the table. She went into the kitchen to help her mother and aunt get dinner ready.

By seven o'clock, the rain was coming down in sheets. Kaia had just set a plate of fried chicken next to the other dishes on the table when at last the men appeared, stomping their boots and exclaiming about the thunderstorm that had come up over the channel. They slipped out of their dripping slickers, leaving pools of water in the foyer.

"We didn't catch any fish all day, but it was great out there," Mark said as he came forward. "Looks like there's plenty of food, though."

He flashed a grin at Kaia—it was what she'd been waiting for all day, she realized. His hair was shining with raindrops, his face flushed with excitement.

"Don't you men want to get some dry clothes on?" Jean asked.

"Hell, no," Mark said, winking at Kaia. "You'll just have to take us as we are."

She smiled at him, meeting his gaze; she was more than happy to take him as he was.

Nico looked weary as he walked toward the table. "We can change clothes later."

"Fine with me," Monty said, following Nico and surveying the food. "I'm starving."

"Come as you are," Elisa said brightly. "Just as I always say. And everything is piping hot." She rushed to the kitchen, returning with dish towels for the men to dry their hair. Kaia and her mother helped Elisa bring the remaining dishes to the table.

Once they'd all seated themselves, Elisa crossed herself, then began passing the dishes around. They all loaded up their plates and began eating, everyone seemingly as hungry as Kaia was after her hike.

After a few minutes, her mother patted her mouth with her napkin and turned to Nico. "I'm going to have to make a couple more phone calls tomorrow. I have to check on the Mannington deal—you know, the sale of that office building uptown. I may have to go back sooner than I thought."

"You could hike over to the Andersons again to use their phone," Nico said.

Kaia stared at her plate, picturing her mother making her phone call in the morning, then coming back to pack her things. Her mother had no doubt memorized the train schedule from Boston to New York. Nico would row her over to the Cape Cod dock; as a realtor, he obviously understood the urgency of business matters. Kaia imagined a taxi waiting for her mother on the other side of the channel. The whole scenario made Kaia sick—the utter predictability of her mother's behavior, the familiar sense of desertion.

"I'd rather make my calls from the Cape," her mother said. "I'd also like to pick up a newspaper. I have no idea what's going on in the world."

"I'm afraid to find out what Carter's up to now," Nico said.

"I'm sure he's pushing for more nuclear plants," Mark said. "In spite of the Three Mile Island disaster."

"I thought Carter was supposed to be an environmentalist," Kaia said.

"That poor Silkwood woman," Elisa said, looking up with a rather sad expression, "and all those people poisoned with plutonium."

"The nuclear plants should be shut down," Monty said. "Every one of them."

Mark glanced at him. "I agree. The companies should be prosecuted. I'd like to go after the corporate criminals, the ones who dump toxic waste into the rivers and ocean."

"Environmental law is a good thing, but I've been thinking of taking up poverty law myself, or maybe defending Native American land rights."

"Whatever rings your bell," Mark said.

Monty grinned. "A lot of things ring my bell, actually." He leaned forward to peer at Elisa. "This chicken is delicious, by the way."

Elisa smiled, a crinkly network of wrinkles radiating from the outer corners of her eyes. "Thank you. I've been cooking all day. There's cherry pie and pecan pie, and—oh, I forgot to bring out the bread! It's cheese bread—you'll love it, Monty."

She scraped her chair back and stood up, stumbling over Kaia as she tried to get out between the two chairs. Her long skirt caught under one of the legs.

"Slow down, Elisa," Nico said. "There's no rush."

"Cheese bread sounds great, Mom," Mark said.

"So does cherry pie," Kaia said. "It smelled so good when I came back from my walk."

Elisa disengaged her skirt and hurried toward the kitchen, tapping Mark's shoulder as she passed him. When she returned with the bread, she sat down and arranged her napkin on her lap, peering down in silence. Elisa looked a little upset—her moods seemed to change so quickly, Kaia thought. Maybe she was just embarrassed at appearing clumsy.

They worked their way through all of the food—the cheese bread, the casseroles, green salad, yams, chicken, potato salad, beet salad, garlicky green beans, macaroni and cheese. It seemed excessive, but everything was delectable, especially the maple-syrup-dipped fried chicken.

"It's supposed to clear up tomorrow," Nico said. "Maybe we can all go down to the beach, have a picnic or something. And Kaia can work on her tan." He looked at her and fingered his moustache, as if to hide his smile.

Kaia shrugged, trying to shake off his stare, and took a bite of the spinach casserole.

After dinner, she helped wash dishes with Elisa, while the others settled into the living room. Her aunt dashed back and forth between the dining room and kitchen to retrieve more plates, then began drying the dishes and silverware while Kaia washed. Elisa's motions seemed frenetic; she was setting each piece to the side then grabbing another one as fast as Kaia could wash it.

"It's just so wonderful to have you here with us," Elisa said, speaking rapidly. "And to have another woman in the house—besides your mother, of course. Nico and I are hoping you can come out more often. You'll probably want to visit your mother in New York, and you've got to come to Bangor and see us, too, whenever you're out here."

"I'll try to, but I'm not sure Dad will let me."

"We'll arrange something, we'll be sure to do that. We just love seeing you."

Elisa became increasingly edgy, chattering about Mark and Monty and their plans to go to different law schools, and how she was going to miss Mark so terribly and how she hoped he would get to see a lot of Kaia and her father in Berkeley. It scared Kaia, the way her aunt had gotten into such a nervous state—maybe it was what Mark had said, that the mania just built up sometimes, possibly because there were so many people around.

It was at least an hour later when Kaia finished helping her aunt put away every last dish and scour every surface clean. Kaia finally left Elisa vigorously mopping the kitchen floor. In the front room, her mother and Nico were sitting on the sofa with their backs to Kaia. As Kaia passed quietly through the room, she heard her mother say to Nico in an undertone, "It's good for her to work off some energy. Just let her be."

Kaia went upstairs. She desperately wanted to talk to Mark, but she couldn't find him. Apparently he and Monty had gone out somewhere. Without her, again.

8

Elisa sat at her desk the following evening, writing fast, thrilled to put the finishing touches on her play. She could hear the others talking and laughing downstairs, none of them at all aware she'd been preparing for this—her entrance, her triumph of theatre. A few minutes later she sailed down the stairs in her scarlet kaftan, her vitality surging back, along with the warmth of the sherry she'd been sipping all day. She told herself she could control this feeling that had been dormant for weeks—what was it? A heightening, or a kind of elation? A fierceness?

Clutching her sheaf of papers and rushing into the front room, her heart pulsing with excitement, she found the young people soberly playing cards. Jean sat next to Nico, talking to him in her conspiratorial murmur, the air rank with the smell of fried fish from dinner.

"Time for a little theatre, everyone," Elisa announced, surveying the bland faces surrounding her. "I've written a play."

Jean and Nico exchanged glances—Elisa hated the way they did that. Mark kept his eyes on his cards.

Kaia turned toward Elisa. "A play? What's it about?"

"It's about families," she said, struggling to keep her voice calm. "It's about anger and tribulation and love."

"Why write about troublesome emotions?" Jean said, her face stony in opposition. "It's not therapeutic for the rest of us."

"Why paint pictures, why compose music?" Elisa wheeled around toward Jean, waving her script in the air.

"I'm game," Monty said, but Mark frowned at him.

"Wonderful," Elisa proclaimed, ignoring her son. "It takes place in 1954. Monty, you can be Nathan, the dark mystery man. And Jean, you can be his wife, Emily."

"Just because you took playwriting in college," Jean said, "doesn't give you the right to inflict—"

"You don't have to be in it, Jean," Elisa said. "Kaia can play the part of Emily, whose baby was left alone—"

"Please don't do this," Nico said, his voice filled with alarm. "We all just want to relax."

Elisa felt a flushing sensation under her skin. *Traitor*, she wanted to scream, but she forced herself to stand there in the frigid silence. She stepped forward. "We need to do this now. We need it to illustrate how all of us, the women, pretend to care for each other—"

"Stop this, Elisa," Jean said.

"—while we only want the company of men and adore them too much, and they drive us to be vain and careless."

"Elisa—" Jean pleaded.

"You see," Elisa continued, "when the play opens, Emily's sister, Joyce, and Nathan are persuading Emily to go out for some fresh air, even though Emily tells them, "The baby needs me, I can't abandon my child just because you think I need to go outdoors."

Nico glared at her, shaking his head. The room went quiet, except for the sound of wind gusting against the house.

After an excruciating moment, Elisa turned toward her niece. "Kaia, maybe you'd rather do the sound effects, the baby crying and so on. You see, Emily has gone out and the baby is wailing upstairs—"

"No!" Jean cried in her harpy voice, standing up. "The baby wasn't crying."

"—and Joyce says to Nathan, 'Relax, let the baby settle down to her nap. Leave her alone.'"

"You've got it all wrong," Jean said, her eyes open wide in outrage. "April wasn't crying. You've imagined these terrible things—"

Elisa had to go on, her hands trembling, barely able to hold the script. She glanced at Mark and Kaia, who both looked stricken. But Elisa knew she had to continue. "So then Emily comes back after her walk and finds that Nathan has checked on the baby and given her a bottle of water. So there's a much better ending, you see. Emily returns to her baby and finds she's all right."

"But Elisa," Nico said, "you know how it happened."

"Of course I do." She dropped the pages onto the floor. "Can't you see? I just want to show how it was wrong for them to tell Emily to leave her baby, who was only two months old—"

Elisa could feel the tears spurting out. It all had to come out and have a different ending this time. Her sweet niece was at her side now, touching her arm. Elisa took a long, shaky breath. "Then in Act Two, Joyce and Nathan conspire to send Emily away—leaving her in a horrid clinic again." She stooped to pick up the scattered pages. "Here, I'll read more lines."

Nico stood and came over to Elisa, laying his hands on her shoulders like an orderly and said, "Elisa, I think you should go upstairs and rest for a while."

"First we have to do my play—it demonstrates what I've been discovering the past few days while you were all out fishing and hiking, how we all have to be hypervigilant—"

"Elisa, just stop it!" Jean shouted.

"It's so clear that we have to be careful when people are thrown together in a place like this. Jean, you think there's not enough love to go around. You think it's something tangible that can be taken and that there's only so much of it—"

"You have no idea what I think." Jean came forward, but Elisa sidestepped out of her reach and grabbed Nico's arm.

"Can't you see," Elisa said, "we don't have to do this anymore, abandoning each other when we desperately need one another." She choked back the sobs, thinking of her firstborn with her precious pink cheeks and sparkling eyes and heartbreaking tiny hands and feet. Dropping her hand away from Nico, she covered her eyes with her hands.

"Don't do this," Jean said.

After a moment, Elisa looked up to see her sister standing in front of her with her lips pressed together in a determined line.

"Leave my mother alone," Mark said to Jean.

He came over, taking Elisa gently by the elbow. He tried to steer her toward the stairs, but she shook him off.

"Just wait, darling, I'm not finished," she whispered. "I just want everyone to see things lucidly. Why are they so afraid?"

"I don't know, Mom. Let's just go off by ourselves for a while, okay?"

He took her arm again and she found herself giving in to his steady presence as he led her away, and when she glanced back into the room it was a delirium of lusterless color. Woozy now, she allowed Mark to walk with her up the stairs. But still she couldn't settle down, she had to work off this monstrous energy that was so unlike the euphoria that had taken over earlier today, when she'd floated through the house. She began to stride up and down the hallway reciting the lulling words of St. Paul: "'Love is patient and kind, love is not jealous or boastful, love does not rejoice at wrong but rejoices in the right . . .'" while Mark leaned against the wall watching her, his arms crossed. Finally she slipped into the bathroom and took her Lithium, almost relieved at the capitulation.

Still she had to march up and down, her edginess muting gradually—she could almost feel the artificial tranquility entering her bloodstream one molecule at a time. She moved to the desk in her room, her mind still racing, full of astonishing ideas that she felt compelled to record while Mark sat in the chair beside her. She felt him watching her as she wrote, and after a while he stood up and laid his hand on her shoulder, telling her to call him if she needed anything. He kissed the top of her head and then went out, leaving the door open.

She would delve into the core of things, she decided; she would document everything. Yesterday she'd overheard Jean say to Nico that she was tired of worrying about her all the time. Jean was preparing her for something, some kind of undesirable shift, some terrible desertion.

It was the same when they were girls—Jean traipsing off on her own pursuits, leaving Elisa on her own. Insatiable Jean, going after all the boys, the ones Elisa would moon over but never dream of approaching. And there was always their father in the foreground, urging Jean to play tennis at college, to be on top, to make something of herself. No grad school for Jean, unlike Elisa with her useless M.F.A. in Dramatic Arts. Jean had to start out right away making money—glad-handing, greedy Jean.

Elisa vowed she would simply make her sister go away. She would no longer be subject to her inept ministrations, would accept only God's guidance, God who was the antithesis of death so that believing in Him she would not fear death, with its awesome hypnotic power.

Then Mark was suddenly beside her again. "Here, Mom." He set a cup of fragrant chamomile tea on her desk. She nodded but couldn't stop writing fast in purple ink, page after page.

Her journal, her savior, her prayer.

The next afternoon Jean and Nico went down to the beach with the boys, leaving Elisa at the picnic table. But at least Kaia had stayed to help clear away dishes. Elisa watched listlessly as her niece scraped leftovers into a bowl.

It had ripened into a humid afternoon, and, soporific from her medication, Elisa planned to take a nap. No one had said anything about her behavior the previous evening; they were probably just used to it.

"Why don't you come out on the beach with us today?" her niece asked.

Maybe she *should* at least try to join everyone, Elisa thought, for Kaia's sake, if nothing else. "I guess I could," she said with a sigh.

Kaia peered into her face. "You're not too tired, are you?"

Elisa touched her niece's satiny cheek. "I'll be all right."

They strolled with linked arms down to the beach, the sun angling across the radiant sand. There were Jean and Nico sitting on a knoll above the beach, Jean nudging him with her elbow, then the two of them waving in unison. Elisa bent her head and shut her eyes, trudging past. Perhaps she was wrong in thinking that Nico and Jean had gone beyond the limits, and that they were conspiring against her. It couldn't be.

Out on the sand, Monty tossed a football to Mark. Elisa watched her bare-chested son hurl the ball back, his forehead scrunched in concentration as he tracked the ball's spiraling path through the air. How serious he was. Even when he played his guitar—handling it as if it were his baby—he was so very solemn, playing his odd little tunes. But it was easy to love someone who was serious, who would not take anything lightly. Even when he mentioned her Catholicism, Elisa knew it was merely a protest—he wanted her to accept his own reality. Maybe he saw her faith as a barrier between them. But she was simply more in tune with the dangers of life than other people were. Prayer could protect her. The earnestness, the meditation, the focus of prayer.

With their lunch of cold chicken, everyone had drunk some Carlsberg, even Kaia—and Elisa had enjoyed some of the honey-tinged beer herself—if only she could recapture the feeling of pleasantness that had come over her just a short while ago. Mark and his father had guzzled the beer as if they were in an inane contest. Not Monty, though; he didn't drink any beer at all. He didn't have that need to compete with Nico, to beat him at everything, as Mark did.

They all knew what they shouldn't do and did it anyway.

Monty ran down the beach and caught the ball. He tossed it back, then waved at Elisa and Kaia. "Come join us!" he yelled.

Mark turned towards Nico and Jean and shouted, "Hey, Dad, if you guys play, we'll have enough for a game. Come on down."

"Okay," Nico yelled back. He sprang to his feet and headed down the slope. Jean followed him, both of them in khaki Bermudas—like children dressed by their mother, Elisa thought.

"It'll have to be touch football," Jean shouted.

"Fine with me," Mark called out, then turned toward his little cousin. "You playing, Kaia?"

"Sure." She grinned and jogged over to him.

Elisa saw something lovely pass between the two cousins, almost as if one of them had blown an invisible kiss at the other, and it pleased her to imagine it.

"Mom," Mark called out, "you can keep score, unless you want to play." He torpedoed the ball to Monty.

At least he'd thought of her, though of course he knew she wouldn't want to play. "I'll just cheer you on," she called back. She gathered her skirt in one hand and clambered up the knoll.

Monty tossed the football into the air and caught it. "How about Nico and Kaia on my team, and Mark and Jean on the other?" he said.

"That's no good," Jean said. "It should be Nico, Kaia and I against you two boys."

"Okay," Mark said. "The two of us against you three."

Elisa settled onto the sand to watch. Nico had the ball and was hunched down with Kaia behind him—goodness, she was so close to him—Kaia in her T-shirt and the briefest of shorts that showed off her shapely legs. Next thing Nico was shooting the ball to Kaia, who caught it and ran. Kaia threw the ball to her mother, who sprinted until Monty caught up with her on his ostrich legs and tagged her on the back. Hah! No touchdown for Jean.

As the play continued, Kaia didn't always catch the ball but certainly ran fast, darting around the boys and passing the ball like a hot potato straight back to Nico or Jean. It was easy to see Kaia as a ballerina, leaping with her lithe, strong legs. And Mark ran with such glorious ease for someone his size, so much of his weight in his arms and shoulders, his feet hardly touching the sand. It became a dance of leaps and lunges, shouts splitting the air. For a moment Elisa felt disoriented, as if she were somewhere else, watching a performance, rather than sitting on this hot beach.

Kaia caught another pass from Nico and ran with the ball. Mark chased her and then threw his arms around her legs and took her down. Oh my! Kaia landed on her back and Mark pinned her down between his knees, toying with her while she lay clutching the ball to her chest.

"Let me up!" Kaia screamed, but she was laughing. Of course she knew Mark wouldn't do that until he felt like it. And he could so easily pluck the ball from her grasp if he wanted to—both of them prolonging the contact, legs and hands and arms—Kaia no doubt enjoying the delicious heaviness of male limbs pressing against her.

Nico yelled at Mark, "Hey, no tackling! This is touch football."

"Get off of her!" Jean shouted. "You're crushing Kaia!"

Anyone could see Mark was not crushing her.

Nico ran toward the scrambling couple and grabbed Mark's shoulder, trying to put a stop to this horseplay.

Mark shook off his father and grabbed the ball from Kaia as he got to his feet. He pulled her up by the hand, and loped away, tossing the ball to Monty.

It was obvious Kaia could hold her own in all of this roughhousing, not allowing herself to be batted around like a shuttlecock. Elisa was reminded of herself at that age, vulnerable but spunky. And it was so very clear that Mark was incapable of hurting his little cousin.

*

After dinner they all lingered in the dining room with their coffee—how delightful it was simply to linger, Elisa thought. And everyone's mood had changed. Mark and the others were more subdued now than they'd been this afternoon, undoubtedly worn out now by the heat and activity. The tension Elisa had sensed since the beginning of their holiday was gone.

"Mark and I have been talking about a camping trip, a sail around the other islands," Monty said.

"Why don't you come along, Kaia?" Mark asked, turning to her at his side.

"That sounds great." Kaia glanced at her mother, who was frowning, then back at Mark.

He smiled. "I'm sure you'd have more fun than staying here."

"What a lovely idea," Elisa said, but Nico glowered at her. He obviously didn't want the young people having too much fun.

"Of course Kaia should go," Elisa couldn't help exclaiming.

Nico stared at Mark. "How long a trip would this be?"

"Just a night or two."

"Why not a day trip?" Nico said. "We don't get to see Kaia much, you know."

Mark took a gulp of his coffee. "It won't be that long."

"I don't want you getting into any trouble out there," Nico said.

"Trouble?" Mark said with a faint sneer, tensing his jaw.

"You know what I mean."

"No, I don't."

Nico leveled a look at Mark. "Out on the water, or on the other islands. You have to watch out. It's not the safest environment for Kaia."

"It's hardly dangerous."

Kaia stared, pleading, at Nico. He grasped his coffee mug and brought it to his lips, taking a drink.

"I suppose Kaia could go," Jean said to Nico.

"Thanks, Mom." It was if her mother had offered her an unexpected gift.

"Just be careful," Nico said, glaring at Mark, then set his mug down hard. "And make it a short trip."

Nico was being so ridiculously protective, as if he were Kaia's father, Elisa thought. Sometimes it seemed the young people needed protection from the older ones more than from each other.

"Good," Mark said. "We'll get the boat ready tomorrow and leave the next day."

Elisa caught the glow of satisfaction in Mark's face, and the frustration in Nico's.

This time her son had won.

9

Mark absently broke up some driftwood, tossing the pieces onto the fire. Farther down the beach, Monty was showing Kaia how to assemble the tent poles and anchor the older canvas tent. Monty had been the same way on the boat—teaching her the basics of sailing—and she'd seemed engrossed in all of it. Mark had spent his time on the boat enjoying the sea air and watching every move of Kaia's tan little body in her black bikini.

Earlier the three of them had finished their supper of baked beans, Polish sausages, and the Boston brown bread Elisa had sent along. Now the sky was darkening and Mark wanted to keep the fire going until they turned in. A chilly, invigorating breeze came off the ocean, blowing smoke into his face.

Picking up his guitar, he began strumming a Latin tune, glancing up now and then to watch the other two. As he played, he wondered why he was constantly thinking about his cousin, intrigued with her every gesture, her soft voice, and the way she looked at him so intently. His conduct, he thought, had been commendable, considering the way he felt, other than a minor lapse or two—there was that walk on the beach that evening and the ill-considered kiss on the knee, and then the time he tackled her during the football game. She hadn't seemed to mind any of that, though.

Once the canvas tent was set up, Monty started putting up the dome tent. Kaia came over and stood a yard away from Mark. When he glanced up from his guitar, she was shivering in her sweatshirt, hugging herself. She smelled like the beach, and her legs were sandy up to her bikini bottom.

"Could you show me a few chords sometime?" she asked.

Mark nodded and kept playing, humming to himself as he tried to quiet his stupidly thumping heartbeat, while he finished the tune. "Why don't you just sit down over here." He pulled a camp chair closer to him.

When she'd settled down, he handed her the guitar.

"Okay," he said, "let's start with a G chord. You know the strings?"

She shook her head. "I'm not sure."

"Here." He reached over and showed her where to put her fingers, arranging her hand in a curved position, lingering a second or two longer than was strictly necessary. He gave her the pick. "Now strum all of the strings."

She did it in a mellow way, offering her own take on the chord. He could see she had a natural touch.

"You've done this before," he said.

"I had a few lessons once."

She had a slight smile on her lips as she concentrated on her playing. He had the impulse to brush the sand off her legs just to feel her smooth skin. He thought of Barb, who had a swimmer's sturdy legs—a tall, striking girl. She was nothing like Kaia. His cousin had her own kind of self-possession—a solitariness, a waywardness he could relate to. There was more to Kaia than to other girls he'd known, even though she was so young.

She glanced up and caught him staring at her. She rested her hand on the guitar, her eyes wide. "I have to admit something," she said.

"What's that?"

"I've been a little afraid to get to know you better, even though we're cousins."

"You have?" He tried to say this matter-of-factly, while his heart kept pummeling away inside his chest.

"I have, actually," she said with the barest upturn of her lips. "My friend Sigourney says things become ordinary once you know someone really well. Or else it turns into the kind of thing where you go nuts thinking about them all the time."

"So either things turn out to be dull, or you get completely obsessed?" What exactly were they talking about here?

She played a chord, then glanced up at him. "Something like that."

He paused, pretending to evaluate the merits of each alternative. "I think I'd rather be obsessed, wouldn't you?"

"Hmm." She kept her eyes on him, as if thinking hard. "Sure. Ordinary doesn't appeal much to me."

"What does, then?"

She looked down, picking out a few notes on the guitar, her manner maddeningly casual. "I guess I'd go for intensity."

"What kind of intensity?" he couldn't help asking.

She strummed on the guitar a couple of times. "Not the way my mother is, that's for sure. Mom goes after what she wants, big financial deals, stuff like that. I care more about other things, like people."

Kaia sounded so naive when she said that, it stopped him for a moment. "I can see that in your mom," he said. But he was barely listening to his own words, thinking more about the way her lips would feel if he were to bend over and kiss her, cousin or not.

"And your mom, too," Kaia said, "she's so passionate, but in a different way than my mother."

"Absentee mothers," he said under his breath.

"What do you mean?"

"My mother was never totally there for me. She was a psych case, a problem. I love her, but I could never count on her."

"I'm not close to my mom anymore, especially since she moved across the country," Kaia said in a wistful voice.

"I can see that." He didn't want to talk about mothers, though. "Here, let's try another chord."

After a while, Monty came over and threw himself lengthwise on the sand, watching as Kaia strummed a series of chords. "Hey, sounds pretty good," he said.

She beamed at Monty, and all Mark could think was that he wanted her to smile at him that way, without holding back. She played the series of chords again with less hesitation. Then Mark taught her to play the first part of a Mama Cass tune, and Kaia sang the words softly. Her voice was pleasant to hear, though she occasionally veered off-key, and that amused him. He could sense the feeling in her as she sang, and she became more confident as she went along.

She finally handed the guitar back to him. By now the sky was an inky blue and the fire had contracted into embers. He wished the two of them were alone together.

"So you guys are staying on Pine Tree for a while?" Kaia asked.

"Only a couple more days," Monty said, sitting up.

"Too bad," she said.

It *was* too bad, Mark thought, especially since Kaia was going to stay on here after they left. But Monty's parents were expecting them up at the St. Lawrence; the trip had been planned weeks ago.

"I hear your dad's a law professor," Monty said to Kaia. "Constitutional law, right?"

"Yep. You're going to law school, too, I heard."

"Northeastern. Mark's the one who got into the hotshot school."

Mark shook his head and poked around in the fire with a stick, stirring up sparks.

"Mark got A's without even studying," Monty said. "He spent all his time playing the guitar and training for wrestling matches."

Kaia turned to Mark. "You were a wrestler?"

"He always manages to come out on top," Monty said. "Does all right in the women department, too."

Mark glared at Monty. "What in the hell are you talking about?"

"I guess it's mainly Barbara," Monty conceded, grinning.

"I told you that's over."

"You just said you didn't want to bring her here."

It was true, he hadn't actually broken things off with Barb. But he hadn't had any inclination to see her during the summer, either. Each time she'd called him, suggesting they get together, he'd begged off, saying he was too busy. In his mind, at least, that meant it was over.

Mark stood and stretched. "Anyway, we should turn in. You can have the old tent, big boy."

Monty drew in his chin with a weird half-grin. "I thought that one was for Kaia. I'm sure she doesn't want to share the dome tent with anyone. Especially with you—not with all the snoring you do."

"The dome's bigger than the canvas tent. Anyway, I don't want Kaia to be alone in there."

"Why not?"

"I just don't," Mark said, raising his voice.

"Kaia's a big girl," Monty said, "in case you hadn't had a chance to notice."

In the shadows, Mark could make out a sneer on his face.

Kaia stood up, her lips pursed, and tugged her sweatshirt down over her hips. "I don't really care."

"There are animals on the island," Mark told her. "Even the raccoons can be pretty aggressive. You'd be better off in the dome so we can all get some sleep."

Kaia pushed her hair off her forehead. She glanced from Monty to Mark, her face lit in the flickering embers. "I guess the dome, then," she said in an offhand way.

Monty shook his head. Mark watched as Kaia gathered up her sleeping bag and pack and made her way toward the dark hemisphere of the tent, as if it were inconsequential, which tent she slept in and who would spend the night in it with her.

Once she'd slipped into the tent, Monty stood up, frowning, to face Mark across the smoking fire pit. "This is a really bad idea, you know," he said, his voice rough.

"I just want to make sure she's all right." Mark struggled to keep his face impassive.

"Jesus Christ, she's your cousin. And she's sixteen."

"Doesn't seem to stop you from leering at her all the time," Mark said angrily.

"You're hopeless, man." Monty snorted and strode away toward the old tent.

Mark kicked a few stones into the fire pit, then doused the burning embers with a pot of water. He gave Kaia a few minutes to settle in, then went over and climbed into the tent. She was lying in her sleeping bag, facing away from him. He rolled his bag out, got in, and lay on his back with his hands under his head.

After a while, he heard Kaia shift in her sleeping bag. "Why did you do that?" she asked, peering over her shoulder at him.

"What?"

"Make Monty sleep in the other tent."

"Like I said, it's not that safe. Your mom wouldn't be too happy if you got attacked by wildcats or something."

"Wildcats?" She sounded skeptical. He could just make out her face in the moonlit tent.

"Probably not, but you never know." There might be deer, skunks, maybe a fox or two, rabbits, turtles. Nothing very dangerous, he would have to say, if he were being completely honest.

She was silent for a while, then rolled over, facing him. "Are we going to get into trouble for this?" Her tone was low and conspiratorial.

"For what?"

"For *this*."

It was pathetic, how little it took to make his pulse quicken—even the mere suggestion that they were doing something illicit. "I doubt it. Unless you're a bigger security risk than I thought."

She laughed. "I would never tell anyone anything, would you?"

He imagined all sorts of things she might mean. "Course not."

She let out a long sigh. "I just wish we weren't cousins."

He was relieved she was actually talking about this—it was something he'd been afraid to face head on. He propped himself up on his elbow and looked into her face. "It doesn't matter," he said firmly.

"It does to other people."

They were both silent, and he laid his head back down on the pillow and sighed.

"I guess you must have a boyfriend, or dozens of them," he said after a while.

"Hah! As if my dad would let me."

"Really? You're almost seventeen, aren't you?"

"Dad says he's not ready for me to date. Last semester, though, there was a boy who liked me."

"Only one?" Mark didn't like to think about boys liking her.

"Yeah. He called me after school was out in June. He wanted to go to a movie with me." She giggled. "He told me he'd been riding his bicycle past my house at night for weeks, trying to catch a glimpse of me."

"Poor kid. So what did you tell him? To go to hell, I hope."

"I told him I couldn't date. But I had no desire to go out with a guy like him, believe me."

"So what kind of guy would you want to be with?"

She shifted onto her back. "I don't have much experience in that area." She turned her head toward him. "But I know I've never been loved by anyone the way I want to be," she said very softly.

"You know how you want to be loved?" He'd lowered his voice as well.

"I just have a feeling about it."

He wished he could be the one to love her the way she wanted, whatever that turned out to be. As he lay there, he tried to keep his breathing normal, but the wrong kind of thoughts kept coming at him like buckshot.

"Kaia," he said quietly, without knowing exactly what he was going to say or do.

She moved her head, and in the bright moonlight coming through the screen he could see her hair spread out over the white pillow. Without premeditating he found himself moving closer, and he reached over to place his hand on her cheek. She inhaled sharply. He raised himself on his forearm and bent over her, his face a few inches from hers. Still she said nothing, but she was looking into his eyes. He kissed her lightly on her brow, then on her lips.

"Is this okay?" he asked.

She nodded and blew out her breath. He kissed her again on the lips, more slowly this time, then brought his face to her neck, breathing in the delicate ripe-pear scent of her skin. He reached into her sleeping bag and eased his hand under her sweatshirt. When he rested his hand lightly on her stomach, she gasped softly. Her breathing became quicker while he searched her face in the dim light. She didn't seem afraid, and he wasn't thinking about what the hell he was doing, he just kept his hand there in suspension and imagined he could feel her pleasure thrumming under her skin. Then he started moving his hand up toward her breast and touched the bare underside—she wasn't wearing her bikini top.

She grabbed onto his arm, digging in with her fingers. "Don't, Mark," she whispered.

He groaned, disgusted with himself, and rolled away from her. "Sorry." He got up and stumbled out of the tent and headed down the beach, running. The cool sand shifted under his bare feet, and after a minute he moved onto the dense sand near the water and ran faster, hoping to wear himself out. He tripped over some driftwood and a sharp pain shot through his big toe, but he kept jogging. He kept replaying what had just happened in the tent. Why had he touched her like that? What was he actually planning to do, for Christ's sake? His little *cousin.* What he did was way beyond anything she would have wanted. Or was it? He recalled the way she'd nodded her head when he'd asked if it was okay, and her gasp when he'd laid his hand on her stomach. And what had she meant when she asked if they were going to get in trouble for this?

After a while he felt calmer, though still sick about the whole thing, and he headed back, jogging at a good pace on the slick, packed sand, the broken shells sharp against his feet. When he entered the tent, she was quiet and still. He lay on top of his sleeping bag, hot and breathing hard. His whole body was tense, his stubbed toe throbbing, and he knew he wouldn't be able to sleep. Kaia shifted around in her sleeping bag and yawned, and after a few minutes, her breathing became smooth and rhythmic. He loved having her just inches away from him, even if it meant he wouldn't sleep all night.

For a while he lay there listening to the slapping of the breakers and the wind gusting against the tent. He thought back to that first boat ride with Kaia, when she'd arrived at the Cape and he'd given in to the impulse to tease her a bit during the trip over the channel. It was as if he'd poked his finger into the cage of a skittish bird, trying to provoke a flutter out of it, its heart pulsing away at his touch, and then had tried like an idiot to get it to hop trustfully onto his finger. Kaia was like that—an exotic, untamable bird, alert to him in a way he liked. She'd been a little afraid of him, he thought, until that first night when she'd turned her back on her mother and walked out into the storm with him.

Feeling restless, he turned onto his side. Kaia was facing away from him, her arm on top of her sleeping bag, her sweatshirt sleeve pushed up to her elbow. He could see the outline of her shoulder rising and falling. He sensed everything acutely—the smell of seaweed, the scent of her skin and hair, the sound of the waves roaring and crashing, the coarse feel of sand between his toes.

"Kaia, are you awake?" he whispered. She didn't seem to move. After a few moments, he reached over, raising himself on his elbow, and placed his hand lightly on her forearm, and she twitched under his touch. Her breath became almost inaudible, and he thought she might be awake now. Her skin felt cool, and he curled his fingers more firmly around her slender arm. She groaned softly, and after a minute shifted onto her back. He took his hand away and lay back down. A moment later she turned her head toward him, opening her eyes, then reached out and took his hand, pushing her fingers through his and holding his hand companionably, as if they'd been together like this many times before.

After a few minutes she shut her eyes and started to breathe more heavily, and her hand loosened under his. He felt incredibly good about having her to himself for the hours ahead. To his surprise, he found that he could relax now, and he let out a long, low sigh.

10

Kaia lay in her sleeping bag with her arm covering her eyes, listening to Monty and Mark argue. She heard her name a few times and heard Monty call Mark an idiot, but couldn't make out most of their words. She hadn't been awake when Mark left the tent earlier this morning, and now she was trying to remember exactly what had happened during the night. She hadn't slept very deeply, and she still felt suffused with Mark's presence. She thought of the way he'd kissed her and touched her and how delicious it had felt. The impulse to turn to him had been powerful, difficult to resist. It was supposed to be scary the first time a guy touched you like that, probably wanting to go all the way, but she hadn't been afraid. He just went too fast and she didn't have time to think about what would happen if she had turned to him, moved into his arms.

She reached under her sweatshirt and ran her hand over her breasts and wondered what they would feel like to a man. Then she heard the swish of the tent flap and Mark poked his head in, staring at her as she slid her hand down. He crawled inside, bringing with him the smell of singed firewood. He reached under his sleeping bag and found his sweatshirt, then pulled it on over his rugby shirt. His jaw was covered with dark stubble.

"Are you going to stay in here all morning?" he asked, his voice a bit gruff.

She sat up and pushed a strand of hair behind her ear. Mark knelt down close to her, peering into her eyes.

"I'm sorry about last night," he mumbled.

She frowned, wondering if he regretted the whole thing. "It's okay."

"Come out and have some breakfast," he said more gently.

After he left, she found her jeans and pulled them on, then crawled out of the tent and walked toward the ocean. A wind was blowing in, the sea riffled like coarse watercolor paper and saturated with deep colors—teal, parakeet blue, slate—the sky's colors reflected in the sea. Sanderlings ran back and forth with each wave, then took flight all at once toward the ocean. The dunes up the coast were washed over with a rusty glow. She didn't believe she would ever return to this place, and she wanted to memorize every detail.

Turning toward the campsite, she caught the aroma of coffee percolating on the grill. Mark was crouched down, stirring the fire with a stick. Monty sat cross-legged on the sand, eating from his plate. He nodded as she approached; she'd never seen him looking so grim.

Mark silently dished out some ham and eggs for Kaia and for himself. After they'd finished, they all sat drinking coffee without speaking, the two guys not even looking at each other.

Mark got up and looked toward the sailboat. "We should head back to Pine Tree soon."

Monty let out a low whistle. "Great. That's just great." He stood up and took a carton of orange juice from the ice chest, then strode toward the water.

Kaia wanted to put her arms around Mark and hug him, but his brow was furrowed, his mouth an unyielding grimace.

"Mark?"

"It's all right." He stared at her, running a hand through his hair, as if debating with himself what to do. Then he turned and jogged down the beach, kicking up sand.

He obviously didn't want to talk to her, and that hurt. What was going on with him? For several minutes, Kaia watched him running away.

Then Monty returned to the campfire.

"Aren't we going to camp out another night somewhere?" she asked him, trying to keep her voice steady.

"We were going to do some fishing south of here, and camp on a different island. I guess we'll make up our minds once we've packed up."

Kaia got up quickly. She crawled into the tent and found her father's 35-mm. Canon and loaded it with black-and-white film. She hadn't taken any photos since she'd come to Pine Tree, but now she felt compelled to make a record of some kind, though she wasn't sure why. Moving mechanically, she took a few photos inside the tent—the screened window filtering the cloudy sky, the rumpled sleeping bags and clothing, Mark's tennis shoes and her own sneakers. But it seemed like a pointless thing to do. Pictures couldn't capture Mark's particular scent, and even Ektacolor wouldn't have reproduced the exact hues of his skin and eyes.

Outside, she had Monty pose next to his tent with the sailboat anchored in the background. How depressing to discover herself documenting her life, storing up images for afterwards—just as she had in the days before her mother went away. She should never have pinned her hopes on anyone. No one, except her father, apparently liked her enough to stick around.

During those weeks in January before her mother left, Kaia had begun, in a casual way at first, to take pictures of her in various places: Mom drinking coffee at the kitchen table, Mom in front of the de Young Museum, Mom working in the upstairs room, which she used as her office and bedroom. A few times Kaia set up a tripod and used the delayed shutter release to include herself in various shots. She took several rolls of black-and-white film, telling herself it was merely an artistic project.

Her mother never commented on this bizarre behavior. After she left, Kaia would often study the photos, observing the way she and her mom appeared happy in them, as if they were part of any family doing ordinary things together. Kaia wished now that there had been more pictures from when she was in elementary school, when her mother had spent more time with her—taking her shopping or to ballet lessons or out for pizza.

Kaia returned to the tent to pack up her things. By the time Mark returned, most of the gear was piled on the beach. Once they'd broken camp and boarded the boat, Mark took the helm. They headed up the Cape in the direction of Pine Tree, rather than southward as they'd planned. No one said anything about it. Monty chatted with Kaia a bit, but Mark hardly spoke at all, his face averted except for occasional glances at her.

During the next couple of hours, she stared at the islands they passed, trying to distract herself from the nearly physical ache that gripped her. She had no idea what was going on, but whatever was wrong had to be partly her fault—maybe for somehow coming between the two guys.

Mark never allowed Monty or her to take a turn at the tiller.

At the cottage, Kaia found Elisa standing quietly at the front window, gazing toward the dock where the guys were unloading the boat. Her aunt's face brightened as she turned, and she came over, her arms outstretched, to give Kaia a hug.

"We've missed you so much," Elisa said. "Things have been pretty dull around here. How was your trip?"

"It was shorter than it was supposed to be."

Elisa raised her eyebrows.

Kaia glanced away for a moment, then back at her aunt. "Where's Mom, by the way?"

"She went back to the city to take care of some business matter. She said to give you her love."

Kaia felt a tight constriction in her chest. "I think I'll go upstairs."

Her aunt reached out, brushing Kaia's arm as she rushed out of the room.

Entering her mother's bedroom upstairs, Kaia caught the floral scent of her mother's Eau de Givenchy. Tears built up in her eyes as she searched the room. Gone were the elegant clothes, the silk scarves, and all of the accessories for her mother's meticulously designed life. Her mother was obviously no longer willing to waste her precious time on an island with a bunch of problematic relatives—Kaia included.

She went to her own room and found an envelope propped on the pillow. She opened it and ran her eyes over the enclosed sheet of paper:

> Sweetheart,
>
> I'm sorry I had to leave so suddenly, but I was needed back in New York for a major deal that was in danger of falling through. I'm glad we were able to spend some time together here. It's beginning to feel as if you're truly a part of my side of the family.
>
> I'll call you when you're back in Berkeley. Take care of yourself.
>
> Lots of love, Mom

Kaia ripped up the letter, throwing the pieces into the wastebasket. Why had she thought it would be any different this time? Even the bit of time they'd had together she'd been forced to share with the others. She clearly didn't figure in her mother's scheme of things.

But now at least she wouldn't have to catch her mother frowning, her face etched with frustration when she glanced at her, as if to remind her that a girl should learn to cope, should be independent, "gutsy" in the face of whatever challenges might be slung at her.

Kaia recalled now the welcoming feel of Mark's touch in the tent. If only she could have his arms wrapped around her now, comforting her. But he would soon be gone, and it seemed that he'd already distanced himself from her. She almost wished she'd never come here.

The only person who truly wanted to be with her was her father—her father who was no doubt eagerly awaiting her return.

11

The gray, damp morning pressed down on Mark as he climbed out of the rowboat at the Cape Cod dock. He felt like such an idiot, giving up the extra days he could have spent with Kaia on Pine Tree. And he still hadn't managed to make things right with her, even though he'd talked to her a couple of times. But they hadn't had a real chance to be alone again. He should never have agreed to leave for the St. Lawrence River so soon.

Nico got out of the boat after him, then Mark took Kaia's hand, steadying her as she stepped onto the pier. Monty followed them all to the parking lot, where the Saab was parked.

"It's been a blast," Monty said to Kaia, stopping and bending to give her a hug. "You keep in touch, kiddo."

"Okay, I will."

"Hey, my turn," Mark said from a few yards away.

She came over, carrying herself in that erect way that made him see the ballerina in her. Impulsively he bent and kissed her, feeling her lips again, her cheek cool under his hand. At that moment he didn't give a damn about what his old man or Monty thought. Kaia stepped back, running her eyes over his face.

"Bye, Mark," she whispered, then reached forward, hugging him tightly, the first time she had done that. It felt so good he just kept holding on, not caring about anything except the feel of her light frame pressed against him, until she eased out of his grasp.

Jesus, what was he supposed to do—say good-bye to her, and then wait for her eighteenth birthday to start seeing her again? His little cousin. Without thinking he hugged her again and kissed her on the lips, then made himself step back, taking hold of her arms. Leaning forward, he whispered in her ear, "Just wait for me, babe, okay?"

With a startled gasp she stared up at him, her lips starting to form some words. Then Mark sensed his father's hard presence behind him and dropped his hands away from Kaia. A blast of wind flung a few sloppy droplets of rain over all of them. When Mark turned around, Nico was frowning but gave him a brisk hug, pounding him on the back.

"Send a postcard to me in Bangor from the St. Lawrence, all right?" his father said.

Then Nico wrapped his arm around Kaia's shoulders and hustled her down to the pier, so damned impatient to take her away. Mark watched as the two of them climbed into the rowboat and pushed off from the dock. When they were out on the water, Kaia turned and waved at him, and he waved back at her, his heart hammering away inside his chest like a goddamned gong.

PART TWO

BERKELEY

1980 TO 1981

1

From the entryway, Mark searched the hazy interior of the restaurant for Kaia and her father. "Kaia likes to eat Mexican," David had said on the phone, naming the airport restaurant where Mark was supposed to meet them. Mark didn't care where they were going to eat, he just wanted to see Kaia. It had been two months since Pine Tree. They had exchanged postcards and a few phone calls during the summer, and he'd found himself thinking about her constantly.

The restaurant was nearly empty and lit with a few red chandeliers. Mark didn't see Kaia or David anywhere. A hefty, middle-aged waitress led him to a booth near the bar, where a couple of guys were smoking and watching a boxing match. The air was stuffy and warm, and Mark was perspiring as he slung his gear under the table and sat down. He asked the waitress to bring him a Coors draft. It was 3:20 p.m., Maine time, so just past noon in California. David had told him he might have to wait a while, since Kaia had her Saturday morning ballet class.

Mark ate the basketful of tortilla chips with his beer and then scanned the restaurant for the waitress, who had disappeared. After a few minutes he got up and crossed over to the bar.

The bartender was probably thirty, with platinum bangs splayed over black eyebrows, her hair pulled back. She was tall and skinny, and up close her thick makeup made her face look like a mask.

She slid a paper coaster in front of him. "Coming or going?" she asked with a grin.

"Excuse me?"

Cocking her head, she wound a strand of hair around her finger with some delicacy. "Arriving or departing?"

"Arriving. Just waiting for someone." He knew he sounded gruff, but he didn't feel like chatting with the woman.

"Another Coors?"

"Sure."

Turning away, she drew the beer, standing with her hip thrust to one side, her weight on one leg.

She set the beer in front of him. He noted with distaste the frosty-blue eye makeup, the dark-red lipstick, the chemical smell of her perfume. Why couldn't women just look natural?

"Where you from?" she asked, resting her hands on the countertop, displaying her long, red-lacquered nails.

"Maine, as a matter of fact." He took a long drink and glanced to the side, where a gray-haired man sat a few seats away, a cigarette in one hand. The skunk-like odor of the smoke made Mark recognize it as a Kent cigarette, the brand his dad used to smoke. Mark had always detested the smell, the way it clung to everything in the house, including Nico's clothing.

"So what are you doing in California?" the bartender persisted.

He wished she would just go away—take care of the other customers, anything. She merely stood staring at him with a smile that struck him as overly familiar.

"I'm starting law school in Berkeley." He felt foolish for blurting it out; it was only bound to prolong the talk.

"Wow, impressive," she said with a smile, and then headed toward the other man at the counter.

Mark quickly drained his glass. What he wasn't going to mention was his biggest coup—getting his uncle to let him rent the upstairs apartment in his house in Berkeley. He thought of Kaia's tawny, smooth face and the way it felt when he'd kissed her in the tent at the Cape. He wondered how it would be to see her now; he'd been obsessing about it during much of the plane trip.

When the bartender returned, he pushed his glass toward her and turned away, gazing around the restaurant. She drew another beer and set it down in front of him, pressing her midriff against the counter.

"So how long does law school take?" She leaned forward with her elbows on the countertop, her blouse straining against her chest. "Until you're a lawyer, I mean."

"Three years."

"Then back home?"

"Probably not." His parents probably assumed he would be returning to Maine every summer and then after he graduated. But he realized now that had no intention of going back.

The woman glanced toward the entrance, and Mark turned to look. A couple stood there, silhouetted against the bright corridor. He stared for a moment, then recognized Kaia and her father. He lifted his glass toward the bartender. "Put it on my bill."

She winked at him, and he headed toward the entrance, his heartbeat accelerating when he caught sight of Kaia looking in his direction. As he approached, he saw that she was wearing a low-cut top that showed some cleavage and a colorful woven jacket that hung open. She wasn't smiling, but the curve of her cheeks softened her face, and her wavy hair floated over her shoulders like a cape. She appeared older than she had at Pine Tree. He shook hands with his uncle and noticed that he was as tall as David now.

When Mark faced Kaia again, he was taken aback by her slight frown. "Kaia," he said, making his voice upbeat. Standing there with his hands balled at his sides, Mark was conscious of David's watchfulness.

"Mark," she said in a flat tone. Still no smile.

Flustered, he let his eyes linger on her face a moment longer, then motioned toward the booth where he'd left his gear. Kaia and her father followed him, and the two of them sat down together on one side of the booth. Mark seated himself across from them. As Kaia slipped out of her jacket, he saw that it was a shimmery leotard she was wearing, and no bra—or not much of one, anyway—so that her breasts and nipples were clearly outlined. *Jesus.* He moved his eyes to her stony face.

David glanced down at Kaia's leotard. "You should put your jacket on. It's cold in here with the air conditioning."

She crossed her arms—a move that only emphasized her cleavage. "I'm fine."

When the older waitress appeared with more tortilla chips, David asked for a pitcher of Dos Equis and an iced tea for Kaia. They all ordered their food—combination plates for the two men and a cheese enchilada for Kaia.

David stretched his arms over his head and clasped his hands behind his head. "Classes start on Wednesday," he said to Mark, "so you've got a few days to buy your books and settle in."

Mark nodded. "First thing I need to do is to get some transportation."

"You want to buy a car?" David asked.

"Yes—just something cheap and dependable. I sold my motorcycle back in Boston, wasn't worth the cost of shipping it."

"I thought you spent the summer in Bangor with your folks."

"No, I stayed in Boston. In July I spent a couple of weeks at the St. Lawrence River." Mark glanced at Kaia. "You know—with Monty." He looked back at David. "Monty was at Pine Tree when Kaia was there."

"I told you about him, Dad," Kaia said. "He's the one who loves sailing."

"So did you, as I recall," Mark said. "Monty's starting law school at Northeastern in a couple of weeks, you know."

"Yes, I know." She was slumped down on the bench now, her arms still crossed. She seemed to be hanging on to some grievance with him, but at least she was making eye contact. She'd been so friendly the few times he'd talked to her on the phone over the summer—nothing like this. It gave him a sick feeling, not knowing what was going on.

For some reason the blonde bartender brought the pitcher over herself, and made a ritual out of pouring the beer slowly into the two frosted mugs, smiling all the while. Then she winked at Mark and said in a sultry voice, "Hey, good luck with law school. Let me know if you need anything else."

Mark nodded at her, then caught a flash of anger in Kaia's glance as the woman walked away. What was the problem here, exactly?

"Tomorrow I'll take you to look for a car," David said rather curtly, as if offering from some imagined duty.

"Great." Mark leaned back and took a drink. "So you're teaching Constitutional Law again this year?"

"Yep." David shook some salt into the palm of his hand and sprinkled it onto the tortilla chips. "You won't be taking that until your second year, though." He chomped noisily on a chip.

They talked more about law school for a while, but Kaia remained quiet, just sipping at her iced tea and glancing frequently toward the entrance, as if she wanted to make her escape.

Finally their food arrived. Mark happened to glance over at the bar, and caught the bartender grinning at him. Kaia turned toward the bar, then met Mark's eyes, her lips pressed together in a hard line. He raised his eyebrows at her, but she just glanced down at her enchilada and began eating.

After finishing all of the food on his plate, Mark drank still another glass of beer, though he was starting to feel a little high. He'd probably drunk one too many, trying to get past his nervousness at seeing Kaia. When the bill came, he reached for it.

"No, I'll get it," David said.

"Nope." Mark reached for his wallet, glanced at the check, and slapped down a few bills. He pushed the tray towards the edge of the table.

David frowned. "I'll get the tip, then." He got to his feet and threw a five on the table.

Mark stood up, swaying a bit, and faced his uncle for a long moment. He realized he was actually taller than David and definitely outweighed him.

"Let's get out of here," his uncle said.

Kaia stood, slinging her jacket over her shoulder toreador style, and David placed his hand on her upper back as they made their way toward the exit, with Mark following behind. Kaia seemed rather slight next to her father, and Mark noticed that David was limping a bit. Mark traced the outline of Kaia's body under the clingy leotard and snug jeans; she was wearing some little heels that clicked on the tile floor as she walked. Once they were in the airport corridor, Mark moved alongside her, but she ignored him.

This was not what he'd been expecting at all.

2

As the car turned into the driveway, Kaia wondered what Mark would think of the old house after not seeing it for eight years. Perched at the top of the sloping lawn, it looked rather shabby and needed paint. She told herself she shouldn't care what Mark thought, anyway. He wasn't the same as she remembered him—he'd almost seemed like some kind of barfly when she'd first seen him sitting at the bar, chatting with the blonde bartender.

"Your room is upstairs in the loft," her father told Mark, once they were all inside the house. "Just go to the back, turn into the hallway—"

"Aren't you even going to take him upstairs, Dad?" She couldn't believe he was being so rude.

"I'm sure he can find it."

Kaia glared at her father for a few moments, then shrugged. "I guess I'll show him, then."

Without comment she led Mark through the house and into the rear hallway, passing the open door of her bedroom. She ran up the stairs and waited at the top for him, her heart fluttering away despite her annoyance with him. There was no doorway to the loft; the stairs led directly into the spacious room. When Mark came up, he set down his duffel bag and guitar and took a few moments to scan the area. His gaze stopped at the stained glass at the end of the room.

"Nice window," he said.

"I found it at a yard sale." Kaia recalled her excitement at the find, several years ago, when she and her dad were looking for some camping equipment. She'd loved its geometric design and the beveled glass pieces, and had convinced her father to buy it and have it installed.

She followed Mark's eyes toward the slender table she had set next to the bed and the vase filled with yellow, coral and red roses from the garden—she could smell their fragrance in the balmy afternoon. She'd ordered the navy velvet comforter on the bed and the embroidered pillows from a catalogue. On the other side of the room sat the armchair her father had brought upstairs and an old oak desk she had re-stained for Mark. This was the first time the room had seemed truly livable. Her mother, in the months before she'd left, had used it as a bedroom as well as an office; then it had seemed characterless, with its filing cabinets, steel desk, and the bed with its gray blanket. Her mother was always on the phone or busy with paperwork during those months, and Kaia had felt excluded.

Today she'd wanted to photograph the room with its lacy curtains billowing in the breeze through the open windows, but she hadn't had time before her ballet lesson. She'd wanted to capture its subdued colors, its angles, the fantastic quality of light, to preserve it as it was on the day of Mark's arrival. *Numinous, luminous, phantasmagorical* were the words that had come to her as she'd taken one last look at the room this morning. Now, as she watched Mark's face brightening with pleasure, and despite her aggravation with him, a part of her still wanted him to love the house, so that he would want to stay.

"Cool," Mark said, his voice low, turning to her.

It was the way he said it that reminded her of the way he was at Pine Tree. Of course he'd meant the room was attractive, but she could tell he'd meant more than the furniture and the décor. He seemed to be including the two of them being together in the house, and his taking over this room. And now she felt his eyes meeting hers and then tracing her forehead, her cheeks, her lips, as if deciding where to kiss her.

He smiled, then, reluctantly it seemed, turned away and walked over to the kitchenette with its miniature refrigerator, which she'd filled with a few bottles of beer she'd brought from downstairs. He opened the refrigerator and peered inside.

"Hey, great." He looked over at her. "Thanks."

He crossed over to the rear door and stepped outside, onto the balcony. "Kaia, come here," he called to her.

She went out and stood next to him at the railing; they looked over the immense yard with its old tree house, where she used to play. Mark stood so close she felt the static electricity from the hair on his forearm. The only sound was the buzz of a power mower a few houses away.

"It's just the way I remember it," he said.

She met his gaze, and he smiled again, in a lazy way.

"Mark," she said after a few moments, "I was wondering something. Do you go to bars a lot?" She knew it sounded infantile, but she wanted to know.

"Hardly." He squinted at her. "Why?"

She hesitated, then said, "You were awfully friendly with that woman at the bar. Do you always hang around in bars and flirt like that?"

"What—you mean with the bartender?"

Kaia nodded, scrutinizing his face.

"She was the one who was being too friendly—I was just trying to be polite."

"Oh, I see." Kaia wasn't completely sure she believed him. "I mean the way you were smiling at her and everything. And she knew about you going to law school."

Mark frowned, looking puzzled. "I wasn't flirting."

Kaia kept her eyes focused on his. "I just thought it was weird the way she came over and winked at you."

"Is that why you were acting that way in the restaurant?" he asked.

She looked away. "You seemed like a different person, that's all."

"I'm sorry you got that impression." He reached out and squeezed her bare upper arm. "I just went over to the bar to get a beer. I was a little nervous about seeing you. I was glad to get away from the woman."

"Okay, then," she said, but felt her heart thundering away. The talk had gotten so personal so quickly, and he was standing so close to her, still holding on to her arm.

"Kaia," he said with an insistence that startled her.

She faced him for a moment, then turned away from the railing. It scared her, his sudden intensity. "Let's go inside," she said.

As they stepped back into the room, he rested his hand lightly on her shoulder. She realized she'd never even seen Mark in a situation with other women around, out in the world like that—she'd only known him on the island. When he was around other people, that wasn't necessarily the same Mark she knew. She told herself that the way he was with her now, when they were alone together, was the way he really was. But she wasn't sure, and she couldn't quite erase the image in her mind of Mark toasting the bartender.

"You haven't seen the bathroom," she said. Now she wanted him to take in everything—the royal-blue towels, the sandalwood soap, the sparkling tiles—everything she'd prepared for him. She'd spent hours cleaning the bathroom, which they had used in the past as a darkroom.

"Actually, I wouldn't mind a shower," Mark said.

"I'll go downstairs then."

"No, wait. I'll just be five minutes."

She shook her head and started to move toward the stairs.

"Kaia, come on, just stay for a while, okay? It's been so long since I've seen you."

She shrugged and said okay, but it meant everything to her that he wanted her to stay up here. She sat in the armchair and stretched out her legs on the ottoman. He hesitated, then headed for the bathroom with his duffel bag.

Hearing the shower curtain draw shut, she recalled how he'd looked in swim trunks during their camping trip—his skin tanned russet, the curly hair on his chest, the muscles in his legs and back working as he did various chores around the campsite. When she heard the water running, she imagined the hot water soaking into his skin, and pictured him coming out of the bathroom with a towel wrapped around his waist.

She wondered if he was thinking about her now.

3

David paced back and forth in the front room, favoring his left foot, since he'd sprained his right ankle a week ago playing tennis. He was trying to overcome his desire for a whiskey, since it was too early in the afternoon to start, and he'd had all that beer at the airport. He hadn't envisaged his nephew as a fully-grown man, and didn't like the way Mark kept staring at Kaia. Why in the hell had he allowed Mark to move in with them? He shouldn't have let Kaia blackmail him, claiming she'd go to New York to live with her mother if she didn't have someone to talk to once in a while. As if he would even consider letting Kaia leave.

He still wanted that drink, and went across the room to pour himself a generous glassful, then drank it quickly and started on another one.

The upstairs shower went on and he wondered if Kaia could still be up in the loft. He set down his glass and strode to the back hallway, passing her empty bedroom, then stopped at the foot of the stairs.

"Kaia," he hollered. It was quiet for a few seconds, then he heard her walk to the top of the stairs.

She stood gazing down at him, hands on hips, a resentful frown on her face. "What," she said in a flat, irritated tone.

"What are you doing up there?"

"Nothing."

"Come downstairs."

She hesitated, then started down the steps and sauntered past him in the hallway. He followed her into the den. She turned around to face him in her low-cut leotard and tight jeans. Why did she have to dress like that? He should have made her change before they drove to the airport.

"Listen, Kaia. Mark is going to need his privacy. This won't work if you're up there bothering him."

"*Bothering* him," she snorted. "Jesus, Dad, he just got here."

"Don't talk to me that way." Just a few years ago, he would have pulled her over his knees in a second, giving her some good hard whacks for that.

She tried to move around him, back toward her room, but he grabbed her arm and blocked her way. "Upstairs is off limits, you understand?"

"Why?" she said, right into his face, and tried to shake off his arm.

Holding on to her, he felt her arm stiffen. "Mark's an adult now, and it's not appropriate for you to be up there bugging him."

"I wouldn't dream of *bugging* him." The impudence was back in her voice, her eyes narrowing. "Besides, I don't see why I shouldn't be allowed to go upstairs. This is my house, too."

He let go of her and folded his arms across his chest. "Just remember what I said." He waited a moment before stepping aside, then watched as she tramped past him toward her room.

"You ruin everything," she mumbled.

"What?" He started after her, but she slipped into her bedroom, shutting the door, and he stopped himself, expelling a long breath. It was a good thing for her she hadn't slammed the door. Standing outside her bedroom, he turned and looked up the stairway. He couldn't believe he'd agreed to let his nephew stay in the house. It galled him to think of Mark up there taking a shower, already making himself completely at home. It felt like a trespass, a particularly disturbing one at that.

David returned to the front room, threw himself into his armchair and ran his hand through his hair. He picked up his drink and finished it. Since Jean had left in January, he'd become content for the first time in years, having Kaia to himself, the conflicts with Jean finally over. And Kaia seemed to be doing fairly well, even if she wasn't deliriously happy. Then, in August, Elisa had called and mentioned the possibility of Mark staying with them when he started law school. "Mark doesn't know anyone in Berkeley," she'd said, "except for the two of you. If you could possibly accommodate him for just a short while, until he gets his bearings . . ."

Elisa was such a charming woman, always gracious whenever he'd spoken with her, despite her mental problems. And she was so persuasive on the phone, suggesting that Kaia should stay connected with the other side of the family. He said he'd think about it, and when he mentioned the conversation to Kaia, she didn't seem at all surprised about the idea. She said casually, "Maybe Mark could help with the chores, like taking out the trash and mowing the lawn."

Against his better judgment, he'd given in and called Elisa back. "I guess he can stay for a few weeks. I suppose Jean's old office could be a separate unit." But afterwards, when he'd started to have some serious qualms about it, it was too late to back out of the stupid plan. By then, Kaia seemed so enthusiastic about the idea of having her cousin stay in the loft, and had thrown herself into fixing up the room. It had shaken her out of the lethargy she'd fallen into after her return from Pine Tree. But now she seemed so full of herself, heady with some new power. So like her mother in some ways.

David rubbed his face with his hands, feeling the intrusive presence of his burly nephew in the house like a heavy pressure on his shoulders. He wondered if Kaia and Mark had cooked up the plan themselves and then conspired to have Elisa call to propose it. For the first time in a long while he had the strong desire to have someone else, an adult, to talk to—someone who would be objective, yet sympathetic. Certainly not Jean, though. He couldn't talk to her about anything anymore. Maybe he would call his friend Chandi, who always seemed ready to listen.

He'd met Chandi Gupta almost a year ago, at a bar association holiday party—she'd first caught his attention across the room because of her striking looks and her cobalt-blue dress. She was talking with two men in dark suits, one of whom David knew. Easing his way into the group and the conversation, he'd been impressed by her intelligence and poise. They'd exchanged business cards, and in February she'd been the one to call him, suggesting they meet for lunch. After their congenial meal, he hadn't called her until July, though he wasn't sure why he'd waited so long—perhaps he was preoccupied with taking care of Kaia. Then while his daughter was at Cape Cod, he and Chandi had gone out for a thoroughly enjoyable dinner, and he'd been intending to call her again.

But for now he really needed to have another drink, after this rather trying afternoon. Then he would consider calling her.

4

Kaia threw herself down onto Sig's bed and watched as her friend put one of the Beatles records on the stereo. Sig's dyed black hair was turning reddish and growing out blond at the roots, and she'd recently added another silver stud to the three in her left ear. Last year at Brookfield High she'd caught Kaia's interest because of her black clothing, combat boots, and violet lipstick; only a couple of the other students looked like that. But Sig didn't hang around with the Goths at school; she couldn't stand that they were so anti-culture, since she liked to read Baudelaire and T.S. Eliot. She had started a poetry group; Kaia went to a meeting with her once. It was such weird stuff the students wrote and recited, with images of death and alienation, that Kaia hadn't gone to any more of the meetings.

Sig dug into her dresser drawer. "Voila!" She held up three thin joints fanned out between her tapered white fingers. "Thai sticks." She brought an ashtray over to the bed, stretched out next to Kaia and lit up a joint.

They lay on their backs, smoking dreamily while Paul McCartney sang about Rocky Raccoon. "This is luscious," Sig remarked.

"What is?"

"The pot, the music." Sig let out a long sigh. "Just being here with you."

Kaia had never tried a Thai stick before and it surprised her, how quickly it made her high—after only a few puffs. "The smoke is rather stinky and potent."

"Like men," Sig laughed. "Stinkily potent."

"*Oui, comme mon cousin.* He's not stinky though." Kaia passed the joint back.

"You mean he's potent?" Sig took a long hit, squinting at her through the smoke.

"Potent? Jeez, I don't know." Kaia considered how much she should divulge about her total preoccupation with Mark since his arrival last week, even though he hadn't been around much—he'd been busy looking for a car and then starting classes. "He's a strong presence, that's all."

"What kind of strong presence are we talking about?" Sig sat up, holding the joint in one hand.

"You know, manly, I guess. Like my dad, but in a different way. Mark's not gruff like Dad; it's just that he's sort of strong and intense, and he's living right upstairs from me." What she felt about Mark was uncategorizable, actually.

"Oh, no, two manly presences. Poor you."

Sig never wanted any other presences to come between them, Kaia knew that. Sig wanted the two of them to be inviolate, closer than sisters.

Kaia took the joint and sucked on it, then let out her breath and eyed her friend. "It's complicated being around men."

"Who would want to be?" Sig was stretched out on her side and blinked languidly, displaying her iridescent-white eyelids. "I feel sort of washed out around them sometimes, as if I'm a watercolor painting being covered over with oils. Defaced, almost."

Sig's face was a gyre of emotions like a rippling silvery pool—Kaia felt she could almost reach out and dip her hand into it.

"Some men are so domineering, like my dad," Kaia said, and handed the joint to Sig.

"I don't even remember much about my dad, except that he used to hit me and my mom."

"Yeah, I know," Kaia said, touching Sig's hand.

Sig took another hit and blew out the smoke. "How old is Mark again?"

"Twenty-two, almost twenty-three. I barely knew him until July, when I was at his family's summer cottage at Cape Cod."

"Wow, a summer cottage. You didn't mention that. Are they rich or something?"

"Not especially. It's been in the family forever. They call it a cottage but it's actually enormous."

"Nice." Sig's voice had a pinched edge to it that made Kaia uneasy.

"It was fun, camping and sailing with Mark and Monty—Mark's roommate from Boston U."

Sig's eyes widened, appearing topaz in the greenish light. "So you got to know those guys pretty well. Your cousin must be fascinating, in a manly sort of way."

Kaia shook her head. It was a delicate thing, talking about Mark, given all the possibilities and ramifications.

"Oh, well," Sig said, putting out the joint. "Time to do the Rorschach thing."

Kaia laughed. "Sounds like a dance. Is this really okay as a science project?"

"Why not? It's an experiment." Sig pointed with her pen to the reproduction of an inkblot in her open book. "Okay, here's the first inkblot. Tell me what you see."

Kaia examined the blot, but was finding it hard to focus. "I see a squid. It looks like a squid."

"That's not bad." Sig jotted down "squid" in her notebook next to "K. Matheson." She put her pen to her lips. "And what do you associate with this image of a squid?"

"Okay, let's see. Blackness. Creepiness."

Sig printed "blackness & creepiness" under a column headed "Reaction/Interpretation." There were other columns for age, gender, occupation and comments. She held her pen poised over the notebook. "Go deeper."

"Deeper? It's just an inkblot." Kaia sighed. Sig actually seemed to be taking this stuff seriously. "Okay, okay. Its edges are creeping out. It's surreal."

"Don't watch me write. Just react."

"Actually, I don't even know what a squid looks like."

"That's okay. It's the first impression that counts. What else does it make you think of?"

Kaia studied the inkblot. "Darkness, the end of something. Okay? Is that good enough?"

"God, are you depressed or something?"

Kaia shook her head. She didn't think she was, but she'd felt down at times this past week, with Mark coming and going without much contact with her; she was always longing to see him. He was gone for hours, especially since he'd bought the Mustang convertible on Monday. Maybe the darkness was her father's somber presence, always watching her. But it seemed like more than that, having to do with Mark, how he seemed almost afraid of himself, of what he might do. There was fear in his eyes when he looked at her. Now she felt the terrible dread that he would keep his distance.

Sig was making a notation in the notebook. Kaia just wanted to lie here, listening to Lennon sing that everybody had something to hide. It seemed so true, it was beautiful.

"That's enough, I guess," Sig said.

"Are you sure Mr. Hodges said this was all right for a science project?"

"As long as it's an experiment or an investigation. But we need to get some interesting results."

"Maybe we need more interesting subjects." Like Mark, for instance. He was a mystery to her and she would be happy to delve into him. But he would think this project was silly.

"You're quite interesting enough," Sig said, as she flipped to another page in the library book where she had underlined some passages in turquoise ink. "It says the best use of the Rorschach test is to reveal creative potential."

"Well, do I have creative potential or not?" Kaia asked.

"That's what we have to decide later on, after we get all the results and compare them."

"I've already sent the inkblot to my aunt."

"Cool."

Kaia had considered having her father do the inkblot test, but he was just her father, a known quantity. It was obvious he wanted to control everything in her life and would always be an obstructionist. She could see her situation so clearly now—she wanted to enter Mark's world and leave her old one behind, but her father was always near the door, blocking her way, wanting to keep her cloistered, bound to himself. Yes, that was it, that was the problem; that plus Mark's weird distance.

Sig wrote her name in the notebook. "My turn. What do I see?" She studied the inkblot for several seconds. "It appears to be the unknown," she pronounced in an ennobled tone.

"Yep," Kaia said, shutting her eyes and letting her head sink into the pillow. "The great warp of the unknown."

5

Mark entered the house through the back door, the hallway dazzling in the late-afternoon light. Peering into Kaia's bedroom, he was surprised at how disappointed he was to see she wasn't there. Since he'd moved in two weeks ago, he always looked forward to his return to the house, hoping to find her alone. But she was often gone, or David was working in his office at home. Mark registered the silence in the house, the feeling of vacancy in her absence.

Stepping into her room for the first time, it felt a bit illicit to be there without her knowing. He caught a lush scent—something like ripe mango or pineapple—a fragrance that triggered memories of her on the Pine Tree beach with the tropical suntan oil glistening on her brown legs. A poster of *The Rolling Stones* hung on the far wall above the double bed with a jumble of blankets and clothes piled on it. A purple armchair was nestled in a corner; he'd seen Kaia curled up in it reading when he'd passed her open doorway.

Some framed photographs caught his eye—large black and whites hanging on the wall nearest the door. One of the photos depicted a pair of grungy tennis shoes and a pair of smaller sneakers on top of a sleeping bag. He was startled to recognize his and Kaia's shoes in the tent at Cape Cod. Another photo showed Monty standing by the canvas tent.

Moving along the wall he saw two shots of himself on the boat—God, he looked so cold, staring out over the water. She'd obviously taken the photos on the trip back to Pine Tree, when he was so absorbed in his own chaotic feelings about Kaia and was furious with Monty. How had she ever forgiven him for ruining their time together like that? The photos seemed unexpected, exposing a hidden side of her that observed what was going on, but held something in reserve, merely capturing the moment. Still, it seemed clear that the camping, the sailing, their time in the tent, had meant something to her, possibly as much as all of that meant to him.

Kaia's light footsteps echoed through the den, and his pulse quickened—so she was home after all. He stepped out of her room just as she appeared in the hallway.

"I thought I heard you." She sounded breathless, her eyes focused on his.

"I was looking for you."

Kaia tilted her head to the side with a slight smile, like a mischievous child. "I gathered that, since you were in my room."

"Right." He shrugged. "What are you doing later?" He glanced at his watch. Five-thirty. David would be coming home soon.

"Not much."

"How about a drive down the coast? I haven't been to the ocean yet, and you haven't been for a ride in the Mustang." He was trying to sound casual, but his heart was pounding away at the thought of taking her away somewhere in his car.

"I should ask Dad."

"We won't go too far. You could leave him a note."

She stared at him. The skin on her chest gleamed above her scoop-necked sweater, and he caught the same heady scent he'd smelled in her room. "I shouldn't just take off like that." She grinned. "It would be wrong."

"Would it?"

"Maybe not," she said slowly, as if considering. "Just a short drive, though."

"Great. Wear something warm. I'll go up and get changed." Swinging around, he sprinted up the stairs. He'd been intending to take Kaia for a drive ever since he'd bought the car over a week ago; he'd obsessed about taking her somewhere, anywhere, as long as it was away from David.

After changing into warmer clothes and splashing on some aftershave, Mark found Kaia downstairs, sprawled in an armchair in the den, one leg splayed over the armrest. The sight of her like that made him want to swoop her into his arms. She raised her eyebrows at him while the rest of her face remained still—a calm, curious look—pretty damned self-assured for a girl her age, and much more confident than she'd been at Pine Tree. He supposed she was more sure of his interest now. She had to know at some level how her looks, her gaze, the way she carried herself, all of that, had a killer effect on a guy. At least it did on him, despite the fact that she was in fact his little cousin.

She had changed into jeans, cherry-red cowgirl boots, and a blue sweatshirt—even her outfit sparked something in him, as if she'd chosen it especially for him.

"All right," he said, grinning. "Let's blow this firetrap."

On their way out, Mark noticed a note labeled "Dad" propped against the vase on the dining room table, and he wondered how she had explained this little outing to her father. Once they were in the car, backing out of the driveway, he asked her what she'd written.

"Just that I was going for a drive with you."

"That's all?" he asked.

"And that we'd be back soon."

"That's about right."

As they headed down the hill with the convertible top down, the wind in his face felt good, refreshing. Steering through the Berkeley streets, he glanced periodically at Kaia's profile, or at her trim thighs outlined in her jeans. Soon they were driving onto the freeway and over the Bay Bridge into San Francisco, riding past the Transamerica pyramid and other skyscrapers, Kaia's hair flowing behind her in a loose, sexy way as she squinted into the wind. Once they were out of the city they picked up speed.

Soon they were cruising down the coastal highway with an incredible view of the blue-green ocean. It was the first sense of freedom he'd had since he'd arrived; he'd been overwhelmed with all the reading he had to do for law school, and found he could only concentrate when he was at the law library, away from the house, away from Kaia. The work was always hanging over his head, and was only marginally interesting. Now he felt he could forget the law books, his gruff uncle, even his own doubts about what he was doing with Kaia. It seemed as if his whole purpose in coming to California was for this drive with her, and for whatever was going to happen next.

"Where are we going?" she yelled into the wind.

"To Half Moon Bay," he shouted back. He'd heard someone mention it and knew it was south on Highway 1.

"That's pretty far."

"We're halfway there, I think. We'll just get a bite to eat and head back."

Feeling relaxed as he navigated the curves of the highway, he took in the blaze of ocean, the fishy seaweed smell, and the soft round hills on the left. A fragment of doubt about what he was doing irritated him from time to time, though, like a speck of dirt in his eye.

It was still light out when they reached the outskirts of Half Moon Bay. Spotting a pizza place, he pulled into the parking lot. He helped Kaia out of the car, and she stood there facing him, a mere foot away, her hair whipping around in the sea breeze. He removed his shades.

"I didn't know we were going to be gone this long," she said. "It was a beautiful drive, though. Maybe we should head back now."

"It was farther than I thought. It won't take long to get a pizza. Are you hungry?"

She nodded. He touched her shoulder, wanting more than anything to pull her close and kiss her. Instead he made himself turn toward the restaurant, shifting his hand to her upper back.

The windowless place was full of people, and several of them, probably locals, stared at Kaia and him as they walked up to the counter. Was it because he was so much older than Kaia, and still had his hand on her back? Was there some kind of guilty look about the two of them?

Mark ordered what Kaia wanted—a mushroom pizza—and carried their drinks to a booth in the back. He drank some of his draft beer, watching Kaia sip iced tea through a straw. He traced his eyes over her high cheekbones and her sleek, expressive eyebrows. She peered back at him, as if trying to interpret something in his face, then turned away to glance around the room.

After a minute, she turned back to him and reached for his beer mug, pulling it from his hand. She took a long drink of the beer, then held the mug close to her chest with a defiant grin. He leaned over to take it away from her and she laughed, holding it off to the side at arm's length until he pried it from her grasp. He set it down sharply, spilling some of it, then leaned further over the table and kissed her on the mouth, steadying her chin with his fingers, her lips wet and tangy from the beer.

"Mark!" she laughed, drawing back.

He blew out a long breath. "You know what you are, Kaia? You're a closet flirt."

"Huh! Blame me, why don't you. A closet flirt!" She was smiling widely now, her face flushed. "What in the hell is that supposed to mean?"

"I just made it up. I guess it's someone who seems shy but smiles a certain way and dresses sort of sexy, and acts a little bit sexy, too. It fits."

"I am *not* a closet flirt," she said, making a laughable attempt to sound indignant. "I don't believe in flirting, anyway. Goddamn it, Mark, you're so full of shit."

"Such bad language, Kaia. Somebody ought to whip your ass."

"My dad probably will once he finds out I'm with *you*."

"Sorry. I just felt like kissing you. At least your dad won't know about that."

"I would never tell," she said.

"I would hope not."

"Well, if I'm a closet flirt, you're a fairly overt one, I'd say."

He slouched back in the bench, eyeing her. So far she could just pass this off as her older cousin getting a bit impulsive on her. But of course he wanted more than that, and she knew it.

"Okay, so I was overt."

"Rhymes with pervert," she said in a merry tone, pleased with herself.

He cringed and turned away to survey the room. People were filling the nearby tables, and the rowdiness in the room was ratcheting up.

She reached across the table for the mug and he slapped her hand away. "Uh-uh, mind your manners, little one," he said.

"Killjoy." She stretched out both hands toward him. "All right. Please."

He wanted to take her hands in his, but instead he placed the mug in her hands and leaned forward. "You poor thing," he said, keeping his voice low. "Hanging around with perverts and begging for alcohol. What would your friends say?"

"I don't have any." She took a drink. "Except for Sig, of course."

"Who's that?"

"Just a friend I hang out with. I've told you about her. We drink wine once in a while, smoke pot, listen to music."

"Wicked girl."

"Yes," she said. "So very wicked."

It was a devilish side of her he hadn't experienced so vividly before, and it stirred him more than he liked to admit. "Your dad would be pretty mad if he found out you were smoking dope and drinking wine, wouldn't he?"

"Yes, my daddy would be very mad indeed. Actually, he's going to be mad about tonight. You said we were just going for a short drive, remember?"

"So we're in deep shit, I reckon," he drawled.

"Especially since I usually go out with him on Friday nights. I sort of forgot about that."

"Let's just hope he doesn't kick me out of the house."

"He wouldn't do that."

"Why not?"

"Because I want you to stay."

He studied her for a few seconds, hoping he was right about the subtext—that she liked him a lot, at least enough to want him to stick around. "Actually, my dad was against me staying in your house," he said.

"Why would your dad be against it?"

"He didn't want the two of us getting too close. He seemed to think there was something going on at the Cape. After the camping trip he had a little talk with me, said I'd better act responsibly when I got to Berkeley."

"You never told me that."

He shrugged. "I don't pay any attention to what he says."

When the pizza came, Kaia took a slice, bit into it, then dropped it onto the plate. "Yeow! It's burning hot." She wiped her fingers and mouth with a napkin.

"Are you okay?"

She nodded her head. After a minute, Mark took a slice and began eating it. It wasn't half bad, except for the slimy mushrooms. He would have preferred sausage, but he wanted Kaia to have whatever she liked.

"Mom wants me to go back East next year for college," Kaia said.

He didn't like the sound of that at all. "Are you thinking of applying back there?"

"Maybe. But of course Dad wants me to go to Berkeley and live at home. He thinks I'm too young to be on my own. He thinks I need to be protected."

"From what?"

"From men like you," she said with a sly grin.

He couldn't believe she was being so bold. "Do you need protection?"

"I don't need to be protected by anyone, just because I'm a girl. I can take care of myself. I wish I could make him understand that."

"Would you do that, live at home with him next year?"

"No way. I want to live on campus, wherever I go. Maybe San Francisco State."

Mark kept his eyes on her. "That's not so far."

"Nope, it's not," she said, with that beautiful smile of hers.

Later, when they left the restaurant, it was dark and foggy outside. Standing next to the car, Mark took off his denim jacket and helped Kaia into it, then squeezed her shoulders from behind.

She spun around, peering into his face. "Old Spice. I like it."

"*Do* you." He kissed her on the lips, more deeply than he had before.

She kissed him back, lingering, then pulled away. He opened the car door for her, and after she was settled in, he pulled the convertible top back in place. As much as he'd enjoyed the blast of ocean air slapping against him on the ride down the coast, it would be too cold for Kaia with the top down now. Once they were on the road, he opened the windows a crack, letting the cool, fresh air blow in, and Kaia didn't seem to mind. They didn't talk much, but Mark glanced at her from time to time, enjoying her presence as they moved along the winding highway, then back through San Francisco and into the Berkeley hills. When they pulled into the driveway, he was relieved to see that David's Volvo wasn't there.

"I wonder where Dad's gone," Kaia said. She hopped out of the car and searched down the street, as if expecting him to come zooming up the street any second.

Mark walked around the car and placed his hand on the side of her face. "Don't worry about him, babe."

She nodded, but looked serious, and hurried toward the front door. He followed her into the kitchen and watched as she took off his jacket and flung it onto the counter. She jabbed at a button on the answering machine, and David's stern voice came on: "Kaia, I got your note. I'll talk to you about it later." In the second message he sounded irate: "It's almost nine o'clock, Kaia. You'd better be back by the time I get home."

Kaia stared at the phone. "I wonder where he's calling from," she mumbled.

Mark reached out to touch her hair, but she ducked away, her face drawn.

"That was really stupid of me," she said. "I should have asked him first."

"You think he would have let you go?"

"No."

"You're old enough to go out."

"You'd think so, wouldn't you? Dad doesn't like the idea of guys hanging around with me, even guys who are just friends."

"I wouldn't either, if I were him. But I'm just your cousin."

The barest hint of a grin came over her face. "He doesn't like cousins, either."

Mark reached out again to touch her, and this time she let him run his fingers through her tangled hair. "Anyway, this wasn't really a date," he said softly.

"Why did you kiss me, then?"

"I meant as far as your dad's concerned, it was just your harmless cousin taking you out for pizza."

"Harmless. Hah!" She gave him a quick kiss—too much like a dismissal. "I'm going to bed. I don't want to deal with Dad tonight."

She started to move past Mark, but he grabbed her by the arm and turned her around to face him. "Didn't you have fun?"

"Sure."

Cupping her face with his hands, he kissed her, more sensually than he'd dared before, and she made a sound of surprise, or maybe pleasure, he couldn't tell which. He wrapped his arms around her, feeling her slender frame against him as they kissed, and pulled her more tightly against him.

"I have to go," she said, then wrenched herself away and ran toward her room.

He headed after her, but she slipped into her bedroom and shut the door. He stood in the hallway for a few seconds and could sense her standing silently on the other side. Then he went back to the kitchen to retrieve his jacket. He caught Kaia's scent on it, and it seemed like evidence of something illicit. He certainly wouldn't want David to find it there.

He felt like a thief, a goddamned intruder. She was too young, obviously naive and scared. He was a complete idiot. He'd have to back off—way off. But he wasn't sure if he could, living in the house with her, now that he had started something more intense than anything he'd expected. He had never thought he would fall in love, in fact he had never believed there was such a thing as falling in love. Was that what this was? Was he actually falling in love—with his sixteen-year-old cousin, for Christ's sake?

6

When the phone rang in the kitchen, Kaia was curled up on the den sofa, still in her pajamas, reading the *Chronicle.* It was probably a wrong number or someone selling something, she thought, and let it ring a couple of times. She'd awakened early, immediately remembering the ride with Mark to Half Moon Bay, and picturing his face as he'd bent to kiss her. It was hard to get the details of the evening out of her mind—it was impossible, actually.

The phone stopped ringing and started again, and then her father walked stiffly, still limping a bit, into the adjoining kitchen. Even this early on a Saturday morning, she had to admit he looked rather dapper in his cords and blue polo shirt, his brown hair neatly combined. No one would guess he stayed up late drinking every night. She'd heard him come in last night, but he'd left her alone, for some reason.

He glared at her from across the room as he picked up the receiver, issuing a grumpy hello into the phone.

"Yes, Jean, he's settled in, all right," he said a minute later, his voice reeking of sarcasm. He cast a severe look at Kaia.

She shuddered, dreading what was coming next. Once he got off the phone, he would start grilling her, spoiling her whole beautiful evening with Mark, making it sound sleazy. He seemed to think every male in sight was out to steal her precious virginity.

"What I mean," her father continued in a louder voice, "is that your nephew has made himself quite at home here. Last night he took Kaia on a ride in his convertible to God knows where."

Mark came running down the stairs and appeared in the den, barefoot and unshaven, in his jeans and a gray sweatshirt. His eyes immediately fixed on Kaia's, with barely a glance at her father. He broke into a smile as he came over and stood in front of her.

"Hey, what's up?" he asked in a low, familiar tone.

"Mom's on the phone." Kaia was suddenly conscious that her face was unwashed and her unbrushed hair a snarly mess. Her heart thumped away shamefully as she watched Mark amble over to the kitchen counter. He poured himself a cup of coffee, then came back and sat next to her on the sofa, perhaps a foot away. She felt safer now with him beside her, his arm close to hers, and she absorbed his comforting earthy smell.

"I had no idea they were planning this," her father said into the phone.

"We weren't planning it, Daddy," Kaia said. She got up and shuffled in her slippers over to where her father stood. "Let me talk to Mom."

He grunted a couple of times into the phone, then said with irritation, "Your daughter would like to have a word with you." He kept his eyes on Kaia as she took the receiver from his hand and cradled it against her shoulder.

"Hi, Mom."

"Hello, Kaia. How's everything?"

"Fine. Just fine." Kaia pictured her mother's smile, her chic brown hair feathered around her face, her hazel eyes.

"I'm sorry we haven't had a chance to talk much lately, sweetheart. But what's this thing about going out with Mark?"

"It was nothing. We went on a drive and had pizza. And it was *not* late." Kaia frowned at her father, who stood over her, hands on hips, scowling, so close she could smell his shaving cream. His face was clean-shaven and pink. "I usually go out to dinner with Daddy on Friday," she continued, "so I guess he was upset about that."

Her father shook his head.

"Kaia, listen," her mother said, in an urgent tone. "Don't go out with Mark."

"I didn't."

"He's your cousin and he's twenty-two years old."

"I know that, Mother. So what?"

"I don't want you spending a lot of time with him. I was against this from the start."

"Against what?"

"Mark moving in with you and Dad."

Kaia was silent for a moment, then said in a low voice, "I have to go. I'm not even dressed yet. Here's Dad." Kaia shoved the phone at him and returned to the sofa, curling her feet under her. Mark placed his arm behind her, on the edge of the sofa.

"What's wrong, sweetness?" he whispered.

She shrugged, her face hot. "It's just that Mom hardly ever calls, and when she does, she just gives me a hard time."

Her father made a few more comments into the phone, then said, "All right, I'll deal with it. Bye." He came over and stood in front of the two of them, folding his arms across his chest, a nasty frown on his face. He appeared massive, looming over them.

"Well?" he said loudly. "What was the idea, taking off like that?"

"I'm sorry, Dad. Next time I'll ask first." She couldn't make herself sound contrite, though. Why should she be sorry? Other girls went out all the time.

"There's not going to be a next time."

"Jesus, Dad," she muttered and reached for a Kleenex from the side table. She blew her nose while he glared at her.

"I'm sorry we didn't let you know." Mark's voice was calm. "But I know what I'm doing. I've been driving since I was fifteen. I don't take chances."

"I don't care. I don't want Kaia riding around with you. Where did you go, anyway?"

"Down the coast a ways," Mark said.

"*Where* down the coast?"

"To Half Moon Bay," Kaia said with as much poise as she could muster.

"Half Moon Bay—so you were gone for hours?" her father asked incredulously.

"We got home around nine," Kaia said. "But where were you, Daddy?"

He glanced away, tensing his jaw, then back at her. "Never mind."

She reached for Mark's coffee cup and took a sip, tasting its bitterness. "Jeez, you're in a good mood."

"Don't talk to me that way," her father shouted, taking a step toward her.

She was afraid that even with Mark right here next to her, her father was going to pull her off the couch and do something humiliating—maybe start one of their shouting matches where he tried to subdue her by the sheer force of his fury.

"It was really nothing," Mark said.

"It's not something to be taken lightly, and you know it. You'll just have to find other things to do with your time, Mark, otherwise you'll have to live somewhere else. This arrangement was supposed to be temporary, anyway."

Kaia glanced at Mark, who merely nodded slowly at her father.

"And by the way, Kaia, you're grounded for a week."

"*Grounded*. I'm too old for that. And you never said I couldn't go for a drive with Mark."

"You knew I wouldn't allow it. That's why you snuck off like that."

"I didn't sneak off. I left a note." She stood up, handing the cup back to Mark. Her father scanned her from head to toe, apparently just now noticing that she was in her pajamas.

He shook his head. "The only place you can go after school next week is to ballet. Now go get dressed. And don't run around the house like that."

She almost said, "Like what?" But she knew he was one step away from losing it. She glared at him, shot a glance at Mark, then stalked off to her room and slammed the door, just wanting this whole scene with her father to be over. Mostly, though, she was afraid her dad would actually kick Mark out of the house. So she and Mark had to be careful, that was all.

7

Elisa glided into her shiny kitchen, thrilled to have the day to herself. But how she missed her darling Mark! What a pleasure it had been to feed her son during his sojourns home during the summer! Feast after feast, her homemade cinnamon rolls dripping with wonderfully sweet frosting, chicken cacciatore, ham sandwiches—she could always make him happy with her food.

There sat Nico's Italian coffee—as bracing as espresso—in a carafe on the counter. But why had he left it there? To tempt her? Sometimes when he forgot and left some, she allowed herself a little, at least when her moods had flattened out, but had they? Today she'd gotten out of bed like a normal wife, sat at the kitchen table in her midnight-blue pajamas reading the Entertainment section, and had seen Nico off with a kiss.

Now she poured herself a demitasse of his deliciously rich brew. She had been feeling almost overpleasant lately, nothing pathological though—she took the pills when she remembered. Nico's coffee would be sure to keep her spirits up, piercing through the lapses into gloom, as did the occasional glass of wine, in spite of what Dr. Sandburg had said about intoxicants and stimulants—attracting her with their very illicitness, their promise of escape from the monotony of normalcy.

The day to herself—what a delight! She would steep herself in pleasure, like fragrant tea leaves in steaming hot water, while Nico was at the office. She would forget the world, its stark invasive presence. So lovely when no one was watching her, judging her. She threw open the kitchen window and inhaled the nippy October air, gazing at the sodden sky with its iron-gray clouds. A solitary truck rumbled dejectedly down their narrow street.

In the living room she put on the album of Celtic folk songs with lyrics she couldn't understand, and she started dancing in her silken pajamas to the resonant women's voices, the whining of violins, the beating of myriad drums, the whistling of pipes. She twirled around and around, then sprinted up the stairs to her bedroom. Looking through her closet, she pushed aside the flaxen linen dress—much too dull! Fingered the velour turtleneck—no—and went through the array of vibrant clothing. Then she pulled out the floral silk robe with its shimmering orchids and pointed stamens, teal vines spreading over the black background, golden flowers like stars.

She slid out of her pajamas, dashed over to her dresser and slipped into scarlet panties, stretchy and sheer, the matching lacy bra, and finally the silken robe, a whisper on her skin. Reveling in her own delectable scent of sleep and lavender soap, she stepped into her satin slippers. Twirling around, waving her arms through the air, she caught herself in the full-length mirror and laughed, fluffing her coppery hair off her neck, letting her robe fall open. There were her long, freckled legs, her breasts brimming out of the lacy cups, the brilliant robe with its exuberant flowers, vivid as life itself, as if Nico had selected each blossom for her from a street vendor in the *Quartier Latin*. She was a painter then, a budding playwright, a dancer, Nico so much in love with his new bride, his Elisa, the two of them so in love with Paris. And Nico so pleased at having captured her, even when she left him asleep in their room on the Seine while she visited all of the boutiques on an entire boulevard, finding the marvelous lingerie and hats and stockings and the enchanting floral robe. Elegance, beauty! Exuberance! That's what Paris was about!

Running downstairs and into the kitchen, she poured more coffee into the china cup, the aroma of the dark liquid melding with the scent of pines and grass in the moist Bangor air coming through the window. It had begun to rain, the drops pattering on the roof, so she closed the window and watched for a moment as a few crystalline drops flowed down the pane. She picked up the cup, savoring its glossy contour, the metastasizing warmth of the radiant fluid, and as she drank, she took in the sharp heat of the drink in her mouth and throat and stomach—how miraculous, how spectacular! She would enjoy herself, and the light rain, even though it undoubtedly presaged the pounding onslaught.

What bliss, to enjoy oneself. What else mattered, beyond this sense of elation—which of course could turn extreme and terrifying if one wasn't judicious. Setting the cup down on the countertop, careful not to shatter it, she decided to be moderate, just as Dr. Sandburg had prescribed—she had to learn to be temperate, so that she could accept a certain stasis in order to plod onward in the humdrum way other people did. Ah! But how dreary to be tethered, to be diluted by the outside world, away from this internal landscape that was *seine schöne Seele*—her own lovely soul!

She knew what she would do, she would add just a touch of Bailey's Irish Cream to counter the effects of the caffeine and create a certain vital balance. She was glad she'd thought to buy the Bailey's yesterday along with the groceries—it now sat under the sink behind the cleaning supplies, a mammoth bottle made for generous appetites, for life-embracing, sensual people. She poured some of the creamy liquid into her cup just as the kitchen phone rang, a biting noise that made her hand jerk so that some of the liqueur splashed into the saucer.

She picked up the receiver. "Yes?"

"I tried to reach you all yesterday afternoon." It was Jean, her harsh tone so terribly jarring.

"Why?" Elisa asked.

"I was just wondering whether you've heard from Mark."

"Of course, just a few days ago."

"Oh, I see. So how does he like living in Berkeley with David and Kaia?"

Elisa sensed a trick question. "Just fine."

"I'm sure he must be busy with his studies."

"Oh, quite." Elisa could hear her sister breathing into the phone, rather unpleasantly.

After a pause, Jean said, "Apparently Mark took Kaia out for a drive Friday night, down the coast to Half Moon Bay." She cleared her throat. "I'm concerned they're spending too much time together."

She sounded so authoritarian, always trying to keep things within the proper bounds. How could David ever have tolerated her? How could anyone stand her, a woman who had no appreciation for passion or beauty? How was it that Jean had turned out that way?

"Mark is going to be twenty-three this month," Elisa said, hearing the crispness in her own voice. "If he takes Kaia on an occasional drive, I'm sure he'll be careful. I don't really think we should be interfering." Elisa could tell by the way Mark talked about Kaia, the way his voice on the phone went soft when he said her name, that he loved his little cousin, and what was wrong with that? Why label or categorize something as exquisite as love?

"You see, Jean," she went on, "passion is not a disease, it's a holy thing. God gave it to us to enjoy. It's all that matters." She knew Jean hated religious talk, but the words were finding their own devious escape. "We should love ourselves, too, as spiritual beings—"

"Elisa, are you taking your meds?" Jean interrupted in her awful grating voice.

"Of course I have," Elisa screamed, and slammed down the phone. She would not listen to her sister any longer.

She stood for a moment, drinking from her cup, savoring the sweet satiny slide of the liquid over her palate. God couldn't mean to deny her this heightening, this ecstasy of the senses. When the phone rang again, she paraded past the screeching instrument, carrying her cup and saucer in ceremonious steps, the ringing less harsh as she moved up the stairs and into her study. She sat at her desk with the pen, paper, and Kaia's letter lying before her, irresistible. Now she could write freely, unhindered by the others with their constant aggravating concern.

Her niece was like her, Elisa could see that. The very fact that Kaia had sent her the inkblot—it was something she herself might have done, sending inkblots to various people for their interpretation. What an absolute delight. Elisa leaned forward, her body tinged with a covert thrill. The inkblot appeared a bit blurry, wavering around the edges. She would have to do without her glasses, exercise her eye muscles along with her mind. She reached for the red ballpoint pen and wrote "October 9, 1980" in tall, loopy script on a yellow legal pad, admiring the ornamental lines on the paper.

> Dear Kaia,
>
> Thank you so very very much for thinking of me. I can see the dancer, the creative soul in you—it comes from my mother, your grandmother, who was like you and me in so many ways. But don't be afraid, Kaia, to go out into the world, to be active, to take part, to risk everything!

Elisa took a sip of her drink and thought of finding the quintessential poem by Pablo Neruda to copy out, something that captured the momentousness and utter sensuousness of love. But did Kaia know Spanish? The poems were certainly most elegant in their native expression.

Elisa began writing again:

> You are so clever, Kaia, with your special project. You say I should just give my first impression

> of the inkblot, and any associations that come up. Well, here we go. I'm opening the inner envelope now.
>
> Aha, my first impression—a couple bowing to each other after a fight that is still unresolved because at the same time they are pulling at something between them—a baby in a basket? Oh but there's a butterfly floating over the baby that shows a fantasy of joy, and there are virulent ravens trying to tell them something quite ominous. It could be women pulling at the basket—I see now that the figures have pointed breasts.
>
> There. Is that enough? Such a lovely person you are, Kaia.
>
> Your Loving Aunt, Elisa

She stood up, trying to master the tremor in her hands as she gathered the pieces of paper and slid them into a manila envelope. After scribbling Kaia's address on it, she found a sheet of old butterfly postage stamps in the desk drawer, tore off several and placed them in a rainbow shape above the address.

She kicked off her slippers—they would only hamper her. That's what shoes were, restraints to keep women from dancing, from running until their breath was gone! Dashing downstairs in her bare feet and out into the rain, she shoved the envelope into the mailbox at the curb and flew back inside, the droplets of rain running down her face. Entering the kitchen, she poured herself a cupful of the Bailey's and drank it in a milky stream, letting the liqueur wash over her tongue, her teeth, her gums.

Then she was leaping up the stairs with the bottle in her hand, not feeling the weight of her body, only the dynamis of her long-strong legs, and she began to write in her journal with her bleedingheart ink, writing about Nico and the way he wore a psychic raincoat so that he wouldn't get wet from her tears and how he would hide under a clear umbrella, deflecting the rain, so that he could watch her with his eyes of aquamarine without ever getting soaked.

She heard the car pulling into the garage and then Nico was coming into the house—Jean must have called him—but Elisa knew she could thrive in this inkblot world forever. She couldn't stop writing—it was all so crucial and her thoughts might slither away. The front door closed and the hangers jangled as Nico hung up his coat and then there was silence while he stopped, no doubt listening for her. She paused in her writing and heard the squeak of his leather soles on the stairs as he trod slowly, keys clinking in his pocket, and when she glanced up and saw him in the doorway she jumped up and ran to him, her robe flying around her thighs, and threw her arms around his neck. He kissed her and took her by the hand into their bedroom and drew apart her robe because he loved her so much when she was so utterly loose and open. Then he was slipping off her bra and panties and his mouth was on her breast, loving her the way he always did, the severe persistent heat of his mouth and hands on her so that she knew he would stay with her and take care of her, not send her away this time, would never allow Jean to come and leach the color away, sucking it all for her greedy self from their cobalt sky.

8

Kaia had never seen Tilden Park so stunning, so lush with color, had never glided through it with the wind lifting her hair off her neck, the top down in a convertible. They plunged past golden meadows, tall eucalyptus trees with their pungent, silver leaves, gnarly oaks huddled together like old men beneath the ceiling of pale aqua sky, Mark navigating his cool car with its ease and power. All week she'd been thinking about him, re-living every detail of their drive to Half Moon Bay, and this afternoon her mood had lifted when she'd walked up the hill and caught sight of his Mustang parked in their driveway.

She'd found him in the den—he'd obviously been waiting for her, and he'd asked her to take a drive in the park with him: "Just for half an hour or so." She'd calculated the margin of time before her father would arrive home, and had agreed, trying to hide her excitement. After all, she was no longer grounded, technically speaking. This time she would make sure she got back in time for the usual Friday night dinner out with her father.

Mark pulled over and stopped in a vacant lot at the top of a hill. "Your turn," he said.

"What?" She couldn't see his eyes very clearly behind his dark glasses and wasn't sure what he meant.

"I'll teach you. There's hardly any traffic."

"I don't have a permit. Dad won't let me drive until I'm sixty."

Mark laughed. "Don't worry about that. You don't need a permit."

"This is a terrible idea, Mark."

"I've been told I'm full of terrible ideas. But it's perfectly safe here. And it's an automatic—it should be easy enough. I just thought you'd have fun driving."

She hesitated for only a moment. "Okay, but just a small practice run."

Grinning nervously, she got behind the wheel. Mark gave her instructions, and she began to drive around the lot in slow motion, practicing forward and reverse. Soon she was pulling onto the road and driving at a cautious pace, the breeze swirling around them, dried eucalyptus leaves pirouetting in the air before them.

After ten or fifteen minutes, Mark motioned toward a parking lot by the carousel and told her to pull in. When she parked, she pressed too hard on the brake and the car lurched to a stop with a loud screech. Across the lot, a mother glanced at the car and hastily pulled her toddler close.

"That's okay, you'll get used to it," Mark said, reaching over and squeezing Kaia's shoulder. "Ice cream?"

They bought chocolate cones and sat in the car, licking the melting ice cream and watching the children on the merry-go-round. She wished she could stay here with Mark as long as she wanted, without worrying about her father and everyone else. When they'd finished their cones, Mark started the engine and drove up into the hills, parking near the pint-sized steam train.

He removed his sunglasses and studied her face, then leaned over and started kissing her gently, then more deeply. A boy had tried French kissing her in the school parking lot during a dance last spring, and she hadn't liked it, his tongue cold and quick. But this was different—Mark's mouth on hers warm and delectable, even more so than when they'd kissed before. He ran his hand over her, brushing her stomach and breasts with a light, electric touch, then reached up under her sweater, spreading his fingers over her ribs. His hands on her felt competent and strong as he edged his fingers under her bra and touched the underside of her breast, making her gasp, then he leaned closer and caught her by the back of the neck with his other hand and kissed her again. After a minute she made herself pull away, even though she didn't want him to stop. They were both breathing hard.

"You scare me, Mark." But he didn't, really. It was something else, a thrill more than fear. Just because he wanted to make out with her didn't mean he was taking advantage. She wanted this as much as he did.

"I scare myself sometimes."

They watched a couple leading their child by the hand toward the train, and a mother wrestling a stroller into the trunk of her car. Kaia wanted to feel Mark holding her again, but she didn't know exactly how far he meant to go. She wanted him to do everything to her and be everything to her, but that couldn't happen. At least while she was living in her father's house. And Mark was her cousin; she couldn't forget that little problem.

"We should go back," she said. "I don't want to get into trouble."

"Just a few more minutes." Mark reached over, stroking her cheek with his fingertips. "I've been wanting to spend more time with you. Especially since our drive last week. I've been thinking about you ever since Pine Tree, actually."

She studied him carefully, not really surprised, since she'd been thinking of him constantly, too. "Why didn't you call me more often during the summer?"

"I figured you'd think I was completely out of line. When you sent that postcard to Monty and me at the St. Lawrence, I thought you might even like Monty."

"It was you I wanted to hear from." She'd sent the postcard, depicting the Big Sur coastline, and had written, "Why don't you guys come out and see me sometime?" She'd acted on an impulse she could express to both of them, but not to Mark alone.

"You got my postcards, didn't you?" he asked.

"Yes." There had been three sketchy updates of his summer, scrawled on ordinary post-office cards. They were all treasured relics, hidden now in her desk drawer.

"Well, I'm here now," he said.

"I don't like doing this behind my dad's back. I'm afraid we'll get caught."

"There's no other way, babe. No one would understand how we feel." He leaned over and kissed her softly.

There was something exciting about him calling her "babe" as he had a couple of times before, as if she were his, and especially in the way he said it just now, with so much affection.

"Let's go home," she made herself say.

Once Mark had switched on the ignition and they were riding along in his Mustang, she recalled the way he'd taken off his shades to look at her, and the delicious, almost physical alarm it had caused in her when he'd leaned over to kiss her. As they drove, clouds slid across the glowing sky, and the breeze sent sycamore leaves scurrying across the road. She found herself memorizing the feel of the wind in her hair, the sight of Mark's forearms gripping the steering wheel, and the view of the brilliant fields and trees in the afternoon sun like a painting by Monet.

9

Lying on his bed each night, Mark would remember how it felt when he'd held Kaia in Tilden Park. And she was so pretty, with that flirtatious grin she would flash behind her father's back, her turquoise eyes showing her vulnerability, yet daring Mark to take hold of her. He would often get up at night, unable to sleep, and would pace around his room, drinking beer, immersed in his thoughts. He couldn't seem to separate the incredible magnetism between them from everything else he loved about her. There was something unique about her, a sultriness, an alert intelligence that drew him in.

Once he went downstairs after midnight and stopped outside her room, listening to her sonorous breathing interspersed with funny little snores. He leaned his forehead against the door, asking himself what in the hell he was doing, and made himself turn away. But did he really need to keep away from her? Why? He would never hurt her. He loved her. Lots of cousins had love affairs. Some even got married.

Fatigued from lack of sleep, he couldn't focus on the legal cases he was reading; phrases like "incorporeal hereditaments" and "detrimental reliance" flashed across his mind like fragments of nonsensical cartoon dialogue. And he couldn't get into the law—it was so medieval, the whole set-up, the rich man always taking some poor man's land based on some archaic legal theory. As Professor Lopez said in Torts class the other day, the lawyer who came out on top was the one who fought tooth and nail and had the law firm with the biggest clout to back him up—that's how the judicial system worked. Mark wondered sometimes if he was staying in law school just to be near Kaia. And he missed the times back on Pine Tree when they'd been out on the water or on the beach together, with nothing to do but enjoy themselves.

He hadn't been able to find Kaia alone since their drive in the park last week, but at least he could look forward to dinner with her and David most nights at the house. Kaia usually cooked, often with her dad's help, but sometimes David prepared meals by himself, especially when Kaia had a lot of homework.

One evening, over the skirt steak David had broiled, they all began discussing the rat Kaia said she'd heard in the basement when she was down there doing laundry.

"You're imagining things," David said.

"And I also heard one several times in the wall of my bedroom," Kaia said, casting a disgusted look at her father. "There are rat droppings in the basement."

"Let's not talk about this at dinner," David said.

Kaia's face turned a bit pink, but she didn't reply.

"I can go down to the basement to check it out," Mark offered.

"Go ahead if you want to," David said, "but I doubt there are any rats down there. Anyway, I can't make it down the steps too easily, until the sprain heals."

The next morning Mark bought a trap, put some cheese in it and set it in the basement. By evening when he returned, there was a huge rat in it, repulsive with its long rubbery tail. When he asked David how to dispose of it, his uncle said sharply, "Bury it in the backyard. Deep, so the neighborhood tomcats won't dig it up." And he told Mark not to tell Kaia, saying it would upset her.

But Mark did tell her, and she seemed grateful. He couldn't understand why David had allowed rodents to invade his home, especially since it was so offensive to Kaia to have the ugly pests around.

Then one evening after classes, Mark went to the gym to work out, and when he got back to the house, it was almost eight o'clock. David was sitting in the room off the living room he used as an office, with the door open of course, and was reading a journal. He glanced up and nodded somberly at Mark as he passed. In the kitchen, Mark found Kaia washing the dishes, standing at the sink with one bare foot wrapped around the other ankle. She glanced over her shoulder at him.

"I didn't realize how late it was," he said, and took a step toward her. "Sorry I missed dinner."

"There's a message for you—Petra called," she said, spitting out the name and flinging an arm toward the counter. She returned to the dishes, working quickly and splashing the water noisily.

Mark picked up the note with the phone number and shoved it into his jeans pocket. "It's not important." Petra was just a law student he barely knew; she was probably calling about the study group she was putting together.

He glanced around the kitchen and didn't see any food left out. "Well, I guess I'll go out and get a bite to eat, then."

Kaia didn't even turn around as he left. She was probably mad because he hadn't called to say he'd be back later than usual, or was it because some female law student had called? It was nothing to get pissed off about. Why couldn't she just say what was bothering her and get it over with? It seemed so immature. But then she wasn't all that mature. Only sixteen, for Christ's sake—although turning seventeen next month.

He went to a pub for a sandwich and a few beers, and when he returned around ten, he saw the light under Kaia's bedroom door and thought of knocking. He felt he shouldn't have to explain about the phone message, but he would if it would do any good. But David had stationed himself in the den, so there was no chance of having a private chat with Kaia.

During the following week, she was quiet during dinner and retreated to her room right afterwards, hunkering down with her books for the evening, barely exchanging words with him when he passed her in the house. At dinner one night she mentioned she was busy working on her college applications, but he had the definite sense she had changed her mind about him. She never gave him a chance to be alone with her to talk.

It was painful, this sudden coldness. It reminded him of his mother, the way she would switch moods like that, for no good reason. When he was a kid, Elisa would move from one of her rapturous states into complete withdrawal, and he was always afraid she would plunge into one of her severe depressions. He'd learned to monitor her moods, to try to keep her on an even keel as much as possible, and not to jolt her with sudden changes or anything upsetting.

Of course Kaia was nothing like his mother, but he didn't like the way she was acting.

The house was dark Thursday night when Mark parked on the street, but the porch light was on—maybe Kaia had gone out to dinner with David. Mark had lost track of time while he was at the law library and hadn't eaten since noon; his stomach was tight with hunger. Damn—he'd forgotten to call Kaia, to tell her he was going to be back too late for dinner again.

As he approached the front steps, he heard voices. In the lamp light he could see Kaia sitting on the deck in a shimmery leotard and jeans, a sweater wrapped around her shoulders, her legs stretched out in front of her. She kept her eyes on him as he climbed the steps, but she didn't smile. Then Mark saw someone in the shadowy part of the porch, and it gave him a sick feeling. The guy was sitting with his back against the wall, only a few feet away from Kaia. He looked about twenty, and was holding a beer bottle.

Mark stepped toward Kaia, so that he was standing over her.

"Hi, Mark," she said in a neutral tone. "Gary gave me a ride to ballet." She glanced over at the guy and said, "This is my cousin Mark."

The guy nodded at him, and Mark's midsection tensed up.

Kaia gave a high, self-conscious laugh. "I'm locked out. I forgot my key."

Mark reached for her hand. She hesitated for a second, but then took it and let him pull her up.

"Let's go inside," he said.

The guy got to his feet. "Hey, what's happening, man?" He was tall and lanky, with dark, greasy-looking hair.

"I need to go in now," Kaia told him. "Thanks for the ride."

"No problem." The guy took a long look at her, then headed down the steps.

Mark unlocked the door and waited, his body rigid, as Kaia stepped past him into the house. He flipped on the light, and she spun around to face him from a yard away. There was something defiant but excited in her gaze, and he could smell beer on her breath.

"Jesus, Kaia, what in the hell are you doing? Who was that guy?"

She shrugged. "He's just a neighbor. He was washing his car when I walked by and we just started talking. Then I told him I was late for ballet, and he offered to drive me there and wait for me."

"You just went off with some strange guy?" He was straining to keep his voice even, but it came out sounding harsh.

"God, Mark, you sound like Dad. Gary's not a stranger. I've talked to him before."

"Really. Well, I can drive you any time, you know, anywhere you want to go."

She lifted one shoulder and stared at him, as if his offer were of little consequence. "Dad will be home soon. He went out to dinner with his friend. I need to get some clothes on." She pulled the pins out of her hair and shook it loose around her shoulders, then just stood there, searching his face.

What kind of game was she playing? "Let's go upstairs for a minute. I need to talk to you," he said.

"I told you, I have things to do." She started to back away from him.

"Come on, Kaia." He reached out and placed his hand on her shoulder, but she turned away, then strutted ahead of him in her tight jeans. He followed her through the house until she slipped into her bedroom. As he stood in her doorway, she turned and met his gaze. He wanted to take her in his arms and erase what had just happened on the porch, and ease the tension of the past few days.

"Well?" She raised her eyebrows, her eyes darkening. "I have to take a shower now and change." She threw her sweater onto a chair.

"Come upstairs with me."

"No way. Dad would skin me alive if he found me up there."

"Just for a minute." He stood there, his arms held stiffly at his sides.

She stared at him, then let loose with an exasperated sigh. "Okay," she said, and edged past him, heading up the stairs. He started after her. She climbed up a few steps, then stopped and whirled around.

"Maybe we should get something to eat first," she said brightly. "We could talk in the kitchen."

He took another step up the stairs until he was eye level with her chest and could smell her sweet, heady scent; he was only a few inches away. "We can do that in a couple of minutes," he said as calmly as he could, his heart rate picking up. "Let's go on up." He cupped her elbow with his hand.

She turned and ran up the stairs. When he entered the loft, she was standing in the light of the floor lamp with her arms crossed, facing him, her jaw set. He walked over to her and took her by the upper arms, feeling the resistance in her tight muscles.

"What are you trying to do, Kaia?" he said quietly.

"What do you mean?"

"You've been acting so cold to me lately. And then riding around with some guy you barely know, flirting your ass off."

She stepped back, freeing herself from his grip. "I was not flirting."

"Damn it, Kaia, you can't do this to me. You know what guys are like."

"Is that what you're like?"

"No." He saw where she was with men now—open, wanting something, but not sure what. He lightly brushed her hair off her shoulder, feeling the delicate fluff of it on the back of his hand. He took her gently by the arms again and bent to kiss her, barely grazing her lips.

"Mark, don't."

He tried to kiss her again, but she averted her head.

"You can't do this to me," she said, scowling.

"Do what?"

"Take me places, kiss me the way you did, and then go out with other women."

"What are you talking about?"

"You've got women calling—"

"What?"

"You know, that message?" Kaia's voice was shaky. "That woman who left her number? I don't know why I even wrote it down. Then after I gave you the message, you went out and were gone for hours."

He blew out a long breath. "God, Kaia, is that what's been bothering you? She's just a law student. She was getting a study group together for the Contracts exam. I didn't want to be rude, so I gave her my phone number. But I had no intention of going. I didn't even call her back. I just went to a bar and had a couple of beers and a burger. I'd rather be here with you, any night of the week." He grasped her more firmly, leaning over her. "I have no interest in her or anyone else."

Kaia shook her head slowly as she looked into his eyes. "I don't know what you want."

"Everything."

"That's not possible, Mark." Tears were building up in her eyes.

"Why couldn't we have everything?"

"You're my cousin, remember?"

She was crying now. Letting go of her arms, he cradled her cheeks in his hands and brushed her tears with his thumbs. "Jesus, don't worry about things like that. Don't you feel how we are together?"

She nodded her head slightly.

"You get upset with me so easily, Kaia. I need someone I can count on."

"Don't you think I need someone like that? I don't trust anyone. My mom doesn't care about me, and my dad just wants to control everything I do."

Mark pulled her closer and kissed her. "Kaia, I love you."

She blushed, studying his face.

"Every night," he said softly, "I have to stop myself from coming into your room." He wrapped his arms around her, her breasts pliant against him. He bent down and kissed her on her neck and face until she twisted her head away.

"Dad's going to be home soon." She sounded breathy and excited, and it made him think David was the only obstacle.

"He'll probably be out for a while with his woman friend."

Kaia pushed at his chest, and he let her slip out of his grasp. He waited a moment, then moved toward her, wrapped his arms around her and kissed her again. He loved the feel of her light torso against him, making him aware of his own strength. He hooked his thumb under her leotard strap and pulled it down, exposing her breast, making her gasp. Then there was the sound of a car swerving into the driveway, the wheels spitting gravel into the underbelly of the sedan, and he groaned as Kaia drew away from him, her hair mussed, her face flushed. She swiftly pulled up her strap.

In seconds she was gone, down the stairs. David marched through the house, his footsteps repugnant, with their irregular, limping rhythm on the hardwood floor. Mark strode the length of the loft, breathing hard, then back to the spot where he and Kaia had been together just a moment ago. He imagined he could still feel the warmth of her body and smell her scent. He'd gone way too fast with her. She was too young, and she was his cousin. She'd never had a lover, or even a boyfriend. God, how could he ever have her to himself? Especially if she wouldn't trust him.

He took a beer from the mini-refrigerator and slung himself into the armchair. Now he was afraid of what he might do if he got her alone again, afraid he might push her into something she wasn't ready for. He thought of his father, with his affairs. The other night his mother had called, hysterical because Nico was out late and she couldn't reach him at the office. She kept saying, "It's her, it's her, I just know it." Mark didn't even want to think about it, he just wanted his father to stop doing whatever it was he was doing.

Mark knew he would never be like his father. If he could just have Kaia, that would be enough. She seemed to be afraid that he would go after other women, but he would never do anything like that, anything that would ever hurt her.

If only she believed that.

10

"I'm an egomaniac," Kaia said.

"I am, too," Sig said in a dreamlike voice. She was sitting in a lotus position on the floor in Kaia's room, holding a joint in one hand, her fingers extended gracefully, the other hand under her elbow, her pose etched in the green light of the lava lamp.

Jazz from the stereo surrounded them. The rain on the roof sounded like corn popping, its rhythm blending with the syncopated percussion of the music, and then the keyboard became dominant, rollercoastering up and down the scale.

Sitting on the floor opposite Sig, Kaia watched as her friend took a hit; she had an artistic way of smoking, as if sipping champagne. The pleasure of the act flooded her face. After a few moments Sig passed the joint to Kaia.

"An occasional egomaniac," Kaia amended, and took a hit. The smoke tasted metallic, like ginseng tea. "I just want my friends to be here, around me, always."

"Wouldn't *that* be cool."

Sig understood what was significant, didn't concern herself with trivialities.

"Do you know what Mark called me?" Kaia asked.

"No idea."

"A closet flirt."

"Why would he say that?" Sig took the joint from Kaia.

She shrugged. "I don't even believe in flirting."

"It wouldn't be right," Sig agreed in a lofty tone, then sucked hard and blew out the smoke in a single blast. "But at times you do in fact flirt, even with Mr. Brown, and you've got this mischievous little smile." Sig grinned, opening her eyes wide in an obvious attempt to imitate Kaia. "Maybe you don't even realize it. And boys always stare at you, wherever we go. Older men, too. It's kind of disgusting, really."

"What are you talking about?" Kaia was sure she never consciously flirted with their photography teacher. He *was* rather cute, though.

"Nothing. Just forget it."

"I don't know what gave you that idea," Kaia said.

"Never mind. Let's just enjoy ourselves. The pot, the music. The rain . . ."

They sat there listening to the music for a while. Kaia closed her eyes, focusing on a horn that was sirening loosely in spirals; then the electric guitars and bass came in.

"Before it was more bossa nova, more rhythmical," Kaia said, "but then it gets wild and intense. I like it."

"Clarke influence. The bass, the hand bells."

Kaia stood up, aware of the density of her body, a compact weight she had to maneuver off the floor. She left the room and returned with a carton of half-and-half, a bottle of Kahlua and two goblets. She shut the door to keep the smoke from spreading throughout the house.

"Aren't you afraid your dad will find out?" Sig asked.

"About the Kahlua? Nah."

"But he'll smell the grass."

"I'll air out the room." Kaia poured out two rather ample drinks, the viscous cream swirling into the Kahlua. They drank some of the rich sweet liqueur.

"Your dad's kind of strict, isn't he?" Sig asked.

"Sometimes."

There was a sound of footsteps climbing the front steps, and Kaia raised her head, listening to the clicks of the door lock. She realized the music had stopped. Mark usually came in through the back door, but now she heard his boots clomping on the floor as he came through the front room and past the kitchen. Sig and she stared at each other as Mark walked into the hallway, then stopped outside Kaia's room.

He tapped on the door, and when she answered, he opened it and stepped in. He stood there in his leather jacket and looked around the room, taking in the paraphernalia strewn over the floor—the matchbox, the baggie of grass, the Zig Zags. "So. Wednesday afternoon."

"Could be a song," Sig said.

"This is my cousin Mark," Kaia said. She wondered if Sig thought he was sexy—kind of a craggy guy with his sideburns and moustache, standing there in his faded jeans. "Mark, meet Sig. Why don't you join us?"

"Thanks." He took off his jacket and sat down on the floor, checking out the half-smoked joint on the saucer.

"Have some," Kaia said.

Mark lit the joint and took a hit. They sat there smoking for a while, and Kaia saw that he had crossed over some boundary. She observed this quite clearly, almost as if it were a physical transmigration. They were instantly friendlier, intimate, the three of them in the same space.

No one spoke while they passed the joint around. Sig stared at Kaia with eyes that were wide and shiny. Kaia crawled over and flipped over the Chick Correa album. The music began with a horn that sounded like a lowing bull. But did bulls low, or just cows, or was it some other animal altogether? Chimes and the bass, then a pipe solo.

"Hey, it's Chick," Mark said. "Who's on the guitar?"

"Al Dimeola," Kaia said.

"Yeah, I can hear the soprano guitar." Mark took a hit and offered the joint to Sig, who shook her head, then he gave it to Kaia, his hand lingering on hers for a moment.

Kaia checked out Sig's face, the way her lips were drawn into a bizarre twist.

Sig clambered over to the purple armchair in the corner and sat down. Kaia thought of the chair's color as aubergine—she loved the hushed velvetiness of the word. Sig sat there, taking stock of everything. There was tension in the muscles of her face, in the rigidity of her expression, as if she were confronting a snake, a live spitting cobra, sent by someone in a box, a thing that might be lethal, oozing poison or contagion. Kaia thought she herself might be hallucinating. She had never been in a situation like this before, wanted by two people. In demand. Even her mother, now that she thought about it, had seemed to slide away from her so easily, leaving only her father to love her with his constant growl of fierceness. And Mark had added a new element to the situation. Kaia saw her own life moving onto a different track, and Sig was not there with her.

"Maybe we could all go out for a drive," Mark said after a while.

"It's raining," Sig said. "In case you hadn't noticed."

"True," Mark said. "Sounds like it's coming down pretty heavy." He took Kaia's glass from her hand and drank some of the Kahlua.

"You two go cruise in the rain if you want to," Sig said. She leaned forward, picking up her neon-green sneaker. "Or you could go streaking in the rain."

Kaia laughed. "No, let's stay here. I'll get us some good munchies."

Sig followed her into the kitchen. They foraged for food, then Sig tapped Kaia on the shoulder. "He's kind of voracious, isn't he?" she whispered, as if they were spies.

"I guess."

"I picked up on it right away."

When they returned to the bedroom, the jazz had stopped and Mark was still sitting on the floor, his head propped against the wall. They all sat in a circle and ate squaw bread with peanut butter, and drank Darjeeling tea steeped with whole cloves.

"What should we do now?" Kaia asked, after they'd eaten all of the bread.

"Whatever we want," Mark said.

"What a concept," Sig said.

"I wonder what it'd be like to spend a month like this," Kaia said, "doing whatever we felt like, listening to music, filling the refrigerator with the most delicious foods we could find. Just eating, drinking, smoking, without having to worry about the time or Dad coming home and wrecking things." She rose slowly and went over to the bed, lying down on her back.

"And without having to air out," Sig said.

"Why can't you live like that?" Mark asked.

"Yeah," Kaia said, "like an animal in the wild, except with human interests, since we probably have more complex brains."

"What else would you do?" Sig asked her.

Kaia lay still, closing her eyes for a moment. "I'd spend time with my friends, paint pictures, dance."

"What—ballet?" Sig said.

"God, no. Something interpretive maybe. Not like ballet—it's way too structured."

After a few minutes, Sig stood up, picking up her book bag. "I'd better get home, sweetpea, so you can clear up this mess before Santa Claus comes home jingling his bells."

"No, no, it's Rudolph with the jingling bells. Or is it Mr. Bo Jangles?" Kaia raised her head from the pillow. "Wait a second. Mark can drive you."

"That's okay. I'll just take the bus. You guys are too out of it." Sig ran her eyes over both of them before making her way out of the room.

It disturbed Kaia to watch Sig leave, shutting the door behind her, as if she were a much older, disapproving person. Kaia saw herself doing everything wrong, as if she were a rather incompetent actress in a play she didn't comprehend. When she was alone with Sig she felt different from who she was with Mark, or who she was with her father. What was she then? Some kind of chameleon, apparently. She was almost seventeen, but had no clue what was going to happen to her. Not the slightest idea. Up until now she'd been thrust into the path of others without any say.

"Airing out time," she sighed, sitting up.

"It's only four-thirty," Mark said.

She got off the bed and sat on the floor next to Mark. He took her by the hand and pulled her up, so that they were both kneeling a few inches apart, and she raised her face to his. He kissed her, then pulled her against him so that her cheek rested against his chest.

"Let's just stay like this," she said, closing her eyes.

"Okay." He kissed the top of her head.

After a long while he let go of her. "What do you want to do?" he asked.

She shook her head. "You have to go so I can clean up in here."

He placed his hands on her shoulders, then stood up. "All right, but I'll help you," he said, and drew her to her feet.

Her only wish then was that her father would never come home.

11

David thought Kaia looked particularly pretty, her face serene as they worked together in the kitchen preparing the *coq au vin*. In her sky-blue T-shirt and snug jeans, her hair piled loosely on top of her head and face flushed, she was so very lovely.

She peered up at him. "Are you nervous, Daddy?"

"Not really. Are you?"

"Course not," Kaia said. "I just thought you might be, since we're having Chandi over for the first time."

"Nope." He laid his hand on his daughter's shoulder. "I'm looking forward to it, in fact."

It was late October, and he'd finally decided to have Chandi Gupta over to the house for dinner and to meet Kaia. During the past several months, he'd met her for casual meals, and it had always been collegial. But when he pictured the way she smiled at him, her head tilted to the side as she met his eyes, he wondered if she might be starting to think of him in a somewhat different way.

He glanced up from chopping carrots and watched Kaia walk into the adjoining den and flip over the album—Beethoven sonatas—on the stereo. Confident of her taste, he'd left it to her to select music for the evening. The two of them had become almost like a married couple in some ways since Jean had left—the way he and Kaia liked to listen to the same music or read in the evenings, the times they cooked meals like this one together or shopped at the farmer's market on Saturday mornings. Things had shifted, though, since Mark's arrival two months ago. Now Kaia seemed to have less inclination to do things with her old dad, and David was regretting that. Fortunately Mark had left around noon today to study at the library, leaving them to do their shopping and dinner preparation. David was grateful to have a few hours alone with Kaia, and she had offered to make a special coconut bread, now baking in the oven, its sweet, toasty aroma filling the house.

Returning to the kitchen, Kaia stirred the onions in the pan, her face moist and pink from the heat of the stovetop. She was a good cook, and knew instinctively how to add just the right amount of fresh rosemary and thyme to the dish. He came up next to her and gently squeezed the back of her neck, and she flinched, as if startled out of a daydream. He relaxed his hand, resting it there, and she edged away from him and took a sip of the special Zinfandel he'd bought for tonight. During the past year or so, he'd allowed Kaia to drink some wine with dinner, and he figured it was all right—the Europeans let their kids have wine fairly young, and it didn't seem to be a problem. Besides, he didn't like drinking alone. He was on his second glass now, not to mention the two Scotches he'd drunk before starting on the wine. He reminded himself not to overdo it.

"Smells good," he said, and Kaia smiled at him, her lips sparkling with some kind of glossy lipstick. His daughter seemed to be more confident, more womanly these days, somehow. "What should we do next?" he asked.

"You could start on the salad, Father dear."

Just that small dose of affection made him inordinately happy—for once he hadn't caught any sarcasm in her voice.

Kaia went to her bedroom and returned a few minutes later wearing a silky, turquoise blouse—rather low cut—that seemed as if it might float off her shoulder any second, velvet pants, and the pearl earrings he'd given her last Christmas. He watched as she tied an apron around her slender waist. Then he heard the obnoxious rumble of Mark's old Mustang as it pulled into the driveway, and he silently cursed his nephew for coming back early. But then he checked his watch and realized that Chandi would be arriving soon.

As Mark entered the kitchen, David caught the exchange of glances between the two cousins—the open smiles, the raising of eyebrows. There was a brand of familiarity between them he couldn't stomach. He was surprised to see Mark set a bottle of Sterling Cabernet on the counter.

"Maybe we can have some of that with dinner," David said.

"That's the idea," Mark said.

"We're actually kind of busy in here."

"I'd be glad to help with something," Mark said in an offhand way.

"In a few minutes I'll be ready to put the lattice crust on the pie," Kaia said. "Maybe you can help with that."

"That sounds like something you should do yourself, Kaia," David said.

"I can show Mark how to do it right." She glanced slyly at her cousin. "Or he shall have no pie."

Damn, that sounded so suggestive, David thought.

Mark laughed. "Can't say I've ever made a pie. But I'll be glad to give it a shot. First, though, I'll take a glass of that wine to get warmed up." He indicated with a nod the open bottle of David's pricey Ridge Zinfandel. He plunked himself down on a bar stool on the opposite side of the counter, and Kaia poured him a full glass.

David chopped at the scallions, slicing down hard with the knife. There sat Mark with his salacious smirk, staring at Kaia while she returned his look. David wished his nephew would just take his wine upstairs and do whatever the hell it was he did up there.

Right at seven, the doorbell rang and David went to the door. Chandi stood on the porch wearing a blue-green coat and a gorgeous smile. She appeared so youthful for a woman in her late forties, with her cropped, black hair and tawny skin. Black eyeliner emphasized her cola-brown eyes, and she wore red lipstick, which made a rather dramatic statement. As she stepped into the foyer, he took her coat and kissed her on the cheek, inhaling her citrusy scent.

"You look lovely, Chandi." In fact he had never seen her look quite so striking.

"Thank you, David." He loved the melodic lilt of her voice, her Anglo-Indian accent.

She glanced at the dining area, where Kaia had set the table with a blue tablecloth, white china, and a colorful bouquet of flowers in a lavender glass vase. "This is such an inviting room, David. And whatever you're cooking smells so good."

"Thanks. We're making *coq au vin*." As he led her into the kitchen, he was grateful for the Beethoven playing in the background—he was sure Chandi would appreciate it. "Well, come and meet Kaia," he said.

As David introduced his daughter, Chandi took Kaia's hand in both of hers, smiling and studying her face intently. Kaia then introduced Mark as her cousin, and Chandi shook his hand.

David poured Chandi a glass of wine and topped off his own, emptying the bottle. "A toast. To friends and family, and especially to these two beautiful women."

"And to all such gallant men." Chandi touched David's glass with hers.

"Yes, to beauty," Mark said, raising his glass and smiling at Kaia.

She looked down, sipping from her glass; a glow of perspiration clung to her forehead like a mist.

If only his nephew could be excised from this picture, David thought, leaving just Kaia and Chandi here with him. It might be like that in the future—having both his daughter and Chandi in his life. There would have to be a reapportionment, a kind of redistricting, you might say, of their relative influence, with Chandi possibly taking over some of Kaia's strong emotional hold over him. Feeling rather effusive in his pleasant, alcohol-induced state, he could almost see it happening; he saw himself as absurdly fortunate, containing so much in his near grasp, as if he were a bankrupt man about to inherit a fortune.

Once they were all seated, David met Chandi's gaze across the length of the table. "Well, shall we?" he said, and handed the ceramic pot of *coq au vin* to Kaia.

He took a thick slice of Kaia's warm coconut bread from the basket. He was proud of his daughter, so clearly a sensualist, a girl who loved the aroma and taste of delicious food, and she seemed so eager to please him by catering to his guest. As Kaia brought her wine glass to her lips, he saw that she'd painted her fingernails an extravagant shade of burgundy, rich against her tan skin—she always had that golden tint, even now, in October.

"David tells me you're studying law at Boalt," Chandi said to Mark, once they'd all loaded up their plates. "How do you like it so far?"

"It's pretty much what I expected. Lots of reading, not too difficult; mainly digesting the concepts and the case law."

"You'll probably be taking Constitutional Law from David next year."

"I suppose so. No one else teaches it." Mark looked down at his plate and began eating.

"Chandi's an attorney," David said. "She knows all about the grind of law school."

"Dad says you do children's rights cases," Kaia said to Chandi.

"That may be glamorizing it a bit. Sometimes I represent the children, but more often the court appoints me to represent the parents in abandonment and neglect cases."

"I told Kaia you've been fighting for more rights for the children when the county takes them away from their parents,"

David said. "To provide the children with more procedural rights, their own attorney, that kind of thing."

"I do have one case where I'm raising those issues. I have a client, a migrant farmworker, who's in danger of losing all rights to her children because she left them in foster care while she worked as a harvester."

"Do you think you'll get her kids back for her?" Kaia asked.

"I don't know. It's an uphill battle once the county moves in. These cases can sometimes go on for years, once they reach the higher courts."

"Your work sounds interesting," Kaia said.

"I keep telling Kaia she'd make a great lawyer," David said. "She's got a good, analytical mind, and likes arguing a point to the bitter end." He smiled at his daughter to emphasize he was teasing.

She frowned slightly. "You're the one who likes to argue."

"What about that debate we had just the other night about the election?"

"So what? That was just politics."

"That's what I mean—you like to argue about politics and the news. Anything like that, as well as what college you want to attend."

"But Dad—"

"Sorry I mentioned the college issue. Let's save that for another time, shall we? I think we were discussing whether you would make a good lawyer."

Her face reddening, Kaia stared at her plate, her fork suspended in the air.

"I'm mostly interested in trial work, myself," Mark said, and took a second slice of the coconut bread. "I'd like to get some practical experience while I'm in law school."

"You have to learn your Evidence and Civil Procedure before you take Trial Practice," David said.

Mark turned to Chandi. "I'm mainly interested in public interest litigation. Some of the professors do pro bono work for the Sierra Club or the ACLU. I'd like to work for a firm like that." He picked up the bottle of Cabernet and started refilling the glasses.

"That's enough for Kaia," David said. Why in the world did Mark think it was up to him to pour the wine, simply because he'd brought it? David shook his head in amazement at his nephew's lack of manners.

Mark filled his own glass and set down the bottle.

Kaia smiled at Mark. "It's all right. I don't plan to get drunk."

"Better not," David said sternly. Kaia was leaning toward Mark, showing way too much cleavage. The blouse was totally inappropriate. He should have made her change.

"I'd like to get involved with environmental lawsuits against the big corporations," Mark said. "It's pretty disturbing what the chemical companies have gotten away with—as they did at Love Canal."

"Saving the planet's great," David said, "but upholding constitutional rights is something you might consider, too." He knew that sounded rather pompous, but he didn't give a damn.

"The people who lived near Love Canal had rights," Mark said. "They had to hold an E.P.A. official hostage before the Feds did anything to evacuate them."

"Holding someone hostage is an incredibly stupid way to protect constitutional rights." David was aware that his voice was growing louder. He took a bite of the chicken, barely tasting it.

Mark shoveled in a mouthful of food and glanced at Kaia, who raised her eyebrows at him.

After a few moments of silence, Chandi asked David, "How did you wind up teaching Constitutional Law, David?"

He took a quick drink from his wine glass. "I was a criminal defense attorney, and started teaching Trial Practice at Boalt part-time. When an opening came up for a tenure-track position in Constitutional Law, I applied for it."

"Don't you miss actual lawyering, though?" Mark asked David.

What nerve. *Actual lawyering.* What was the problem with his cocky nephew? Didn't Mark see how impudent he was coming across? If he did, he obviously didn't care. Trying to stifle his anger, David said, "Wouldn't be any decent lawyers without some good instruction. Anyway, I've got other things going, like trying to get some new clinical programs started, so students can get the kind of practical experience they need."

"Heard it's not going to happen," Mark said. "That it's all talk."

"It's a hell of a lot more than talk," David said, taking another gulp of wine. "We'll manage to get it done somehow, unless Reagan gets elected and federal funding is cut."

"Looks like he will," Mark said.

"No way. It would be the first time an incumbent was ousted since Herbert Hoover," David said. "I can't believe anyone would be idiotic enough to vote for a right-winger like Reagan."

"Carter's a goner," Mark said.

"I seriously doubt it," David said, then turned to Chandi. "Did you watch the debates Tuesday night?" he asked.

She looked up. "Yes, I did. I was disappointed in Carter. And he's been so ineffectual in trying to get the hostages out of Iran."

"But it wasn't his fault the helicopter crashed," Kaia said earnestly. "And I'm sure Reagan wouldn't do any better in a situation like that."

"What could anyone expect from an ex-movie star?" David said.

Kaia took a sip of her wine and smiled at Mark, and he grinned back at her. The two of them were certainly enjoying each other's company. David just hoped Kaia would get over this infatuation or whatever it was, so that she could concentrate on her schooling. And Mark was going to have to find his own place. Very soon.

David picked up a piece of bread and buttered it, then met Chandi's eyes. A slow smile formed on her lips, and, in spite of the tension at the table, David forced himself to take a deep breath, and smiled back at her.

David sauntered along with Chandi, her arm linked through his, and gazed up at the ink-black sky, dotted with stars. He was glad his ankle was nearly healed now, and he could walk without discomfort, no longer forced to hobble along like an old man. He loved this time of the evening and being out in the cool night air with Chandi—she'd talked him into a stroll around the neighborhood while Kaia and Mark did the dishes, and now David felt relieved to be out of the charged atmosphere of the house. He had the surprising sense that Chandi and he were more or less a couple, and he wondered how that had come about. A few weeks ago, the night Kaia took off to Half Moon Bay with Mark, Chandi had invited him over for an impromptu supper at her house, and something in their relationship had seemed to shift in a more romantic direction then. That evening she'd worn a red, clingy dress and an exotic perfume. And her voice seemed softer lately when she spoke to him, on the phone or in person.

"Have you had time to delve into *Lord Jim*?" she asked now, peering up at him in the glow of the streetlights.

"Yes, I've started on it." He'd borrowed the book from her that evening at her house and had read only a few chapters so far. "I'd forgotten so much of the story since I read it years ago. I must admit, though, I'm finding it rather depressing."

"I guess it can be."

"The guy's a real brooder."

"That's Conrad, all right. His characters tend to be that way."

David slowed his pace, fixing his eyes on the sidewalk ahead of them. "It was interesting, the way guilt drove him for so long. He couldn't rid himself of that terrible guilt."

"Yes. Like so many strong emotions that can take hold of one. Guilt, jealousy, anger."

"Yes—anger," he said. "That's a hard one, and of course every parent knows about guilt."

"I can imagine. But you seem to be a dedicated father."

David shook his head. "I don't know how well I'm doing as Kaia's only functional parent."

"Really?"

"I've been thinking something is wrong, that she isn't really doing that well."

"Kaia seems like a happy girl."

"I don't know." He turned to Chandi as they walked along. "I woke up last night in the midst of a horrible dream about Kaia. It jolted me awake. I felt an almost physical dread, and I had to get up and have a drink. I wandered around the house for a long time before I went back to bed."

He was silent while they crossed over to Indian Rock Park, then said, "From what I can remember of the dream, I was visiting some foreign city with Kaia, a huge, mazelike city with canals. It didn't seem like Venice, though. Could have been a place like Amsterdam, I suppose. I've never actually been there, but in the dream it seemed like a very bleak city with canals and concrete buildings and walls. I was supposed to meet Kaia at a café, but she didn't show up, and I started to panic."

David tried to recall more details as they ambled along. "The last time I saw her in the dream," he said after a moment, "she was wearing heavy black eyeliner and looked tall and pale, nothing like her real self. I had the impression that I didn't know her anymore, and that she was beyond my grasp. And when I couldn't find her, I became frantic and started to run along the canal, searching for her, convinced she'd gone swimming with some strange man. I had the strong urge to dive into the canal but I couldn't see her anywhere. Then I started running faster and became convinced she was dead, that this man had harmed her or killed her. When I woke up, my heart was pounding away like a bass drum." He felt completely churned up now, back into the disturbing mood of the dream, his heart rate accelerating as it had during the dream.

Chandi turned to him, her eyes wide in the hazy light.

"It was the worst nightmare I've had in a long time," he said, shaking his head. "It's rather Freudian, isn't it?" Feeling self-conscious now about divulging his foolish dream, he said, "Maybe the man in the dream was Mark—he seems to be around all the time, and spends way too much time with Kaia."

"It's your dream," Chandi said in a subdued voice. "I don't know what it means, or how it could be Freudian."

David wasn't sure what he meant either, except that he did sense at times that his daughter was slipping away from him. He couldn't really explain that to Chandi; it was rather personal, and difficult to articulate. And Chandi didn't have any children, had never been married. "Maybe if Jean were still here, there would be more balance in Kaia's life." He glanced at Chandi. "Kaia's been lonely much of the time, and I think she misses her mother sometimes. That's all I meant."

"It's all right, David, I really don't mind if you talk about your ex-wife."

He stopped and faced her, placing his hands on her upper arms. "You are such a lovely woman, Chandi."

She tilted her head. "Thank you, David." She sounded surprised by his compliment; he realized he rarely expressed those kinds of sentiments to her, or possibly to anyone.

He leaned over and kissed her lightly on the lips, a warm sensation, and her lips pressed briefly against his. He'd only kissed her before on the cheek, and only a couple of times. As she drew away, she smiled at him.

"We can't really spend much time alone together in my house, with Kaia and my nephew around," he said. "And your house—I wouldn't want to impose on you."

"You would never be imposing, David."

He turned and started walking with her again. "How about spending some time together tomorrow night, then?"

"Yes, you could come over for some chai."

He smiled and put his arm around her. "That would be wonderful." It made him anxious, taking this step, but he also wanted to do this, at least part of him did. It didn't seem like the wisest thing, leaving Kaia to her own devices, and if he were to be gone all evening, it might be inviting trouble. He would insist she go to Sigourney's house, or that Sig come to their house to keep Kaia company.

Kaia wasn't quite seventeen, after all, and she needed his love and protection as much as ever. Perhaps more than ever.

12

During most of November, Kaia spent her evenings on her homework and filling out college applications. She had little time for anything else, but she still went to ballet lessons two days a week. They'd hardly even celebrated her birthday. Mark took her out one afternoon to buy a pair of pink ballet slippers as a present, but they'd ended up making out in his car, which had completely derailed her concentration for the rest of the day. When he occasionally suggested they get a pizza or a hamburger in the afternoon, she refused. It was way too distracting to be with him.

She was anxious to finish her applications so that she could think more seriously about what she and Mark were going to do. She always felt his presence in the house, upstairs or at times when he walked down the hallway past her room. Even when he wasn't around, she would catch herself daydreaming about him, imagining the way he looked at her so attentively, and recalling his kiss and the heavy, warm feeling of his arms wrapped around her.

In December, two weeks after her birthday, Kaia found a large package on the porch with no return address. At first she thought it was from her mother, though her mom had already sent her a check, a week after Kaia's birthday. She opened the enclosed card:

Dear Kaia,

HAPPY HAPPY BIRTHDAY!! Hope you had a marvelous time.

I'm sorry this didn't reach you in time, but I've just finished the quilt. I spent hours embroidering the flowers—gardenias just for you! I'm always trying something new, and quilting is so different for me, so calming, and I often need that.

Mark says he might want to spend some time at his grandfather's cabin in northern Maine next summer, and I thought you could go up there for a visit—it's heavenly! It would be a wonderful vacation for you before you start college in the fall. You could stay up there for as long as you like. Of course it's a little rustic, with no electricity, but it's Mark's favorite place, and I'm sure you'd love it.

Write and tell me what you've been doing, and make that stern father of yours lighten up a little!

Nico sends his love, too.

Hugs and kisses from both of us,

Elisa

Kaia opened the box and gasped as she spread the quilt on her bed. Each teal-and-purple square had a large white gardenia embroidered in its center, with a border of bright blue. She turned the quilt over and ran her hand over the purple satin backing, then held the exquisite quilt to her cheek.

She found some stationery and wrote back:

Dear Elisa,

Thank you for the gorgeous comforter! The silky side feels wonderful, and your design is beautiful. It must have taken you a very long time to make. It's the most beautiful gift I've ever received.

I spent my birthday weekend printing photos in the basement with Dad. On Friday night he said he wanted to photograph me in black and white. The one he picked to enlarge is half in darkness, and in soft focus, like a glamour shot—not like me at all. Dad thinks he's Pygmalion or something.

Please write again soon.

Love, Kaia

13

Later it would seem to her that it had happened randomly, yet inevitably, like an El Niño, or a Santa Ana wind swirling around them, gathering into a storm. A few days before winter break, Kaia finished sending off the last of her college applications. She'd applied to San Francisco State, Stanford, Berkeley—to make her dad happy—and Columbia, to satisfy her mother. Relaxed for the first time in weeks, Kaia went to the dance studio to limber up. Sometimes after ballet she liked to soak in the tub, but today after a short session she wanted a hot, invigorating shower.

Letting the steamy water spray against her back and legs, she immersed herself in its heat, enjoying the toned feeling that came after dancing. She turned and let the water mizzle her face, her breasts, her stomach, a surge of pleasure passing through her body. The water penetrated her shoulders, soaked down into her flesh, her blood jumping to the surface of her skin. She worked the shampoo through her hair, and lathered carnation-scented soap into her skin.

Thinking of Mark, she imagined spending an evening with him in a dark restaurant, talking, a candle throwing shadows over his face like a painting in *chiaroscuro*. She recalled his embrace in the loft a few weeks ago, could almost feel the pressure of his mouth, the sturdiness of his body against her. She rinsed out her hair and let the water flow over her face and body.

A sudden sharp knock made her jump, startling her out of her reverie.

"Yes?" she called out, thinking it might be her father.

The door opened part way. She peeked through the foggy glass enclosure—it was Mark, his brown hair and denim jacket unmistakable.

"I'll be out in a minute," she said.

"I need to talk to you." His voice was low and insistent.

She turned off the water as he opened the bathroom door wider—she could see his face more clearly now through the glass and realized he could see her entire body, although obscured by the steam on the glass.

"Hand me a towel." Her legs were trembling.

He came into the room, shutting the door behind him, and pulled a towel off the rack. She slid open the glass door and took the towel from him, then quickly wrapped it around herself and stepped out. He grabbed her by the shoulders and spun her around, pressing her against the bathroom door, the water from her hair sluicing over her shoulders. He kissed her, and she closed her eyes, kissing him back.

After a moment, she drew away. "I need to get my robe. I'm freezing." She opened the door and rushed toward her bedroom. She had told Mark that morning that her father had a faculty meeting and would be coming home late, so Mark had probably taken that as an invitation—and she realized now that it was. She'd wanted to spend time alone with him; and now that he was here, it both thrilled and frightened her.

By the time he reached her room, she had dropped the towel and slipped into her terry robe. She felt warmer, now that she was dry and the heat was on in the house. Then she heard Mark coming down the hallway.

He came up to her and slid his hand inside her robe, finding her breast. She pulled back slightly, though his hand had felt good. He took her by the elbows and kissed her. "I want to see you." He spread open her robe.

For a few seconds she held her breath, embarrassed—he appeared so rapt as he ran his eyes over her body. She stepped closer and he kissed her, sliding his arms inside her robe again and pulling her against him, his jacket and jeans rough against her skin.

"We have plenty of time," he said.

She nodded, although she wasn't sure how long they would actually have. "I have no idea what I'm doing," she said.

"Don't worry, Kaia. I love you so much."

"I love you, too, Mark."

He put his arm around her as they walked out of the room and climbed the stairs. He helped her out of her robe, lifted her in his arms and swung her onto the bed. He bent to kiss her, then took off his shirt and shoes and stood there in his jeans, gazing at her as she lay there with her arms folded over her breasts. She wasn't afraid, not exactly, just acutely aware of him viewing her naked body, and conscious that her heart was beating fast. She'd wanted this to happen, and she wanted Mark to be the one. But what if her father came home unexpectedly? She told herself that was extremely unlikely, but she couldn't help imagining his enraged face if he discovered her with her cousin.

Mark stepped out of his pants. Kaia forced herself to take deep breaths as she watched him. He lay down next to her, sinking his face into her neck, kissing her on her mouth and face, smoothing her wet hair away from her forehead. When he pressed the length of his body against her, she could feel all of the textures of his body, the heat of his skin, and she took in his baked-bread aroma. His face was tense with pleasure. For a brief moment she thought she heard a sound downstairs, but decided it was just the normal creaking of the old house.

He switched on the cassette player next to the bed and the sound of Neil Young's tenor rolled over them. Taking his time,

Mark moved his hands and mouth over her with a kind of reverence. She touched his shoulder, his arm, not knowing what to do, absorbing the sensations. He ran his hand along her stomach, rubbing it softly, lightly pinching her skin. She listened to Neil Young's voice, concentrated on the slow rhythm of the tinny harmonica, the music reverberating in a steady beat.

Mark's hands were gentle, careful. He lavished baby oil on her and it felt good, the way he presumed to take control of her body. Thrilled to be able to touch him, she traced her hand over him. He put on a condom and lightly, patiently, caressed her.

Another ponderous song came on, about a dream and a promise and a man. She inhaled deeply as Mark leaned over her on one extended arm and looked into her eyes, the sun through the window throwing his face into partial shadow, the clear azure of his eyes capturing the light. And then he was over her, and she clutched at his back, breaking into a sweat. A moan escaped from inside her, and tears welled up in her eyes. He pulled back a little and became still. He looked into her face and kissed her. Reaching her arms out to his neck, she pulled him down against her, and after a while she instinctively began to move her hips in a rhythm like a sensual dance, and then everything became a blend of music, scents, heat, her legs quivering as she dug her heels into his back.

He went on, measured, making a low sound in his throat, his mouth on hers. Everything slowed down as she took in every nuance of sensation. Then, finally, he threw his head back and cried out, startling her.

Afterwards he kissed her face, her breasts, her belly. Then he lay there, his moist skin against hers, and caressed her almost listlessly, then more insistently, until she lost herself in a flood of whiteness while the brisk air from the open window rushed over her face and her breath caught—so incredible that now everything that mattered began here, with him.

14

During Christmas break, Kaia's father flew with Chandi to Seattle for a few days to visit Chandi's relatives, leaving Kaia to stay with Sig. Mark had returned to Maine—Kaia's father had insisted on it. She was sure, though, that her father didn't actually know what was going on between Mark and her.

On a Saturday afternoon, Sig and Kaia were supposed to be working on their history papers but didn't feel like it, so they curled up on the sofa and wrapped themselves in a comforter and listened to the Beatles on the radio. Ever since John Lennon had been shot in November, they'd been listening to Beatles music as a tribute.

The phone rang next to Sig, and after several rings, she turned down the volume on the radio and answered. "Just a minute," she said a moment later in an irritable tone, narrowing her eyes as she handed the receiver to Kaia.

Kaia wondered if it could be her mother calling. Her mother hadn't even considered coming out to California for Christmas; as usual there was a major deal pending. Her mother had sounded peeved when Kaia had told her she couldn't spend the holidays in New York.

"Kaia," Mark said on the phone.

"Hi, Mark," she said softly, thrilled to hear his deep, affectionate voice. "Where are you?"

"I'm still in Bangor. Monty's here, too. We're going to visit his family in Connecticut in a couple of days."

In the background, Monty yelled, "Tell her it's too bad she's being held hostage in California."

It made Kaia happy to picture Monty's long-toothed grin and narrow face. It would have been fun to fly back to Maine with Mark and spend time with him and Monty, but there was no way her father would have let her go.

"I wish we could talk without everyone else around," Mark growled.

"Okay, okay, I'm leaving," Monty shouted. "Watch out for this maniac, Kaia."

"See you later, Monty old boy," Mark said.

After a few seconds of silence Kaia asked, "So how's your mom doing?"

"About the same. I think Dad was just making things sound worse to make sure I came home. At least she doesn't seem to be drinking."

"That's good. So what's the plan?" Self-conscious with Sig sitting next to her, Kaia kept her voice low.

"I can't say it over the phone—it would make you blush over every part of your body."

"No, really, Mark."

"It's going to work out."

"I think Dad's starting to suspect—" She glanced over at Sig.

"We can always get an apartment together."

"Oh, sure." She gave a short laugh. "I'm not too excited about cohabiting with a corpse."

Casting a frown at Kaia, Sig got up and padded into the kitchen.

"Come on, babe. It's just a matter of time. Whenever you're ready."

"Hey, Mark, let's talk about this when you get back. I gotta go." She paused. "I love you," she whispered.

"What?"

"I love you," she said, spacing out the words.

"I love you, too, Kaia."

After they said good-bye, she leaned her head back against the couch with a sigh.

Sig came over with two opened bottles of Budweiser and flopped down on the sofa. Her face was drawn and pale, in contrast with her spiked black hair, which she'd dyed turquoise on the tips, so that she looked like a tropical bird. She handed one bottle to Kaia and took a sip from her own. "My, that was rather interesting."

"Was it?" Kaia could tell she was hurt; Sig seemed to feel that their friendship was some kind of secret society for just the two of them.

"So you're in love with your cousin." Sig crossed her arms.

Kaia took a sip of the beer, then looked at her.

"Why didn't you tell me?" Sig asked.

"I thought you'd figure it out. And besides, I knew what you'd say."

"What—that you're both pervs and that he's a creep?"

"You don't even know him," Kaia said angrily.

"Is that why you haven't had time to see me very much lately?"

"I'm here now." Kaia reached over to touch her friend's arm. "You're my only friend, you know. We're both sort of outcasts." Kaia attempted a grin, but Sig just glared at her.

"Is that why you like me? Because we're both nerds and never get invited to parties?"

"No, you're just really cool, and great in so many ways. And we understand each other like no one else does. Who wants to go their dumb parties, anyway?"

"Everyone at school admires you, though," Sig said. "You got elected Class Secretary just because someone nominated you and put you on the ballot without your even knowing about it.

Lots of kids would be friends with you if you wanted them to be. You're just too stand-offish."

"I'm not interested in them. I don't need them."

"What about Mark? You seem to need him, from the sound of your little chat just now."

Kaia shrugged, not wanting to talk about this. She knew Sig wouldn't be able to handle it.

"He's your cousin," Sig said, "and he just wants to fuck you. He probably already has."

Startled by Sig's hostile tone, Kaia met her eyes but said nothing.

"*Jesus*, Kaia." Sig scowled. "You don't tell me anything. I thought I was your best friend."

Kaia paused, considering what to tell her. "It's only been a few times."

Sig shook her head with a smirk of disgust. "He's just a testosterone machine. You said he's been leering at you from the minute he arrived."

"Not leering, just lustful. Enthusiastic."

"Extremely lustful and enthusiastic, I'd say."

"What's wrong with lust, anyway?" Kaia said. "Everyone seems to think sex is evil or something. It's not anyone's fault, it's the hormones." She felt disloyal to Mark, trivializing their lovemaking that way, but Sig wouldn't understand if Kaia tried to describe how otherworldly it felt to be with him, and how Mark loved her the way no one else could, and how she loved him just as much.

"Right," Sig said flatly, but with the hint of a resigned smile. "You can blame it on the pituitary."

"And the hypothalamus, right? Isn't that what controls the pituitary?"

"Yeah, but what controls the hypothalamus?"

"Who knows," Kaia said, grinning.

Sig shook her head. "I guess I'm a little slow. I should have figured out this was happening. But it's not going to last, then how are you going to feel?"

"I don't know what's going to happen."

"What will you do if Papa Bear finds out?"

"What will Papa Bear do?" Kaia said. "That's the real question."

15

Kaia had always known she could get into trouble with her father quite suddenly—in a minute or even a split second. His mood would change that rapidly, sparking into an angry, sometimes physical conflict. A severe glance and a grab of her arm was sometimes enough to silence her, although she wasn't always sure what he was thinking or what exactly he wanted from her—she usually just registered the disturbance between them and tried to deflect his fury. She was well aware that behind his desire to control her, there was a fanatic strength to back it up. But sometimes she couldn't help confronting him.

But by the end of December, she'd become aware of a shift in the atmosphere at home. Since Mark had returned from Maine after Christmas, her connection with him felt stronger, while her dad's vigilance had subsided; there was an odd, rather determined calm about her father, as if he'd decided something.

They spent New Year's Day at home with Chandi and Mark, drifting in and out of rooms, eating snacks and drinking wine, watching football, taking walks. In the evening, Chandi left, and a few minutes later her father ushered Kaia into the living room, leaving Mark in the den watching TV. Her dad shut the door leading to the rear of the house and, with a grim face, gestured for her to sit on the sofa, then sat in his armchair near her.

This was it, she thought. He knew.

"I want to tell you something, Kaia." His voice was strained as he held her gaze.

"What?" She examined his eyes, the deep chevron lines in his forehead. He looked tired, but serious, and it made her more than a little apprehensive.

"I've decided it's time for Mark to find his own place."

She inhaled sharply, then dropped her eyes, biting her lip. How much did her father know?

"Why are you doing this?" she asked him.

"I've been thinking about this for some time. Mark has been hanging around the house too much, and it's disruptive to our home life. It was only supposed to be a short-term arrangement, anyway."

"Disruptive? I hardly see him at all."

"I don't think that's true, Kaia. But in any case this is what I've decided, and it only remains to tell him."

"No." Kaia stood up, balling her fists. "You can't do this."

He shook his head, his jaw tightening. "I'm giving him a week to move out."

"What? I don't understand this at all."

"You'll just have to live with it, Kaia." He stood up and gripped her by the arms. "And you are not to go anywhere with Mark anymore—or see him."

She yanked away from him. "What? Why not? Mark is my cousin."

He placed his hands on her shoulders, pressing down. "It's not appropriate for you to be spending time with him."

As she stepped back, his hands dropped away. "Mark's the only friend I've got, other than Sig. You've made sure of that. You don't even let me date or go to parties."

"What are you talking about? I let you go to that dance last spring."

"Wow. One dance during the whole time I've been in high school."

"That's beside the point. Anyway, I have a feeling you've been spending time with Mark the past couple of months because I've been so busy, or maybe because I've been seeing more of Chandi."

Kaia frowned at him, mimicking disgust. "That's completely ridiculous." There was a tiny irritation of truth to it, though. It was sort of a neat balance: her father had Chandi, while she had Mark. But her dad would never understand about her and Mark. Every moment they could, they wanted to be together. She was sure her father had never felt that passionate about anyone.

"In any event," he continued, "it's just going to be you and me for a while, so you'll have to get used to it."

She placed her hands on her hips. "What about Chandi?"

"That's irrelevant." He strode over to the liquor cabinet and opened the glass door, then snapped it shut. He leaned with his hands on the marble top, then came over and stood in front of her, shoving his hands into his pockets.

Despite the familiarity of his rugged face and widow's peak, he seemed like a stranger to her in his coldness; his anger was what she knew, not this hard determination.

"Dad?"

"What," he said flatly.

"I'm going to live with Mom, then. I can't stand it here."

He stared at the floor for a few seconds then leveled a hard look at her. "No, you are not. And don't ever try to threaten me."

She glared at him. "But—"

"This is what I've decided, Kaia. There's nothing more to be said. And you are not going to New York." With that, he swung around and left the room, banging the door shut behind him.

She held her face in her hands and started to cry, then raised her head to listen to the sound of the two men talking in the den over the noise of the television. After a minute, she heard her father shout angrily, "She's under-age, I hope you realize."

The sickening thought came to her that her father might actually prosecute Mark if he knew for sure what was going on. Her father probably had the idea that if he got Mark out of the way, everything would return to the way it was before Mark had moved in with them. But that would never happen. Mark was a part of her life now. She would never forgive her father for this.

Stepping toward the living room door, she strained to hear their conversation. They were arguing, but she couldn't hear everything they said. She turned, wanting to get away from her father, and headed out the front door. She would take a long walk, even though it was dark and cold outside, and try to calm down. If her father saw how truly upset she was, he would guess the truth about Mark and her. Maybe he already had.

Kaia hadn't expected Mark to be waiting for her in his Mustang when she passed through the school gate with Sig; she hadn't heard from him since he'd moved out two weeks ago. But there he was, waving at her from his car, which was parked across the street. Sig placed her hand on Kaia's arm, as if she could somehow stop her, but Kaia said good-bye and rushed across the street, then hopped into Mark's car.

He turned to her. "I've missed you, Kaia."

"I've missed you, too." She didn't want him to know the full extent of her misery during the past two weeks, since he hadn't made much, if any effort to contact her.

"Let's go somewhere," he said, and when she nodded, he started up the engine, drove her to nearby Live Oak Park, and parked on the street.

She was nervous that someone she knew might see them here, but couldn't think of another place to go.

He leaned over and kissed her, bracing her chin with his hand. "Why don't you come over to my apartment so we can talk?"

She felt a delicious heaviness inside, her body remembering what it felt like to be with him. "I'm supposed to be taking the bus home. Then I have to go to ballet."

"When else can you see me, though?"

"I don't know. But I've already missed all of my lessons the past two weeks, waiting for you to call in the afternoon."

"I tried once and just got the answering machine. I guess you weren't home yet. And I didn't want to get you into trouble with your dad. I couldn't tell when he might be there."

Peering into his eyes, it was hard not to give in to him; but the fear of her father finding out about this was lodged like a foreign object in her chest. "I just can't right now, Mark."

"Come on, Kaia. You've got a couple of hours, right?" He gently touched her neck. "Just come over and see where I'm living. I'll get you home in plenty of time."

"I don't want to lie to Dad. I'll get into serious trouble with him if he finds out."

Mark bent over and kissed her again, then drew back a bit, his face a few inches away.

She sighed. "All right. But only for a little while."

He drove down the commercial strip of College Avenue, then turned onto a side street and pulled into a parking lot in front of a group of white stucco buildings. Walking through the courtyard, they passed a dry swimming pool, then climbed up to the apartment, their footsteps ringing on the metal stairway. As they entered the living room, Kaia caught the musty odor of mildew, and surveyed the gray walls with the paint peeling off in patches. In a corner a few law books and legal pads lay scattered on the carpet, a brass lamp sitting next to them. There was no furniture of any kind. She couldn't stand the thought of him living alone in this dump.

Mark turned to face her from a mere yard away, his arms at his sides. "I love you so much, Kaia. Do you realize that?"

She wanted to wrap her arms around him but was afraid of what it might lead to. "I know, Mark. I love you, too. But this whole thing has been so hard for me, especially when you were living with us."

"Really? Is that how you think of it? Hard for you?"

She could see she'd hurt him. Although she had missed him terribly, there was some relief now from the anxiety and guilt that she'd felt when he was living in the house. "I was always afraid Dad would catch us together."

He stepped closer. "I hate being away from you. I need to see you, Kaia."

She took a step back. "I don't know how we can. Dad will find out if we keep seeing each other. I'm only seventeen, Mark."

"Right. How serious can a seventeen-year-old girl be?" A slight frown crossed his face.

"What's that supposed to mean?" She was trying to keep her voice neutral, as if merely asking for an explanation, but it hurt that he would say that. He had to realize how much she loved him.

"You're young, that's all. You probably want to date a bunch of guys, go to dances, do all that high school stuff. It's your senior year, after all."

"Of course I don't. All I ever think about is you. I've been in love with you ever since Pine Tree."

Mark took a deep breath and let it out slowly. "Then what I want is for us to see each other as much as we can. And Mom says I can live in the cabin in Maine for the summer, so—"

"I know. The last time she wrote, she said we could stay in Grandpa's cabin if we ever wanted to. I was surprised she suggested that."

"You know how my mom is—anything goes if there's love involved."

"But Dad would never let me go."

"Let's forget about your father for once, okay? We can work it out." He bent to kiss her, then slipped his hands under her sweater, taking her by the ribs and pulling her towards him. "I want you to be with me all the time." He kissed her on the neck, then took her hand, tugging her toward the bedroom.

"You can't do this, kidnapping me like this."

"You can say no."

She couldn't help smiling as she peered up at him. "Do you have an actual bed?"

"You ask a lot." He led her into the bedroom, and they lay down on the mattress on the floor. Stretching out on top of her, he kissed her. He took off her sweater and bra, then his mouth was on her breast, and he ran his tongue over her midriff, sending shivers of pleasure through her. Kneeling over her, he pulled off her pants, buried his face in her belly, then stood and took off his clothes.

"Be careful, Mark."

He crouched over her, his eyes on hers. "I'll take care of everything, Kaia."

She raised her head to kiss him and then, after he'd slipped on a condom, she was sliding against him, lifting her hips to press against him, and all she was conscious of then was that she wasn't going to deny herself Mark, and everything that was between them.

16

Even from the top row of the stadium-style classroom, Kaia could see the outrage in her father's face, his gaze lighting on one student after another as he paced back and forth lecturing.

"You don't take away a person's freedom and property, even in time of war, because of his or her race and without due process of law." He turned and stopped behind the podium, grabbing the edges and leaning forward. "That is something that may not be done in a free country with a constitution designed to protect all of its people from arbitrary and tyrannical acts."

He was lecturing his Constitutional Law class about the Japanese-Americans who were imprisoned in camps during World War II. He was twelve years old at the time of the internment, he told the class, and remembered thousands of people, including several of his neighbors, being taken from their California homes. It was something Kaia had heard him rail against in the past. He began pacing again, speaking about the people who had lost everything, who had no one courageous enough to stand up for them in the face of this insult to democracy and plain human decency.

Kaia was glad she had come to sit in on his class. This was much more interesting than she'd expected, and she felt proud of her lanky father in his pressed cords, navy turtleneck sweater and sports coat. He moved energetically across the room and back, occasionally checking his notes on the podium. He had seemed so pleased when she'd appeared in his office earlier in the afternoon and told him she needed to do research for a paper on the Equal Rights Amendment. He offered to find some references for her, then invited her to sit in on his class. He really believed in these things—freedom of speech, due process, equal protection. Her father was a feminist, too, at least in theory—he said it was clear that women had to be treated as equals.

Not teenage daughters, though, she thought, as she watched him lecture on civil rights with so much enthusiasm. But she had to admit there was definitely something worthwhile in fighting for the constitutional rights of oppressed people.

In the weeks that followed, she started going to the law school more often, and would occasionally sit in on one of her dad's lectures, and he would always glance up and nod at her. She found she was beginning to understand something about due process and equal protection, and recognized that there were practical applications in the real world.

Whenever she could, she would meet Mark in the library or in the courtyard outside while her dad was in a meeting or teaching. Her father had found some books for her so that she could work on her term paper in his office. He often looked suspicious when he returned, but he probably figured not much could be going on in the short time he'd been gone. He was completely wrapped up in the textbook he was writing and seemed distracted much of the time, and he never asked her if she'd seen Mark in the halls; he probably didn't want to know.

One day when she met Mark in the courtyard at Boalt, he took her to the stacks in the library to show her the new study carrel he'd managed to get for himself; most of the other first-year students had carrels in the main room, but he'd lucked out when a carrel became available in a secluded part of the library.

He'd hung an Indian-print bedspread across the opening, as a few other students had done in other parts of the library. The carrels in the vicinity were hardly ever used, Mark told her. This remote section of the library housed only old law reviews and rarely used books. Supposedly no one ever came by.

Mark took her by the hand behind the curtain and sat down in the chair, pulling her onto his lap. He kissed her, and when she responded, he moved his hands inside her blouse and onto her breasts. When they made love it was fast and exciting—satisfying in a different, thrilling way. But in the middle of it she flashed on her father's furious face, and afterwards she felt shaken at having taken such a risk.

In the weeks that followed, Mark and she met whenever they could manage it, stealing time for sex, usually at home when her father was out—Mark would park on a side street and stay only an hour or two—and once in a hidden glen in Live Oak Park, an encounter that left grass stains on her bottom.

One afternoon Mark arranged to meet her at his carrel while her father was in class. "Here's something—" He inhaled deeply. "Don't laugh."

He had her sit down and showed her a list he'd written, summarizing the marriage laws for the fifty states. He pointed to a few states with stars next to them. "These are the places where you can get married without parental consent, even though you're under eighteen."

Shocked, she gaped at him in silence for a few seconds. "What are you saying?"

"You just need a court order or a permit from the Clerk of the Court."

She frowned. "But we're cousins, Mark."

He pointed to a column on the right, entitled "Cousins." There were X's next to about a third of the states. "These are the places where it's legal for first cousins to marry. The marriage would be honored in most other states." Standing next to her, he ran his hands through his wavy, mink-brown hair, searching her face.

She tried to think. "Are you talking about now?"

"Maybe this summer. We could stay in the cabin together and then live together wherever we wanted, without any hassles."

"You mean we would just run away? I didn't know you were thinking about that. Jesus, Mark."

He looked hurt, and bent over her, laying his hands on her cheeks and kissing her. "Your parents will get over it. You love me, don't you?"

"Sure I do, but I can't get married now."

"This is the only way we can have a life, Kaia. Now. I don't want to wait for years, until you've finished college."

"I couldn't do that, Mark. My parents would never forgive me."

"It would be all right, once they understood you would still be going to college somewhere. We could live wherever we wanted. They couldn't do anything about it."

"We wouldn't have any money. They would never help us."

"I'd get a job. I don't even care that much about law school. I could just as easily do something else. And I'm sure you could get a scholarship."

"You'd give up law school?"

"I don't even like it. I think I'd hate being a lawyer. I would rather do some kind of work where I could be active and work outdoors. I'm not the type to live my whole life wearing a suit and doing paperwork in an office."

"I knew you didn't like reading all those law books, but I never realized you hated it that much. When did you start thinking about this?"

"Ever since classes started last fall, I've had serious doubts. But I wanted to give it a year, and stay out here to be with you. Anyway, we could still come back to Berkeley if I wanted to finish law school. I could get loans, and my parents might help out."

Kaia ran her eyes over Mark's face. She had never seen him look so animated, or so desperate. Cousins marrying. It would be impossible for their parents to accept, even if it was done legally. "What about the genetics? I want to have kids, Mark."

"Don't worry so much. That won't be a problem. We can have kids some day." He kissed her. "I want to be with you all the time, wake up with you every day, not have your dad always interfering with us. Don't you want that?"

"Of course I do. I hate sneaking around behind his back." She sighed, wanting more than anything just to have him wrap his arms around her and not have to worry about anything. "I love you, Mark. And I'll think about it, okay? But I have to go. Dad's class will be over soon."

"Yes, think about it. Seriously." He handed her the list.

"Okay." She kissed him, then sprinted down the aisle and up the rear stairway to her father's office. She had barely picked up a book and flung herself into a chair when she recognized his footsteps coming down the hall. She let out a long breath.

Marriage. It had little to do with being in love, as far as she could tell. And Mark wasn't leaving much room for her to figure out what she wanted to do or when she might want to do it. She needed to finish high school, go to college, get started in a career. At a gut level, though, she was sure what she wanted now—somehow to see more of Mark, so that she wouldn't always be waiting for him, dying to be with him. She wasn't prepared to leave her father's house, though, not yet. It was her home. And she couldn't bear the thought of giving up everything—her dad's love, her mom's trust, maybe even Sig's friendship, and college.

Still, she felt a tremor of excitement at the thought of running away with Mark and marrying him, a thrill she savored until the moment her father swung the door open, leveling one of his impugning glances at her.

"Hello, Father," she said with a nervous grin. She liked seeing her dad in his office and pretending she was one of his law students. He didn't seem to be so severe with her when she came to see him like this; he even seemed proud to have her here, working on her paper and occasionally coming to his class.

"Hello, Kaia. What have you been up to?"

"Not much." She was still smiling, thinking of Mark and what he'd proposed. She turned her focus to the book lying on her lap unopened. "Just doing some research," she mumbled.

But she had something of her own now, a possibility her dad knew nothing about, a fantasy he could not intrude upon, a dream that would make her ecstatic each time it came to her.

17

Kaia was sitting propped against some pillows on her bed, daydreaming about Mark as she watched the February wind whip around the branches of the tree outside her window, when suddenly the door flew open, and her father stepped into the room, glowering.

She glared back at him. "Don't you ever knock?"

His frown deepened as he came over to her and snapped open a folded sheet of paper. She smelled whiskey on him, even though it was early on a Saturday afternoon.

"I want to ask you something, Kaia."

"What?" She leaned forward and tried to read the paper he had in his hand; she was afraid this had something to do with Mark.

"Why haven't you been going to ballet?" His gaze was pointed at her face.

She shook her head slowly.

"Tell me, Kaia."

She tried to think as she peered up at him. "Why are you accusing me like this?"

He dropped the paper to the floor, and in two swift strides pulled her off the bed and onto her feet, the way he used to when he was about to swing her over his knees. "Just answer me, Kaia. What in the hell have you been doing with your afternoons?"

She stepped back, jerking her arm away. He grabbed her upper arms, digging his fingers into her flesh.

"Stop, you're bruising me."

"Answer me. Have you been seeing Mark? At the law school or anywhere else?"

"Of course not." She flushed, glancing into her father's eyes, then focused on the gray sideburns standing out from his jaw. She hated him, with his whiskey breath and his belligerence.

He tightened his grip. "You're lying, Kaia."

"I am not." She shook her head, trying in vain to break away from him. She felt justified in lying to him. He had no right to interrogate her in this way.

"Sit down." He pushed her onto the bed, bent to pick up the paper, and thrust it in front of her face.

She took it and started reading. It was a letter from the Bay Area School of Ballet, dated February 20, 1981:

> Dear Mr. Matheson:
>
> We are concerned about Kaia's spotty attendance at ballet classes since the start of the year. In January she attended only two lessons, and only one this month so far. Kaia has been with us for several years, and we hope she will be able to continue with classes. As you are no doubt aware, we will be performing Romeo and Juliet in August, and Kaia could still prepare for a part.
>
> Please let us know if you have any questions or concerns regarding her lessons.
>
> Sincerely yours,
> Melissa Kingsley, Director

Kaia tossed the letter onto the bed and crossed her arms.

"Well?" her father said. "What have you been doing with your afternoons?"

"Nothing. I've just been here, doing homework and things."

"I don't believe you, Kaia. Why haven't you been going to your lessons?"

"I'm not that interested in ballet. I just got tired of it. Mom was the one who wanted me to do ballet."

He stepped toward the window, then swung around. "You'd better stop lying to me, Kaia. I know you've been seeing Mark. Why else would you stop going to ballet without telling me? What do you see in him, anyway? And what kind of twenty-three-year-old man goes after his young teenage cousin?"

Kaia glared at her father in disgust. He couldn't possibly understand how she felt about Mark.

Her father threw himself into the armchair, dwarfing it with his broad shoulders, and eyed her with a perplexed frown. "What am I supposed to do with you? You realize I just want to protect you."

"I don't need to be protected."

"Of course you do."

"You're being ridiculous. You don't get it, do you? I just want you to leave me alone."

He rose swiftly from the chair and moved toward her with his arms tensed at his side. "No, I don't get it—why you're lying to me and doing things behind my back. You are not giving up ballet. You need something useful to occupy your time. I'll make it my job to deliver you to your lessons and anywhere else it's absolutely necessary for you to go."

She stood up. "I don't want you to drive me anywhere. I want to get my license and drive myself."

"We're not going to talk about a license until you show some responsibility. You have way too much freedom as it is."

"You're acting like my prison guard, Dad."

"*What?*" he said, gawking at her.

"That's what you're doing. And I'm not going to perform anymore. I'll go to lessons, if that's what you want." She crossed her arms. "But I'm not doing *Romeo and Juliet*, Dad."

"Why not? At least it will keep you busy."

"If you try to make me perform, I'll quit ballet."

"No, you will not," he said, leveling a look at her.

Then he strode out of her room, and she shut the door and leaned against it, breathing heavily. At least he had no concrete evidence that she'd been seeing Mark. But now she would have to continue ballet lessons—in order to get her father off her back—which would waste two precious afternoons she could be spending with Mark. And if her father started driving her everywhere, how would she ever be able to see Mark at all?

18

When the acceptance letter from San Francisco State came in late March, Kaia didn't tell anyone except Sig. She didn't want to be pressured by her father, and didn't even want Mark to influence her decision. Of course Sig thought it was great that Kaia got in. A week later, the UC Berkeley acceptance came, along with a rejection from Columbia, and she realized she had to tell her father. As soon as he stepped through the front door that evening, she told him she'd been accepted at Cal.

"I knew you'd get in," he said with a broad smile. "I'll take you out to celebrate, anywhere you'd like to go."

"Let's just wait a few days, okay? I still haven't heard from Stanford."

"I'm just proud of you, that's all. We'll go out and have a fancy dinner somewhere."

"Dad, I have to tell you something. I applied to San Francisco State, and I was accepted there, too." She managed to get this out quickly before he interrupted.

"Why on earth did you do that?" He sounded perplexed by this odd bit of information—as if it were a piece of a puzzle that didn't fit into his over-all design.

She explained that her photography teacher, Mr. Brown, had earned his MFA at SF State and thought she might like the Art Department, the campus, and living in San Francisco. "He said I'm a talented photographer," she added, then realized how irrelevant that would seem to her father.

"But you're an excellent student, Kaia. That's the main thing. And you can take photography at Berkeley. Why would you even think of choosing SF State over a world-class university like Cal?"

"I might want to major in Art, and SF State has a really great program."

He stalked over to the hutch, splashed some whiskey into a glass, and took a long drink.

"I need to think this over on my own, Dad." If he wanted to get drunk and rant and rave, she thought, that was just too bad.

He took another swallow of his drink. "There's nothing to think over. It's simple. You'll go to Berkeley and live at home."

She hated the way he issued orders about things that should be up to her, like what college to attend, and whether or not to take ballet, and whether or not she could see her own cousin.

"I don't want to go to a school where you're teaching," she said, trying to stay calm. "And I do not want to live at home."

"You wouldn't be taking any classes from me, at least in your undergraduate years. And you're much too young to be on your own."

"Millions of college students do live away from home, you know."

"That doesn't mean you will. You'll be younger than most freshmen. Living at home for a year or two won't kill you."

"You have it all mapped out for me, don't you?" she said fiercely, and took a deep breath. "I want to take a look at SF State, Dad. You're just being a snob about this."

"Kaia, I am not wasting my time and yours looking at a school that's not even in the running. I can't believe you had the audacity to apply there behind my back."

"I guess I'll have to go see it on my own, then."

"Don't bother. You're not going there."

"Don't you even care what I want? Don't you see how unfair you're being?"

He eyed her for a few moments with a baffled expression on his face, swallowed the rest of his drink, poured another one, and headed for his study.

"Dad!" she called after him. "Why do you always walk out like that?"

He turned around, his face hard, his lips curled downward. "There's nothing further to discuss."

✳

Early the following evening, Kaia came home to find her father with Chandi in the kitchen, the two of them drinking wine. Chandi looked especially striking in her coral pantsuit and gold bracelets. Dad was lucky to have an attractive woman friend like Chandi—someone who would actually put up with him.

"Where have you been?" he asked Kaia.

"Sig took me over to San Francisco State to take a look around."

"What?" he said, his voice rising. "When did you decide to take this little excursion?"

"Since you wouldn't take me, Sig drove me after school."

"I've told you, it's not in the running."

"I actually liked it a lot. So as far as I'm concerned, it *is* still in the running."

Ignoring her father's incredulous stare, she pictured the campus with its looming pines, eucalyptus trees, twin residence halls and modern buildings. It was barely a mile from the ocean. She could study French, Poli Sci, Literature, Art and Dance—there were courses she wanted to take in so many departments. For the first time, she was truly excited about going off to college. Some of the students there were dressed in black with combat boots, the girls wearing heavy black eyeliner and metal jewelry like Sig, a few guys sporting mohawks or long, shaggy hair. She and Sig passed a group of shirtless, sun-tanned guys in jeans playing hacky sack on the quad, and Kaia caught the strong scent of pot smoke. It was easy to picture herself there with Mark when he came to visit, the two of them sitting on the grass, enjoying each other's company without her father's interference.

Chandi gave a sympathetic smile. "It's a big decision you have to make, Kaia."

"Yes, I know. And I've thought a lot about it."

"You should have talked to me about this before going over there on your own," her father said. "What's the point, anyway? You've been accepted at Berkeley. You haven't even heard from Stanford."

"Actually, Dad, I did get an acceptance from Stanford. But I don't want to go there. I've decided on State."

"You've *what*?" He came a step closer and peered down at her. "You got into Cal and Stanford and you want to go to some state college?"

"So you really liked the campus, then, Kaia?" Chandi asked.

"I loved it. That's where I want to go." Kaia glanced from Chandi to her father.

"Over my dead body," he said. "You can't just decide your whole university career out of spite."

"It's not out of spite," Kaia said, and then turned and strode out of the kitchen toward the rear of the house. "That's where I'm going, Dad, and you're not going to change my mind."

"We'll talk more about this later," her father called after her.

As Kaia entered her bedroom, she heard Chandi say in a quiet voice, "These days a young woman has the right to make her own decisions, David."

"Apparently she's not mature enough to make the right one by herself. And she needs to live with the one parent who gives a damn about her."

"She's nearly eighteen, you know." Even from Kaia's room she could hear the strain in Chandi's voice. "When I was that age, I decided to leave India and attend Oxford, against my father's wishes."

"That's irrelevant. This is a decision Kaia and I are going to have to make on our own."

"You're getting all churned up about things again, David. And you've started drinking a lot."

"Not that much. It's only because I'm concerned about Kaia's welfare."

There was silence, the two of them apparently contemplating the brazenness of this particular lie. Anyone had to see, Kaia thought, the kind of obsessive control her father exercised over her. He obviously wanted her here for his own sake—to keep her with him as long as he could. Couldn't he see how futile that was?

The argument with Chandi moved into the living room, and after a while Kaia left her room and walked quietly to the open doorway and stood listening. Her father sat in his chair, his hands gripping the armrests, with Chandi standing over him. The scene reminded Kaia of the arguments her parents used to have before the divorce.

"There are limits to what you can do, David," Chandi said in a pleading tone. "There are boundaries. It's pathological, the way you won't let Kaia go."

Her father dragged his hand down over his face, distorting his features.

"You don't understand," he groaned. "Kaia is simply not mature enough to be living on her own, doing whatever she wants with whomever she wants to do it. She's barely seventeen, you know."

Chandi turned, registering Kaia's presence.

"Dad," Kaia said, stepping into the room. "I'm not going to Cal or Stanford. If you won't send me to State, I'll find some other way to go there. I can get loans and a job. I'll do whatever I need to do. And I'm sure Mom will help me."

He stared at her, speechless for once, his face twisted into a frozen grimace.

She spun around and rushed back to her room. Now she couldn't wait to call Mark and tell him the good news. He would be as thrilled as she was that in a few months she would be living in San Francisco, only a few miles away from him, finally out of her father's clutches—and attending the college she wanted.

19

David watched as Chandi picked up her glass of Merlot and leaned against a cabinet, crossing her legs at the ankles. Even for this casual dinner at home, she was wearing a lovely knit dress that clung to her curvaceous figure rather nicely, along with dressy sandals and dangling gold earrings that shimmered when she moved her head.

He went over to her, placed his hands gently on her cheeks and kissed her on the lips. "You're very special to me, you know, Chandi," he said.

Her eyes widened, and she drew her chin back. "And you are to me, David." She said this rather politely, then turned away and stirred the Brazilian stew on the stove.

Maybe she felt a bit shy, he thought, after his impulsive display of affection in the midst of preparing their dinner. Or, more likely, she was surprised that he'd said she was special to him, as if he were leading up to something. Maybe he was, subconsciously. After all, they'd been dating for several months now.

It had been a good evening up to this point, and he'd made sure to keep the booze to a minimum—only one Scotch and a glass or two of wine so far. He'd left the beef out of the stew for Chandi's sake, and had added bay leaves and chili peppers along with the black beans and vegetables, the delectable aroma of the food now permeating the kitchen air.

He was glad he'd arranged for Kaia to stay over at Sig's for the weekend, so that he could have Chandi over for dinner and overnight, then tomorrow they would drive to Carmel to stay at his favorite hotel. During the last few days he'd cut back on his drinking, and was letting Kaia's college issue ride—at least until next week, when she would have to send in her response to Cal. He would send it in for her if necessary. And certainly Stanford would be better than a state college, although it was nearly an hour's drive from home, and he'd have to buy her a car so that she could commute. He suspected his recalcitrant daughter had already sent in her acceptance to San Francisco State, but that could easily be rescinded. He would see to that once they had their final discussion about Berkeley. But tonight, at least, he didn't have to deal with the college issue.

When the stew was ready, he and Chandi sat down at the dining room table. In its center sat the white roses David had bought earlier.

He raised his glass. "To our weekend."

Chandi raised hers and took a sip. For a short while they ate in silence—everything had turned out just right, David thought: the potato-flour rolls with sweet butter, the salad, the spicy stew and saffron rice.

"By the way," he said, "my textbook's been accepted for publication." He'd just found out this afternoon and had saved the news as a surprise for her.

Chandi smiled, lifting her glass again. "That's excellent, David. You must be so pleased." Now that they were sitting in the dining room, she sounded rather formal and seemed even less at ease than before.

A few minutes later, she said, "Oh, no. I forgot. I've left Mandrake in the house. He needs to be let out."

"Do you really have to go over there?" She had agreed to spend the night here in his house for the first time, and he hoped she would simply forget about the damned cat. His own king-sized bed was so much more comfortable than her smaller one. Besides, he hated the way Chandi allowed the enormous cat to jump on her bed, even while they were making love.

She sighed. "Maybe I'll just call my neighbor."

"Yes, that would be better."

After they had finished their dinner along with more wine and then some ice cream, David had the sudden idea of showing Chandi the photographs he'd taken of Kaia. Chandi might like to see what his daughter was like in years past, so beautifully captured in the black-and-white pictures. When he stood up he swayed a bit and felt woozy, but managed to usher Chandi into his bedroom, where the framed photos hung on the wall. He pointed out the portrait of Kaia at thirteen, serenely lounging on the sofa, reading, and the other photographs he'd taken more recently.

"They're lovely. Professionally done." But Chandi's speech was a bit slurred, probably from all the wine, her brow slightly wrinkled, as if she were puzzled.

She leaned forward to examine the 8x10 photograph that hung over the bed, the portrait he'd taken of Kaia when she'd turned seventeen last November. It was a view of her face and upper body in soft focus, light glinting in her eyes, her skin shimmering in her low-cut black dress. He was sure Chandi would never have imagined Kaia so glamorous looking. But now Chandi was biting her lip and heading for the door, and David had no idea why.

He followed her into the kitchen, where they made tea. He tried to figure out the reason for her abrupt change of mood, but could only attribute it to her apparent intoxication.

"Are you feeling all right?" he asked her.

After taking a sip of her tea, Chandi said, in a rather hoarse voice, "David, maybe we shouldn't be seeing so much of each other."

"What? I don't understand."

She set down her cup and touched him on the arm, as if to placate, but it came across as condescension. "You still have Kaia to consider, and I don't quite see where I fit in."

"Kaia would love having you around more, I'm sure. You're a good role model for her."

"Is that it?" Chandi said curtly, stretching out her hand and splaying her fingers in an unattractive gesture. "That's not what I want, David—to be a role model for your daughter. Is that it? A good influence?" She inhaled sharply with a half-sob.

Good God, what had he said? He shook his head. In his fuzzy-brained state—too much booze, he realized now—he still couldn't fathom what was going on. "No, that's not it. It's just that I admire you so much, Chandi. It's been good for Kaia to know a woman lawyer. That's all I meant."

But the wine seemed to be making Chandi more emotional than he'd ever seen her before, her eyes now filled with tears.

"Let's go sit down," he said and steered her into the living room with his hand on her back.

Beside her on the couch, he shifted his legs to relieve the discomfort of his boxer shorts riding up on him. He wanted to loosen his belt after all the food and drink he'd consumed, but he felt constrained. They sat in the dim light of a table lamp, his hands clasped between his knees, his enthusiasm for their evening evaporating.

"I think I should leave, David. I don't feel that comfortable staying over now."

"What's wrong? Don't you want to go to Carmel?"

"I don't think so."

"Why not? Why the sudden change?"

"I just think it's for the best." Her expression was neutral, impossible to read.

He stood up and began pacing around the room. "But we've planned this, and I've been looking forward to this weekend. I love your company and everything about you."

He continued talking to her in an urgent voice, as if he could convince her by the sheer force of his energy to stay with him. She merely followed him with her eyes as he traipsed back and forth across the floor. Couldn't she see how hard this was for him, displaying his feelings like a goddamned supplicant? He stopped in front of her and shoved his hands into his pockets.

"I need someone to keep me on the right course," he said. "I was hoping, in fact, that we might think about moving forward with our relationship."

She stared down at her shoes, running her hand up and down her bare leg. Finally she peered up at him. "David, I think instead we should back up a little, at least until Kaia goes off to college."

"Things may not be so different then—she'll probably go to Berkeley and live at home. So why shouldn't we go forward now?"

"I'm just not ready for that. You need to focus on your daughter's needs right now. There will be so many changes when she starts college in the fall. And you told me not long ago that she might still be seeing Mark, and you've been so upset about their relationship—it's impacted ours in so many ways."

"I don't think she is, after all. If you were around more, things would be more stable; it could be a real home for all of us." His voice was getting louder, and he heard his own pitiful desperation in it.

"I don't see it happening that way. You're upset so much of the time. I know you worship Kaia, and she's a lovely girl, but you need to allow her to become an adult, apart from you. As I've intimated before, the closeness you want so much with her is unhealthy. You don't own her, David."

He shook his head forcefully. That was not the situation at all. It was Kaia who owned him.

"And you've been drinking way too much," Chandi added.

"I'm not drunk now, if that's what you think. Really, it's not a problem. I'll do whatever it takes." He sat down on the sofa and took her hands. "I love you, Chandi."

He wrapped his arms around her and kissed her, then he heard footsteps on the front porch, and the door flew open. The foyer light switched on like a spotlight; Kaia stood there gaping at the two of them.

He got up and crossed over to her. "Chandi and I were just talking."

"Don't worry, I won't interrupt, then," Kaia said.

"What's wrong? I thought you were staying at Sig's." He could tell he was slurring his words, and he felt embarrassed.

"I'll deal with it," she said in a choked voice, and sidled past him, then hurried out of the room, shutting the door firmly behind her.

Chandi came over to him. "I should go."

David let out a long sigh. "Please stay, Chandi. We can still have a nice weekend together."

"I don't think it's the best thing, especially now that Kaia's home, and she's clearly upset. Go to your daughter."

"It's okay. She obviously doesn't want to talk right now. We won't bother her. And we need to leave early for Carmel. I'll drop Kaia off at Sig's in the morning."

Chandi allowed him to wrap his arms around her but said nothing. Her body felt rigid and unyielding.

"Neither of us should be driving, anyway," he said. "We've had all that wine. Please, Chandi, stay here tonight."

She exhaled slowly. "All right. I suppose it would be the best thing. Then we can talk about Carmel in the morning."

He kissed her on the forehead. "I'll get your bag from the car."

But it all seemed so damned awkward, somehow. When he returned with Chandi's suitcase, she emerged from his bedroom with a solemn expression on her face.

"David, is it possible—is there another room where we could sleep?"

He set her suitcase down on the floor, examining her face for a clue.

"I wouldn't feel comfortable in there," she said. "Maybe we could use the upstairs room."

Then he understood. She had never slept with him in his bedroom, which had been his and Jean's. In fact Chandi had probably never even stepped inside the room until this evening, when he'd shown her the photographs.

"Why didn't I think of that? We never use the upstairs room, and there's still a bed up there." He drew her to him and kissed her. "Of course we can sleep up there."

But as they walked down the rear hallway past Kaia's room and climbed the stairs, David dreaded the thought of sleeping in Mark's old bed—it reminded him how disturbing it had been to have his nephew in the house, lurking around Kaia all the time. Still, he wanted to alleviate the strain between Chandi and himself. Possibly if they slept up here as she wanted, she would feel better about the whole situation.

They undressed quickly in the cool, moonlit room. Under the sheets Chandi's legs brushed against his, her bare breasts and stomach pressing lightly against him. He ran his hands over her, kissed her, inhaling her delicious nutmeg-like scent.

"David?"

He kissed her again on the mouth, not wanting to spoil the mood by talking.

She pulled back, resting her head on the pillow. "You love her so very much, don't you," she said in an unfamiliar, slightly plaintive tone.

"Kaia?" he said, surprised at the question. "Of course I do."

"All those pictures in your bedroom. It's quite something. Did you have them hanging over the bed when Jean was living here?"

He wished she wouldn't go on about it. "Not the most recent ones." He stroked her arm and kissed her again on the lips.

"We should have gone to my house tonight," Chandi said. "We would have had more privacy there. I feel as if there's a third person here."

"I'm sorry about that. Kaia was going to stay over at her friend's house. They must have had an argument."

"I don't feel we're alone. She's right downstairs."

"Don't worry, she can't hear us." He cupped her breast with his hand, trying to focus himself.

She suddenly broke away from him and sat up. "What's that?"

He'd heard it, too—some scratching, skittering sound. "It's probably a cat on the roof." Dismayed, he sensed the mood slipping away, perhaps irretrievably.

"No, it's a smaller animal, or several of them. Rodents of some kind."

"Maybe it's a squirrel," he said.

"Not at night. They're probably tree rats." Chandi lay back down and David placed his hand on her tensed arm. He could just barely make out her vigilant expression in the dim light as she listened to the pattering.

"See, there it is, again," she said. "It definitely sounds like more than one. You can't have rats around the house, David. It's appalling. Kaia told me Mark caught one in the basement."

"I'll take care of it, whatever it is," he said in a low voice, squeezing her arm gently.

After a minute or two, he leaned over, kissing her on the cheek. With his head next to hers on her pillow, he detected the same honeysuckle essence of his daughter's shampoo that he'd caught earlier when he'd driven her to Sig's. He wondered if Kaia had been sleeping up here, or taking naps in this bed. He loved the familiarity of her scent, but it distracted him to imagine his daughter's young face on the pillow.

After a while the pattering receded, and he ran his hand over Chandi's thigh, enjoying the feel of her smooth skin, and anticipated her soft caving-in to him, as if for the first time. For a minute, she lay there immobile, but then she turned, allowing him to wrap his arms around her. But she seemed barely willing, and rather passive.

It was over quickly, and afterwards Chandi still seemed shut off. Turning to lie with his face in his pillow, David noticed a sour, masculine odor, distinct and repellent, that was not his own. It came to him, in a shock of recognition, that it had to be Mark's odor, and that it had to be recent. It made him sick. Mark hadn't lived here in months. Kaia might actually be seeing her cousin, possibly even having sex with him here in this bed. The thought was utterly revolting. God, how he hated that bastard.

The old anxious suspicions arose, along with the disturbing feelings he couldn't seem to dispel. He pictured Kaia in her room beneath them now, probably upset about Sig, and about Chandi being here. Even now, with this lovely woman beside him and their special weekend ahead of them, he realized he couldn't stop worrying about his daughter.

20

Scallops. God, and the brandy—half a bottle of the damned stuff. David crouched, naked, on the hotel bathroom floor in the dark, repulsed by the stink of his own vomit. Another surge came and he threw up again. Weakened, he flushed the toilet and pressed his forehead on the rim. Chandi was probably awake in the other room, listening to this. How humiliating. He felt as though a large, dull corkscrew were moving slowly in and out of his gut.

Chandi and he had polished off two bottles of wine with dinner, although he'd drunk the lion's share of it. After dinner he bought a bottle of brandy in the hotel gift shop, and drank several glasses of it in their suite. It was too much for his stomach, on top of the scallops in the rich cream sauce.

He hadn't called Kaia yet, out of cowardice, knowing it would make him a wreck if he didn't find her at Sigourney's. He'd started thinking about his daughter soon after his arrival in Carmel this morning, and couldn't help imagining her with Mark. Now he pictured Kaia the way she looked this morning, standing in her bedroom in her robe, just out of the shower, wet ropes of hair lying on her shoulders, looking so innocent and lovely. He'd kissed her and told her to behave herself. Sig had agreed to pick her up later in the morning, and he could only hope that she had, despite the girls' argument last night. Kaia had refused to tell him what it had been about.

He stood up unsteadily, flipped on the light and squinted in the mirror. His face appeared jaundiced in the fluorescent light, and there were ugly bulges under his eyes. He looked like an old toad. Bending over the sink, he rinsed his face, then drank some water and shuffled back into the bedroom. In the faint light coming through the curtain, he could see Chandi sitting up in bed in her nightgown.

"What is it, David? Is it something you ate?"

"The scallops," he groaned, and climbed into bed. "I made such a pig of myself. And the brandy."

"I hope you'll feel better in the morning." There was a clipped edge to her tone, and in the semi-darkness her face was drawn. "I've been looking forward to the champagne brunch."

David emitted a deep, involuntary groan.

"What's wrong?" Chandi asked.

"The idea of more food, that's all. And champagne. I'm thinking we should either drive back tonight or in the morning. It might be food poisoning. I don't want to be this far away from home if I get really sick and have to go to the emergency room."

"Tonight? It's past midnight." She sounded indignant. "I'm sure you'll feel better soon. Are you worried about Kaia? Is that it?"

"That's not it," he mumbled. "I just feel wretched."

Chandi slipped down under the covers. "It would be very disappointing to drive back early tomorrow. Now that we're here, I'd like to enjoy Carmel." There was an unmistakable whine of reproach to her voice.

He grunted, feeling another painful cramp in his gut. She was probably disappointed, too, he realized, that they hadn't made love. He'd fallen asleep as soon as they'd climbed into bed, and then he'd awakened some time later, horribly sick to his stomach.

He reached over and feebly patted her thigh. His only wish at the moment was that this miserable night were over so that he could return to Berkeley, pick up Kaia at Sigourney's, and then keep her safely back at home with him.

21

Mark felt the swell of Kaia's firm little ass against him, her long curly hair tickling his chest as they lay together on her bed, the bedroom ablaze with sunlight. He touched her breast and she placed her hand over his, then she turned over and kissed him, her eyes in the sunlight an unbelievable sky-blue. After a few moments, she rolled onto her stomach, and he rubbed her back between the shoulder blades and along her spine, the way she liked it.

She got up and put a Dylan album on the stereo next to the bed, turning up the volume so that the music filled the room, then got back into bed and inched forward into Mark's arms.

"I love you, Kaia," he said loudly over Dylan's raspy voice.

"I love you, too."

He caressed her, kissing her, then gently moved her so that she lay face down and he stretched over her. Moving unhurriedly, he straddled her and pulled her up by the hips so that she was on all fours, her back smooth, curving outward at the hips. He squeezed her shoulder, and made himself go slowly, her back rippling in motion with him.

A moment later Kaia screamed as the door burst open.

It was David, bellowing, "Get off of her, you bastard!" He stormed into the room, his reddened face a grotesque scowl.

"Jesus," Mark said, kneeling upright. He grabbed at the sheet to cover himself.

"Get away from him, Kaia!" David yelled, then pointed at Mark, shouting, "You goddamned bastard, get out of my house right now before I kill you."

"Go away, Dad!" Kaia was huddled on the bed, naked and trembling visibly, her arms across her breasts.

David banged his fist against the wall and took a couple of steps forward. "Get off of that bed and put some clothes on, Kaia!" he shouted.

"Leave us alone," she said shakily. "I'm not getting up until you leave my room."

"I said to get up and get dressed!" David roared.

He glowered at the two of them for another few seconds, then turned and marched out, slamming the door shut, the force of it vibrating through the walls. They could hear him stomping toward the front of the house.

Kaia turned off the stereo. Her face was splotchy, her whole body shaking as she started to dress. She kept saying, "Oh, no, no, no," like a hysterical child.

Mark got to his feet and pulled on his clothes, a physical dread passing through him. A minute later he heard David's heavy footsteps striding toward the den and into the hallway, stopping outside the bedroom, and then his uncle began banging on the door with his fist.

"Kaia!" he hollered. "Have you got your clothes on?"

"Wait!" She stood in the middle of the room in her jeans, naked from the waist up, her eyes darting around the room until she spotted her sweatshirt on the floor. As she bent to pick it up, the door swung open and David strode into the room, his face contorted in rage. Barely glancing at Kaia as she pulled on her sweatshirt, he lunged at Mark, grabbing him by the shoulders and shoving him against the wall.

"I'm having you arrested," he yelled into his face.

Mark pushed him away and clenched his fists, realizing how easy it would be to get into a stupid fight with his uncle. David stood there, breathing heavily, his feet braced apart, his fists clenched like a cop in a street confrontation. Mark stepped around him and jammed his feet into his sandals.

"Mark," Kaia said hoarsely, "you've got to leave."

"I'm not leaving you alone with him."

"You sure as hell are," David shouted. "Get out of here right now!"

"Please just go, Mark," Kaia pleaded.

"Are you sure?"

"Yes." Tears were streaming down her face.

"All right."

Mark turned to David, who stood a mere yard away from him. "You'd better just leave her the fuck alone," he said right into his face.

The two men stood glaring at each other for several long seconds, then Mark lunged past David without looking at him and stepped out into the hallway. "I'll call you later, Kaia."

"No you won't," David yelled.

"Like hell I won't," Mark shouted back, then stomped out through the back door. He tramped down the driveway and got into his car, sick with the thought of what would happen to Kaia and him now.

Shaking with fury, he turned on the ignition and drove down the hill.

❋

"When did this start, Kaia?"

She wanted to cover her ears, but didn't dare. Sitting down on the bed, she gazed at the floor, placing her trembling hands on her knees. Her father had seen her, and seen Mark and her together, so exposed—that was the most sickening thing.

"Answer me," her father barked. "When?"

Kaia glared at him. His jaw was tight, his eyes watering. She had never seen him this upset before. She hated him. He had ruined everything, the day and night she'd spent with Mark, their lovemaking, everything.

"December," she whispered.

"All this time? How could you do that to me, Kaia?"

She shook her head. It obviously had nothing to do with her father.

"The bastard," he said, his voice choked. He took a few steps away from her and spun around. "I'm taking you down to the police station. I'm going to press charges against him."

"I'm not going."

"If I say you are, you are. And I'll make sure you never see him again."

"We'll get married, then they won't prosecute him."

"Don't even think about that." He came over and stood in front of her, scowling. "You're not pregnant, are you?"

"No," she said in a small voice.

He grabbed her arm, pulling her to her feet.

"Let go," she said. "You're hurting me."

He released her arm, but remained standing over her, his face a couple of inches away from hers.

"Did he ever force you, or pressure you?"

"Of course not."

"He got you drunk—it amounts to the same thing. I saw the empty wine bottle. I can get him on statutory rape and contributing to the delinquency of a minor. I can get him on a lot of things."

"I wasn't drunk."

He stared at her for several long seconds. "I'm calling your mother."

"Don't do that, Dad."

He turned, his jaw hardening. "You're telling me what to do or not do, after this?"

Afraid to move, she searched his face and tried to gauge the degree of his anger, the extent of his self-control. He stood there, clenching and unclenching his fists.

"Just don't try me, Kaia."

He stomped out of her room and went into his office, and slammed the door.

22

Jean took a sip of her Chardonnay, which was mediocre at best. Nico really didn't know his wines. And the restaurant he'd chosen was cramped with tables so close together that the waiters brushed the backs of chairs as they moved about, their trays held high not for flair but to avoid banging the heads of diners. The red overhead lamps cast a sickening pink glow over the table. Why hadn't Nico chosen a nicer place, with booths, where they could have talked more privately, instead of this strip-mall restaurant on the outskirts of Bangor? And he'd made her come all the way from New York to Maine rather than meeting her in Boston. It rankled, to say the least.

"I didn't want to tell you all of the details over the phone," she said, keeping her voice low, "but David found the two of them in Kaia's bed together."

Nico leaned forward, frowning. "They were actually—?"

"Yes. Apparently he got food poisoning in Carmel and went back home earlier than he'd planned."

"When I talked to Mark he said he wasn't doing anything wrong." Nico shook his head. "Must have been a real shocker for David."

"I'm sure it was," she said bitterly.

Nico sloshed the pallid Chardonnay around in his glass and took a long drink. After the waiter took their orders, Nico leaned back in his chair, scanning the room. Such an attractive man, Jean thought—the olive skin, the black hair with a touch of white in the sideburns, the open-collared blue shirt that set off his eyes. But he was visibly tensing his jaw as he observed the other diners, and it made him look a bit hard.

He finally met her gaze. "What does Kaia say about all of this?" he asked.

"She wouldn't speak to me. And David said he's going to get Mark expelled from law school."

"He has no right to do that," Nico said angrily. "I've told Mark if he wants to stay in Berkeley, he has to stop seeing Kaia."

"You think that will stop him?" Jean took a gulp of her wine. "What if Kaia gets pregnant?"

"They're not stupid, Jean. Anyway, let's not worry about hypotheticals." He polished off his wine and set the glass down.

"You don't worry about anything, do you, Nico? Kaia and Mark are much too closely related to be involved like this."

Nico glared at her without responding.

"She has your eye color, Nico."

"Jesus Christ. Don't pull that on me." He poured himself a full glass of wine and downed half of it. "You know this is sheer speculation," he said in a nasty tone. "You always said Kaia couldn't be mine."

"Now I'm not so sure. She didn't get those bright blue eyes from me. And David's eyes are a darker shade of blue. In fact, his are two different shades of blue."

"So what? Yours are a shade of blue, aren't they?" He peered at her for a moment.

She frowned in disbelief. "Hazel, depending on the light. God, Nico, don't you know?"

"This is stupid. Dark blue, light blue, who the hell cares? Maybe it was some blue-eyed ancestor. And Elisa has blue eyes."

"Kaia looks a lot like you, Nico. It's become obvious. Kaia's complexion, too—she's always had that Mediterranean look."

"You mean that gorgeous California tan? Come on, give me a break." He finished his wine, then signaled for the waiter and ordered another bottle of the same Chardonnay.

"We can't just stand by and hope they'll stop seeing each other," Jean said after the waiter had whisked away the empty bottle. "Especially if you and I are going to move ahead the way we've planned."

"Sometimes, Jean," Nico mumbled, "I don't know what in the hell you're talking about."

"I think you do," she said, and sat back in her chair. She'd obviously made him defensive by bringing up their own situation. He was so volatile, and emotional—but that's what had drawn her to him in the first place. Her attraction to him had come to a head, she recalled, at an especially fraught time, when Elisa was in the hospital for Mark's birth. Jean remembered drinking Bordeaux with Nico at his house that evening, just a few hours after the birth, celebrating with a mixture of joy and relief, when she and Nico had somehow ended up in bed together. She recalled too vividly how they'd visited Elisa later that night at the hospital, and how she'd stared at them in confusion through the haze of painkillers she'd been given for the Caesarean section. Maybe the wine had tinged their lips scarlet, or maybe Elisa had smelled the wine on their breath when they'd bent to kiss her.

Jean now watched blankly as the waiter set their entrées in front of them. Nico immediately plucked the sprig of parsley from his plate, dropping it disdainfully on the tablecloth; he'd always hated hackneyed presentations.

"And the wine I ordered?" he said gruffly to the waiter.

"I'm sorry, sir, it's coming," the waiter said, nodding as he retreated.

They waited in silence until the wine came, then started on their halibut.

"I think you should go to Berkeley and find out what's going on," Jean said. "If Mark is still bent on seeing Kaia, you've got to make him come home."

Nico leaned back in his chair. "I'm not having him drop out of law school and ruin his entire future because of this little peccadillo."

"You call this a peccadillo? My God, Nico, what are you thinking?"

He glared at her. "What I'm not going to do is tell Mark that he may be engaged in an incestuous relationship—which of course is ridiculous, anyway. Mark would hate me for the rest of his life."

"It *is* incestuous, no matter how you look at it. The whole thing is so low-class, even if they're only cousins—it makes me gag. Appearances do count, Nico, as I'm sure you realize." Jean leaned forward. "You simply need to have to have a serious talk with Mark."

"And tell him what, about this possibility you've suddenly imagined?" Nico scowled. "And then expect him to keep it from Elisa?"

"Maybe. But in any case, at some point we'll have to tell them."

"Oh, no, we won't." He eyed her coldly. "It would utterly destroy Elisa. She'd never be able to handle that."

Jean couldn't believe he was being so adamant. "They will all have to deal with it at some point. We can't even think about getting married if Kaia and Mark are carrying on. We would all look like hicks—cousins having sex, and their parents marrying each other."

He expelled a long breath. "You're right, we would. We'd look like a bunch of goddamned hillbillies." He took a gulp of his wine and set the glass down smartly. "That is, if anyone knew about us."

"So you agree, then, that this can't continue."

"It can't and it won't. Mark is too smart for that." Nico's face was contorted in an ugly frown. "But if you ever breathe a word of this speculation of yours, or tell anyone about us, it'll be over for us."

Jean flushed. "Nico, how can you say that?"

He braced his hands against the edge of the table. "You just want to use this episode to crack things wide open. And frankly I'm not ready to do that. Elisa is way too unstable."

Another couple was being seated at a nearby table. "We should talk more about this later, maybe at the hotel," Jean said, straining to keep her voice even.

"There's no point in discussing it any further. And if Mark sees Kaia on the sly once in a while, it's not the end of the world. He'll get over it."

"On the sly." Jean sat back, fuming. "God, Nico. Just like you. Everything's all right if no one finds out."

"Let's finish our dinner and get out of here." Nico ate rather quickly, then threw his napkin on the table. "Elisa thinks I'm meeting with a client at the office. I don't have time to go to the hotel."

"Yes," Jean said angrily. "I'm sure Elisa will worry." She drank the remaining wine in her glass.

Jean sometimes wondered what it was Nico liked about her—the dependable sex, maybe? Or was it her "hard intelligence," as he'd once referred to it? Maybe she was just a sane version of Elisa, someone he could depend on to be rational. At times Jean suspected that she'd been used in some way—perhaps even to keep Nico's marriage intact, to keep him from straying to other, less discreet women. At other times, she saw herself in the role of Nico's steady companion, and Elisa, ironically, as the intoxicating mistress. If only things could be resolved, made less perplexing and painful. Her sister was an albatross, a problem that would never go away.

Nico shifted sideways in his chair, one hand in a tight fist on the table, and turned his head away. It struck Jean that David had occasionally assumed the same averting posture during the final months of their marriage, when they were fighting so much.

Now she had the impulse to take hold of Nico's hand, make his fist soften under her touch, but she sensed he would resist.

"I don't think we should do anything right now," he said in a quieter, more resigned tone, meeting her gaze. "Let's see what happens in the next couple of weeks."

Now, at least, he sounded more like someone conferring with his lover, rather than a man who had come to resent her. It was a rare thing, the kind of love that flouted everyone's beliefs and expectations, the intense kind of love that she and Nico had always shared.

But suddenly, Jean realized, their love seemed so terribly fragile, and so very elusive.

23

Jean waited in her rental car in front of Kaia's school, and imagined her daughter coming through the gate flaunting one of her jewel-toned sweaters—perhaps the emerald-green or ruby-red one. Kaia had such a flair for the vivid, a taste for everything sensual and dazzling. No wonder she was so attracted to Mark, with his simmering sexuality, so much like his father's. Still, Jean thought her daughter would have had more sense than to sleep with her cousin.

Angling the rearview mirror to check her makeup, Jean noted unhappily the wrinkles around her eyes, etched in the harsh sunlight, and her dry lips. She powdered her nose and put on fresh lipstick, hoping to appear more alert than she felt after the flight from New York. It had only been four days since Mark and Kaia had been caught *in flagrante*, but it seemed longer, probably because of all the heated arguments with David and Nico since then. According to Nico, Elisa didn't feel anything needed to be done about the situation—she felt Kaia and Mark were engaged in a beautiful love affair and should be left alone. Unbelievable. But Elisa didn't know everything, and of course she had no common sense whatsoever.

After a few minutes, a bell rang and students emerged through the gate in clusters. Jean finally spotted Kaia, wearing a black tank top and jeans and strolling with another girl—that friend of hers with the violet hair.

"Kaia!" Jean called out.

Her daughter stopped and gazed at her for a few seconds, then crossed the street and peered through the open driver's side window. "What are you doing here, Mom?"

"Don't worry, nothing has happened. I just flew in, and I told your father I would pick you up. I need to talk to you."

"About what?"

"Let's go find a place to sit and talk."

Pressing her lips together, Kaia turned and waved to her friend, then climbed into the car, tossing her book bag into the back. As Jean started the engine, Kaia rolled down the window and stared off to the side. They drove in silence for a few minutes until they reached Solano Avenue. Jean found a spot in the shade in front of Café Carlos, where they used to eat as a family.

"What are we doing here?" Kaia asked.

"We could go in for a drink, or something to eat."

"I'm not hungry." Kaia sat with her hands clasped in her lap, her bronze arms tensed, her face frozen.

"Kaia," Jean said as gently as she could, "it's very important that you realize what you're doing."

"You flew all the way from New York to make sure I know what I'm doing?"

Jean nodded, keeping her eyes on her. The flight had been impulsive, and she hadn't even told Nico she was going. But since he wouldn't deal with this, she had to.

"This is no one else's business," Kaia said.

Jean studied her daughter's satiny young face. Despite her honey-toned complexion and small stature, Kaia reminded her of Elisa sometimes—the mysterious inner life, the similar gestures—for instance, the way Kaia had just now turned toward her with a puzzled frown, her head cocked to the side, a look filled with complicated emotion. So much like Elisa, and perhaps like their mother.

"You have to be wise about this," Jean said, straining to keep her tone reasonable. "Love has to work into the over-all scheme, into your whole life."

Kaia gave a brisk shake of her head. "No, Mom. Love comes first. Of course I'll have a career, but my life is not going to be based totally on making money, or being a success in the business world."

"That's not what I'm saying," Jean said, dismayed at her daughter's bitterness.

Kaia grabbed the door handle. "I'm going to get a drink." She opened the door and stepped out of the car.

Jean got out and followed her into the market across the street, where they bought cans of Coke. They strolled along the sidewalk, sipping their drinks.

"Your father says you've even talked about marrying Mark," Jean said.

Kaia took a swig from her can.

"If you ever had a child with him, God forbid," Jean went on, "you'd multiply your chances of passing on any bad genes. And seventeen is simply not old enough to think about marrying anyone."

"Jesus, Mom. Bad genes?"

"You must realize there are genetic problems when cousins have children together. There could be birth defects . . . "

"Stop it, Mom. This is so ridiculous."

Jean got a Kleenex from her purse and slowed down, wiping her forehead. The sky suddenly seemed to radiate extraordinary heat. She wanted to find a place to sit down. "Let's go back to the car. It's much too hot out here."

Kaia spun around and started to stride down the block, as Jean hurried to keep up with her. Once they were settled back into the car, which thankfully was parked under a tree, Jean opened the windows and forced herself to take a deep breath. She turned to her daughter.

"Listen, Kaia. I came here to tell you that there's another reason you've got to stay away from Mark—for good. I've been involved in something you're not going to understand. It's related to your Uncle Nico."

"What about him?"

"Well, for quite a long time there has been a strong feeling between us, and—"

"I don't want to hear this." Kaia looked down, her jaw tight.

"I have to tell you, because we've been seeing each other for a long time now, and at some point, I hope in the near future, we're going to get married."

"*What?*" Kaia gave a short, scoffing laugh. Then she said fiercely, "Tell me you're joking, Mother."

"I'm not joking."

"You came out here to tell me you're having an affair with Nico and that he's going to divorce Elisa and marry you?"

"I'm telling you this because any relationship you have with Mark would have consequences."

"What? You mean because Mark would be my stepbrother then?" Kaia gaped at Jean. "You have to stop doing this, Mom. He's married to your sister, remember?"

Jean forced herself to go on. "There's much more at stake here than you know," she said with slow emphasis. "If you and Mark continue to see each other, it will be extremely destructive, not just for you, but for everyone else."

"What do you mean, destructive?"

"There are things you don't know, that you can't possibly understand." She knew she was prevaricating, but at the moment she couldn't force herself to inform her daughter of the remote possibility that she could be Nico's daughter. If Kaia would just promise not to see Mark anymore, Jean thought, she wouldn't have to tell her. Besides, if she did tell her, Nico would be furious; he was probably going to be extremely upset anyway when he found out she'd told Kaia about their affair.

Kaia fixed her eyes on her for several seconds. "So that's why you left me and Dad, because you wanted to be with Nico."

Jean shook her head, at a loss for words.

"So it wasn't for your stupid job after all."

"I left in large part for the job," Jean said, trying to keep her voice steady. "The divorce would have happened in any case."

"Who else knows about you and Nico? Does Dad know?"

"No. And I don't think you should tell anyone yet. Let Nico tell Mark in his own way, when it's the right time." In fact Jean wasn't sure Nico would ever tell Mark, and he'd forbidden her to tell Mark herself. In any event, Kaia would tell him eventually.

"So you divorced Dad and left me alone with him so you could have an affair with your own sister's husband. And then when you finally come out here to see me, it's because you want to wreck my whole life—"

"I'm not trying to wreck your life. That's the last thing I want to do. I'm trying to protect you."

"*Protect* me!" Kaia inhaled sharply. "That's insane. How long have you been seeing Nico, anyway?"

"For a long time.

"When? When did it start?"

"We fell in love after he and Elisa had been married only a few years."

"Before you met Dad?"

"Yes," Jean said, holding Kaia's incredulous gaze.

"How could you do that?" Tears streamed down Kaia's cheeks. "That's utterly disgusting," she said, her voice raspy. She leaned over the seat and grabbed her book bag, jerked the door open, and lurched out of the car.

"Wait!" Jean called out.

"So you're not going to tell Dad and Elisa about this?" Kaia asked through the open door.

"Not yet. Only if you see Mark again. Then everyone will need to know. This just can't go on."

With a horrified look, Kaia took a step backward. "So you're blackmailing me."

"Kaia, please get back into the car. I really don't think you understand."

Kaia stood there with her hands on her hips, breathing hard. "You're hateful," she said, then slammed the door and bolted, sprinting up the sidewalk.

Jean sat there stunned for a few moments. It was a mistake, coming here. She should have done this over the phone.

By the time Jean moved the car into the congested traffic, Kaia was nowhere to be seen. She drove toward the house, which was only a couple of blocks away, her mind flashing on Kaia's stricken face. As terrible as this confrontation had been, though, it had been necessary. She drove slowly, searching along the street, peering up Black Path, which led to their house, then headed toward Indian Rock Park, but didn't see Kaia anywhere. When she drove up their old street, she was surprised to see David's Volvo parked in the driveway—he must have come home early. She drove past the house, searching for any sign of Kaia, then parked on the street.

She walked to the front door and tapped, using the old-fashioned knocker. Shifting from one foot to the other in her pinching high heels, she rapped again. The last time she'd walked out through this doorway, she'd apparently given up the right to enter without knocking.

After a minute, she heard David's heavy footsteps and tried to steady herself. The door opened, and there he stood, gaping at her.

"May I come in, please, David?" she asked.

He stood with his feet braced apart, the blazing sunlight on his scowling face. "What in the hell happened?" he asked.

"Is Kaia here?"

"What did you say to her?"

"Why? What did she say?"

"Don't be coy, Jean," he snarled. "She comes in here like a zombie, won't talk to me, then runs to her room in tears. I looked in on her a minute ago and she's just lying on the bed, sobbing. I'm not going for a change of custody, if that's what you want."

Jean cleared her throat. "No, I just told her that she had to stop seeing Mark."

"I've already made that absolutely clear to her," he said with a sneer.

"Maybe she needed to hear it from me. And there are more pressing reasons than you realize, David."

"Like what? And why should she listen to you, for Christ's sake—the absentee mother?"

"Can I please come inside so that we can discuss this? And I must talk to Kaia."

He remained standing in her way, his face frozen in a mean grimace. "Seeing you was traumatic enough for Kaia."

This was too much, David barring her entry to what was once her own home, as if she were some obstreperous person who needed to be handled—like someone peddling magazines, or a Jehovah's Witness.

"Listen, David," she said, "I'll be leaving for the airport soon. I need to talk to my daughter."

"Kaia obviously does not want to see you."

"I am not in the mood to argue with you. Just step aside." She placed a foot on the threshold and to her astonishment, he took a step forward so that she was gazing up at him, eye to eye.

"You've done enough harm," he said in a hard voice. "I'm managing things."

She took a step back. "How can you manage anything, with your drinking and your overbearing behavior—"

"Just get out of here, Jean. I mean it. I'm not listening to any more of this."

Stupefied, Jean gawked at his flushed face, trying to recall why she had ever loved this man. "Let's not do this, David."

He started to close the door.

Jean stretched her arm out, calling, "Kaia," a wail that came out involuntarily as David shut the door. She heard him lock it with the deadbolt. Pressing her hand against her mouth, she stood there trembling for several seconds.

She rushed to the car, fumbled to insert the key into the ignition, and drove off.

Maybe Kaia had already gotten the message, Jean thought. That was why she was so distraught—at the very least she had understood that there would be serious repercussions if she continued to see Mark. If there was the slightest hint that the two were seeing each other again, Jean figured she could step in then.

Perhaps she had done enough, at least for now.

24

"David, you simply cannot win a hundred percent in this situation," Chandi said, face-to-face with him in the kitchen. "You've got to back off."

They were in the midst of preparing a supper of pasta and salad, and David had been hoping his daughter would come out of her room to join them, but now he and Chandi had launched into yet another argument about Kaia and her damned cousin. Yesterday Chandi had said that cousins all over the world had relationships and even got married. She didn't understand how repugnant this was to David, especially considering what his nephew had done to Kaia.

He was exhausted after four days of bloody Armageddon since Chandi and he had returned from Carmel—their heated arguments, the screaming matches with Kaia, his discussions over the phone with Jean. Even Nico had called, lambasting him for going to the dean about Mark—what nerve, when Mark was the one at fault in this whole situation.

"Certainly there are ways to make sure Kaia and Mark don't see each other," Chandi said now. "But you don't have to go crazy over it. You act as though Kaia belongs to you, and she simply does not, at least not in the absolute way you seem to think."

"How would you know? That's how it is with children—they do belong to their parents."

Her jaw set, Chandi swung away, grabbed her purse from the counter, and rushed through the living room and out the front door.

Immediately ashamed at having flung his angry words at her, David went after her, but she didn't even turn around when he called out to her. She simply got into her car and drove away. He'd never considered how painful it might be for her as a single woman of forty-five to be reminded that she would never be a mother.

He went to get himself a drink, his third Scotch since he'd arrived home this afternoon, but he felt he needed it, even more so after Chandi's upsetting departure. Sitting in the living room, he thought over what she'd said. It was easy for her to tell him to stop yelling at Kaia, but Chandi didn't have the vivid picture in her mind of his daughter on all fours, with Mark going at her like an animal. Kaia obviously needed a very firm hand at this point in her life.

David squeezed his eyes shut, trying instead to retrieve an image of Kaia when she was younger, her lovely hair winding down to her waist. He recalled how she would sometimes ask him to brush the tangles out of it, and how gratified he was to oblige, since her mother never seemed to be around, or available for that sort of thing. Once he'd opened the bathroom door to find Kaia at thirteen standing naked at the sink, just out of the shower, her back to him. It was so striking, her long wet hair, and so overwhelming, her blossoming femininity, that he just stared for a moment at her. But the expression on her face was scathing when she turned around to see him standing there, his hands hanging at his sides. Now he tried to erase the image of her angry face from his mind, along with the disturbing one of Kaia with Mark.

He told himself that after he'd finished this one last drink, he would go to Kaia's room and talk to her, try to make her see that he was just trying to take care of her in the best way he could and that he loved her very much. But he was afraid she would give him the same accusatory look as she had that time when she was thirteen and he'd seen her naked in the bathroom.

Maybe Chandi was right, that he'd have to find a way to loosen his grip on Kaia—at least once he made sure Mark was out of the picture.

*

"I feel terrible," David said to Chandi, who sat across from him in a booth at The Raven the following evening. "It's clear to me now that I shouldn't have dragged you into all of this."

Chandi took a sip of her espresso, peering at him over the brim of the cup, but said nothing. David detected something judgmental, and certainly distant, in her stare. He knew he looked haggard—he'd seen himself in the mirror before he left the house—the droopy folds in his face, the puffiness under the eyes, his sagging mouth. He hoped Chandi couldn't smell the whiskey on him, but surely she understood the state he was in after everything that had happened.

"Jean and I should have worked this out with Kaia by ourselves," he said. "I'm sorry I got you involved."

"But you haven't tried to work it out with anyone." Chandi's cheeks were flushed, and there was a look of barely contained frustration in her expression.

He reached across the table and took both of her hands in his. "I guess I've been pretty difficult these past few days."

"Yes, you have." She drew her hands away. "And you've been drinking so much. Even before this thing with Mark and Kaia."

"Not that much."

"You've even been drinking this afternoon, I can tell."

It bothered him the way the women in his life, even Kaia, made such a big deal about his drinking. He'd never considered it that excessive. It was merely something he enjoyed and felt he deserved, or needed at times, in order to relax.

"This is a very tough time for me," he said. "I'm doing the best I can—I just want to get Mark permanently out of the picture. I have to feel Kaia is safe before things can get back to normal."

"Going to the dean, and threatening to prosecute your own nephew—you're being insanely overprotective, David."

"It's a fatherly instinct to be protective."

"She's nearly eighteen." Chandi paused, staring intently at him. "Your love can injure her, you know."

"That's ridiculous," he said, wiping the perspiration from his forehead with a napkin. "Anyway, I'm sorry I've been so upset all week. I certainly don't expect you to see my behavior as a small thing, but you must realize it was an aberration, not my usual self at all."

She met his eyes, her lips pursed. If only she would show some of her old feeling for him, some tiny sign of affection. But perhaps it was too soon to expect that. He pictured the appalling scene when he'd yelled at her and insinuated she knew nothing about being a parent.

"Why don't you say something?" he pleaded.

Chandi raised one shoulder dismissively. "I don't see any possibility that the dynamics will change," she said in a terrible, resigned tone.

"There was no excuse for letting myself go on like that." He grabbed her hand. "I just hope you can forgive me."

She slipped her hand out of his grasp once again. "It's not a question of forgiving you. The fact is, I don't believe it will ever work out for us."

It scared him—the way she had delivered her flat, lawyerly assessment of their relationship. Didn't she have any feeling left for him at all? "We can still make it work," he said.

She blew out a long breath. "No, David, I really don't think we can. It's as if you're carrying some misbegotten torch for your daughter, and that seems to be the only thing that matters to you."

"What? I have no idea what you mean." David shook his head, dismayed at her resistance. "Chandi, I just hope you're not going to let this one incident—"

"It's not just one incident," she said with considerable force. "It's many in the course of the past six or seven months. I can no longer tell myself things will be different in the future. That's simply not the case. You're still trying to force Kaia to live at home and attend Berkeley, when that clearly is not what she wants. Nor is it the best thing for her."

She sounded so harsh, so cold—he wished she would be her usual, kind self. He moved his hand to his chest, feeling an almost physical ache. "Please, Chandi, you must realize how much I want you in my life. I've decided to let Kaia go to San Francisco State and live in the dorm. I told her last night. So she won't be around as much, and we won't be arguing about her anymore. Things will be better in the fall."

Chandi coughed and took a sip of her coffee. "They won't be that different, David." She met his eyes and paused for several seconds. "But we can try to be friends, and colleagues." Her face was frozen now in a taut grimace, as if dealing with a problematic client, as if she'd made this trite suggestion just to be civil.

"Surely you don't mean that." Couldn't she see how much he cared for her? A sharp prickling of panic was building up in his chest.

He dreaded what might come next—the stiff, formal hug, and then the pain that would settle in once he got home, even with a few more drinks inside him. He stood up abruptly and strode out of the coffee house. He'd forgotten where he'd parked and had to search up and down the rows for it, his vision blurred with tears. He thought of Chandi sitting there, glaring stonily at him as if she hated him. Did all of his women hate him? How had it come to this?

At last he found the Volvo, got in, and drove distractedly toward the house. Trying to clear his mind, he told himself that possibly Chandi would come back to him later on, when this mess with Kaia and Mark was resolved. And once Mark was gone, Kaia would eventually get over this ridiculous infatuation with her cousin. Then, David felt, he might somehow be able to repair his relationship with his daughter, and with Chandi. His entire focus for the present, though, would have to be on Kaia—where it had to be at this vulnerable point in her life.

25

The moment her father left the house to shop at the farmer's market Saturday morning, Kaia phoned Mark. "I have to see you. Dad's gone out. Can you please come over?" She knew she sounded desperate but couldn't help it. She missed him so much and had felt so isolated since her father had found her and Mark in bed together.

At least Sig had gotten over their fight last weekend, when Kaia had told her she wanted to be with Mark while her father was in Carmel. Furious, Sig had said a lot of hateful things about Mark, and had ended up driving Kaia back home in vengeful silence. But now Sig seemed to have forgiven her; she felt sorry for what Kaia was going through with her father.

Mark showed up at the door fifteen minutes after Kaia's phone call. He stood there on the porch in his gray T-shirt and jeans, searching her face for a long moment. She let him into the house and hugged him, burying her face in his shirt, comforted by the feel of his arms around her and his familiar salty scent.

"Are you okay?" He pulled away to look at her again.

"Not really. Let's go somewhere. I don't have too much time before Dad gets back."

They drove to Grotto Rock Park, a few blocks away, and parked at the curb. They climbed into the back and held each other. He put his hand under her chin, moving her face toward him, and kissed her.

"What's wrong?" he asked.

She tried to think, distracted by the pleasure of his kiss. "My mother came out here on Thursday."

"Really? Why? Does she want you to move to New York?"

Kaia shook her head, glancing away. "No. That would interfere with her plans."

"Her plans? What do you mean?"

"It's complicated." She couldn't bear to tell Mark about her mother's affair—it would hurt and infuriate Mark, and there was no telling what he might do. She shuddered inwardly, thinking of her mother's threat to tell everyone about her affair with Nico if Kaia didn't stop seeing Mark. Kaia had never perceived her mother as ugly before, but now she did, picturing her in the car that afternoon—the angry lines in her forehead, the mascara smudges beneath her eyes, the expensive hairdo sprayed so much it remained rigid whenever she moved her head.

"Complicated? I don't get it."

"Everyone is so set against us—they think our relationship is abnormal."

"You can't listen to them."

She took a deep breath, trying to keep from breaking down. "I think Dad really will have you arrested if you don't leave the state."

Mark took her hands in his and stared fixedly into her eyes. "I know that, Kaia."

"I would never testify against you, though."

"The D.A. could subpoena you and make you testify. And besides, your dad's testimony would be enough. And yesterday the dean called me into his office and said I'd be expelled if I'm convicted. Your dad told him what happened. I might even go to jail. And I could never become a member of the Bar, with an offense like that on my record."

"I can't believe Dad would actually press charges."

"I think he'll back off if I leave the state. Kaia, I'm going to have to go back to Maine."

"I don't want you to leave, Mark. If Dad does go to the D.A., I think you should fight it."

Mark shook his head. "There's no good legal defense. And the whole thing would tear us apart. I'm driving back to Maine tomorrow." He kissed her, his lips lingering on hers. "I want you to go with me, Kaia."

She examined his face to see if he was serious. "You know I can't do that, Mark. Maybe later, but not now."

"We could get married in Rhode Island, with permission from the Court Clerk. How is that wrong, Kaia? Just tell me that."

"Dad would be so furious, he'd find a way to bring you back to California to prosecute you."

"Not if we're married. The whole thing would be moot then."

"I can't marry you, Mark." She started to cry. She couldn't tell him what her mother had said. It would kill him. It would destroy what they had, poison the past, ruin everything. She pressed her hands against her face, trying to regain control. After a few seconds, she dropped her hand. "I can't have your children, Mark."

"Kaia, Kaia." He stroked her hair then wrapped his arms around her again, kissing the top of her head. "You can have anything you want. They don't understand how we feel about each other. Being cousins is no big deal. Lots of cousins marry—all over the world, in fact. It's legal in a lot of places."

"Doesn't it matter at all to you, that we're related?" Then a horrible possibility flashed across her mind, and before she could think, she blurted out, "What if we were brother and sister?"

Mark gaped at her. "That's ridiculous. We wouldn't feel the same way about each other then."

He was right, she realized. And her mother would have told her if there was any possibility that she and Mark were more closely related than cousins. It *was* a ridiculous thought.

"I can't give up everything right now," she said, wiping away her tears.

"We can have what we both want. You could still enroll in a college somewhere, and I could get a job. We could live in Maine or anywhere."

She pressed her face into his T-shirt, then, a moment later, looked up at him. "Dad agreed I could go to San Francisco State. I think he was afraid I'd never forgive him if he didn't let me go there. I sent in my intent to register yesterday. And I'll be living on campus."

"What's more important, Kaia?"

"We'll find a way to be together, but not right now."

"I want to be with you, Kaia, and I'll do anything to make that happen. You're going to have to decide."

"How can I decide anything right now? I haven't even had time to think things over. And I have to get back to the house. If Dad sees you with me, he'll have you arrested."

"Okay, then," Mark said sadly. He kissed her again.

"What are you going to do, then?"

"You know what I want to do." It was that low, seductive voice she found nearly impossible to resist.

If only she could run away with him and ignore all of the consequences. "I mean what are you going to do in Maine?"

"Grandpa's going to let me stay in the cabin. I'll refurbish it—clean out the mold, do some repairs, put a coat of stain on the wood. Dad wants me to go to law school in Maine or New York."

"Are you going to do that?"

"It's too late to transfer for the fall. Anyway, I'd rather live at the cabin and get away from the all of the pressure for a while." He paused, then took her by the shoulders. "Come with me, Kaia."

"I need to go to college, Mark. But you could come out to see me once I'm living at the dorm. We'll still be able to see each other."

"Is that all you want? To see me once in a while?" He sounded incredulous.

"I thought you'd be staying in Berkeley, living right across the Bay. Then we could have seen each other all the time."

"I can't stay in California, Kaia."

"I do want to see you as much as I can. We can talk about it later. Let's start driving back to the house, please, Mark."

He let go of her and started up the engine, and they drove in silence. He parked a block away from the house. Mark began kissing her, but after a minute she forced herself to pull back. He held her face in his hands, his eyes fixed on hers.

She kissed him, then got out of the car and ran down the street—luckily her dad's car wasn't in the driveway. She went into the house and upstairs to Mark's old room. Flinging herself onto the bed, she stared at the ceiling, breathing fast but trying to steady herself. It had felt so wonderful to have Mark's arms around her and to be with him. If only her father hadn't caught them together, and if only her mother hadn't come out here with her disgusting story. How could her mother have done that to Elisa? Her father would be devastated if he found out about her mother's affair with Nico. And then of course Elisa might find out.

But what could be done about it? Maybe, Kaia thought, if she just went off to college and told no one about her mother and Nico, all of their lives wouldn't be damaged any more than they already had been. She and Mark could decide later what they wanted to do, how they could be together without all of the complications.

That was all she could hope for right now.

PART THREE

BERKELEY AND SAN FRANCISCO

1981 to 1985

1

One Sunday in June Kaia decided to bake bread. She'd found a bread cookbook her mother had left behind on a high shelf in the kitchen—it looked as though it had never been used. It must have been a gift from someone who didn't know her mother very well; Kaia couldn't recall her ever baking anything.

Kaia first tried out the recipe for Irish Soda Bread with golden raisins, and that afternoon she and her dad each devoured several hot, delectable slices straight from the oven with lemon butter, accompanied by his blackest coffee. It surprised her, the way he seemed so gratified, as if she were making the bread just for him. The following week, she moved on to bread made with yeast, and soon started creating her own combinations of ingredients. Once she tried a mixture of oats, dried apricots and dates, another time rye bread with orange, anise and cranberries. She loved the simple, physical pleasures of kneading the dough, forming the loaf, and taking it out of the oven in a cloud of fragrant steam, the sweet aroma circulating through the house. Her father was always drawn into the kitchen as if by a siren's song, to find out what she was baking.

As compulsive as it seemed, her breadmaking was one of the few things that made them both happy, at least momentarily. Most of the time they simply passed their days quietly in a sort of truce, interacting only when necessary; her father still seemed disappointed in her, obviously because of her involvement with Mark, as well as her choice of a college; and of course he was sad because she was moving into a dorm, away from him, in a matter of weeks.

She wished she could be baking the bread for Mark, and she thought of him constantly, picturing him alone in their grandfather's cabin in rural Maine. She wanted to share everything with him. After he'd left, she had managed to rent a post office box so that she could get letters from him. It was in Sig's name, since she was eighteen and had a driver's license for identification. Kaia rode over to the post office on her bike whenever she could, and in May she was overjoyed to find a long letter from him in response to hers. He was refurbishing the cabin and was planning to start a garden, he'd written, and more than anything he wanted her to be there with him. She'd sat on the lawn outside the post office and read his letter over and over, tears streaming down her cheeks.

After her graduation in mid-June, Kaia had started working for her dad in his office, doing some filing and typing. He paid her for the few hours she worked and promised to give her some legal research to do, updating the case law for his latest law review article. She was glad to have some extra spending money, and enjoyed having a job for the first time. Her dad seemed to like having her company at the office, especially since he wasn't seeing Chandi anymore and seemed lonely much of the time.

One evening Kaia told her father she wanted to learn to make Indian bread, and asked her father if he minded her contacting Chandi to see if she would teach her how to make *naan*. He shrugged and said it was all right with him. When Kaia phoned her, they made a date for the following Saturday. They spent the morning making the dough and forming it into flat rounds while chatting about Kaia's college plans and Chandi's legal work. After the *naan* came out of the *tandoor*, Kaia sat with Chandi at the kitchen table and sank her teeth into a piece of the warm, chewy bread, shutting her eyes and savoring the subtle texture and flavor.

Chandi laughed. "This is so delightful, Kaia, seeing you enjoy your food so much."

Kaia opened her eyes, surprised. "I've always loved food, and cooking."

"It didn't seem that way a couple of months ago. You were getting so thin. I'm glad to see you putting on a few pounds and filling out. You look almost robust!"

Kaia smiled. "I never thought I'd be called robust. I guess it's because I'm not dancing now. And I plan to eat lots of *naan* in the future. I'll have to save up to buy a *tandoor*." She couldn't help thinking how much Mark would enjoy being here now, eating the *naan* with them, and she felt again how much she missed him.

"You can always come over here and bake." Chandi paused and peered into Kaia's face, perhaps catching her pensive look. "You're missing Mark still, aren't you?"

Tears brimmed up in Kaia's eyes. "Yes, but we've been in touch." She inhaled sharply, wondering if she should have told Chandi this.

Chandi touched Kaia's arm lightly. "Don't worry, I won't tell anyone."

As far as Kaia knew, her father and Chandi weren't even talking; Dad wasn't the type to chat on the phone. But in any event, she felt she could trust Chandi.

Besides baking, Kaia derived some pleasure from doing the simple legal research for her father. She drove the Volvo for practice as much as possible, with her father navigating, and he agreed she could get her license soon, and drive his car when she was home on the weekends, obviously a bribe—anything to get her to come home.

Then, in July, Chandi announced she was going to India for three weeks to visit her family, and asked Kaia if she would take care of her cat. Kaia talked her dad into letting Mandrake stay in the house with them, arguing that Chandi's tom would take care of any rats still infesting the house. At first the giant tabby started sleeping in the den, and then at the foot of Kaia's bed; she loved the sound of Mandrake's purring, like a miniature engine idling. One afternoon Kaia found him sitting smugly on their front doormat, a mangled, bloody rat hanging from his mouth. Luckily her father was at home and took care of it. Kaia suspected, though, that Mandrake had only caused the rats to hide; she was afraid the infestation would surface later on.

When Chandi returned from India, she hired Kaia to help with a stained-glass window she was designing for her living room. Chandi used some of Kaia's suggestions for color, and once the glass cutting began, Kaia enjoyed the process of wrapping copper foil around the edges of the cut pieces of glass, and then placing them on the large graph paper design on the worktable. Chandi would solder the pieces together after they were all cut and foiled and laid out together in an elaborate floral design. She promised to give Kaia a chance to try her hand at soldering.

Chandi had converted her screened patio into a studio so that there was enough ventilation to blow away the smoke and fumes. Sometimes the scent of roses and magnolias floated in from the backyard, and Kaia loved to gaze at the small pond with its water lilies and the redwood hot tub surrounded by flowerbeds. Chandi invited Kaia to bring her swimsuit over so they could soak in the hot tub, and they often enjoyed doing that after working for a few hours.

One Saturday afternoon, after Chandi had cut out a long piece of yellow glass for the border of her piece, she straightened up, rubbing her lower back, and pushed her dark hair off of her forehead.

"You really enjoy this stained-glass work, don't you?" she asked Kaia.

Kaia glanced up from her foiling and nodded.

"I'll help you design a piece of your own if you'd like," Chandi said.

"That'd be great."

"Let's take a break. I want to tell you something." Chandi sat down in a chair and stretched her legs out on the ottoman, and Kaia seated herself in the chair next to her.

"Kaia, I just want you to know that I admire the way you stood up to your dad about where you wanted to go to college. It really took guts."

"Dad's still upset that I turned down Cal. I just hope he doesn't start drinking a lot again when I leave."

"That's up to him." Chandi's face turned serious. "You do need to be away from him, you know."

"He seems so depressed sometimes, I'm sure he'll be lonely when I start college and live in the dorm."

"Really, Kaia, you can't let his problems control you."

Kaia sighed. "You're right, I do need to be on my own."

After a few moments' silence, Chandi said, "Turning down Stanford, too, that was quite something. I went to law school there. I was accepted while I was still at Oxford, and was thrilled, but frightened, too, about coming over here by myself, even though I was twenty-one at the time. My father went into an absolute rage over it, as he had when I'd decided on Oxford. But I'm glad now that I came here, and stayed."

"You don't seem like a lawyer. You seem so artistic."

"I enjoy helping people with their problems, but I also love spending time here, doing some of my projects. You don't have to do just one thing to be happy."

"And you don't mind living alone?" Kaia hoped she wasn't being too personal.

"At times, but there are benefits to being independent. Sometimes I wish I'd had a child or two, but my life would have been quite different. It's such a huge commitment." Chandi gazed out into the garden.

"You have some regrets, though?"

"Not really," Chandi said, turning back to Kaia. "I like my job very much. I was just thinking about Roberta, the client I told you about last fall—the migrant farmworker who left her kids in foster care." She let out a long sigh. "As it turned out, we lost at trial, and the judge cut off all of her legal rights to her kids. Roberta and her boyfriend had been arrested in a stolen car when they were driving up north to work in the orchards. She almost went to jail, but the worst thing of course was losing her children. So now we're appealing the judge's decision."

"It's terrible that her kids have to stay in foster homes. Do you do a lot of trials like that?"

"Mostly we do appeals, and not much of the nitty gritty trial work. Sometimes I call our firm Lofty Towers."

Kaia laughed. "It must be exciting, though."

"Sometimes. Anyway, when we get the trial transcripts from Roberta's trial, I may need an assistant to help with some of the preliminary work. Maybe you'll have a few hours free later in the summer, if your dad doesn't keep you too busy with his work."

"I'd like that."

"Meanwhile, you'll have to come downtown and see my office. It's right on Market, so I can take you to a smashing lunch at Stars."

Kaia grinned. "But I have nothing to wear."

"We'll have to do something about that," Chandi said.

2

One Friday afternoon, Kaia was lying on her dorm bed, exhilarated and spent from dancing for an hour and a half to the live music of African pipes and drums, her phone rang, and the woman at the front desk told her she had a visitor in the lobby. She pulled a sweatshirt over her leotard and tights, and headed for the elevator. She hoped it was Sig—she hadn't seen her since starting college two weeks ago. But when she stepped into the lobby, Mark was standing there with his hands in the pockets of his denim jacket, looking directly at her. She covered her mouth with her hand, unable to believe it was him. He walked up to her and stood there smiling at her.

"Hungry?" he asked. His gaze was leveled at her, his arms crossed, as if trying to keep himself from reaching out for her. His face was ruddy, his moustache fuller, blending into a new short beard.

"I'm always hungry," Kaia said, barely catching her breath. "But don't take that too literally."

Mark shifted his weight from one foot to the other in his old dusty boots. "Is that a warning, Ms. Matheson?"

"Not really. I just try to keep my appetite reined in. As much as possible, that is."

He laughed, his eyes a clear blue in the overhead lights. Even from a few feet away, she imagined she could feel the heat rising off his arms, his neck, his entire body.

She took two steps forward so that she was a couple of inches away from him. "Of course I don't let just anyone feed me," she whispered.

He stroked his beard, a gesture that made him seem older, and ponderous. "Didn't think you would."

She hesitated a moment longer, then threw her arms around his neck and gave him a long kiss, not caring for once if anyone saw them.

"I'm staying at an inn in Half Moon Bay, by the way," he said after a few moments, "in case you wanted to check it out."

"I'll get my bag. Be right back."

As she rode in the elevator to the fifth floor, her heart beating fast, she told herself this was the kind of thing she could handle without being thrown totally off balance. Mark and she would share a few meals, sleep together, and wake up the next morning in the same bed. There would be the thrilling rush of it, the mellowness of lying in his arms, and then the point when they would return to their usual lives. They were on their own now, away from the theatrics of their families. Her father would never know.

When she returned with her overnight bag, Mark took her to his rented Datsun and drove toward the coast on Highway 1. He suggested they have something to eat at a café he'd found after driving from the airport to Half Moon Bay the previous night. Soon they were winding past miles of eucalyptus groves, and then they caught a view of the glistening teal-green ocean. Kaia was reminded of the afternoon a year ago when Mark had taken her in his Mustang to Half Moon Bay for pizza. That was undoubtedly the reason he'd chosen to take her there now.

They cruised down the coastal highway with the velvety brown hills on their left and the ocean on their right, talking mostly about Kaia's first weeks of college. She told Mark about the African dance class with students providing live music. "I like it so much more than ballet."

"Good. I'm glad." He reached over and squeezed her thigh. "Did you get my last postcard?"

"Yep. It's been hard not being able to talk to you."

"I still can't get phone service at the cabin."

When they reached the café, they found a booth and Mark sat next to her, his thigh and shoulder pressing against her. They ordered spaghetti and meatballs and shared Mark's glass of wine, while Kaia talked about college. The most interesting class, she told him, was Society and Politics, where they discussed topics like the E.R.A., nuclear disarmament, and gay rights.

"Cool," Mark said, putting his arm around her shoulders. "I'm happy you're enjoying it."

"I've been super busy, though. And I haven't gotten to know many people yet."

"Do you have a roommate?"

"I did for a few days. She arrived from China after I moved in, but she didn't speak English too well and missed her family, so she went back home. I tried introducing her to people, but I think the culture shock was too much for her."

"You'll get a new roommate, then?"

"I'm not sure, but I think I'll have the room to myself." She took a bite of the meatball. "So what's it like at the cabin?"

"The cabin's fairly old and weathered, so I cleaned it up and put a coat of red paint on it. After the ice melted on the lake last spring, the hills turned green. It's beautiful there. I love it. I've gotten into some gardening—a few vegetables so far—and I think I wrote you about restoring antiques. I'm actually getting some business and selling to some stores in town."

"Isn't it kind of lonely at the cabin?" She took a sip of his wine.

He shrugged. "I'm used to it, I guess. But it would be so much better if you were there with me."

"I wish I could be."

He looked down, stirring the spaghetti around in circles on his plate. "I've started designing and making some furniture, too. I'm thinking of staying out there for a while."

"You don't miss law school, then?"

"Not really. I love what I'm doing, and living out in the country."

As he told her more about his life at the cabin, she could picture the kind of life where you would greet the morning with a naked stretch, tend to the garden, do some carpentry, and then prepare a lunch of freshly-baked bread, goat cheese and apples. Later you might meander down to the lake for a swim or to sail, then return to the cabin to prepare a supper of trout and freshly picked vegetables. Finally to bed, relaxing in the light of an oil lamp. A simple life with no need for a telephone or TV or even electricity. It seemed so wonderfully peaceful compared to her hectic college life in the noisy city.

Once they'd finished their meal and had climbed into the Datsun, Mark inserted the key into the ignition and turned to Kaia. "So what now?"

She imagined the sensation of his lips on hers, the feel of his hands moving across her body. "Where is this inn you were just telling me about?"

He grinned and started up the engine.

They drove to the outskirts of Half Moon Bay and up into the hills above the ocean, then wound along a dirt driveway to a yellow, two-story farmhouse with a wrap-around porch.

"Who else knows you're in California?" she asked as he pulled in front of the inn.

"Not a single person."

He carried her bag up to their room on the second floor, which was furnished with antiques and redolent with the scent of seasoned wood. Kaia took in the dankness of the plaster walls, the fragrance of fresh linens. It was still early in the evening, and pale sunlight filtered through the lace curtains, creating an intricate pattern over the interior—a frilly veneer over the somber dark of the room. With its wooden floor that listed to one side, the room seemed to lack solidity.

A flicker of fear passed through her, and she felt herself wavering. What if her father did find out about this? What would he do? Have Mark arrested? Her father might try to force her to live at home. And how was Mark going to fit in with her life, now that he'd apparently come to reclaim her?

She sat on the edge of the bed, brushing the thin chenille spread with her fingertips, and tried to focus on the coolness, the vacancy of the room, the feeling of the moment before.

"Is there a bathtub?" she asked, conscious of the anxious tone in her voice. "I'd like to take a bath or shower."

"Down the hall." Mark handed her a towel and a bar of soap. "Shampoo?"

She nodded, and he gave her a tube of Prell.

"Need any help?" he asked, tilting his head.

She shook her head. "I think I can handle it."

In the bathroom she undressed and lowered herself into the clawfoot tub as it filled. She watched the spout disgorge a thick stream of hot water that surged around her hips, her back, her breasts. She leaned back, soaking her hair, which was longer than it had been in years—nearly to her waist. Light filtered through a stained-glass window, and there was a quietness to the room, an indistinctness to the atmosphere, as if in a museum or church. She pictured Mark in the room, waiting for her. He seemed different now, with his Zen-like calm. Maybe it was the months spent at the cabin, outdoors all the time, with no one around to hassle him, no pressures. He'd always seemed happier outdoors, especially at Pine Tree. She wondered if she could ever live like that in a cabin in the country. And she also wondered if Mark would really want to stay there for a long time, and try to support himself with his antiques and furniture making. She was more attracted to him than ever, if that was possible; he seemed much more open and relaxed than when he was living in the Berkeley house and going to law school. Maybe they could make it work, somehow.

An image of her mother's face intruded, her skin like worn, pale shoe leather, her gaze grim and disapproving. During their brief phone calls during the summer, her mother had never said anything about Mark or Nico or Elisa. In spite of herself, Kaia felt a sudden inkling of shame. She'd been trying to stifle the recurring sense that there was something else her mother hadn't told her—some other reason Kaia shouldn't be involved with Mark. But even though Mark and she were cousins, how could seeing him hurt anyone, as long as she didn't get pregnant?

She shampooed and rinsed her hair, then rested her head back on the edge of the tub, sliding her shoulders and neck into the water, her tension washing away.

When she got out, she wrapped the towel around herself and crept down the hall, carrying her clothes. As she entered the room, Mark rose from an armchair and advanced a few steps. She loosened the towel and tossed it aside. He came over and bent to kiss her. She felt cold, standing there naked, and slipped under the sheets, and he quickly took off his clothes and climbed in after her. He stretched out on top of her and placed his hand beneath her hip, moving her into just the right position, then propped himself on his elbows and searched her face, his lips just inches away from her mouth. She lay there, feeling Mark's heat seep into her skin.

"Are you about to take liberties?" she asked.

"Oh, yes, Kaia. Many, many liberties with you."

"God, I love you so much, Mark."

"I love you, too, Kaia. I always have, always will. You know that, don't you?"

"I can't see you during the term," Kaia finally told Mark on Tuesday morning, in the hotel's breakfast room. "I'll flunk out. I'm behind in my reading, and I've missed my Monday classes."

"You'll catch up. I'll take you back to campus and maybe we can just see each other at night for the next few days."

"It would just make it harder when you leave, Mark. And I won't be able to concentrate on school."

"I can't stand to be away from you, Kaia. Don't you want to be together all the time?"

"Of course I do. But I have to stay in college and get my degree."

"You could do that anywhere. There are colleges in Maine, you know."

"I like it here, Mark, and I can't make any big decisions right now. We'll see each other again soon. We'll find a way."

He looked miserable, but she insisted he take her back to San Francisco.

Two hours after he dropped her off at the dorm, he called her from the airport while waiting for a standby flight. "Are you sure you want me to leave?" he asked.

"No, of course I don't, but I can't—"

Then his flight was called and he had to hang up. Sitting at her desk in her dorm room, Kaia wondered if she'd made a huge mistake. Picturing Mark's face, so full of affection, she put her head down on the desk and fought back her tears. She wished she could be on that plane with him right now, and wondered if she simply lacked the courage to live her life the way she wanted to.

It didn't help, either, that since Friday her father had phoned several times, leaving messages for her at the front desk, asking her to call him. But of course he couldn't possibly know how she had spent her weekend.

3

On Thanksgiving Day, Kaia and her father prepared their dinner—a diminutive turkey with two yams and a couple of other traditional dishes. As she watched him guzzle the Chardonnay, she thought they should have invited Chandi; it would have been more fun, and maybe it would have put a damper on his drinking. She recalled the delicious dinner they'd had at Chandi's house last March, when Kaia and her father had arrived to the spicy aroma of curry and peppers. They had all made *samosas* in the kitchen, drinking glasses of Gewürtztraminer while the other dishes simmered on the stove.

"Do you ever see Chandi, or talk to her?" Kaia asked now.

"Not really," her father said, glancing down at his plate.

"You're still friends, aren't you?"

"In theory." Still avoiding her eyes, he took a long drink.

"Dad," Kaia said a few minutes later, over the cherry pie, "I'm thinking of getting a part-time job."

He raised his eyebrows and shoveled a large piece of pie into his mouth, taking his time before answering. "Why would you want to do that? It would only interfere with your studies."

"I need some spending money. And I want to save up to buy a car."

"You don't need a car right now. Don't I give you enough money?"

"Not enough to buy a car. Anyway, I was thinking I might call Chandi to see if she still needs an assistant."

He stared at her with a puzzled expression. "I don't think that's a good idea, Kaia."

"I can phone her myself, you know. I'm not asking you to call her."

"You can always work for me on the weekends if you want some legal experience. And of course I'd pay you for your time."

"I'd like to work in a regular law office, Dad. I'm going to call Chandi, to find out if she needs someone to help with that farmworker appeal."

Her father's jaw tightened, but he merely picked up the wine bottle and refilled their glasses.

*

When Kaia phoned Chandi the next day, it turned out the transcripts in the farmworker case had finally come in, and Chandi said she was in dire need of some help. Kaia couldn't believe her luck. Chandi would pay her a decent hourly wage, and Kaia could start next week.

After classes the following Wednesday, Kaia took the M-car from campus to Chandi's office south of Market. Kaia was given an office to herself for the afternoon, although law students would sometimes be sharing it. She spent most of the time reviewing appeal briefs to get an idea of how to summarize the evidence presented in the trial court. At five p.m., she left the office and wrote Mark a letter while she sat on a bench, waiting for the M-car back to campus:

December 3, 1981
Dear Mark,

I miss you so much. If only you were living here, close by.

Something great has happened. Chandi has hired me to work as her assistant, so I'll be able to save up to buy a car, and maybe fly to Maine for a weekend in the spring. I have a long winter break coming up—five weeks—so I'll be able to work extra hours then.

Chandi's office is on the eleventh floor of a high-rise downtown. Remember when she told us about the case of the farmworker whose children were taken away from her? Well, they lost at trial, and I'm working on the appeal now. My first project is to summarize each witness' trial testimony.

What are you doing, now that it's wintertime? Tell me every single detail so I can picture you in your snug little cabin!

Love and kisses, Kaia

A week later, she received his reply:

God, Kaia, I miss you more than you would believe. I think about you constantly. Just say the word, and I'll come out to see you. Or I'll buy you a ticket to fly out here.

I've weatherproofed the shed where I do my carpentry and restoration work, and I'm taking in more projects lately.

You should see it here—there's a thick blanket of snow on the ground. A few idiots come through on their snowmobiles, but otherwise it's quiet and peaceful. The roads are often blocked, so sometimes I can't get into Beaulieu to call you or get my mail.

I didn't spend much time in Bangor at Thanksgiving. Your mom didn't come this year, so you could have come, and slept in the den (and had a night visitor). We've got to do something about this,

> so we can see each other more often, or even better, be together permanently. Is that something you ever think about?
>
> It sounds like the firm you're working for is doing some good things. I'm glad you're enjoying it—whatever gets you up in the morning. Just make sure you have time for me. I think of you all the time, Kaia, picturing you here with me at the cabin and waking up together every morning.
>
> All my love, Mark

During winter break, Kaia took BART from Berkeley each weekday into downtown San Francisco to work at the office. The dorm was shut until the end of January, when classes would start again. Working was better than hanging around the house, and Kaia was finding the legal work interesting; she could see that lawyers actually had the power to help people. And she found that reading the transcripts of the trial was quite absorbing.

One Saturday during the break, she invited Sig over to bake bread. Sig had been taking art classes at City College while living at home. She walked through the door wearing a green tie-dyed sweatshirt and jeans with frayed holes, her dyed black hair longer now and tinged magenta at the tips. Kaia rushed to her and hugged her.

In the kitchen, they talked about their classes while they made pumpkin bread. When it was done, they talked while they ate warm, thick slices with apple butter. Kaia's father was outside raking leaves, and probably hadn't yet smelled the bread baking; Kaia was grateful for the chance to talk to Sig alone.

"So have you met anyone?" Kaia asked her friend.

"You won't believe this, but I've actually been seeing someone—my ceramics teacher—for the past month or so."

"You didn't tell me about that," Kaia said.

"We haven't exactly been talking much—you weren't in your dorm room the last few times I called. But here's the bad part about Brian—he's married and has kids."

"That must be tough."

"I don't think I'll be seeing him anymore. He couldn't figure out a way to see me during winter break. I guess he thought it was too risky to sneak off, with his family at home all the time. And to tell you the truth, I've been getting a little tired of the whole student-teacher relationship bit. And men in general. They're all kind of jerks."

"Not all of them," Kaia said.

"You mean Mark?"

"Yes, and there are other guys who aren't so bad, either. I told you Mark was here in September, but I'm not sure when I'll see him again, and I can't really think about anyone else."

"Too bad. Can't get over him, huh?" Sig studied her face.

Kaia shook her head. She didn't even want to try to get over Mark. It was something Sig would never understand; she still seemed to resent Mark because Kaia had spent so much time with him during their senior year. If only Sig would get over it, they wouldn't always have that between them. Mark wasn't going away, Kaia was sure of that.

4

In late February, Kaia learned that Roberta Barrett, their farmworker client, would be coming into the office to consult with Chandi about her case. An hour before her appointment, Kaia went in to talk to Chandi.

"I'm wondering if you'd consider letting me start doing some legal research on Roberta's case," Kaia said. "I'm taking Legal Writing and Research and Pleadings now." She'd learned about the Paralegal Program at SF State and had signed up for the law classes in addition to her regular courses. She would earn more money as a paralegal, and it would be more challenging than just reading transcripts.

Chandi crossed her legs with her usual aplomb, her bronze face curtained by black hair that shimmered as she tilted her head. "I think you could try doing a little research. I'll give you an issue to start on."

"That sounds great. And can I sit in on the conference when Roberta comes in?"

"Yes, of course. I'd like you to be there."

Roberta turned out to be a tall, hefty woman, close to forty, dressed in a dark-blue polyester pantsuit, her expression rather impassive as she shook hands with Chandi and Kaia. After she sat down, Roberta immediately began to talk about her kids, and how much she missed having them live with her. She told them that the children's father had long ago moved away and couldn't be located.

"I want to get my kids back right away," she said, leaning forward. "Why is this taking so long?"

Chandi explained to Roberta the process of researching the law and writing briefs, then waiting for the judges to set a court hearing on the case; it could be many months before a judgment came down. "Meanwhile, you should try to visit your kids as much as you can. That will be in your favor if the case goes back to the trial court."

"I've got a job as a motel maid, and I'm seeing my kids as much as I can." Roberta settled back in her chair. "Now I have money for the bus and to buy a few things for them."

"That's good," Chandi said. "I'm glad the foster parents are cooperating with visitation."

This poor woman, Kaia thought, working so hard, who wanted her children back more than anything. Roberta had made just one big mistake, leaving them temporarily in foster care in order to pick cherries, but she'd needed the money for her kids. Kaia felt a constriction in her throat, thinking of her own mother who had so many options yet had chosen to leave her, and for no good reason.

"When I get my kids back," Roberta said, "my mother can help take care of them so I can still work. So, anyway, what comes next in my case?"

"If we win in the Court of Appeal, there will be a new trial, and you'll have another chance at winning custody."

"Do you think we might lose?" Roberta asked, alarmed.

"I can't guarantee anything," Chandi said quietly. "We'll do our best, and meanwhile you need to keep your job here rather than leaving the state to pick cherries again, all right?"

"I'm not planning on goin' nowhere, with my boyfriend in jail here in San Francisco. We're gonna get married as soon as he gets out, maybe even have a kid or two." She grinned, happy at the thought, displaying tobacco-stained teeth. "If I ain't too old by then."

Kaia recalled that Roberta's boyfriend had been arrested for car theft when he and Roberta were driving to Washington to work as harvesters. Kaia didn't understand how a mother could get herself into a situation like that and risk losing her kids. It was incomprehensible, too, that Roberta would consider having more kids with a convicted car thief when she couldn't even keep the children she already had. But it seemed best for her three kids to be together again, and Roberta was obviously motivated to get them back. Hopefully she wouldn't abandon them again.

"Miguel got five years, didn't he?" Chandi asked.

"Yep, but he'll be out in three with good-time credits," Roberta said. "I can wait."

"I'm glad you've found a job and can see your kids. Meanwhile we'll keep working hard on your case."

When Roberta left, Chandi closed the door and sat down at her desk. "That's the most difficult part of the job," she said to Kaia. "Offering encouragement when you don't actually feel it's warranted."

"You don't think we'll win?"

"This appeal has nothing extraordinary about it, except that I asked that separate attorneys be appointed for each child, and the motion was denied. Each child might have different needs, so there should be separate lawyers for each child, so that the court can then decide what's in the best interest of each child, even apart from what the parent wants."

"Sounds like a good issue."

"It's a long shot. There's the practical matter of getting the county to pay for more appointed lawyers. Poor people aren't exactly the courts' highest priority."

"I just hope we can do something," Kaia said. "It's the kids I really care about—they've been separated from each other and from their mom for over a year now."

In fact the case had tugged at her heart from the moment she'd heard about it, when she had just met Chandi. Maybe, if they won the case, Roberta would do a better job taking care of her kids, then just possibly the children would forget the time they'd spent in foster care while their mother ran off with her lover. That was what Kaia fervently hoped would happen—a good result for the abandoned kids.

"We'll try our best," Chandi said, a bit sadly though.

Kaia hadn't heard from Mark in weeks, either by phone or letter, even though she'd written him several times. It was six months since he'd taken her to the inn at Half Moon Bay last September. She was trying, unsuccessfully, most of the time, to keep him submerged beneath her consciousness, Triton-like; she knew she wasn't yet ready to have him rise up and take over her land life. At times though, alone in her dorm room, she felt rather unhappy, and wondered if he might be seeing someone.

In March, she enrolled in a modern dance class through the City Rec Department, wanting to limber up and counteract the nervous energy engendered from over-caffeination and the haphazard intake of food. Dancing lifted her spirits. Ecstatic one evening after class, she thought of Elisa, who had been a dance instructor. She wrote her aunt a quick note:

March 12, 1982
Dear Elisa,

I miss you all so much, especially now—it's been so long since I've seen you.

I've been working hard on my legal job and classes and needed some exercise, so I'm taking a modern dance class. Today there was reggae music—this kind of dance is so different from ballet. Ballet seems like a strait jacket, practicing the steps over and over to perfection, compared to the leaping-soaring feel of interpretive dance.

Mark told me you used to teach dance. Do you still?

Much love, Kaia

The following week she received Elisa's reply:

March 19, 1982
Dear Kaia,

Your note made me so very happy. I sometimes get rather down in the dumps, so I don't teach now, since I never know how I'm going to feel on a particular day. But when I'm feeling better I dance alone in the house, at times slowly to Eric Satie, other times bounding madly through the front room to Tchaikovsky. No one else knows about this—don't tell!

Never stop dancing, Kaia! We all love you.

Always, Elisa

The letter alarmed Kaia, and she thought of writing to Mark about his mother's depression, but he already knew about her mood swings. And Elisa didn't want anyone to know about her solitary dancing and her bad days. Kaia figured she would wait until she heard from Mark to ask him how his mother was doing. He did say he occasionally visited his parents in Bangor. Still, Kaia kept thinking about Elisa's letter. If only she could see her aunt again, and see Mark.

5

After much deliberation, Kaia decided to declare a major in Political Science. There was a gravitas to it that appealed to her, a solid connection to the real world, the world inhabited by Roberta and her children. Kaia's favorite course this semester was Contemporary Issues in American Politics, and she especially liked her instructor, Mr. Davidson, a guy in his late twenties with a magnificent mane of red hair. He insisted his students call him "Tom."

The first time Kaia went to his office, in early May, to talk over ideas for a term paper, it reminded her of her pilgrimages to her father's office during high school. When she rapped on Tom's open door, he sprang to his feet, greeting her with a cheerful smile, as if he'd just been hoping she would come by for a chat. Stacks of books and papers sat on the floor and tables. Dust coated every surface except for his desk.

Kaia had some ideas for her paper, but in the midst of discussing them with Tom, she found herself fixating on his languid brown eyes. He was so striking—tall, lean, commanding, like a tennis player. His skin had a slightly weathered look. He might even be thirty, she decided; at least five or six years older than Mark. She wondered why guys her own age didn't appeal to her so much.

Apparently sensing something in her gaze, Tom said, "Do you want to go for coffee, or maybe just take a walk while we chat?"

"Sure," she said.

She was surprised to discover how much she enjoyed strolling around campus with him, talking about politics, and in the following weeks she went to his office several times to talk about her paper. She devised her own topic, about women in professions, how family life was being transformed by feminism. They had many debates about the topic, and also revisited some of the other issues Tom liked to discuss in class—the way Reagan was cutting social programs in favor of arms; why people were driven to organize and limit each other's lives through laws; the merits of socialism vs. capitalism; and topics in the news. It felt adult and worldly, debating with Tom in his office or over coffee at the student union. Sometimes their meetings made her think of her father and miss him a little—his energetic presence, his strong opinions, his authoritative intelligence.

Kaia glanced up from her Poli Sci exam and found Tom smiling at her from the front of the classroom. She returned to the essay she was writing, trying to refocus her thoughts. She hadn't been to his office for several weeks. But last week he'd stopped her after class to chat, and she'd mentioned she was moving to an apartment closer to the office, where she had a full-time summer job. Tom had immediately offered to help move her out of the dorm with his pickup, but she hadn't given him an answer. Her father certainly wouldn't like being usurped in that way; he'd made it clear he wanted to move her himself. And since he had agreed, amazingly, to let her have her own place instead of moving home for the summer, she wanted to let him help her with the move.

She was one of the last to finish the exam, and when she took her bluebook to the front of the classroom, she dropped it on the table with barely a glance at Tom, then dashed out of the room. As she left the building, she heard Mark call out her name. She spotted him leaning against a monolithic cement planter, wearing khaki trousers, a black shirt and sandals. He took a few strides toward her, grasped her by the shoulders and bent to kiss her.

"I'm here to drive you, Ma'am," he said with a smile, "anywhere you'd like to go." He was squinting at her in the sun.

She could barely speak, she was so happy to see him. "Any suggestions?" she managed to ask.

"I'm full of suggestions," he said in a low voice, "but for right now, I hear the camping's good up near Mendocino."

"How did you know when my finals were over?"

"You told me the classes you were taking, so I just called the Registrar's Office to find out your final exam schedule."

She took his arm and headed with him toward the dorm. "I have to move out of my room by Sunday."

"We could spend a couple of days camping first."

She heard a man call out her name, and when she turned around, she caught sight of Tom loping toward them with a stack of bluebooks under his arm.

"I just wanted to talk to you about something," he said, out of breath when he caught up with them outside the residence hall. "Have you got a minute?" He glanced over at Mark.

"This is my cousin, Mark Karadonis," she said. "My Poli Sci instructor, Tom Davidson."

Mark nodded, frowning. Neither man stuck out a hand.

"I hate to interrupt," Tom said, "but I need to discuss something with you, Kaia."

"Go for it," Mark said, placing his hand on her shoulder.

"Actually," she said to Tom, "we're about to drive up the coast to go camping."

He raised his eyebrows. "I thought you were moving into your new apartment—right after finals, you said. We could do it this afternoon—I've got my pickup here."

"Thanks, but that's all right." She just wanted him to shut up and go away. "My dad's planning to move me out."

Tom shrugged and fixed his gaze on Mark for a moment before turning back to Kaia. "Just thought I'd offer. Give me a call if you need any help."

"Sure, thanks," Kaia said, and turned away.

Mark dropped his hand from her shoulder as they walked into the dorm lobby.

"Can you wait here?" she asked. "I just have to throw a few things together."

Mark nodded, looking unhappy.

In her room, she threw some clothes into her duffel bag, then hurried to the elevator, still nervous after the encounter with Tom. She wondered what Mark thought about her relationship with her instructor—if it could even be considered a relationship. He was an acquaintance, that was all, and her teacher.

Mark glanced a few times at Kaia as he drove, but she seemed to be avoiding his eyes. Finally, he asked her, "Who in the hell was that guy, Kaia?"

"I told you, he's my Poli Sci instructor." She gave him a cautious look. "I didn't go out with him, if that's what you think."

She was flushing, Mark noticed, but what did that mean?

"Were you planning to?" he asked.

She hesitated a moment, shifting in her seat. "No."

He tightened his fingers on the steering wheel. "Why was he offering to move you into your new apartment? Why would an instructor do that?"

Kaia glanced away, then turned to meet his eyes. "I was talking to him after class last week and mentioned I was moving. I never agreed to let him help me."

He wanted to believe her, but the guy was obviously quite familiar with Kaia and was making a move on her. There were probably other guys doing that, too. And Mark didn't like the way she'd introduced him as her cousin. That rankled. But he didn't want to think about it anymore. Besides, he had things of his own he didn't want to discuss, and he felt uneasy about pointing the finger. He should have come out here sooner, with or without an invitation, even though she always seemed so busy with work and classes.

As they drove north, they sat out the hours, talking only now and then about inconsequential things. The scenery along the coast was beautiful, and Mark tried to immerse himself in the sight of the jade-green sea. He realized that he'd missed the sense of its vast openness and the smell of the seaweed in the air. He didn't go to the Maine coast that often, and it was different from the California coast—the northern Atlantic seaboard was more rugged, less hospitable than the Pacific.

For a while they listened to a country-and-western station on the radio, but the lyrics were too sappy; even Johnny Cash was irritating. Too much about lovers cheating on each other. And about loneliness—Mark knew enough about that.

By the time they'd reached Mendocino and found a campground, it was nearly dark and there was a chilly dampness to the breeze. They set up the tent he'd bought on the way up the coast, and laid out the new sleeping bags, zipping them together. The smell of the moist soil and resiny pines made Mark feel calmer, back in his element.

"I'm freezing," Kaia said. "Let's get in the sleeping bag and warm up."

He had no argument with that. They climbed in with their clothes on, and when Kaia moved into his arms, hooking her leg over his waist, all that mattered was holding her and being with her again. They quickly undressed, then Mark pressed her close, the length of her body warm and smooth against him, and they stretched out their lovemaking for as long as they could.

Afterwards they shared a beer, and eventually they both cooled down and had to put their clothes back on, then reclined in the sleeping bag without any talk. Only a short while before, Mark had been so completely focused on the pleasure of making love with Kaia, but now he was starting to feel troubled again. He recalled her flustered look when that guy had approached her, and then her vagueness when she talked about her campus life during the drive up here. Were there other men she went out with? Mark couldn't stand the thought of it. Why couldn't she just come and live with him? But she'd said so many times she loved SF State. And he couldn't move out here to live—he had established his life in northern Maine, and was supporting himself with his furniture making.

"Why didn't you write to me for so long?" Kaia asked all of a sudden, her voice wavering. She raised herself on one elbow, staring at him. "Have you been seeing someone?"

He couldn't lie to her. And she'd probably sensed something, since he hadn't said as much as he might have about the instructor.

"There was someone, but it was nothing."

She sucked in a breath. "Nothing? What's that supposed to mean?"

"It was over almost before it started. Do you really want to hear about it, Kaia?"

He could see her nodding in the dark, her face drawn.

"All right," he said, sighing. "This woman who works at the co-op where I buy my supplies, she was interested, I guess." He remembered how the tall, slender cashier in blue jeans had looked into his eyes, rather meaningfully he thought, while helping him pack his groceries—a task the customers were supposed to handle by themselves. Pretty lonely at the time, he'd liked the thought of female company. He'd been surprised by her obvious interest, especially since she was older; he'd noticed a few strands of silver in her straight black hair. He'd introduced himself and then spontaneously asked her out to lunch, which wasn't like him at all. But he hadn't seen any harm in lunch. Her name was Frida. That was how it had started, anyway, but he certainly wasn't going to tell Kaia any of the details.

"I went out with her a couple of times," he said, "but I couldn't go on with it. It was easy to back off, figuring I was going to find a way to see you." He couldn't tell Kaia that he'd wanted to go to bed with the woman one night but then her teenage son had been home. And after that, Mark just couldn't get into it, thinking about Kaia and how he might be destroying everything they had if he got into a relationship with the woman. The whole episode had poisoned him with guilt.

"What was she like?" Kaia asked sharply.

"In her thirties, nothing out of the ordinary. I didn't care about her, Kaia."

"Don't tell me her name." She lay back down and took a deep breath. "Is that why you haven't been writing?"

"You didn't seem to care whether you saw me or not. I said I'd come out any time you wanted me to, but it seemed like you were always too busy." Mark reached over and touched her arm. "Nothing happened with that woman, Kaia."

An animal scratched in the leaves outside their tent.

"What's that?" Kaia said. They lay still, listening. "Why did we even come here?" she mumbled, and turned onto her side, away from him.

Mark went outside in his socks, taking his boot with him, and stared at the animal, a huge raccoon with its teeth bared, its golden eyes glittering in the moonlight. He heaved the boot, which landed with a thud right in front of the animal. It slunk away in a smooth, unhurried motion, sniffing the ground as it went.

"They'll gnaw holes right through your tent," he told Kaia, once he'd climbed back into the sleeping bag. "Sometimes they carry rabies."

"Great. Now I won't be able to sleep." She was still turned away from him.

"Babe?" he said after a while.

"Hmm?"

He put his hand on her shoulder. "I don't want to see anyone else."

She rolled over to face him. "I don't, either. So we won't. But I don't understand how you could have done that." There was that quiet wistfulness in her voice that always got to him.

"I'm sorry, Kaia. I love you more than anything or anyone."

She peered at him in silence, as if trying to determine whether or not she could believe him, or trust him, and that hurt.

6

Kaia's father was upset, she could tell, when she said a friend was helping her move, but she got off the phone before he could press her for details. Mark spent two more days with her in the city, but then had to leave to get back to the cabin. She began working at her summer job, doing research for another brief in Roberta's case and also working on a new child abandonment case. She tried to keep busy, occasionally having dinner with her father, and going to flea markets or movies with Sig on the weekends. But she was always thinking about Mark.

He flew out again for several perfect days in late August, then fell into a routine of coming every few months, usually when she'd finished her exams, or at the beginning of a term when she hadn't begun to study in earnest. Sometimes he would take her to the inn at Half Moon Bay, which became their special, romantic place, and other times he would stay at her apartment or take her camping, then he would fly back to Maine when she became frantic about classes and work. His visits were the main thing she looked forward to, and savored for a long time afterwards.

Besides her Poli Sci classes, she continued to take law classes in the Paralegal Program. She'd been able to save some money, so Chandi took her shopping for a car one weekend and they found a cheap '72 VW bug convertible, red with a black top. When Mark flew out to see her, they often took drives along the coast or to the wine country. Elisa was the only one who knew about Mark's visits, and she was sworn to secrecy.

Sometimes Kaia would meet a lawyer at work or someone at school who seemed interested in her, but then Mark would call and the sound of his voice would erase any thoughts of going out with another man. Besides, they'd promised each other they wouldn't see other people. In spite of her busy schedule, though, she often felt lonely, especially at night, reading law books in her apartment.

One evening after work, near the end of her second year, she had dinner with Chandi at a small Peruvian restaurant in the Mission District. After a few glasses of beer, the conversation came around to Mark, and it was a relief to be able to talk to Chandi about him. Kaia confessed that she'd been seeing Mark all this time, which didn't seem to surprise Chandi. Kaia told her, in so many words, that she wanted independence, but was drawn to Mark's tendency to permeate every cell of her being.

"Yes, I could see it was like that between you two," Chandi said. "But have you dated other men at all?"

"Not really."

"Why is that?"

"There are only two men in the world who could ever love me so intensely." Kaia was astonished to hear herself say this so smugly, as if it were self-evident. She'd never put it into words before, even in her own mind.

Chandi took a sip of beer, then set it down. "You mean, of course, Mark and your father."

"Yes."

"Could it be," Chandi said carefully, "that you've kept other men at a distance, believing that these are the only men who could love you as deeply?"

Kaia shook her head, feeling rather like a stubborn child, refusing to confess to a small crime of which she was patently guilty.

They continued to talk about men, and finally Chandi said, "Maybe you should give the relationship a real try, Kaia. Spend the summer with Mark, see if it can work out in a practical way. Find out if it can last."

"We can't," she said. "We both have our own work, and besides, Dad would kill me." She knew, too, that staying with Mark for a whole summer would only deepen their relationship and make it nearly impossible for her to return to California. She could never explain to anyone how each time Mark came to visit her it was as if he'd brought her a ripe peach when she was parched and withering away, and had fed it to her in sweet, fragrant slices—how could she ever resist him? Their short visits never seemed enough for either of them. They were completely immersed in each other, forgetting everything else for the few fantastic days they spent together. There was nothing Mark didn't know or sense about her. He remained her incredibly magical man, her sexual shaman.

She just wanted to finish her degree before making any rash moves. And at some level, at least, she knew she was merely postponing a decision about him.

One evening in October of Kaia's junior year, Elisa phoned, full of excitement, inviting her to come for Thanksgiving. Elisa rarely called, and she was in a particularly effusive mood. Without much thought, Kaia accepted. She had savings now and simply wanted to go, in spite of the way she knew her parents would react. Mark would be there, and she would see her aunt and uncle for the first time since Pine Tree. After two and a half years of Mark's sporadic visits—the last one was during the summer—it felt wonderful to write him that she was flying out to Maine to see him and his parents.

"Kaia, this is a terrible idea," her mother said on the phone, after hearing about Elisa's invitation, no doubt from Nico. "Will Mark be there?"

"Of course—he always goes home for Thanksgiving. Are you going to be there, too? I guess that would be awkward."

Her mother was silent, obviously evaluating the subtext in Kaia's remark, and then said, rather huffily, "I won't be there. It would be too much for Elisa to handle a lot of guests."

"A lot of guests? That would be you and me, Mom." It was her imperious mother who would be too much to handle, with her repellent, secret agenda. Even though she hadn't seen her mother in over three years, Kaia didn't want her to be there. It would ruin everything.

Kaia ended the conversation, then screened her calls and refused to respond to her father's irate phone messages during the days prior to her flight. He would never change, never let her out of his radar if he could help it. At least her mother had made no new threats about what she would do if Kaia went to Bangor. Her mother probably wouldn't divulge her own affair with Nico to everyone unless she knew for sure that Kaia was involved with Mark—that was what Kaia kept telling herself, anyway. And it was possible, too, that her mother was no longer involved with Nico. Kaia could only hope—fervently—that this was the case.

Sitting next to Mark in the airport terminal, Elisa felt a bit under the weather as they waited for Kaia to emerge through the gate. The sense of doom had ushered itself in like a drunken party crasher, its arrival triggered several days ago by Nico's booming voice, radiating incredulity and outrage: "But Mark's going to be here, too, isn't he?"

Of course their son would come home for Thanksgiving. Elisa hadn't asked Nico whether it would be a good idea to have their darling niece come for Thanksgiving, and when Elisa told him she'd invited her, Nico had treated her like a troublemaking, unthinking wife, as if she'd gotten them into some truly horrible situation.

But then doomsday had in fact arrived—David calling, and Nico conferring with Jean on the phone as if this were the Cuban missile crisis and bombs were about to be dropped. Jean simply couldn't see the difference between something that was sordid and something that was exquisitely beautiful. Of course Jean and Nico had no idea Mark was still seeing Kaia; they were just afraid something would start up again between the two cousins. Poor wrongheaded Nico, pacing the upstairs hallway late last night, then conspiring on the phone with Jean.

Elisa tugged at Mark's sleeve when she caught sight of Kaia walking through the gate. Her niece's face opened like a poppy in the sun when she spotted them. It cheered Elisa, seeing the loveliness of Kaia's smile and the same joyful anticipation in Mark's eyes. He'd been under such a strain since his arrival two days ago, her strong, handsome son, his expression pinched when his eyes met his father's, the two men always in opposition. If only they would see things the same way. How sad it was to see such a paucity of affection—what an utter waste.

And now Kaia in her wool coat was hugging Elisa, and then embracing her brawny cousin, kissing him on the lips, and again it lifted Elisa's spirits. She truly didn't mind sharing her son with Kaia; she could almost see herself handing him over to Kaia for safekeeping, his happiness preserved like pristine water in a well.

Mark drove with Elisa in the back seat of her tiny, red Cavalier, the two cousins murmuring in the front, their utter joy and contentment palpable. But after the initial excitement of Kaia's arrival, Elisa sighed, starting to feel down in the dumps again. If only this dense pressure would disappear, she thought, this heavy mass impinging slowly on her like a wall of clay. It must be like death—being unable to escape its nauseating clutches, its suffocating entrapment. It had to be a bad batch of medicine, the Lithium not working anymore, failing to bring that bright state she welcomed as her own version of sanity.

Then Mark swerved rather quickly into the inky wet driveway, aware no doubt of Nico waiting for them with his hard stance and furrowed brow. It was raining now, the cool drops splashing onto Elisa as Mark gently helped her out of the car. Perhaps he sensed the riptide pulling her under, though she'd hardly been drinking at all. Most of the time she was too spent to even pour herself a glass.

Nico met them in the foyer, his hands shoved down his pants pockets, and Elisa could see him trying to contain his impulse to take Kaia tightly in his arms—their shining niece, older now, a grown woman. He drew Kaia into the living room with his arm around her shoulder as Elisa trailed behind, the cat scampering alongside uncle and niece, trying to work its way between them.

Nico had made a fire, and oakwood smoke wafted through the air. They sat in the room lit by a single lamp and flickering flames, no one wanting to stir up the fire to a brighter glow, all of them perhaps preferring the dimness. Nico refused to look at Elisa except for an occasional glance, and hardly looked at their son. Kaia was the only one with much to say, telling them about her studies and her apartment in San Francisco. Such a dear.

Elisa felt she'd done enough, no longer able to abide the undercurrent of Nico's resentment—as if it were such a terrible thing to invite Kaia here while Mark was at home. Elisa stood and announced she was going to bed, and they all stared at her in silence for a few moments before saying their goodnights. Fine, let them figure out the next step. She hadn't the wherewithal to decide anything.

Mark leaned against the kitchen counter, sipping the strong coffee he'd brewed. He heard the water go on upstairs, and then the sound of knocking pipes behind the walls—probably Kaia taking a shower. He wished he could join her up there. Last night Nico had brought blankets and a pillow into the den for Kaia, and twenty minutes later she'd come upstairs. What a farce. But at least, Mark thought, he'd had Kaia to himself all night.

Elisa drifted into the kitchen in her yellow robe, her face a sickly white, her hair hanging unkempt around her shoulders.

"I was about to start the turkey," Mark said. "Didn't you buy one, Mom? And the rest of the stuff?"

"I didn't. I'm so sorry, darling."

"But Dad said you went shopping yesterday."

"I only got food for dinner last night. That was all I could manage. I didn't really see the point of lugging all those other things home. Food doesn't matter so much, does it?" She sank into a chair at the table.

Mark recalled the other haphazard holiday meals they'd had in the past when his mother was feeling down. But why hadn't his father done anything about it this time, especially with Kaia here for her first Thanksgiving with them? And why hadn't Nico called the doctor? Elisa obviously wasn't doing well.

"There must be a market open somewhere," Mark said. "Kaia and I can go."

"Yes, good idea." Elisa sighed.

Mark went over to the table and sat down next to her. "Have you been taking your Lithium, Mom?"

She shook her head. "It doesn't work."

"It only works if you take it every day." He reached over and squeezed her hand, and she began to cry, putting her head down onto her arm on the table.

"I took one just now," she mumbled. "But it doesn't do anything for me."

"Should I call Dr. Sandburg, then?"

"No. He doesn't care a fig about me. I just need to sleep." She turned her head toward him, still resting it on her arm, her eyes pink, the skin under them swollen. "Your father gets up at night and—" She stopped, shutting her eyes tightly.

"What, Mom? What's going on?" He said this as quietly as he could, but he felt the old anger toward his father rising in his chest. Mark was unable to forgive him for the way he treated her—the womanizing, especially, and then keeping her supplied with alcohol when it was the worst thing for her.

"He makes phone calls downstairs late at night, and then of course I can never sleep." She continued to cry softly.

"Tell him to stop doing it, Mom. And I'll tell him, too."

In the next moment, Nico stood in the doorway. Mark hated the way he stood there scowling at them.

"You can see your mother is overwrought," Nico said. He came over, placing his hand on her back, and bent to kiss her cheek, but she recoiled, turning her head away.

"Don't speak of me as if I weren't here," she said in a faint, hopeless tone. "I just need some sleep, with you prowling around the house all night."

Nico frowned but said nothing.

Mark wondered if his mother had heard Kaia climbing the stairs. And had his parents heard their lovemaking? So what? Nico probably knew the situation, and Elisa wouldn't mind.

"You should rest, Mom." Mark stood up, taking her arm gently and easing her out of her chair, and she sagged against him. He started up the stairs with her and when he glanced up, he saw Kaia coming down, her hair dripping wet.

"Mom just needs to lie down," he said.

"Dry your hair, dear," Elisa said to Kaia. "There's a blow dryer—" She dropped her gaze, as if trying hard to remember something.

"Thanks, Elisa. I'll find it." Kaia threw Mark a stricken look.

"I'll be downstairs in a while," he said as he passed her.

In the bedroom, Elisa took off her robe and immediately started shivering in her flannel nightgown as she climbed into bed. Hopefully she would just slip into one of her trancelike sleeps. Sometimes after sleeping she would awaken from a state like this one, having forgotten her sadness and whatever had caused it. He pulled the covers up to her chin. She appeared even paler now, her skin moist, her red hair silvery at the roots.

He kissed her on the forehead. "I'll turn up the heat when I go downstairs. Kaia and I will cook. I love you, Mom."

Turning off the light, he headed out of the room, leaving the door open in case she called for him.

*

Kaia stood at Elisa's kitchen window, peering out at the steel-dark clouds. It was raining again, more heavily now than earlier, drenching the trees and lawn. Hearing footsteps, she turned to see Mark escorting his mother into the dining room. Elisa was still in her robe, but her hair was brushed, her face calm, though lined with fatigue. Mark helped her into a chair at the table.

Kaia went to take the roast out of the oven. She and Mark had found a neighborhood market open, but there were only a few turkeys, frozen solid as granite. So they had bought a roast instead, along with Lipton's dried onion soup to make gravy, a Mrs. Smith's peach pie, and a few other things.

"This isn't enough," Kaia had told Mark in the store. She'd wanted to create a feast that would rejuvenate Elisa's spirits and make everyone happy. But Mark had assured her it would be all right.

Now the two of them carried the platters of food into the dining room and seated themselves. Nico came to the table with a bottle of red wine and three glasses in his hands. He had been drinking Scotch in the living room during the afternoon, and his face was flushed. He opened the wine bottle while Mark lit the two candles in the centerpiece. Elisa peered into the flames and crossed herself, a limp gesture.

Nico lifted the bottle in Kaia's direction, winking at her. She shook her head, then he cast a glance at Mark, but Mark ignored him. Nico filled a glass to the brim, sat down and took a drink. Kaia passed the rolls to Elisa, who took one and placed it gingerly on her bread plate. Kaia nudged the butter dish toward her, and Elisa turned to her with a startled smile, then bent her head and concentrated on buttering the bun.

Mark took a slice of the roast and passed the platter to his dad. The meat smelled of onions and sat in a pool of greasy broth.

"This is certainly a novelty for Thanksgiving," Nico said, maneuvering a slab of the juicy, pink beef onto his plate. He turned to Kaia. "This looks good, sweetheart."

Embarrassed, Kaia managed a tight smile. He was her uncle as well as her mother's lover, Elisa's husband, and Mark's father. She had no idea how to relate to him—she wasn't sure whether to resent him, love him, or just tolerate him. She wasn't even sure whether Mark cared about his father, and she often wondered if Mark knew about Nico and her mother. Kaia had little appetite for dinner, and wished she could be alone with Mark instead of caught in this confusing situation. She helped herself to a potato and a spoonful of sour cream. It was lucky that her mother wasn't here to criticize the plain food as well as everything else that was going on—it would only have made things worse.

They finished passing the dishes around, helping themselves, and began eating, the only sound the clinking of silverware against the delicate white china.

"So I gather you're thinking about going to law school, Kaia," Nico said after a minute or two.

"Yes, I'm thinking about it."

Mark frowned at his father. "Kaia hasn't decided yet for sure."

Kaia had told Mark she'd applied for law school, but of course he didn't like the idea of her staying in California; he said it would only keep them apart longer. And of course it would, but she needed to have work she cared about, and there were no law schools in the wilds of northern Maine. She kept hoping he'd make his way back to California, although she wasn't sure how that could come about, since Mark loved living on the land in Maine and seemed ill at ease in the city these days. And he was starting to get some significant income from his carpentry business. They were barely able to discuss it without getting into an argument.

Nico glowered at Mark. "Since Kaia has told us all about it, it seems to me it's an open topic of conversation." He turned to

Kaia. "Your mother tells me you've been working on some cases with this Indian lady."

Kaia bristled at the way he'd referred to Chandi. "Her name is Chandi Gupta. She's one of the top attorneys in her field. We've been representing a farmworker whose kids were taken away from her by the county." Kaia didn't want to explain that they'd lost the appeal and were hoping the Cal Supreme would hear the case.

Elisa gasped. "How terrible."

"I'm working on some other cases, too."

The phone rang in the kitchen, the sound reverberating throughout the dining room, and Elisa dropped her knife onto her plate. After several rings, she scraped her chair back.

"Let it go," Nico said sharply.

Elisa started to rise, her lips twisted in annoyance.

Nico got up and bolted for the kitchen. "Never mind. I'll get it."

He picked up the receiver, then walked further into the kitchen, out of everyone's line of sight.

"Hello," he said in a low voice. There was a pause, then he said in a louder voice, "Oh, yes, she's here—we're just having a terrific dinner that Kaia fixed." Another pause. "All right, just a minute."

He appeared in the doorway, the receiver pressed against his chest, staring at Kaia, and mouthed the words "your father."

She shook her head briskly.

He put the phone back to his ear. "Could she call you later, after we've finished our dinner?" A moment later, he pressed the receiver to his chest. "He says it's urgent. He wants to speak to you now."

Kaia got up and strode over to Nico. He cupped her shoulder as he handed her the receiver.

She greeted her father in an irritated tone.

"How could you just fly across the country like that without even talking to me about it?" he demanded, slurring his words.

"Happy Thanksgiving to you, too, Dad."

"What's going on, Kaia?"

"This is stupid." She kept her voice low. "You're not even sober."

"Sure as hell am," he snarled. "Anyway, you have to come home now, Kaia."

"I can't do that right at the moment. Why don't you just leave me alone?"

"Don't talk to me that way. You're just going to have to live at home and commute to campus if you're going to behave like this. You obviously can't be trusted to live on your own."

"Don't be ridiculous. I'm hanging up now, Dad. Good-bye."

Before she reached the dining room table, the phone rang again, and she returned to the kitchen and unplugged it. Another phone continued to ring upstairs.

"Old man's upset, hey?" Nico appeared slyly pleased as she walked past him to her chair.

She sat down, letting out a long breath. "You could say that."

Mark raised his eyebrows at her.

"It's all right," she said. "I'll deal with it."

Nico lifted his glass and winked at her with that familiar glint in his eye. "I'm sure you will, sweetheart."

By evening Elisa was feeling better—at last her Lithium was taking effect. She was reading in bed when the phone rang, and she grabbed the receiver just as Nico was saying hello.

"Hi, Nico." Jean's voice was low and intimate.

Elisa sat up stiffly in bed. "Hello, Jean," she said curtly.

"Oh, Elisa," Jean said in a brighter tone.

"Yes, it's me, and I'm wondering why you keep calling, and so late at night." Elisa had surprised herself with the strong note in her own voice. Mark was right, she didn't have to put up with Nico's phone calls, and her devious sister's intervention.

"Naturally I'm worried about Kaia. I hope you've been keeping an eye on her and Mark."

"Why are you so worried about that?"

"There, you see, it's never been useful to talk to you about the situation," Jean said with exasperation. "Nico, are you still there?"

"I'm still here," he grumbled.

"Really, Elisa," Jean said, "it was misguided, to say the least, to have Kaia stay with you while Mark's at home."

"Nothing's going on with the two of them," Nico said.

Why was he lying, Elisa wondered. He had to know that Kaia and Mark couldn't possibly stay apart when they had a chance to be together.

"I'm thinking of flying up to Bangor tomorrow," Jean said, "to see Kaia before she returns to California."

"Just stay away," Elisa said, her voice rising. "And don't call Nico anymore. We're in control of things."

"Are you?" her sister said. "I don't think so."

"Stop calling. Good-bye, Jean."

"Well, all right, we can talk more in the morning." Jean spoke with that horrid condescension Elisa hated.

"I'll just be a minute longer, Elisa," Nico said.

"No, Nico. Hang up now." Elisa got out of bed and paced back and forth a few steps with the receiver in her hand.

"Fine," he said, "we'll talk tomorrow."

"No you won't," Elisa said.

Jean gasped, then there was a click on the line.

"Nico?" Elisa said. There was only Jean's unmistakable breathing.

Elisa slammed the receiver down and stood there, shaky but triumphant as she heard Nico's footsteps coming up the stairs to her.

*

Around eleven that evening, Kaia was tiptoeing down the hall to Mark's room when her uncle emerged from his room in his bathrobe. He came over to her and placed his hands on her shoulders. In a strained voice he said, “This can’t go on, Kaia. We all love you, but you can’t be with Mark in this way.”

She tried to pull away, but he held on to her.

“There’s a lot you don’t know,” he said.

“Actually, I do know.” She was shivering, but stared directly into his eyes. “Let go of me, Nico.”

His eyebrows shot up and he kept his hold on her in the dark hallway for another couple of seconds, his stale wine breath blowing into her face. Then he released her. She strode toward Mark’s room and entered without looking back, and firmly shut the door.

7

In late January, Kaia found the trial transcripts for a new case on her desk at the office. The client was a schizophrenic whose wife had died and whose legal rights to his young children had been severed by the county. As she read the transcripts, Kaia found herself completely absorbed in the facts of the case. She asked Chandi if they could go back to the trial court to request supervised visits for their client so that he could see his children during the interminable appeal process, so that the kids would at least know their father. And maybe their client would get better, she argued, with the right psychiatric treatment.

"It's a little late to ask for visitation now," Chandi said, "and these types of requests are rarely granted while an appeal is pending. But I suppose we could try."

Still hopeful of success, Kaia drafted and filed the motion, then waited for the Court to decide. A month later the request was summarily denied. Maybe, Kaia thought, if they'd been able to represent the children instead of only their father, the Court would have paid more attention. She felt sorry for the young kids, living in foster care, their only surviving parent mentally ill and unable to see them. But there was nothing to be done except to go through the lengthy appeal process.

Kaia was about to finish her paralegal certificate and hardly felt like a college student anymore. Her legal skills were sharpening, and she threw herself into last-minute research for the hearing on Roberta's case in the California Supreme Court. Chandi had convinced her friend Bruce Fields, a newscaster from the local CBS affiliate, to do a special report on the case for the news hour. It was an important case, since the Court appeared to be interested in the issue of legal representation for children in abandonment and neglect cases. Bruce was going to interview Chandi in front of the courthouse the day before the hearing, and Kaia thought this would be a great opportunity to have Roberta on the air, telling her story.

Chandi didn't think that was such a great idea. "Maybe you could say a few words about Roberta's case on camera," she told Kaia, "but you never know what Roberta might come up with. There probably won't be time to prep her, even if she does show up."

For the interview, Kaia wore a tailored, slate-blue dress she'd picked up on sale at I. Magnin, and Chandi showed up in a dazzling white pantsuit and expensive gold jewelry. Bruce and his cameraman were waiting for them outside the courthouse, but Kaia didn't see Roberta, even though she'd left several phone messages for her.

Bruce was an attractive man in his thirties with an affable smile. Before he started the on-camera interview in front of the courthouse steps, he asked Kaia a few questions about her role in the case, and Chandi told him about Kaia's research skills and her passionate interest in Roberta's case over the past three years.

"We'd better start shooting if this is going to make the six o'clock news," Bruce said finally.

On camera, he asked Chandi about the case and the legal issues involved, and she began discussing the constitutional rights of children who had been abandoned by their parents.

Roberta suddenly appeared, towering over Kaia. "I didn't abandon my children," she said loudly.

Chandi continued to speak, ignoring their client's outburst.

"I want to say something," Roberta said.

Kaia took Roberta's arm and led her a couple of steps forward. This was Roberta's case, and she had a right to voice her feelings about losing her kids. "Our client has something to say," Kaia whispered to Bruce.

He glanced over his shoulder at Roberta, who was dressed in jeans and a stained sweatshirt, her greasy hair pulled back in a ponytail.

"Thank you, Ms. Gupta," he said to Chandi, signaling for the camera to turn back to him, "and now we have the mother, Roberta Barrett, who has lost all her rights to her children, and Kaia Matheson, a legal assistant who has been working diligently on the case."

As the camera swung toward Roberta, Kaia saw Chandi's dark eyes widening in surprise.

"Ms. Matheson, I understand your client has something she would like to say," Bruce said into the mike, then held it out to Kaia.

"Yes, well, this is Roberta Barrett," Kaia said, handing her the microphone.

Roberta removed her sunglasses and squinted towards the camera. "I just want to say that I never abandoned my kids. I left them with relatives so I could make some money workin' in the fields. They wasn't with strangers or nothin' like that. The judge just called it a foster home. And he didn't want us to be on welfare, neither, so I had to work like he told me, and that's what my socialworker kept tellin' me to do, too, so I drove with my boyfriend up north to pick cherries. And now I'm cleanin' motel rooms so I can earn money for my kids. I hardly ever get to see them, and I hope my lawyers can do somethin' about it. I just want my kids back."

Out of breath, Roberta glanced at Kaia, and Bruce took the microphone, tilting it toward Kaia.

"Ms. Matheson, do you have anything to add?"

Kaia took the mike. "We're trying to get a new trial, so that there will be adequate representation for Roberta's children, all of whom have expressed their desire to live with their mother. Roberta Barrett has not abandoned her children; that is a legal fiction. She's taken care of them the best she could while working in the fields. We can't turn back the clock and give our client the time she's lost with her children during this long appeal, but we are hoping to convince the Court to give her another chance to regain custody of them in the near future."

"Thank you, Ms. Matheson, Ms. Barrett, and Ms. Gupta." Bruce said. "I wish you the very best of luck." With that the cameraman turned off the glaring lights and started packing up his gear.

Chandi walked over to them. "You took a chance, Kaia," she said sharply.

"I'm glad we got some of the human side," Bruce said. "It was a pleasure meeting you, Kaia, and you, too, Roberta." He bowed slightly as he shook their hands. "Thanks, Chandi. I've got to run so we can get this on the air."

Luckily Chandi wasn't overly upset about Roberta's part in the interview and conceded it might even be helpful in focusing attention on the case. At six p.m., she and Kaia went into the office lounge and turned on the TV news, joined by a couple of law students. Bruce had cut down Chandi's legal discussion, but aired all of Roberta's and Kaia's comments; the entire piece lasted no more than three or four minutes. When it ended with the camera on Kaia's face, the law students clapped and cheered.

"Well done, Kaia," Chandi said, smiling graciously. "That actually sounded quite good."

8

Finally Kaia's mother wanted to see her. It was mid-June and classes were over; her mother had phoned one evening and invited her to fly to New York for a few days' visit in early July. Kaia was shocked. It was several long years since she'd seen her mother. Even though there had been sporadic phone calls, the invitation seemed to be out of the blue, and Kaia wondered why her mother suddenly had the urge to see her.

Kaia caught her breath and said, "I'm working full-time this summer, Mom. I'm not sure I can take any time off."

"I was hoping you could be here for just a couple of days." Was that a rare note of wistfulness in her mother's voice?

Kaia sighed. "I suppose I could talk to Chandi about it."

"Good. Call me back and I'll buy your ticket."

After Kaia hung up, she realized she might be able to see Mark while she was back East. She got approval from Chandi for a few days off, quickly decided on a date, then wrote to Mark, asking if he could come to see her in New York one day while her mother was at the office, and telling him she could only spend a couple of days there before she had to get back to work.

The day before her flight, Kaia received a short note from Mark: "I won't be coming to New York. A few hours just won't do it for me."

Kaia had thought for sure he would come to see her, and his abrupt note felt like a physical blow. She couldn't bear the thought of not seeing him, and figured she would have to find a way to contact him from New York.

After the long, tiring flight, her mother picked her up at JFK in her silver Mercedes coupe, waiting in the loading zone with the engine running. When Kaia climbed into the passenger seat, her mother was listening with close attention to the news on the radio. It was commentary on the Equal Rights Amendment, which had just failed in its final vote.

"Three votes short," her mother fumed, then leaned over to give Kaia a peck on the cheek before driving on.

After they arrived at the condo, her mother paced around the living room in her high heels, gesticulating with her glass of Chardonnay and railing about the defeat of the ERA. "We only needed three more damned states. Can you believe it?" Her voice resonated in the cathedral-ceilinged apartment with its plate-glass windows.

Kaia had now been at the white-on-white condo, drinking wine, for half an hour and was dying to elevate her feet to the glass coffee table, but dared not. Her stomach was gurgling, and she felt lightheaded and irritable.

"This sounds like a personal failure for you, Mom."

"Of course it is," her mother said with a puzzled frown. "It should be considered a personal failure in the way it impacts every woman."

Kaia cast a pointed glance at her watch. It was now nine p.m. here on the East Coast. "I'm hungry, Mom. What's in the fridge?" Possibly her mother had already eaten.

"I'd forgotten about dinner." Her mother shook her head absently as she seated herself in her ivory leather armchair and drank her wine. "We'll go out and get something to eat in a bit."

Kaia noted that her mother had gained weight, and her short brown hair was dull from too many dyeings. She wore an orange silk blouse, a linen blazer, and a beige skirt that was too short for her. She probably had no time to exercise. Recently when Kaia had asked her over the phone if she still played tennis, her mother had laughed. "That's a California thing," she'd said. Maybe, Kaia thought now, it was acceptable to be pudgy if you dressed expensively enough.

"And there's Phyllis Schlafly," her mother went on, "an activist with a law degree, making speeches all over the country, and then proclaiming the holiness of being a housewife."

Kaia took a sip of her wine. "That is rather ironic, isn't it."

"The point is that women can work, even with a child. They just need adequate day care."

"Or husbands who can spend time with their kids."

"Yes, exactly. As in the case of your father." She took a sip of her drink. "Fortunately he was able to contribute."

Irritated at her mother's dismissiveness, Kaia looked away, scanning the room. Not a single photograph. Not the slightest reminder of the family or their past. Just a huge, framed Lichtenstein print in stark primary colors and black-and-white stripes. Her mother had been enamored with his work ever since she'd seen it exhibited at SFMOMA some years ago and had bought a couple of posters with reproductions; the clean edges and two-dimensionality seemed to appeal to her. But now her mother could apparently afford a real Lichtenstein. Kaia had never liked Pop Art and had never appreciated his work, especially the images taken from the comics: the women's faces with their red lips, the eyes with their cool, pained expression, the flat cartoonish backgrounds.

"I haven't eaten in hours, Mom," she said again, this time in a more accusatory tone. The extremely dry wine seemed to be corroding her extremely empty stomach.

"There's a darling bistro just down the street. We can walk."

"Great." Kaia forced a smile. "I wouldn't mind seeing a little of Manhattan."

"Tonight will be a start. Tomorrow I'll have to go to the office to check up on a few things, but I won't be there too long." She smiled. "I have some ideas for you, some sightseeing you could do in the morning."

Kaia felt her face flush. She'd hoped, foolishly, that her mother wouldn't feel compelled to work as much as usual during their visit. And Mark had refused to see her here. She never should have come to New York.

*

The next morning Kaia found a lukewarm pot of coffee in the kitchen. Her mother had left a note:

> Kaia,
>
> I'm so sorry, but I got a phone call from the office about an emergency that has come up. Escrow is on the brink of falling through on a big commercial account. I have to be there all day to see this through. I'll be back this evening and we can go out for dinner.
>
> Love, Mom

It was their relationship that was on the brink of falling through completely, Kaia thought. A dozen twenties were fanned out on the gleaming countertop next to a list of sights Kaia could take in via taxi or subway. The nauseating display of cash hurt the most—as if money could compensate for the lack of her mother's company. Kaia figured the money was meant for two days' worth of sightseeing. But in a way it was what Kaia had expected, or had feared would happen, in any event.

After staring blankly at the smoggy cityscape through the wide picture window for a few minutes, Kaia tried reading the *Times*. Fifteen minutes later, unable to focus on anything in the news, she went out, found a taxi and headed for Central Park. She started with the zoo, as her mother had suggested, stopping to watch the penguins, polar bears and tigers, but she felt sorry for the animals in their cramped quarters. She wandered along a path and climbed to the top of the castle, taking in the impressive vista of the park and the soaring buildings beyond.

By noon it had become muggy and oppressive. Kaia sat down with a hot dog and absently watched boaters on the lake for half an hour while daydreaming about Mark, then headed back to the condo to take a nap.

That evening she had a late dinner with her mother at a Chinese restaurant. When the waiter came, Kaia was surprised that her mother ordered Tsingtao beers for both of them—Kaia was only twenty.

"The drinking age is eighteen in New York," her mother explained, no doubt catching Kaia's puzzled look. "You would absolutely love everything about New York. Why don't you apply to law school out here? The best schools are on the East Coast, you know."

"Why would I want to do that? So I could live in the same city as you and never see you?"

"I'm sorry about today, Kaia, but—"

"Anyway, I love San Francisco. And I have a good job there."

Her mother blew out an exasperated breath, studying Kaia's face. "There are good jobs everywhere. You should try some place new. Maybe you'd even meet a nice guy out here."

"There are nice guys everywhere, Mom."

"I know a young loan officer you could meet—"

"No, Mother."

"I just thought we might all have dinner together. He's eager to meet you."

"I'm not interested in meeting anyone and I'm not going to live in New York. I came here to see you." Kaia paused. "Is that why you invited me to visit, to have me meet this guy?"

Her mother shook her head brusquely. "I just thought it was something that might entertain you while you're enjoying the city." Her mother sounded a bit deflated. "Everything in New York is so exciting—wonderful people, great museums, so much to do. It's up to you, Kaia."

When they returned to the condo, the phone was ringing, and her mother picked it up in the kitchen. "Jean Stillworth."

When had her mother gone back to her maiden name?

A moment later, her mother said, "Oh, hello," in a sharp tone. "Yes, she is." She tapped with her lacquered nails on the kitchen counter, her mouth a snarl. A moment later she said harshly into the receiver, "You shouldn't be calling here."

Her heartbeat accelerating, Kaia strode across the room and grabbed the receiver. "I'd like to talk privately," she said, her face so close to her mother's that Kaia could smell her scented face powder.

With a theatrical sigh, her mother stalked into her bedroom and shut the door.

"Kaia, it's me." Mark sounded oddly subdued.

"I know. I'm so happy to hear your voice." Her throat felt constricted. "I wish I could have told you earlier I was flying out here, but Mom just invited me two weeks ago."

"Did you get my note?"

"Yes. You sounded rather angry."

Mark was silent for a few seconds, then said, "Look, Kaia, why don't you come up here for a couple of weeks? Just take some time off."

"I can't, Mark. I'm flying back in two days. I have to get back to work—there are deadlines. Chandi didn't even want me to leave right now. I'm really sorry."

There was a long silence, and she realized, unhappily, that she sounded like her mother, with her busy agenda. But it was impossible to stay out here any longer.

"Kaia?"

"What?"

"When are you going to start taking us seriously?"

"Oh, Mark," she sighed. She wanted to be right next to him then, instead of hundreds of miles away.

"Just think about what you're doing, Kaia." He hung up.

She hadn't even had a chance to tell him how much she loved him. She was wiping the tears from her face when her mother emerged from her room and came over to Kaia.

"So you're still in touch with Mark," she said in a low, confidential tone, as if she thought this would make Kaia spill out all of her secrets.

"It's no one else's business, Mom. And what's happening with Nico, by the way?"

Her mother merely stared at her.

"I think I'll go to bed now. Good night, Mother." Kaia went to the guest bedroom and shut the door.

After taking in a few more sights the next day while her mother was at the office, Kaia met her for dinner again. Kaia was getting the impression that her mother never cooked. Kaia realized, looking back on it, that her mother had never done much cooking. She seemed to think food preparation was part of the enslavement of women.

Her mother said nothing more about Mark's phone call. It must have taken an effort. Maybe she was satisfied that Kaia was flying back to California and would soon be far away, out of Mark's reach.

The following morning, Kaia found a note from her mother with another pile of cash saying she had a meeting and couldn't take her to the airport. Even though it was predictable, Kaia was furious. Why had she bothered to come out here at all? Had her mother just invited her out of some kind of belated guilt? Or was it because of the loan officer she wanted Kaia to meet?

At eleven-thirty, Kaia was dressed with her bag packed when the mail cascaded through the slot in the front door. She picked up the envelopes and magazines, looking for something to read, and stood leafing through a *Time* magazine. Then, when she threw the mail on the dining room table, she noticed a white envelope with "N. Karadonis" in the top left corner and a realty office return address in Bangor. Her mother's name and address were scrawled in plain, masculine handwriting. Kaia ripped open the envelope and read the letter quickly:

> Jean,
>
> As I've said countless times, don't call me at home. Elisa gets upset when I take calls downstairs late at night. If we just wait a few more months, things should settle down. I'm sure Mark won't be seeing Kaia anymore. Soon we may not have to worry about a risky situation arising, and especially the possibility you keep mentioning.
>
> I'll try to meet you in Portland or Boston the weekend after next. I can probably drum up some business there. I'll call you from my office.
>
> Nico

Kaia sat down at the table, her stomach tight. What was this possibility he was talking about? That she and Mark would live together, or marry, or that she would get pregnant? And what was suddenly so risky about the situation? Elisa's mental health and happiness had always been in jeopardy.

Kaia knew she couldn't pretend any longer that things would turn out all right. This was hard evidence that her mother and Nico were still involved and making plans for the future. How could they? They had no right. It made Kaia sick to think about what might happen next.

She walked into the kitchen and phoned for a taxi. She didn't even feel ashamed about reading the letter. Opening someone's mail was minor compared to what Nico and her mother were doing. She tore up the letter and stuffed it into the bottom of the garbage can, then headed outside to wait at the curb.

9

When the phone rang at the office one November afternoon, Kaia picked up the receiver and stretched the cord to its full length as she walked over to the window.

"Kaia Matheson," she said. Twelve stories below, a dark-haired woman with a brief case was climbing out of a taxi on Market Street—it took a second or two for Kaia to realize it was Chandi.

"It's me, babe," Mark said.

The mere sound of his voice gave Kaia a plummeting sensation, as if she were parachuting out of an airplane. She leaned her forehead against the glass, absorbing its cool, refrigerated feel.

"Where are you?" she asked.

"In Beaulieu."

Disappointed that he wasn't at the San Francisco airport for a surprise visit, she sat down at the desk and took a deep breath.

"I thought I'd fly out next week, in time to celebrate your birthday," he said.

Her breath caught at the thought of seeing him, but in the next moment she wondered how she could manage to take any time off, with all the legal work she'd been assigned and her mid-terms coming up.

She let out her breath. "That's wonderful." It was what she wanted more than anything, she realized, in spite of everything else.

"I told you I'd come."

It was true; in a recent letter he had mentioned coming out for her twenty-first birthday. She leaned back in her swivel chair, raising her stockinged feet to her desk. "What am I going to do with you?"

"You know what to do with me, Kaia. You can tell me to go to hell if you want to."

"I would never do that."

He was silent for a moment, then said, "I should go. I know you've got important things to do."

"I'm so glad you're coming, Mark."

"November 15. I've already got my ticket. See you, babe." There was a click at the other end.

Mark wasn't flying to California because of her birthday, she was sure of that. He didn't believe in rituals. They just loved each other, that was it. It had simply been too long, and they needed to see each other.

She heard a rap on the door and turned to see Chandi in her chic, mocha-toned suit standing in the doorway.

"Hey, congratulations," Chandi said.

"Oh, right. Thanks." The promotion. Ever since Kaia had earned her paralegal certificate last June, Chandi had been lobbying for a raise for Kaia, and it had finally been approved.

Chandi sat down with a smile that showcased her implausibly white teeth. "You deserve it."

"Thanks. By the way, I've sent in my application to UC Hastings."

"Good for you. I'm sure you'll get in." Chandi sat back in her chair. "Actually, I'm hoping you'll have time to prepare some pre-trial motions for Roberta's case."

"But I've got other deadlines coming up." And Mark, she thought, arriving next week.

"I can reassign one of your cases. I know you want to do more trial preparation, and you've been so invested in Roberta's case."

Kaia sighed. "I'm still hoping that by some miracle we'll get her kids back for her after all this time." The Cal Supreme had sent the case back to the trial court, but now they faced the most difficult part—convincing the judge that Roberta should have her children back.

Chandi lifted an elegant, dark brow. "I hope you're right."

"Roberta's still seeing her boyfriend, Miguel, at the jail," Kaia said. "I talked to her last week."

"We're going to have to keep him out of the picture at trial, or she's going to lose again. Hanging around with a car thief won't help her case."

"All for the love of Miguel," Kaia said, sighing.

"Could be a country-western song." Chandi grinned as she turned away, and then left Kaia's office.

It was amazing how Chandi could keep her objectivity. For some reason, this case had gotten to Kaia. She still wondered what might have caused Roberta to drive off in a stolen car with her lover to pick cherries in another state, leaving her children behind. Obviously Roberta wasn't too smart when it came to grasping long-term consequences. And what if she did get her kids back? Would she wind up abandoning them again? Not all mothers could be counted on, as Kaia was well aware. She had always been sure that when she had her own children, she would be absolutely devoted to them. Lately she'd been noticing a lot of pregnant women walking around—and also a lot of cute, radiant babies in strollers, right out there on the street.

She sat for a long time, wondering what to do about Mark. All she could think of was the way his eyes looked when he smiled at her and the dusty scent of the old denim jacket he was wearing the last time she'd seen him—too many months ago.

*

"I'm here," Mark said on the phone. "I'll rent a car and drive to your office."

"Good, because my car's in the shop. I've been taking the bus."

"I'll be there soon."

Something in his voice had the ring of disappointment. She wished she'd been there when he got off the plane.

"I can't wait to see you," she said softly. "Just honk from the street—it's hard to find parking around here."

Barely an hour later, as she rounded a corner in the hallway, Mark came striding toward her, dressed in his denims and old boots.

Kaia rushed toward him, her heart knocking around like an engine that was seriously out of whack. She swung her finger to her lips, then kissed him on the cheek. She didn't want Chandi to know she was cutting out early, or that Mark was here. She wasn't sure if Chandi had any contact with her father—if she did, she might slip and say something about Mark's visit.

Mark had parked in a loading zone, and when they got into the car, he drove without speaking, apparently concentrating on navigating through the rush-hour traffic as Kaia directed him to a pub she knew. After finding a parking place, they went in and headed for a booth in the back. Mark ordered a beer for himself and a glass of wine for Kaia, then scanned the crowded room.

He finally looked into her face. "When are you going to stop treating me like your dirty secret, Kaia?"

"I'm sorry, Mark. I just didn't want Chandi to know you were here."

"Why not? She's not even seeing your dad anymore."

"I think they might talk once in a while."

"You're turning twenty-one. You can do anything you want."

Kaia let out a sigh. "My dad would disown me if he knew I was seeing you. Anyway, what I want and what I can have are two different things."

He paused, scrutinizing her face. "What is it you want so much?"

She hesitated. "A child," she said after a few seconds. "At some point."

"I've always known that, Kaia. You've always talked about it. And of course we can do that. I'd love it if you had my baby."

She looked around the darkened room, then back at him. "We can't, Mark."

He stared at her for a moment, then said, "Cousins marry and have babies everywhere in the world, Kaia. It's not a big deal." He leaned forward and took her hand. "It would be *fine.*"

Her eyes moistened, and she squeezed his hand. Marriage. Mark's baby. It seemed like a dream. Was it even possible?

Their drinks arrived, and they ordered burgers. Kaia took a long sip of her Chardonnay. Sometimes she was smitten with an almost physical yearning to hold a tiny infant in her arms. What she wanted, fundamentally, was to have Mark's child; she wanted it to be *theirs.* She tried to imagine herself in the cabin, a baby nestling against her shoulder while she tended to the bread in the oven. Could she possibly live with Mark in Beaulieu? Maybe take the Maine bar exam? But besides the possibility of a genetic mishap, there was the whole family opposition, like a glacier that would never melt. She wondered if she would really be able to cut herself off from everyone in that way.

Mark didn't say how long he would be staying, and she didn't ask. He was never one to carry much baggage, but in mid-November there was no reason for him to return to northern Maine any time soon, with the snow and subzero temperatures rolling in. And the only thing she wanted right now was to be lying in his arms.

*

The next day Kaia phoned Chandi, telling her she had to take some time off and asking her to assign her projects to other law clerks. Though sounding miffed, Chandi acquiesced without asking any questions. Perhaps she had seen Mark at the office.

Over the next few days, Kaia attended her morning classes at State, then spent afternoons with Mark wandering through the Japanese Gardens or past the buffalo herds in Golden Gate Park, or if it was especially mild, strolling on the beach. They ate Chinese take-out or pizza, thinking about food only when they became famished. On the foggy November nights, they drank wine and talked, or bundled up and explored the Mission District or North Beach or another neighborhood. One night they dined at an Italian restaurant filled with the rich aroma of mizithra cheese; it was like a dark cave, resplendently lit with candles.

Everything seemed sharp and powerful now that Mark was here. They made love whenever they felt like it—sometimes it was vigorous and intense, other times luxuriant, languid.

One evening after he'd been in San Francisco for a week, Mark mentioned, over a couple of glasses of wine at the apartment, that he might be able to stay out here for a while, with the winter coming on and less to do at the cabin.

She took a sip of her wine. "But what about your furniture business?"

"I can take a few weeks off." There was a slight edge to his tone.

She sighed. She loved having him here, but how could he possibly fit into her hectic San Francisco life right now? She'd been having trouble sleeping, and often felt her stomach tighten when she thought of her neglected job and coursework. "I'm not sure now is the best time, Mark. Let's talk about it later, okay?"

He shrugged, but his face had fallen at her reaction.

Over the next several days, whenever she returned to the apartment, there were messages on her answering machine—several from her father, sounding angrier each time at her failure to return his calls, two from Chandi, and one from Sig. Sig was aware Kaia had been seeing Mark all this time, but she didn't know Mark was here now. Kaia refrained from answering the phone and didn't call anyone back. She avoided calling the office, afraid Chandi might be angry with her. Kaia felt guilty, hurting everyone by her silence, but she didn't want to try to explain what was going on.

Mark called his mother from Kaia's apartment one night, the conversation affectionate and light, then Elisa asked to talk to Kaia and wished her a happy birthday. Kaia's birthday was still several days away, the same day as Thanksgiving this year. Her father would never understand why she was having Thanksgiving dinner and celebrating her twenty-first birthday with "friends" rather than with him, but that was just too bad. She wanted to spend the day, and every day she could, with Mark. She would have to catch up on her work and studies later, after he left. That is if she still had a job and hadn't missed any of her exams.

At the end of November, Mark returned to Maine, and Kaia tried to immerse herself in her legal work and school. As the weeks passed, they kept in contact by letter and occasional phone calls, but it wasn't enough. The San Francisco winter felt bitingly cold and bitter, and she wondered if she could ever stand to get through another one without him.

One Sunday afternoon in the spring, as Kaia was reading a magazine article about the burgeoning arts-and-crafts scene in Marin County, it occurred to her that she might take a jewelry-making or glass-blowing class. A day-long workshop might provide an escape from the pressure of work and classes. They had lost Roberta's case at the second trial, and Kaia was feeling discouraged about the legal system. Now they had to file another appeal, and it didn't look promising.

She was searching the magazine for weekend classes when the doorbell rang and a FedEx package arrived, with Mark's return address on it. Thrilled, she opened the package to find a framed, hand-tinted photograph of a nude woman lying outstretched on the bed, reaching for her infant. Kaia took in the subtle peach tones of the baby, his zaftig arms and legs. A note taped to the back read:

> Kaia,
>
> This photo has been hanging in the cabin forever, and it always makes me think of you.
>
> Everything is possible. It was a tough winter. I miss you.
>
> Love, Mark

She pressed her hand to her mouth, and in a moment tears were brimming up. She carried the photo across the room and propped it up on the mantel. It reminded her of how much she wanted a child, and made her feel that intense love she and Mark had always shared. She didn't know when she would see him again, and had stopped taking the pill a month ago since she didn't need it, and also didn't like its side effects. When could she trust herself to lie in Mark's arms again and still be able to move forward with her life?

After pouring herself a glass of Cabernet, she sat down again, gazing at the photograph. She realized she was merely postponing a decision about Mark, making herself believe she could go on taking him in sporadic doses, like a homeopathic remedy. But she had the sense that one day, through persistence and serendipitous timing, he would inveigle her into forgetting everyone and everything else that mattered to her in order to be with him.

Two days after graduating in early June, Kaia strolled into a travel agency on Market Street. She felt suddenly free, with her degree in hand, and she was ready for a change of scene before starting her summer job with Chandi. Then law school would begin in the fall.

She walked up and asked the tall, wolfish-looking man at the counter, "What's the closest airport to Beaulieu, Maine?"

The man smiled, a collaborative grin that convinced her this was the right path to take. "Let me see what we can find."

After she bought her ticket, Kaia wrote Mark a letter, telling him she was planning to fly out next week.

A week later, she received his postcard: "Can't wait. Love, Mark."

PART FOUR

BEAULIEU AND BEYOND

1985 to 1986

1

As the propeller plane veered into a wide orbit prior to landing, Kaia spotted the single runway flanked by yellow fields and a cluster of airport buildings that resembled an enormous Lego set of white, black and gray. Within minutes the asphalt rose up before the plane, and she braced herself as the plane bumped down and slowed to a roll. The atmosphere in the cabin felt instantly galvanized, like sea air after the roaring crash of waves.

Climbing down the steps, she stood for a moment, moored to the steaming pavement by her weighty duffel bag, the humid breeze blowing her hair away from her face as she scanned the crowd behind the gate, searching for Mark. She imagined him with his wrestler's shoulders, his arms crossed, his head tilted, evaluating her the way he did. It had been seven months since she had seen him. The moment she had thought of coming to Maine, the idea of staying with him in the countryside for the summer had completely taken hold of her. She hadn't considered practicalities or consequences; she'd trusted them both to make things work.

Then she caught sight of Mark standing at the fence; he was gazing in her direction from behind his dark glasses, his hands gripping the railing. He didn't wave or move—it was possible he couldn't see her in the glare of the sun. When she reached the gate and made her way toward him, he broke through the throng of people and strode up to her.

He bent to kiss her, cupping the sides of her face with his hands. "Kaia," he said in a low voice, kissing her again. "You've finally made it." He took her duffel bag and led her out to the parking lot to his dusty blue pickup and helped her into the cab.

He got into the truck and started the engine. "You look good," he said, glancing at her.

"You're just saying that. I'm a mess from the trip."

"Right." He shifted the truck into reverse. "I'm not that complicated a guy, Kaia. I say what I mean."

"I'm just a little jittery, I guess, from the trip."

"I'm a little keyed up myself." He gave a funny half-smile and squeezed her thigh, then turned his attention to the road.

They drove onto the highway, bumping on the rough road past bright-green hills, and for a while they trailed a white truck with a bumper sticker that read, "Question Authority." A black Labrador stood in the open bed of the truck.

"You'll like it here," Mark said after a while. "You'll see how different it is from the city, peaceful and quiet."

Quiet seemed like an abstraction, set against the whine of the engine and the clatter of her anxious thoughts. What would it mean, to spend part of the summer with Mark? She saw that his face and arms were a darker chestnut than they'd ever been. She had the impulse to bring her lips to his arm, feel the web of sun-bleached hair on his forearm and inhale his warm scent, but she held back. It wasn't the right moment. He seemed preoccupied, determined to get her to the cabin. She could always count on that, his determination; it had been there from the start, from the moment he'd rowed her over the channel to Pine Tree Island five years ago.

He accelerated, passing the truck. For a while they drove past ochre fields and undulating green hills, then at last he turned up a long driveway. He pointed out orchards, a garden, and the stone wall he'd built along one boundary of the property. She hadn't anticipated that Mark's landscape would have such an allure for her. He parked the truck outside an old shed. The brick-red log cabin was much larger than Kaia had pictured it, with a sagging barn behind it. When she got out of the truck, she was hit with the pungent odor of hay and fertilizer, the air itching inside her lungs.

Inside the cabin, she surveyed the main room, which was furnished with an old gray sofa, a table and, against the far wall, a narrow bed, Spartan with its plaid blanket and single pillow. The place seemed so clearly Mark's domain. All these years she'd been drawn to this place in her imagination, as if to an intriguing mystery, yet she had resisted each summer and Christmas, afraid that it would feel this good to be in Mark's cabin with him.

Mark carried her bag into a room with only screens for windows; it looked as if it had once been a porch. A double bed took up most of the space and was covered with a primrose-yellow comforter that smelled new. Kaia laughed: the set-up seemed so out of place in Mark's cabin. "Where did you get the comforter?"

He grinned and set down her duffel. "J.C. Penney—bed and all. I've always slept in the main room."

She went over to him and put her arms around his waist, leaning her head against his chest, and he wrapped his arms around her. She loved the comfort of his body against hers, but wondered what he was expecting of her, whether he thought she was going to stay out here permanently. She wasn't ready, though, to talk about it.

Apparently sensing her mood, he took her by the hand and tugged her towards the door and out into the garden, saying he wanted to show her what he'd planted this year.

2

When they returned to the cabin, Kaia said she was hot and wanted to change out of her dress. Mark was hoping it was an invitation, but she slid away from him, and it was torture for him to keep from following her into the porch room. A few minutes later she came into the kitchen wearing a white tank top and shorts. She glanced at him shyly, like a young girl. Running his eyes over her brown legs and bare feet, he wanted more than anything to pick her up and carry her into the other room, but he sensed she didn't want that. He turned and grabbed two beers from the refrigerator.

They sat at the table and she told him about the bumpy flight from Boston, and about the past months of work and classes. She'd given up her apartment in San Francisco and had temporarily moved her things into storage. It occurred to Mark that things had always seemed kind of temporary and unsettled with Kaia. It was killing him, not knowing what her visit was about, but he couldn't bring himself to ask how long she was planning to stay; he didn't want to think about her leaving, now that she was finally here with him.

"So what can I do around here?" she asked in a cheerful voice.

"I'm making some tables for an outfit in Portland right now. The carpentry work is bringing in some good income. You can do some sanding, finishing, that kind of thing, if you want. I do everything by hand. No electricity, so no power tools. And there's the garden—it always needs tending."

"Sounds good. It'll be a change for me." She smiled and stood up, stretching her arms up over her head, her flat tan belly showing, her breasts outlined in her tank top.

She had to know exactly what she was doing to him. He rose slowly from the table.

"I need to take a nap," she said. "I'm not used to this heat. I'm really tired."

"Right. Go for it." But it hurt to see her amble out of the room without a backward glance. Again he had to restrain himself from going after her. His face heated with resentment; he had always been so sure about her, from the time they were together at Pine Tree, and he'd always wanted her. But she didn't seem to need him as urgently as he needed her.

He went to the shed and sawed wood for an hour, then picked some carrots, green beans, and salad vegetables from the garden. Afterwards he took a shower in the stall he'd rigged up outside with a solar heating panel. He was proud of the job he'd done on it and figured Kaia would like taking warm showers. This winter he would have to go back to heating water over the propane stove for bathing in the clawfoot tub—a tedious task, to say the least. Returning to the cabin, he put on a fresh T-shirt and jeans.

He was sliding a thick steak into the spattering oil of the skillet when she came into the kitchen. She appeared calmer, softer, the way she always looked after waking up. He put the other steak in the pan and tossed some chopped garlic on top of it.

"Come on over here," he said.

She walked over to him, and he kissed her on the lips, putting his arms around her. She gave a little groan of pleasure.

"Can I help?" she asked.

He motioned toward the lettuce, tomatoes, and radishes on the sideboard. "You can make the salad."

She prepared the salad vegetables while he tossed the carrots and green beans into a pan with water. Kaia had always liked vegetables, and these would be tastier than anything store-bought. Impulsively he went over to her and pulled her chin up to kiss her again.

"Plates are over there," he said, turning her around by the shoulders and pointing to a cupboard over the sink.

Over dinner, he told her about the other organic farmers in the area and how they had started a seed bank to preserve the original strains, since the commercial hybrids were taking over. He'd thought she might be bored by the details of farming, but she seemed interested and asked a lot of questions. He told her he was growing a variety of legumes, potatoes and other vegetables and fruits. "I still buy meat, cheese, and bread every week or two in town, though."

"Do you ever bake anything?"

He laughed. "Wouldn't know how. I could rig up an oven, though. Maybe a stone oven outside. Can't bake anything with the propane stove. One of these days, I might even get a generator and a real refrigerator, instead of this kerosene job."

"I didn't think about what it would be like here without electricity."

"We don't really need it. The sun can dry your hair." He reached across the table and took her hand.

She squeezed his hand. "Not in the winter, though," she said. "But I guess you probably keep warm and dry with your fireplace."

The corners of her mouth veered up in tiny, pronounced curves, and he could sense the careless energy in her frame that always attracted him. Something about her smooth face, her long wavy hair and fern-like scent stirred him. He recalled the way her

San Francisco apartment had smelled of roses the last time he was there, and the evening she had entered her living room in a satiny kimono that fell open, exposing her full breasts, creamy below her tan chest. He remembered, too, her cool hands on him, soothing, electrifying.

This time she was giving him the chance to have her completely—that was why she had come, he wanted to believe. He had to seize the chance for all it was worth.

After dinner they went outside and picked apples from a tree, then walked down a path to the creek below the cabin. They sat on the rocks, swishing their feet in the icy water, and bit into the crisp fruit, the juice squirting into the air. Kaia seemed more relaxed now, more content, even with the gigantic mosquitoes whining around their heads. She slapped her leg, squishing one into a bloody smear, then wiped her hand on the grass.

"What's winter like here?" she asked.

He laughed. "You don't want to know." This was the second time she had mentioned being here in the winter. He lightly squeezed the back of her neck. "Stay and find out—I'll get you through it, and you could end up liking it."

"I wasn't really thinking of that." She swatted away another mosquito.

"Or we could go someplace warmer for the winter."

They were silent for a while, then Mark said, "Mom was glad to hear you were coming out here."

Kaia gave him a sharp look. "You told her? That means everyone will know pretty soon."

"She won't tell anyone. What did you tell your dad?"

"I just left a message on his machine that I was taking a short vacation. I didn't say where."

"Jesus, Kaia, is that what this is? A short vacation? I didn't think you'd come out here without telling your parents. I thought it was going to finally be out in the open."

"I'm sorry, but it's not. I just don't want to deal with my dad's fury at the moment."

"You'd better call him and tell him to stay out of this. I don't want him barging in on us."

"You don't have a phone."

"It's only twenty minutes into Beaulieu, babe. I could take you there tonight."

"It can wait. I need a few days to enjoy myself before I'll be ready to deal with him."

Mark frowned. She would never stand up to her damned father. She was always so concerned about what he wanted or expected from her. Maybe this was going to be a quick trip for Kaia, so that she wouldn't have to tell her dad about it at all.

"When I phone Dad," she said slowly, "I'll tell him there's nothing he can do to make me leave."

"Isn't there?"

"He might threaten to cut me off financially. But I can get emergency loans for law school, I'm pretty sure. And I plan to keep working, anyway."

So she did plan to go back. At least he knew that now. "I don't want this thing about your dad hanging over our heads, Kaia," he said, suddenly depressed. "I want to enjoy the time we have."

She reached over and took his hand. "I'm sorry, Mark. I'm just a little disoriented right now. I should have told him."

"So how long are you staying?" he made himself ask.

Peering into his face, she said quietly, "A few weeks."

So that was all the time she could spare. He let out a heavy sigh. "I never know about you, Kaia. Do you know how hard that is for me?"

"Well, now that I'm here, we can sort things out, have things more ordinary."

"Whatever the hell that means." It was coming, he knew it then—more pain. She just couldn't free herself from her old man, that's what it was. Even after everything David had done to keep them apart, she was still afraid of her father. And she was stuck in her city life.

After they returned to the cabin, Kaia went outside to take a shower. It was growing dark when she came back in, still in her tank top and shorts. She went into the porch room, where he'd lit an oil lamp next to the bed. He went to the doorway and stood with his arms stretched out on the door frame, watching her search for something in her duffel bag.

"Why don't you come and have a glass of wine when you're finished," he said.

"Sure." She glanced up at him and he caught, with relief, the barest smile forming at the corners of her mouth.

Nestling with Mark on his pillowy couch, Kaia burrowed her head into his chest. She loved being with him in his cabin with its massive stone hearth, its smoke-blackened walls and tall windows, its mingled smells of garlic, wood, and old clothes. He told her their maternal grandfather had bought the cabin in the fifties. The original owner was a glass artist who had etched the front window with its pattern of ferns and berries. The man had designed the window for his wife, who later left him, taking their child with her. When he sold the cabin, he left behind the hand-tinted photo of a nude woman, apparently the absconding wife—it was the photograph Mark had sent to Kaia in San Francisco. She'd studied the photo a hundred times, intrigued by the image of the woman lying on the pale sheets, reaching for the baby who slept a foot away from her on the bed.

"I love that photograph," Kaia said. "But you never told me how sad it was—the story behind it."

"It should be called 'Unattainability.' But only if you know that she later left her husband."

"It's a beautiful picture, the woman and her child," Kaia said.

"There's love in the picture, you can see it." Mark drew her closer, stroking her hair. "You see the wife and baby through the man's eyes when he was taking the photo."

Kaia laid her hand on Mark's belly, squeezing it gently, and he bent down to kiss her.

They sat drinking their Burgundy for a while, then Kaia got up and took the empty tumblers to the kitchen. She was standing at the sink when Mark came up so close behind her that she could feel his heat against her legs and back. He placed his hands on her hips and when she turned around, he put his arms around her, brushing the top of her head with his beard. She reached up and looped her arms around his neck, inhaling the metallic firefly aroma of his skin. He took her by the hand into the porch room and threw back the comforter, and she lay down on the sheet. Bending over her, he quickly pulled off her clothes, brushing her arms, belly, hips, and thighs with his hands. He lowered his face and flicked her taut nipple with his tongue, sending chills through her, then kissed her on the mouth, his tongue pressing deeply into her.

There was a purposefulness in his expression as he tugged off his shirt and slipped out of his pants, then stretched out next to her. He moved closer, tracing the curve of her shoulder with his hand while looking into her eyes.

No one could touch them here, she felt, and the days and weeks lay before them, profoundly new and ungovernable.

The next couple of days felt good to Mark in a physical sense—gardening, having meals with Kaia, feeling her presence, inhaling her sweet scent in the spaces of the cabin, being in bed with her all night, and talking about anything, just to hear each others' voices. In the mornings, after finally leaving their bed, they would go outside, and Mark would sometimes leave his work in the shed in order to stand and watch Kaia kneel by the plants in the garden; she seemed completely absorbed in pulling weeds or watering.

But at times her unreasonable failure to contact her father invaded Mark's mind like a bat flailing about in the rafters of the barn. This refusal of hers remained in his consciousness, and a times he felt an undercurrent of tension between them. It was as if she were slowly making up her mind about him, and whether she would stay with him. He didn't believe she would actually return to California. But she seemed so afraid to stand up to her father and risk estrangement from him. It was painful to Mark, waiting for her to decide just how much she wanted to end the secrecy and be with him, whatever the cost. Disclosing their relationship to her father would be a turning point, somehow, the first step in being together permanently.

He said nothing. He was pitiful enough as it was, the way he always displayed his love, conspicuous as a birthmark—always, it seemed, wanting more from her than she wanted from him. What he really wanted was for her to decide on her own to be with him, but the anguish of waiting for her to do something—to give him an indication of what she wanted, especially after they'd been together for these wonderfully long days and nights—ate away at him, hour by hour.

3

Wading through a pathway overgrown with tall grasses, Kaia could feel the pebbles through her thin buffalo-hide sandals. She caught the odor of wood dust in the warm air from Mark's sawing and sanding, blended with the minty smell of pines and the waft of alfalfa and fertilizer from neighboring farms. The air wavered over the fields, the deep-green trees at the edge a blur; a few violet clouds flickered with distant lightning.

When she strolled back toward the cabin, Mark was bent over, sawing a piece of wood, his bare back a breadth of earthy tan. He turned around, watching as she approached, then he smiled and followed her wordlessly into the cabin. She waited while he went to wash his face and hands in the bathroom basin.

"Let's go for a drive," he said, coming into the main room as he dried off with a towel. "We need to get some supplies in town. We can have lunch, too."

"Sounds good," she said.

They drove in the pickup past the grassy fields with their backdrop of pewter sky, the endless barbed wire fences the only sign of restriction, softened by cornflowers and purple lobelia growing along the roadside. They could drive for miles without seeing anyone, Kaia thought, even in the midst of summer. And in the winter, neighbors would come in their snowmobiles to dig you out of your cabin. She wouldn't have to be always thinking of her next move, planning her career path, trying to maneuver around other people's hopes for her. Here, life was seasonal, lush and pure—so different from her California life in every way. And of course she would be here with Mark. It had seemed a fantasy, before she'd arrived.

"You've changed a bit, Kaia—you seem more careful these days," he remarked, glancing at her. In the shadowy cab, his eyes were a dark, clear blue, his forehead a polished bronze.

"I guess I am different. I'm not so adolescent anymore." She kept her eyes on him. "You've changed, too, Mark. You seem more settled now."

"I'm a small-time farmer and occasional carpenter," he said with a grin. It sounded like a line he'd rehearsed, a rather odd designation he'd chosen for himself.

"I don't quite see you that way. You've always loved the outdoors, I know. But there must be other ways you see yourself."

"I don't spend much time thinking about it."

She was silent for a minute or two. "I guess you don't know many women around here," she couldn't help saying.

"I've formed no outside attachments of that kind, Kaia," he said quietly.

"That's good."

"Right," he said, with a questioning glance. "I suppose it is."

After he parked the truck in Beaulieu, he glanced at her short dress and bare legs, then placed his hand on her knee. As he leaned closer, she caught a whiff of his earthy scent. "Don't tell anyone you're my cousin, okay, babe?" He kissed her on the cheek.

"Jesus," she said, letting out her breath. "You make it sound so illicit."

"It's nobody's business, that's all. This is a small town." He got out of the truck and went around to open her door.

She held her hand to her throat for a few seconds, then climbed out. Maybe it was better to be discreet, but it felt wrong somehow; it tainted everything, just as the secrecy had all these years.

She followed Mark up a stairway to a café above a shop. The place was crowded, with the smell of fried fish in the air. As they walked to a booth in the back, a few people glanced up to watch them, tracking them with deadpan stares. One middle-aged man in overalls checked out Kaia, then winked at Mark. A white-haired woman frowned almost imperceptibly at them as they passed her table. Was the town really that provincial, that people always noticed a newcomer?

Kaia thought of the drive with Mark to Half Moon Bay when she was sixteen, and pictured the two of them entering the pizza parlor, their faces raw from the ride in the open car along the coast. The look of rebellious, masculine triumph on Mark's face must have been apparent to everyone in the place. And she saw herself overflowing with happiness at that moment—they were a pair of exotic birds, synchronized and brilliant. Had there always been some visible chemistry between the two of them? Why couldn't they have been together all these years? Why had she let her parents hold her back?

Mark placed his wide hands next to hers on the table and stared at her. Feeling his interest focused on her, she absorbed the details of his slightly weathered face as if for the first time—the aqua eyes, the rugged brow, the generous mouth beneath his moustache, his beard. She loved every detail about him.

After a while she moved her hands away and twisted her black pearl ring to relieve the discomfort where a blister had formed; it was probably the hot, humid air that had made her finger swell and rub against the ring.

"Why do you always wear that ring?" Mark asked.

Kaia shrugged. "I just like it. Dad got it for me in Hawaii, and he likes me to wear it."

"Is that all it takes?"

She shook her head. Mark had always seen her father as his competitor. Stretching her hands out on the table, she stared at the ring. It was one of several presents her father had bought for her in Maui while attending a conference some years ago. She was fourteen or fifteen at the time. She always wore it on her wedding finger, since it fit best there. The other gifts he brought her were odd: a grass skirt, a bottle of fragrant coconut oil, a life-sized wooden dog you could sit on, with metal teeth in its large mouth for grinding the meat from ripe coconuts.

"Remember the grass skirt I showed you that time?" she whispered, leaning toward him. "Dad bought it on that same trip."

Mark leaned forward, his face mere inches away from hers. "Oh, yeah, I remember," he said in a soft voice.

She had worn the grass skirt and danced topless for Mark in the Berkeley house one afternoon when her father was at his office. How thrilling it was, those times when Mark would come to the house on the sly, or would take her to his apartment—the physical takings, the way he had always tried to close the gates around them. Mark was incapable of giving her up, no matter what; she saw that now. Having staked his claim when she was a teenager, he felt it was irrevocable. She acknowledged, too, her own desire, the feelings for him that would never dissolve, like lacework netted around her heart.

A waitress with dyed, blue-black hair and a complexion like raw halibut appeared, pen poised over her order pad. "How ya doin'?" she asked Mark.

"Not too bad." He settled back on the bench.

After Kaia had scanned the menu, she glanced up to find the waitress staring at her. It was probably startling for a stranger to see how much she and Mark resembled each other—the tawny skin, the brown wavy hair, the bright-blue eyes. Could she tell they were related? Or had she noticed the way they'd been leaning toward each other like co-conspirators, with their hands close to each other's on the table but not touching, then had drawn apart when she'd approached? Even if the woman hadn't seen it now—the furtive aspect to their intimacy—others would catch it another time and wonder what it was about. Or was it just her own paranoia, Kaia wondered. It seemed that she and Mark had always set themselves apart, encapsulating themselves, and their insularity only made them all the more conspicuous.

The waitress shifted her weight from one foot to the other. "The fried smelts are on special today."

"Sounds good to me," Mark said. "Do you want some, Kaia?"

She nodded, not really caring what she ate. He ordered the smelts and two Budweisers.

After the woman left, Kaia asked, "What are smelts?"

Mark laughed. "You'll see."

"I guess there are a lot of people living your kind of lifestyle around here," she said, after a while. "Living out on the land, organic farming." It sounded lame to categorize him that way, but she felt slightly on edge with him here, away from the lull of the cabin.

"What's a lifestyle?" He sounded perplexed. "I live the way I want to. I don't care what people think."

She paused, trying to formulate a question in her mind. "Why do you care if they know we're cousins?"

Mark fixed his eyes on her. "Because people around here are so damned nosy. They might wonder what I'm doing with my cousin out at the cabin. I don't want to be hassled. You have to make a few compromises for that."

Kaia blushed, feeling the force of his intensity. She should have asked him to visit her in California, or in some neutral place like Denver, or in a national park somewhere. Here it would be too easy for him to take her over completely, the way he had when she was a teenager.

"I've written to my parents," she said. "I'll mail the letters while we're here in town."

He nodded, his face relaxing.

"I told them I needed some time out here without being bothered by anyone," she continued, "and that if they tried to interfere, I'd cut off all contact with them."

"Why *are* you here, Kaia?"

She took a full breath and surveyed the room, then turned back to him. "I just want to find out what it's like spending time together without the outside pressures."

"If you mean your parents, I don't think we'll ever get away from them completely."

"Maybe the letters will help. We've both always hated the secrecy. And I like being at the cabin with you, away from them and everything else. I love it there."

"Good. I'm glad to hear that."

But she could tell it wasn't enough. Whatever she said or did was never enough for him. She had come out here to be with him. All this time, there had only been Mark in her life. If she could only make up her mind about what she did want. She knew how painful her indecision had always been for him.

The smelts turned out to be small fried fish, and were served on cafeteria-style ceramic plates. Kaia inspected the peculiar fibrous, yellow-green vegetable on her plate. "What's this?" She held up a stringy bit of the vegetable with her fork.

"Fiddleheads." Mark grinned. "Try one."

"I think not. It smells like canned asparagus."

"Come on," he teased. "It's good for you."

She made a face at him and let it slide off her fork. "Uh-uh."

The smelts, though, weren't too bad—they tasted like mackerel disguised with a cornmeal crust. After they'd finished their food, Mark ordered slices of rhubarb pie à la mode. Kaia ate hers quickly, savoring the glazed tartness of the fruit, the sweet vanilla ice cream melting in her mouth.

"You really tucked into that pie," Mark said.

She laughed, seeing the affectionate humor in his eyes. "I hardly ever eat desserts."

"You deny yourself so much, Kaia." His brow furrowed slightly. "Why do you?"

"Maybe I'm afraid of what might happen if I let myself go. After all, I've made a few mistakes in my life."

"What mistakes?" he asked in a sharp tone.

Disturbed by the quick surfacing of his anger, she looked away. An elderly man at a nearby table glanced at her, then pushed his glasses farther up his nose and resumed reading his newspaper.

She leaned across the table and touched Mark's hand. "I know I should have come out here before," she said in a near whisper. "I shouldn't have worried so much about my dad."

"I thought maybe you came out here because you had nothing better to do."

It was an accusation, the sort of remark that would have been even more jolting if he'd made it at the cabin; it wouldn't have fit in with the loose, comfortable way they moved around each other out there.

"You know that's not true, Mark. I wanted to come, more than anything. But I told you I have to go back to work at the end of July, and then I start law school in September."

"Even though it's a complete waste of time and not what you want at all."

"You always think you know what I want, don't you?"

"I can't believe you want to build a fort around yourself in the goddamned city."

The old man at the other table peered over his glasses at them again and rattled the pages of his newspaper.

"Sure," Kaia said. "That's exactly why I'm here, to build a fort around myself in the goddamned city."

Mark stared at her for a few seconds without speaking.

"You know how much I love you, don't you?" she asked in a low voice.

Mark sighed and took her hand, squeezing it. "I think I do, Kaia." He stood up slowly, took out his wallet and dropped a twenty on the table. "We should get back to the cabin."

When they emerged into the muggy Beaulieu afternoon, they strolled to the intersection and then waited for the light to change. He placed his hand at the nape of her neck, his touch soothing. As the light turned green, they crossed the street and headed down the sidewalk while strangers with their shopping bags and blank stares moved past them.

Kaia saw that she and Mark could never be one with the townspeople. The two of them were drawn more closely together by the peculiar foreignness of the town; they were clearly not a part of it. The cabin had become their province, a circumstance they inhabited, a place where Kaia felt perilously happy.

"What are your plans exactly?" she asked, meaning what were they going to do for the rest of the afternoon. But then she drew in her breath, surprised by the sultry intimation that had surfaced in her own voice. She looked up at him from behind her dark glasses, trying to gauge his reaction as they walked toward the truck.

"You mean what are my intentions?" He squinted down at her. "Just you wait, Kaia," he said, smiling.

4

A week later, on an oppressively hot afternoon, Kaia stepped into a phone booth in Beaulieu, while Mark stood outside with his arms crossed.

"Go away," she said. "I'll meet you in that coffee shop down the street."

"I can wait."

"No. I don't like you hovering." When she shut the door, it instantly felt twenty degrees hotter inside.

Mark stood there for a moment longer, then turned, shaking his head, and strolled down the street. It was around ten on a Saturday morning in California, and Kaia was hoping her father would be off at the farmer's market or playing tennis, so that she could just leave a message on his machine, telling him she knew what she was doing and to leave them alone. On the other hand, she needed to get this over with, for Mark's sake as well as her own. Neither of them wanted her dad coming out here to try to retrieve her.

She dialed the number and pushed open the glass door to let the stifling air escape. Beads of sweat were already trickling down her neck. After a single ring her father picked up the phone and said hello in a gruff voice.

"Hi. It's me, Dad." She could hear him breathing into the phone in the tense silence that followed.

"I figured it might be you," he said angrily. "Why in the hell did you go off like that without telling me, Kaia?"

"You would have tried to stop me."

"I'm your father. I have a right to know where you are. And to stop you from doing idiotic things if necessary."

She pictured her father's scowling face. "I'm an adult, Dad, remember? You can't make me do anything."

"Kaia, I want you to hear me out, all right? Don't hang up. I've been worried sick about you."

"I'm sorry to hear that, Dad."

"You're throwing everything away. Mark is just a hippie drop-out. And he's your cousin, for Christ's sake."

"Is that all you have to say?"

"You need to come home, Kaia. If you don't return right away, I'm coming out to get you."

"Don't be ridiculous. You'd better not." She closed her eyes to shut out the glaring sunlight. "Don't come here, Dad. I'm not going anywhere with you."

"Your home is here, not out in the sticks with him. What about law school? I just know he's going to try to keep you from coming back to California."

"I plan to go back to start law school."

"You think you're going to spend the rest of the summer out there with him and then come home?"

"Not the whole summer. But if you fly out here and try to pressure me, I won't come back."

"Don't try to blackmail me, Kaia. It won't work."

"You're always interfering with my life."

"If you mean I've tried to protect you from that son-of-a-bitch, then, yes, I've interfered once or twice."

"Don't ever talk about Mark that way again," she yelled, her stomach clenching up as if she'd been punched. "Ever. I'll do whatever I want." She took a deep breath and went on hoarsely. "I don't want to live anywhere near you if you're going to try to control everything I do. I am not a child."

"But you've got rotten judgment."

"Thanks a lot."

"Kaia, listen to me. If you don't come back soon, don't ever expect a penny from me again."

"Talk about blackmail! Just leave us alone." She slammed down the receiver and stepped out into the dizzying heat, wiping the perspiration from her face. She stepped over to a storefront and leaned against the plate glass. After a minute or two she walked unsteadily down the sidewalk toward the coffee shop.

When she entered, Mark glanced up from his newspaper at a table near the window.

She slumped into a chair. "Dad threatened to come out here, and I told him he'd better not even think about it."

"That's good." Mark reached across the table, enfolding her hand in his. "The mothers have spoken. These were in my post office box."

An unopened envelope lay on the table in front of him, and next to it another letter.

"I don't think I have the stomach for this right now."

"My mom says she knows everyone is mad at us, but she hopes we have a good summer and sends her love."

"I'll read them later. I just want to get back to the cabin, take a swim in the lake and cool off."

"Sure, babe."

He sounded so optimistic, she couldn't stand to tell him she was afraid her father might actually fly out here and try to take things into his own hands.

On the drive back to the cabin, she read Elisa's letter, then opened her mother's, just to get it over with:

> Kaia,
>
> Don't you see how dangerous this is? I'm disappointed in you. You must return to San Francisco immediately. If you don't return, I'll have

to take any to take every action I possibly can to make sure you leave Maine for good. Everything will have to come out. Dad and Elisa will have to be told the whole situation.

If necessary I'll send money so you can fly back right away.

Mom

Kaia groaned. What was she threatening exactly? To tell everyone about her affair with Nico? Why? How could she be so cruel? But Kaia didn't believe her mother would actually do that, and in any event, Nico would surely prevent her from doing that—he wouldn't want to hurt Elisa that way.

Kaia crumpled the letter and flung it onto the floorboard. Then she picked it up and stuffed it into her purse, not wanting Mark to read it. "Jesus. I should never have opened it."

"Just forget about her." Mark reached over and rubbed her shoulder, keeping his eyes on the road ahead.

"How could she?"

Mark glanced at her. "What did she say?"

Kaia pressed her face in her hands before answering. "She's so disappointed in me. She may have to take some kind of drastic action."

"That's ridiculous. There's nothing she can do."

"I don't know. Maybe I should call her and make some threats of my own."

"Like what?"

"Tell her if she interferes I'll never see her again. In fact, I'll write her and tell her that."

"What if they try to force you to leave?" He turned to her, searching her face.

"I'm going to leave in a few weeks, anyway, Mark," she said quietly, hating to say this but knowing it had to be said. "I need to get ready for law school before classes start, and put some hours in at the office. Why don't you come to California to be with me?" Now it seemed like the only solution.

He shook his head. "What? And live in some apartment in the city? Who would pay the rent? I've established my business here. And I've invested everything in this place. You could go to law school out here. Don't you love it out here?"

"Yes, but not as much as you do."

It seemed that Mark wanted too much now, wanting her to live here with him in Maine and give up her life in California. If she stayed out here, she might never go to law school, never have the career she wanted. She was sure there was no law school nearby.

What he was asking was simply too hard, and too soon.

5

Kaia spent some mornings gardening, and other times she helped Mark sand chairs and tables by hand down to a silky sheen. They spent whole afternoons sailing on the sparkling lake. It was perfect—being in the boat with Mark every day, the water a clear, rippling sapphire, the sun shining on the islet at the lake's center, the trees glimmering like the iridescent feathers of tropical birds. Mark would always take charge of the boat, his broad hands grasping the tiller firmly as he executed one graceful turn after another while lake water sprayed over them. She was happy just to lie back and enjoy the fresh breeze blowing over her.

They would sail for an hour or so and then would find a spot to anchor. Mark would stand, hands on hips, inhaling deeply as he prepared to dive into the icy water. By now, in late July, his body was leaner than it was a few weeks ago—probably from working outside, and the carpentry. Kaia wondered if he followed this pattern every year—becoming slimmer during the warm weather, when he could do more physical work, then putting on a few pounds during the more sedentary winters and frosty springs.

After she watched him dive, she would somehow muster the nerve to jump in after him, not wanting to be left behind to roast in the sailboat, and craving the exhilaration of swimming with him in the bracing water. They usually swam nude, since other boats rarely came by.

Mark had found permanence here; it was beautiful to see him so content. Clearly he was someone who needed to spend much of his life outdoors. Kaia thought about extending her stay through Labor Day. She couldn't stand to think about leaving, and wondered what the fall would be like in northern Maine. They had heard nothing more from their parents.

Then early on a Saturday evening, Nico drove up the driveway in his bronze '57 Jaguar coupe with its top down. Kaia and Mark stood watching from outside the carpentry shed as the car materialized in a cloud of dust—Nico with his shades perched on his aristocratic Grecian nose, the Jag with its voluptuous lines. Leaning on the horn with its high-pitched beep, he pulled up next to them, then climbed out, grinning. He wore a tan jacket and neatly pressed trousers. He strode over to Mark and hugged him, then wrapped his arms around Kaia, kissing her on the cheek.

"What's the occasion?" Mark asked.

"Just a friendly visit."

Mark snorted, shaking his head.

Kaia led the two men into the cabin, and Nico stood for a moment in the main room, looking around. Then his gaze fixed on the porch bedroom with its unmade double bed, visible through the open doorway. He turned back to them, raising his eyebrows.

"So what's going on?" Mark asked. "Is Mom all right?"

"Yes, she's doing fine, considering." Nico rested his hand on Mark's shoulder. "Let's go sit down."

They went into the kitchen and Mark brought some beers to the table. Nico began chatting about the congested traffic on the drive from Bangor, the sluggish sales in commercial property, the fierce thunderstorms they'd had over the summer. He mentioned

Elisa was actually planning to teach a poetry course at Hillcrest in the fall. Kaia asked polite questions while Mark nodded occasionally, grim-faced, his arms crossed.

Nico was handsomer than ever, despite his graying hair and the lines engraved between his eyebrows; he appeared older than when Kaia had last seen him in Bangor at Thanksgiving, almost two years ago. But it was a kind of handsomeness that did not appeal to her, his features too refined, his smile too dazzling. He kept glancing at her affectionately, wielding the same jovial charm he had at Pine Tree when she was sixteen.

"I guess I'm appointed delegate to this convention," he said finally, with a bark of laughter.

"Really," Mark said. "How so?"

"From what I gather, Jean had a hard time keeping David from flying out here to hogtie Kaia and take her home. Jean was afraid of what might happen if he did fly out here, and she talked him out of it, at least for now. Anyway, we decided I'd be the one to come here to study the lay of the land."

Mark frowned. "You have no right."

"You're both taking a big risk—you, especially, Kaia, if you don't go back and start law school."

"Who said I'm not going back to California?"

Mark's jaws tightened. "Why don't you just say what you've decided, Kaia, if you've already made up your mind?"

"Maybe we should just hear what your dad has to say."

"Why listen to him?"

"He's come all this way."

"We don't know what to think," Nico said. He stood up and braced his hands against the back of the chair. He threw a frank glance at Mark. "We're not going to get anywhere here. I have some things I'd like to discuss with Kaia alone. I'm staying at an inn in town and I'd like to take her there for dinner."

"Forget it," Mark said, his voice ratcheting up. He scraped his chair back and stood facing his father. "There is nothing you can say that I can't hear."

Nico turned to Kaia, his face serious. "I want to make sure you have a chance to think this over on your own. And that you understand what's at stake."

"Without my influence, is that what you're saying?" Mark said.

Nico stared at him for a long moment.

Kaia rose from the table. "Let's all go sit in the other room." She walked out of the kitchen.

"We don't need to talk about anything with him," Mark said, coming after her. He pulled her around to face him and peered into her face, his hands on her shoulders. "Kaia, don't listen to him," he said in a low voice.

"It's okay. It'll be fine. What are you afraid of?" She waited a moment, then went over to the sofa and sat down.

Mark spun around and headed out the front door. What did he think Nico was going to do, abscond with her? She sat there taking deep breaths to calm herself.

From the kitchen doorway, Nico stood watching her. He'd taken his jacket off and was wearing a spruce-green polo shirt. "Another beer?" he asked.

She nodded.

A few moments later Nico strolled out of the kitchen and set two beers down on the coffee table, then sat down next to Kaia. They drank the beer in silence for a minute or two, his arm resting behind her. They could hear Mark vigorously sawing wood outside.

"So how do you like living at the cabin?" Nico asked.

She gave a long sigh. "It's wonderful, and so peaceful here. I love sailing on the lake, working in the garden, having fresh vegetables for dinner every night."

"My mother loved gardening, too. You should have seen the gladiolas. And every kind of vegetable."

"I don't know much about her," Kaia said, "except that I was named after her."

"Yes, in fact you were. She was petite like you, too." Nico patted her bare thigh, and Kaia wished she wasn't wearing shorts.

"You've caused quite a stir," he went on, "coming out here like this." He took a swig of his beer. "Your father obviously wants you back in California. I spoke with him yesterday."

She nestled into a corner of the sofa, farther away from Nico, tucking her bare feet under her. "I'm not sure exactly how long I'll stay here."

Nico sighed. "I don't know where to begin, Kaia." His face was flushed, possibly from the beer and the heat. "I know what your mother told you when she went out to see you—just before Mark left Berkeley."

"That was just something to get me away from Mark. It's so ridiculous, about you getting a divorce and—" She paused, holding his gaze. "Isn't it?"

He took another drink, then wiped his mouth with the back of his hand. "I guess I'd have to say it's a problem without a solution." He took her hand, which was balled up into a fist, and kneaded her knuckles with his thumb.

She jerked her hand away. "The solution is obvious," she snapped. "Stop seeing my mother."

Tears cropped up in his eyes—it surprised her; it was rather maudlin of him. He brushed them away and inhaled sharply. "Can't," he said, choking up.

"Why not? Do you really love her that much?"

"Yes. I have for many years. Your mother is a strong, amazing woman, as I'm sure you realize, Kaia."

"You're not going to marry her, are you?" she said in a flat tone.

"In a way I feel as if I'm already married to both of them."

"She never should have told me she was going to marry you. And by the way, Mark doesn't know anything about this."

Nico raised his eyebrows. "What? You didn't tell him?"

"No."

"Mark must suspect—about the affair, at least."

"I don't think so."

"I thought that's why he left Berkeley—because you both saw how impossible the whole situation was."

"My dad was going to bring criminal charges, that's why Mark left."

"But I assumed this other thing was hanging over your heads, too."

"That wasn't the main thing. Anyway, I never told Mark or anyone else about you and Mom. I didn't want to be the one to drop the bomb. And I didn't want Elisa and Mark and Dad to be hurt. I was hoping your affair would just end."

"I know it would be very hard on everyone if they found out about it." He said this in a gentle, reasonable tone, as if he regretted this unavoidable situation—as if he himself hadn't caused it.

"Devastating, wouldn't you say?" she remarked.

Nico nodded slowly. "Elisa couldn't handle it."

"My mother threatened me. She said she would tell Dad and Elisa everything if I didn't end my relationship with Mark for good. But you know what?" Kaia took a gulp of beer. "I think she expected me to tell everyone myself, so I'd be the one tossing the Molotov cocktail. She didn't think I'd keep it a secret from Mark, and she figured Mark would confront you with it and then Elisa would somehow find out and Mom would get what she wanted. But I never told anyone. And Mom assumed I didn't have much contact with Mark afterwards."

"But you were seeing each other all this time?"

"Yes." Through the open window, Kaia could hear Mark hammering in the shed. She looked directly into Nico's face. "All this time I had to keep it to myself. It makes me sick to think how long this has been going on."

Nico leaned his head back on the sofa, sighing. "Shall we have another beer?"

"Maybe we should get something to eat. I don't like drinking on an empty stomach." She'd drunk two bottles already and was feeling woozy.

They moved into the kitchen, and she set out a hunk of cheddar cheese and some bread along with a bottle of beer for Nico. She sat down opposite him and watched as he cut a piece of cheese and a slice of bread and handed them to her, then took some for himself.

"Doesn't it bother you, carrying on with Mark, given this other involvement?" he asked.

"Doesn't it bother you, being involved with your wife's own sister?"

He kept his eyes on her. "Even if it weren't for that, you're much too closely related to Mark to be doing this."

Kaia shook her head, as if she could thus rid herself of the thought.

"You may be too close to have children," Nico persisted.

"I don't know if that's true. Mark says there's not a very high risk."

"Just think about it, Kaia. It's pretty incestuous as it is."

"You don't have to call it that," she said, then paused. "What do you mean, *as it is*?"

Nico sat back in his chair, frowning for a moment before speaking. "The whole situation. Jean and Elisa are sisters. You and Mark share some of the same genes. And you're ostracizing yourselves from the family, from everyone."

"It's not us. We're not ostracizing ourselves. Everyone knows about us now, so it's up to you to accept it or not."

Nico let out a long sigh. Kaia had the fleeting sense that he had come here to tell her something else—but she wasn't sure she wanted to hear it.

"I won't give up Mark, no matter what," she said. "But I don't want him ever to know about you and Mom. Why don't you just stop seeing her?"

Nico opened his mouth, then shook his head.

Outside, the sounds of hammering and sawing had stopped abruptly.

After an extended silence, her uncle asked, "Well, what are you going to do, then?"

"I'll probably go back, even though I've had the impulse to stay out here sometimes. I don't plan to give up everything."

"Good," he said, with too much eagerness. "I'm glad you've settled on that. You'll get your law degree, find a job. San Francisco is a great place to live." He sounded like a salesman, trying to clinch a deal before the customer changed her mind. "And after all of this hullabaloo has calmed down," he continued, "you'll find a way to fit in with all of us, be a regular part of the family."

"Whatever that means," she muttered. As if it could all be so easily resolved, as if her feelings could simply be watered down into some mundane, familial relationship with Mark.

They both turned as they heard Mark enter the cabin. He came to the kitchen doorway, his face shiny with perspiration, sawdust clinging to his hair, and ran a hand over his head.

"So I guess you two have got it all figured out," he said, glowering at his father.

"Not really," Kaia said. "Why don't you sit down and have a beer?"

"No thanks."

Nico stood up. "I should be going." He slung his jacket over his shoulder, and moved past Mark into the other room.

Unhappy about the way things stood, Kaia followed him. "You could stay for dinner."

"That's all right," Nico said, turning to her. "I'll have something at the inn."

She walked with him to the front door, and slipped into her sandals.

"Bye, Mark," Nico called, and strode out of the cabin.

Kaia went after him and shut the door behind her.

When they reached his car, Nico turned to her. "Maybe I shouldn't have come."

"Maybe not."

He put his hand on her shoulder and steered her toward the driveway. "Let's take a little walk."

She wrapped her arms tightly around herself, feeling the chill of the evening breeze on her bare arms and legs as she strolled up the driveway with him.

"Kaia, I don't want you to tell Mark about the affair. Since he never knew about it, there's no point in telling him now. It would kill him."

"You should have thought of that before you started it."

"It started the day Mark was born."

Deeply shocked, she stopped and turned to her uncle. "It's been that long?"

He nodded, then reached out to squeeze her shoulder. "Yes, Kaia. That long."

"Mom never told me exactly when it started."

"Your mother wanted me to tell you and Mark, but he would hate me for it."

"She insisted you tell Mark about it?"

"Yes, but I don't feel it's necessary anymore. You say you're going back to California anyway." They ambled on, then he said, "I could take you to the airport tomorrow, you know."

"It's not as if I've joined some cult and you have to rescue me."

He gave her a curious look of appraisal. She was feeling the beer, and if she sounded adolescent, it was too damned bad.

"When will you fly back, then?"

"My return ticket is for Monday." Two short days from now, if she didn't delay her flight. A gust of wind buffeted them, and she rubbed her arms as they continued to stroll along the stone wall.

"You're shivering." Nico stopped and swung his jacket around her shoulders. He grabbed the back of her neck under her ponytail as they continued a few steps toward the highway.

She turned to face him, freeing herself from his grip.

"I see why Mark finds you so hard to resist," Nico said in a low voice.

She leveled a hard look at him for several seconds, her jaw tensed, then turned and marched back towards the cabin.

"Slow down, Kaia," he called out.

She only walked faster. He caught up with her, and when they reached the roadster, they both stopped, facing each other. He bent and kissed her on the cheek. "Tell Mark I'm sorry for the disruption."

He reached his arms out to hug her, but she took a step back, wanting to get away from him. She'd been mistaken in thinking her old goat of an uncle would have anything useful to tell her. The whole family scenario had the same doomed feel to it that it always had.

He got into his car. "See you later," he said, with a slack, ingratiating smile.

"Maybe," she said, attempting to sound flippant. But what she felt was dismay at having spent any time alone with her uncle. She watched as he backed up the car, turned it around and drove off, bumping down the uneven dirt driveway. He might love his son and love her, too, in his own screwed-up way, but he was a morally weak man.

She walked slowly toward the cabin, and forgot until she stepped through the doorway that she still had Nico's jacket draped around her shoulders.

✻

Mark sat on the sofa next to a glowing lantern, the humid air suffused with the odor of beer and kerosene smoke.

"What was that about?" His voice was a bit hoarse.

She stood across the room watching him in the flickering glow of the lamplight. "Your dad went back to the hotel. You obviously didn't want him here."

Mark stood up, his face impassive. "You've got his jacket on."

She glimpsed down, embarrassed. "I forgot to give it back to him."

He moved a few steps toward her, then stopped a couple of yards away. "He must have told you something."

"Some fatherly advice, that's all."

"About what?"

"About going back to California. I've always planned to go back, you know that."

He shook his head slowly, his jaw tight, his hands on his hips. She let the jacket slide off her shoulders to the floor.

"Let's talk later," she said. "Not now."

"Come here."

She sucked in her breath and walked up to him, examining his face with its pained, angry expression. He waited a moment, then pulled her tank top over her head, unhooked her bra and flung it off. He placed a hand on her breast and kissed her hard on the mouth. After a minute, he picked her up, laying her on the couch, and pulled off her shorts. The muscles of his face and neck appeared taut as he quickly undressed.

He lay down alongside her, running his hand over her breasts, and kissed her deeply. Pulling her against him, he made her gasp, and she focused on the way it felt as he touched her, divesting her of her composure, her self-control. Then he was on top of her, taking her deliberately, as if in a ritual, as though to confirm the way things were between them. It was what she wanted, to be with him like this.

They lay together afterwards on their sides, his body against her back, his arm pressed against her breasts. After a while rain began pelting the roof, and they moved into the porch room. Fresh, damp air gusted through the screen like a moist breath as they lay on the bed, both of them silent and awake for a long while.

6

It was damn irritating, Nico thought, the way the bartender kept darting glances at him. The man's expression turned into a rude stare when Nico ordered another gin and tonic—his fourth or fifth, he was dimly aware. He chomped on some more of the peanuts in the bowl on the counter, the only food he'd had since the cheese and bread at Mark's cabin.

The young bartender came over, wiping his hands on a towel. "I assume you're not driving anywhere tonight, sir."

"This is an inn," Nico said, "miles from anywhere. Where in the hell do you think I'd be driving? I'm stuck here in this shitty hotel." He looked around the bar, and saw that the only other customer had left.

The bartender smirked, quite unpleasantly. "I think you've had enough to drink, sir." He veered away and started rinsing glasses.

"Person has a goddamn right to be served." Nico was aware his speech was dragging, his brain sluggish. "Just give me the fucking G & T to take to my room. Don't need to put up with this horseshit." He held his head in his hands. He truly needed another drink. Didn't want to think anymore about the goddamn fiasco this trip had turned out to be. And all because of Jean's ridiculous notion that Kaia could be his; surely Jean had made it up for her own selfish reasons. Now he was glad he hadn't told Kaia about it. She would have told Mark, and Mark would have despised him. It was bad enough that Kaia might tell him about the affair with Jean. His big fear had always been that Mark would tell his mother and then everything would fall apart.

The bartender spun around, grabbed Nico's glass and made him another drink, then shoved it in front of him. Nico stood up and grabbed onto the edge of the counter, trying to keep his balance. He staggered and spilled some of his drink onto his shirt on his way out of the bar. What a disgusting old fart he was. After hobbling to his room, he sank into the armchair and, fumbling with the phone, put a call through to Jean. He just wanted to get this over with.

"Jean?"

"Oh, Nico, I was just watching the news. So how did the visit go?" He heard the faint sound of ice clinking in a glass.

"Not so great," he drawled.

"You've been drinking."

"Sure have."

"I was just having another Scotch myself, trying to get to sleep."

He snorted. "You sound a little drunk."

"Well, I'm not, really."

"Have to say, I'm just a little upset after all's said and done."

"Why? What did you tell them?"

Nico drank from his glass, rummaging around in his mind for just what had been said. "Just told Kaia it was a dicey proposition, this thing with Mark."

"Nico, I need to know exactly what was said."

Boy, just like her, pinning him down. He tried hard to focus, but the room was spinning. "See, the good news is, Kaia's planning to fly back on Monday, so this'll just blow over. It's all a big fucking deal about nothing."

There was silence at the other end, which he was having a hard time interpreting. His stomach was churning. Even in his drunkenness he could see this was a big mistake, talking to Jean in his present state.

"So you didn't tell Kaia."

That was Jean all the way, going after him like a fucking cop.

"Actually, Kaia and I talked while Mark was outside, about how dangerous it was, blah, blah, blah. The whole damn spiel. Why you ever sent me on this stupid trip, I'll never know. I never believed any of your ridiculous story, anyway. I shouldn't have said anything to Kaia." He hiccupped and took another drink, waiting for Jean to say something instead of just breathing into the phone. "But we can't ever tell Mark anything," he went on. "It would destroy everything. Never, never tell Mark. I've always said you can never tell Mark."

"But Kaia will tell him, I'm sure."

"Is that what you want? To make everything explode? That's very mean of you, do you know that? You can be very—"

"Stop this, Nico. Try to sober up, for Christ's sake. They just need to know, that's all."

"No they don't. If Mark finds out about us, or about your crazy idea, he'll tell Elisa. I just know he will. I better call her now, and tell her the trip went okay."

"Nico, wait, what are you going to tell her?"

"About my little visit with the kids. What else? Got to go now."

He hung up, feeling more miserable than when he'd started the goddamn conversation. He finished his drink, trying to settle his stomach. He was feeling woozier by the minute, but he longed to talk to Elisa. After several attempts he managed to dial the right number and reach her.

"It's so good to hear your voice," she said. "I was asleep, but I was just thinking about you before I went to bed."

"This was so damn hard, coming up here alone like this. And now Mark's mad at me."

"You didn't have to go. Mark must think you're trying to take Kaia away from him." Elisa paused. "You've been drinking, haven't you, Nico." Her voice was more sad than reproachful.

"Yep." He chuckled.

"Maybe we should talk tomorrow when you come home."

"I just needed to hear your voice."

"I still don't understand why you had to go see them, Nico."

"Had to find out if there's a dangerous situation like Jean keeps saying."

"You spoke with Jean?" There was a little whine in Elisa's voice.

"Before the trip. She called me at the office, worried about Kaia."

"So she sent you to see them?" Elisa's voice rose.

"No, no, I wanted to visit them."

"Why can't you and Jean leave them alone?"

"Turns out Kaia's going back to California on Monday. And we want her to stick with that. So don't tell her to stay with Mark, okay?"

"I don't have that kind of influence, Nico. You and Jean are trying to make them feel guilty about something they shouldn't feel the slightest bit guilty about. But what were you saying, about it being a dangerous situation?"

"No, no. No danger, really. Just Jean's stupid idea. Not true at all. This possibility"—he spat out the word—"about Kaia. Jean's full of baloney."

"What possibility?"

Even in his foggy state he could hear the panic in her voice and thought he might have blurted out too much. He groaned. "Don't you know, Elisa?"

"What?" she whispered.

"You know I care about you, more than anyone else, don't you?" He heard her gasp. He had hoped she would say the same thing back to him. Didn't she love him? As much as he loved her?

He felt a horrible siege of dizziness and dropped the phone onto the floor. He lurched onto the bed face down but felt too woozy to reach for the receiver before the whole room turned into a sickening blackish blur.

Elisa sat in bed, shivering in her thin nightgown. After a minute, she dialed her sister's number.

"Nico just called me," she said, then pressed her fingers against her mouth to stop her lips from trembling. She absolutely had to sound calm. "Nico was drunk and I think he may have passed out." She inhaled sharply. "He said something I didn't understand about Kaia and Mark."

"Really? What did he say?"

"He said you thought it was a dangerous situation, that you'd talked about it with him. He wasn't making any sense and then he suddenly got off the phone and I didn't know the phone number or even the name of the inn where he's staying, so I couldn't even call him back."

"What's wrong, Elisa? Are you upset?" Jean was speaking slowly, her words a bit slurred.

"Of course I'm upset. Why are you two always conferring behind my back?"

"It's not behind your back, Elisa. I think he just called me because he was drunk and wanted to talk about the trip."

Elisa took a sharp breath. "You talked to him just now?"

"Yes. Then he said he was going to call you. He told me Kaia was going to fly back to California on Monday. Didn't he tell you that?"

"Yes." Elisa tried to keep the shakiness out of her voice. "But then he said there was some dangerous possibility involving Kaia and Mark. What is this about, Jean?"

Elisa heard her sister taking a drink.

"I don't know," Jean said.

Elisa slid down in her bed, lying on her back now, feeling suddenly weak. "Answer me. It has to do with you and Nico, doesn't it?" She'd always suspected something, and now she was afraid her intuition was right. But what about this "dangerous" possibility?

"Frankly, this isn't the best time to talk about it. Let's wait until Nico gets home. You can talk to him about it—about what he meant."

"Why? You know what he meant, don't you?"

"Didn't he tell you about his talk with Kaia?" Jean asked.

"About what?"

"About this possibility."

"What do you mean?" Elisa whispered. She knew, though, what Jean was intimating. Everyone had noticed that Kaia and Mark resembled each other, but Elisa had always thought it was because they were cousins.

"Really, isn't that what Nico was just telling you?"

Elisa's heart was beating painfully hard. "So there *is* something that's terribly wrong, isn't there, Jean? You and Nico—" But Elisa couldn't say it.

"I thought he told you everything. We weren't sure Kaia would actually return to California, so he had to tell her about that possibility. To make sure she wouldn't carry on with this."

"What possibility?" Elisa's pulse was racing. "They're just cousins. That's all." But they both had Nico's blue eyes.

"Yes, of course they're cousins," Jean said quietly.

"But there's a possibility? Kaia could be Nico's—?" Elisa's throat clamped down convulsively. She caught a glimpse of her own horrified expression in the dresser mirror opposite the bed.

"Don't even think about that, Elisa, please. You can talk to Nico tomorrow and find out what he meant." Jean paused. "Have you taken your—"

"You and Nico? How long has this been going on? Are you still—?"

Elisa heard Jean inhale sharply.

"It wasn't enough for you to let my baby daughter die in her crib—" Elisa said, barely able to choke out the words.

"Please stop this. You're making a lot of assumptions."

"You've already told me enough, Jean. How could you do that to me? How could Nico?" Elisa could hear her own voice rising in a wail. "How could you?"

Jean was silent for a second. "Calm down, Elisa. Please just take your meds and go to sleep. We'll sort this out tomorrow morning."

"How could you?" Elisa screamed, and slammed down the receiver. She turned over, sinking her face into the pillow. She began to sob—great gulping, choking sobs that shook her entire body as she lay on the bed.

7

In the morning, lying in bed, Kaia was reminded of the first time Mark had spent the entire night with her in Berkeley while her father was in Carmel. It was a night much like last night, and she'd had the same sense of contentment after a night of lovemaking—but it had been tainted with a prickling feeling of unease, the same foreboding she felt now.

Mark had already risen and gone outside. She became conscious of the sound of him pounding nails in the shed. Gazing toward the window, where lush foliage crowded against the screen and the sky glistened an eerie pink, she recalled the view of treetops from her old apartment in San Francisco, and imagined her room with her own bed and her antique dresser with its scent of old oak. How strange it would be to see herself again in the dresser's beveled mirror. Mark had no mirrors in the cabin—he had no need for any, he'd said—but she didn't mind brushing her teeth and combing her hair by feel.

Still, she missed being in her own place surrounded by her own things. She would have to search for a new apartment as soon as she got back to San Francisco—she'd given up her old one because she wasn't sure when she would return. It would be too crowded to stay in Sig's tiny apartment for more than a few days.

She got dressed, then went outside with a cup of tepid coffee. The muggy air clung to her arms in a clammy film. In the open shed, Mark had his back to her and was sawing a piece of wood, his muscles working under his T-shirt. When she called out to him, he glanced over his shoulder at her and straightened up.

"I need to talk to you," she said.

His face slackened, and he set down the saw.

A feeling of dread ran through her body—of the next step, of irretrievably hurting him. "I can't stay, Mark. I still want to go back to start law school."

"God, Kaia. I don't believe this. After being together like this all summer—"

"And there's something else. Can we go inside and talk?"

Frowning, he gestured toward the cabin, then followed her inside and into the kitchen. She sat down and he took the chair opposite her.

"Do you know about your dad and my mom?" She forced herself to say this bluntly in order to get it out, but her voice came out normal and clear, which surprised her, even though she'd been rehearsing this conversation for so long.

Mark looked puzzled, as if he hadn't heard right. He was silent for a moment. "What are you talking about? Some fling?"

"It's more than that."

"You can't listen to him. He's a goddamned liar. You can't trust him."

"You didn't know, then."

"That's what he came here to tell you?" Mark's forehead was red and creased into a scowl. "The bastard."

"No. I already knew about it. Mom told me about it."

"When was this?" he asked.

"Just before you left Berkeley."

"So your mother did have some kind of—"

"It's still going on," Kaia said quietly. "That's why she moved to New York. Mom claims they've actually talked about getting married."

Mark stood up, his hands at his hips, his face contorted in rage. "That's ridiculous," he shouted. "There's no way Dad would ever do something like that."

"Before you left Berkeley, Mom made it sound like a strong possibility."

Mark stalked over to the counter, then whipped around. "Why in the hell didn't you tell me about it?"

"I just couldn't. It would have made you so upset, and you might have done something drastic. But that's not all. Mom said she would tell Dad and Elisa about her affair if we didn't stop seeing each other."

"All these years, Kaia, I thought you wouldn't go with me because you didn't love me enough." He came around the table and stared down at her.

"No, that wasn't it. I've always loved you." She reached out for his hand and held it in both of hers, scrutinizing his face. "Didn't you have any idea about this?"

"A few times, I thought maybe something was going on, but I couldn't believe Dad would do that to my mother."

"I had no idea until Mom told me."

"I still don't understand why you didn't tell me." His voice was strained. "For four years now, you've known." He turned away and strode out of the kitchen, pounding the door frame with his fist as he passed through.

Kaia wanted to go after him but remained seated, too shaky to move. After a minute, Mark came back into the room and stood a few feet away from her.

"Don't you see, Mark," she said softly. "If I'd told you, you would have confronted them, and everything would have come out. Mom would have told Elisa. Mom was trying to force Nico to get a divorce. And I was afraid you'd hate me because of what my mother had done."

"I would never hate you, Kaia."

She stood up, facing him. "Mom implied that once they got married, we'd be their stepchildren. We'd be like brother and sister, almost."

"My dad would never marry your mother," he said flatly.

"But I didn't know that then. And I'm still not sure."

"If they keep this up, we'll have nothing to do with them. Anyway, why shouldn't we live any way we want to? Who cares about them?"

"We can't shut them out of our lives forever, Mark."

He shook his head. "I can't believe this. So this is why you insisted on keeping our relationship secret all these years?"

"I didn't see any other way. And besides, if Dad had known I was seeing you, he would have cut me off completely. But I just couldn't keep this from you any longer."

"And what about us now?"

"Ever since that night in the tent with you at Cape Cod," she said, her throat constricting, "I've wanted to be with you. Now everyone will have to deal with it."

He stepped closer. "I wouldn't have given that night up for anything."

"That's the way I've always felt about it, too."

"Something happened. We both felt it."

"It started for me from the moment you picked me up in your boat."

"And for me, too." He placed his hands on her cheeks and peered into her eyes. "How much exactly do you regret, Kaia?"

"I don't regret anything. I can't imagine what my life would have been like without you. But I might if I stay out here now."

Frowning, he dropped his hands to his sides. "Was that ever a possibility, staying out here with me? For good, I mean."

"I've thought of it, of course I have."

"Look, Kaia, what if we were the last two people on earth? Then would you stay here?"

"But we're not."

"We could be, here. Why don't you try it—take a year off and live out here?"

"I can't do that unless I'm willing to give up everything."

"I am. I'm willing."

"I'm going to law school, Mark. I still feel like a teenager with you. I need to have something of my own to do."

"You're a strong woman, Kaia. You've always been the one to call the shots."

She wrapped her arms around his waist and gazed up at him. "After law school, I want to be with you, wherever we can live together. But you know how much I want to have children. And I want your children. I've always wanted that."

"I want that, too, Kaia. We can have kids together."

Then she recalled Nico saying that his affair with her mother had been going on since Mark was born, and the terrible thought came to her that Nico might be her father. But it was too awful to contemplate, and of course—of *course*—her mother would have told her. So it wasn't possible. And to even mention it to Mark would taint their relationship.

"We just have to decide so many things like that first," she said. "Whether we'll get married, would we adopt, that kind of thing. But we don't have to decide all of that now."

He placed his hands on her shoulders. "Why not now? I asked you years ago to marry me. And we can have our own kids, it's not a problem, really, Kaia."

"Can't we just agree to decide that later? I want to be with you. We'll find a way. Isn't that enough?"

"All right." He ran his hand over his face. "All right. That's enough talk. I can't stand any more of this."

"Mark, I'm leaving on Monday." It came out as a near whisper.

He looked away, his jaw clenched, then back at her. "Dad talked you into leaving, didn't he? How could he do that?"

"I'm not going because of anything he said. But you do know he loves us both, Mark."

"But I'm his son," Mark said harshly. "I'll never forgive him for this."

8

Nico awoke at the inn dry-mouthed and with a piercing headache. After drinking two cups of coffee in the restaurant, he packed and checked out. During the tedious drive home, the rain drummed steadily against the windshield, and he tried not to think about his conversations with Elisa and Jean—he couldn't remember much of what was said—but he felt weighed down with dread. He stopped once in a small town to get gas and a burger.

Still feeling depressed as he pulled into his driveway, he braked and climbed out of the Jag. The neighbors' Rottweilers began barking viciously, hurling themselves against the rickety fence, as they did every damn time he came home.

"Shut up!" he bellowed, which only made the barking grow more ferocious. Nico had always considered it unneighborly of the Schmidts to harbor the Rottweilers, and having three of them seemed like overkill. He caught the flash of teeth as one of the hounds attempted to leap over the fence.

A light, cold drizzle was coming down. As he walked to the rear of the car, his legs felt stiff from driving for so many hours. A gust of wind came up, flinging raindrops from the trees onto him.

As he took his bag from the trunk, he began to feel nervous about seeing Elisa. He tried to imagine her rushing into his arms in one of her flowing purple outfits, her lovely auburn hair streaming out behind her, but now it seemed like a ludicrous fantasy.

Bag in hand, he stood for a moment under the mottled gray sky, staring at their old two-story house, its green shingles glazed with rain, the fir branches dripping onto the roof. He felt something like guilt, something akin to the constant gnaw of remorse from his long infidelity. But all he had done this weekend was to try to rescue Kaia and Mark from a bad situation.

Peeking through the garage window, he saw Elisa's red Cavalier parked inside. He trudged up the front steps. The front door was unlocked—unusual when Elisa was alone at home. Stepping inside, he found a lamp burning in the living room, even though it was barely four in the afternoon. He registered the peculiar silence in the house, and it disturbed him, his disquiet compressed like a tumor in a corner of his brain.

He called out, "I'm home, Elisa."

The only sound was the muted barking outside. Elisa was probably napping, he thought. But then surely the dogs' ruckus would have awakened her. Nico heard Piper scampering down the stairs, her claws clattering on the wooden steps, and then the cat appeared around the corner. Slinking over to him, she swiped the length of her furry torso against his pant leg. It was good, Nico felt, that Elisa had her cat for company.

Piper followed him into the kitchen, mewing plaintively while Nico searched for cold wine in the refrigerator. There wasn't any, so he found a bottle of Cabernet in the wine rack and opened it, pouring himself a full glassful. He made a mental note to feed the cat after he went upstairs to see Elisa.

The kitchen was immaculate; she'd apparently engaged in one of her manic cleaning episodes while he was gone. He hoped she'd forgotten what he'd said on the phone last night, his crude attempts to explain everything.

He headed up the stairs with his glass of wine, turning to check whether Piper was behind him, underfoot as she often was.

The cat was crouched at the bottom of the stairs, eyeing him, her tail twitching. The smell of stale incense hung in the air as he neared the top of the stairs. He stopped in the bathroom off the hall to use the toilet, then closed the medicine cabinet door, which had been left open. He washed his hands and felt oddly comforted by the aroma of Elisa's lavender soap.

As he approached the shut door to the bedroom, something shot through his brain like an electric shock. He shoved open the door and stepped into the room. He was immediately hit with the astringent odor of smoke and wine.

Elisa lay on the bed with her eyes closed, her face pale in the light of the bedside lamp. She remained completely still on top of the quilt, and something about it caused a tight feeling in his torso.

"Elisa?"

She didn't move. He felt faint. He set his wine glass on the dresser and rushed over to her, again calling her name, his heart knocking inside his chest. He touched her cheek, which felt cool against his hand. Bending towards her, he saw now that her lips were bluish, her mouth slightly open. Still no detectable movement.

He took her limp wrist and felt for a pulse—nothing—but then he wasn't trained for such things. She had to be alive. He leaned over her with his ear next to her mouth and nose, but couldn't detect any air escaping. His gaze lit on two prescription bottles on the table. He picked them up. Both were empty. "My God," he gasped. Then he noticed the empty Chardonnay bottle, the wine glass, the box of crackers, a candle stub and an incense burner containing a pile of ash.

His hand trembling, he grabbed the phone next to the bed and dialed 911.

A woman answered at once. Tears sprung into Nico's eyes. "My wife," he stammered, "seems to have taken some pills." He stumbled through the necessary information. The woman put him on hold while she ordered an ambulance, then she instructed him on how to check for vital signs, and he did the best he could, his hands shaking wildly as he tried to find a pulse in her neck. Nothing. Then he saw a faint movement, her chest rising slightly, and she gave a soft gasp.

"She's breathing," he reported in a high-pitched, quivery voice.

"An ambulance will be there very soon, sir. Just stay with her, but don't hang up."

Holding the receiver against his ear, he ran his eyes over the length of Elisa's body. She was wearing her favorite light-green cashmere sweater and a long skirt, and her face was made up, though her lips were bare. Her arms lay at her sides, and she wore a pair of woolen socks. He glanced around and saw her shoes next to the bed, several magazines stacked on the dresser, and a book of poems open on the floor. Scanning the room, he saw no note anywhere. Not wanting to leave her side, he sat down carefully on the bed next to her, and laid a hand on her shoulder. He strained to detect any movement and saw her chest barely rising again. There was a tiny sigh, but perhaps it was his own breath; he couldn't tell. Haltingly he related these signs to the woman on the phone.

He became aware of tears flowing down his cheeks while he waited for the ambulance. There was a twitch in Elisa's eyes. *Let her live*, he prayed, *let her live*. When the woman on the phone asked if the front door was unlocked, he ran downstairs to check, then returned to Elisa's side.

He finally heard a siren and went to the window. The ambulance lights flashed spasmodically as the paramedics piled out. The Rottweilers' frenzied barking rose to an agitated pitch. The crew hastily unloaded their equipment and headed for the house. Nico told the dispatcher the ambulance had come, and hung up the phone. As the medics came through the front door, he dashed into the hallway and shouted, "She's up here."

Five paramedics crowded into the bedroom, carrying equipment, all of them young and tall, like a cast of actors in a hospital drama—four men and a woman. The female medic came up to Nico, addressing him calmly as Mr. Karadonis. He attempted to answer her questions while glancing anxiously at the paramedic who was bent over Elisa, checking her vital signs.

"She has a pulse and is breathing," the man reported a minute later, then clamped an oxygen mask over her face.

"Thank God." Nico lowered himself heavily into a chair in the corner. He choked back a sob. They had arrived in time. It would be all right. They were going to resuscitate Elisa.

As the medics gathered around her, Nico numbly fixed his gaze on her quilt. He recalled that she had made it in part from his old shirts and pajamas. She had always loved him so much. She still loved him, he told himself.

"We'll transport her to the hospital now," the female medic told Nico.

"Yes, yes, you'd better do that." His lips were trembling. "She'll be all right?"

The medic raised her eyebrows slightly as she stared at Nico. "We can't tell yet."

Two men placed Elisa on a stretcher and prepared to carry her out of the bedroom. Nico hurried out of the room ahead of them, anxious to get the cat out of the way so that Elisa's rescuers wouldn't trip as they made their way down the stairs.

Outside, the dogs barked furiously, again throwing themselves against the unstable fence. The paramedics slid Elisa into the ambulance as Nico watched. They wouldn't allow him to ride in the back with her or sit in the cab. He got into his car and drove behind them, watching through the rear window of the brightly lit ambulance as a medic ministered to Elisa. They would revive her, surely they would, that was their job. They saved people every day.

At the hospital, Nico filled out paperwork, then paced in the waiting room. He was perspiring, his heart racing. How had he allowed this to happen? Once he got Elisa home, things would be different. He would show her how much he loved her. He would never do anything to hurt her again. His affair with Jean was monstrous. This was all his fault, a result of his terrible judgment. And what *had* he said to Elisa last night?

He sat down and sunk his head in his hands, but he couldn't stand to be near the other people who were waiting for news of their own loved ones. Suddenly feeling feverish, he got up and walked around the room, trying to make himself believe that Elisa would soon be back to her lovely, vivacious self.

After an hour, Nico was about to ask at the desk for an update, when a dark-skinned, middle-aged man in a white coat emerged through the double doors and conferred with the woman at the desk. She pointed to Nico, and the doctor then walked over to him. Nico stopped pacing, and waited. The man's face was drawn and tired-looking as he approached. He placed a hand on Nico's shoulder.

Nico's stomach convulsed.

Staring for a second or two into Nico's face, the doctor said with a Middle-Eastern accent, "I'm sorry to inform you, sir, that your wife has just passed away. It was too late to revive her, I'm afraid. There was very little we could do."

"Elisa? No. Karadonis? She died?" Impossible. The doctor was mistaken. He obviously had the wrong woman in mind, and therefore the wrong husband. The receptionist had pointed to the wrong man.

The doctor nodded and moved his hand to Nico's upper arm, gripping it firmly, as if to calm him. "Yes, sir. It is Mrs. Karadonis. I am so very, very sorry."

Nico flung off the man's arm and staggered toward the door.

"Wait, sir!" the doctor called out, and ran to catch up with him. "Please. We need you to take care of some things. We will help you call a relative if you like. And we can bring someone here, a counselor, someone you can to talk to—"

Dazed, Nico turned and gaped for a moment at the man, then barged through the exit door. It was dusk now, and he stumbled over to a patch of grass next to the parking lot. He fell to his knees, his fists falling to his sides like leaden objects. He bent over and pressed his head against the wet grass, his heart banging in painful thuds against his ribs.

*

At midnight, Nico was sitting in his living room, staring at the cold brick fireplace, when the phone rang in the kitchen. He let it ring a few times, and then finally roused himself to answer it, taking his glass of whiskey with him.

"I've been trying to reach you all day," Jean said. "When did you get home?"

"This afternoon." Recalling his arrival, he felt a dull pain in his chest.

"Was Elisa at home when you got there?"

Nico snorted and gave a high-pitched, hysterical laugh.

"What's wrong?" Jean asked.

He sucked in his breath, then blew it out. "She's dead." He felt brutal, delivering the blunt, unspeakable words to Jean in this way. He didn't even fully sense it was true. But he had no energy left for finesse or kindness.

"Dead? What do you mean?"

He covered his eyes with his hand. "She took every pill in the house—her Lithium, her new pills, and a bottle of aspirin. She's down at the morgue." It gave him an strangely malicious satisfaction to level these facts at Jean.

"Oh, Nico—" she gasped. She was silent for a second, then asked, "Why didn't you call me earlier?"

"I was at the hospital, taking care of things."

"I'll fly up there in the morning." She blew her nose. "Are you all right?"

He said nothing. How could he be all right?

"Have you told Mark?" she asked.

"Mark hasn't got a goddamn phone."

"Do you want me to call anyone? I can phone David, of course. Kaia's flying back to San Francisco tomorrow, so he can tell her when she gets there."

It sickened Nico, the way Jean sounded so damned eager and efficient. "I'll find some way to reach Mark," he said, his weariness weighing on him. "Maybe the sheriff in Beaulieu can go out to the cabin tomorrow. I have to be here to take care of things."

"Okay. I'll make some other calls when I get to Bangor."

"She didn't even leave a note," Nico said, choking on the words. He didn't want to start sobbing again; he'd done so much of that tonight that he felt depleted.

"She did sound upset last night—" Jean started to say, then stopped.

"You spoke to her? When?"

Jean hesitated for a few seconds then said, "She called me right after you'd talked to her."

"What did she say?" His mouth felt dry.

Jean cleared her throat. "She wanted to know if there was something going on between us. I denied it, of course—"

"What did you say, exactly?" Nico shrieked.

"I don't remember the exact words, but she'd figured it out anyway, from something you'd said."

"I only told her she shouldn't encourage Mark and Kaia to stay together. Tell me what you said to her, Jean."

"Not much."

"Did you tell her about our affair or not?"

"Not really. She was very upset, and I tried to calm her down. I just said she should talk to you when you got home."

"So you more or less admitted it, then?" Nico yelled. "You told my manic-depressive wife this bit of news over the phone?"

"No. You told her, Nico. You were completely smashed. She just called me to verify what you'd said."

"I only told her you thought it was a bad situation with Mark and Kaia, but that Kaia was leaving!" he screamed. "Jesus. Did you tell her you thought Kaia could be my daughter?"

"Of course not. Clearly you had already said something like that to her. She kept asking about a dangerous possibility, or something like that."

"I would never have told her about your crazy idea. What did she say about Kaia?"

"I forget, Nico. I just got the impression she had guessed something. She was hysterical, and I just tried to calm her down, saying she was jumping to conclusions, or something along those lines."

"She was hysterical? Jean, why in the hell didn't you call me, or her doctor or *someone*, the police or whatever?"

"I don't mean she was literally hysterical, just upset. I told her to take her medicine and go to sleep, and then she hung up on me. Then I tried to reach you, but at first I couldn't find out where you were staying. I tried all of the inns in Beaulieu. When I found out where you were, you weren't answering the phone in your room."

"Jesus Christ, Jean. What kind of sister are you? What kind of *person* are you?" He slammed down the receiver, his throat raw. He sloshed down the rest of his whiskey and poured himself another glass. His heart still pounding in fury, he had to admit that he didn't recall exactly what he *had* said over the phone last night to Elisa.

He ran upstairs to their bedroom and stood there, his gaze fixed on the bed. He would never be able to sleep in here again. Tears coursed down his cheeks, and sobs broke out from deep inside his chest. He moaned, pressing his hands over his face.

They had killed her. He and Jean had murdered his beautiful wife.

9

In the morning Mark drank strong, hot coffee at the kitchen table, needing it to cut through the smog of his thoughts, and watched Kaia eat the last bit of egg and bread, moving the food to her mouth in a preoccupied way. They had barely spoken since they'd gotten up, and when she'd started packing, her face composed in grim determination, he couldn't stand to watch, so he'd walked out of the room.

After breakfast, Kaia returned to the porch room to take one last look around for her things. Mark followed her, grabbed his keys from the dresser and carried her bag outside.

They climbed into the pickup and he started the engine; it coughed, then idled roughly. He wished the engine would die so that Kaia would miss her flight and have time to think about what she was doing, but it revved up in a loud, obnoxious rumble. He turned to her, trying to steady himself.

"Tell me, Kaia. Are you planning on coming back or not?" It came out gruff and confrontational, but he couldn't help it.

She looked apprehensive, as if she were about to confess to something shameful. "Of course I'll be back."

It sounded so damned polite. He searched her face for signs. She returned his gaze, her jaw set. He wasn't sure whether or not he believed her.

"Kaia, you can't do this to me anymore. Don't ever come to me again unless you plan to stay with me. I can't keep putting my life on hold, day after day, year after year. I can't stand to have you ever leave me again. Do you hear what I'm saying?"

She nodded slowly, her lips quivering. "I told you, I just need to get my law degree. Then we can be together." She said this slowly, deliberately, as if to convince him that she meant it. "I asked you to come and live with me in San Francisco, but you're being so stubborn about staying out here."

"What, do you want me to work in a bank, or something like that? My furniture business is taking off here, and we'll need the income. Why couldn't you go to law school out here?"

"There's no law school around here, you know that, Mark. But there must be some way you could live in California, or you could come for longer periods of time. Please, think about it."

"After the way we've been this summer, how could you even consider leaving? Don't you see that we belong here together?"

She sighed. "Let's not keep arguing about this."

He shook his head and peered through the open side window at the dull grays and greens of the fields, trying hard to blanket his thoughts. He put the truck into reverse and backed up a few yards, slammed on the brakes, turned and sped down the gutted driveway, gravel spitting from under the tires. Then he drove out onto the stretch of highway.

When the sheriff's patrol car stopped Mark on his drive back from the airport, he thought he might have been speeding. The deputy came up to the cab and asked him if he was Mark Karadonis, and then Mark knew it wasn't for a traffic violation.

The young deputy took off his sunglasses and squinted at Mark. "I'm sorry to tell you, Mr. Karadonis, that there's some bad news. Your father called the sheriff's station and wanted us to inform you that there's been a death in your family."

"What?" Mark pushed the door open and got out, his heartbeat racing. It obviously wasn't Kaia, whose plane had taken off only fifteen minutes ago, and he hadn't heard a crash or sirens or anything like that. And they couldn't have gotten to him so quickly.

"Who?" he demanded, his hands on his hips, standing opposite the officer on the shoulder of the road.

"Your father said to tell you that your mother has died, and to come home as quickly as possible. I'm very sorry, sir." The deputy replaced his shades and pinched his nose, glancing down at his feet.

Mark couldn't move, his heart still pounding hard.

The cop glanced up. "Can I offer you some help, to call anyone, or anything?" he asked.

"No." Mark pressed his hand against his stomach, and stood there for several seconds, his legs shaking. "No, no." He shook his head. "I have to start driving." He got into the pickup and, his hands trembling, he started up the engine. He turned the truck around to head for Bangor and accelerated onto the road.

His entire body was trembling now, and he drove blindly, tears obscuring his vision. This was his father's fault, he was sure of it. His only goal now was to hold himself together until he could get to Bangor and find out what had happened. Only then would he believe it was true. His mother dead. He just couldn't absorb it as anything real. His main feeling was rage at his father. His father had to be responsible somehow.

For the next hour or so, he drove fast, going ninety at times, gunning past the occasional car on the road. Then he slowed down, feeling suddenly deflated, tears brimming up again—Kaia gone, his mother dead. How could all of that have happened in one day?

He stopped to call his father from a pay phone, but only got the answering machine with Nico's recorded voice: "We're not home, but leave a message and we'll call you back." A wave of nausea came over Mark, and he couldn't think of any sort of message to leave, so he hung up. He took some deep breaths, then got back into the pickup and drove off. He still didn't fully believe that his mother had died; he had to have it confirmed. An accident? No, more likely an overdose, like the other time.

The second time he stopped at a pay phone, a couple of hours from Bangor, he reached his father. Nico sounded fatigued and said Elisa had taken a lot of pills while he was in Beaulieu. He'd found her lying on their bed, comatose, and she'd died at the hospital. He had no explanation, no clue as to why she had done this. Jean was with him in Bangor.

Tears rolled down Mark's cheeks. After hanging up, he returned to the pickup, where he sat, sobbing, finally believing it was true.

A few minutes later, he forced himself to get back on the road, and then he started to wonder why Jean was already at their house and what she had to do with this. He dreaded seeing her.

When he arrived at the house, his red-eyed father hugged him tightly, patting his back, while Jean stood in the middle of the living room with her arms crossed, observing the two of them. Mark tore himself away from his father's grip and ran upstairs to his parents' bedroom. The room was dark, the drapes closed. The air smelled smoky. He switched on the bedside lamp, then searched the table and dresser top, desperate to find a note. His father came quietly into the room and stood watching, then came up to Mark and laid a hand on his arm. Mark wrenched himself away, frantic to find something.

Nico remained in the room, saying nothing, while Mark searched through his mother's desk and everywhere else he could think of—under the bed, under the pillows, in her dresser. Finally Mark turned around. His father stood there, hands in pockets, with a perplexed, stricken expression.

"Did you already find something?" Mark demanded. "Was there a note? Don't keep it from me. I have to know."

His father shook his head, tears glinting on his sallow cheeks. "Not a thing," he whispered, biting his lip. "Absolutely nothing."

Mark left the room and strode down the hall to his old bedroom, shutting the door. He lay down on his back and stared up at the ceiling, furious with both of his parents. Then he felt the hard object under his pillow. He sat up and uncovered his mother's journal.

He turned on the lamp and flipped through it to the last entry, written in Elisa's slanted script:

> It is hours past midnight, black rain falling. I'm drinking my glass of wine with a Lithium tablet to stay calm, but will soon take all the pills, the ones that anesthetize, the ones that will do what's necessary. With poisoned clarity I write—thoughts poisoned by what Nico and Jean have told me, poisoned by their treachery.
>
> Not the kind of day I expected, though I knew one day things would crack wide open and I would fall through. It is a day with summer rain and not, as I once envisioned, a snowy day with Nico tromping around outside in his galoshes, oblivious. There is a slackness, things do not fit. I can no longer anticipate his return, the proper emotions absent as I contemplate the charade, the deviation that was our marriage. I am estranged now from all of it. I only wonder why—the intricacies of their lies, their brazen deception. I denied all of it for so long, though I had a feeling something was going on. I simply didn't let myself believe it.
>
> What can come of it, this fraudulence? Our love seemed mysterious, shadowy, but is now harshly delineated, a small, paltry thing.
>
> But mostly I think of you, Mark, and our deep steady love. I must remember, too, my baby girl, the sister you never knew, an unfurling bud, with her blossoming allegiances, her soft gaze and lovely face.

Follow your passions wherever they may lead,
Mark darling. Pay no heed to the others.
This journal and this poem are for you alone.
Burn everything. Please.
All my love, your mother

Beauteous
The love I nearly had
That phantom
Vested now in Kaia's
Turquoise eyes.

Mark lay back down and forced himself to take long, deep breaths.

He stuffed the journal back under his pillow, then sat up on the edge of the bed, leaning over and covering his mouth. He tried to force back the tears, but convulsive sobs began to wrack his entire body, and he found there was nothing he could do to stop the onslaught.

10

After flying all day with tedious stopovers in Boston and Houston, Kaia deplaned in San Francisco late in the evening. She searched for Sig but didn't see her, and then was shocked to see her father waving at her. She was outraged that he had come for her and detested the stern look on his face; she was in no mood for a confrontation.

As soon as she reached him, he bent and kissed her on the cheek.

"Sig's coming to get me," she snapped.

"Actually, she's not coming." He shifted his shoulders back, and frowned. "I phoned her and told her I'd get you."

"Why did you do that? I just want to go to her place and go to bed. She said I could stay there for a while."

"I want you to come over to the house, Kaia, at least for tonight." There was something grim in his manner that stopped her for a moment.

"I'm not ready for any heavy talks or anything like that. You can't just force me—"

"I'm not forcing you, Kaia." His voice was unusually calm. "I just need to have you at home for a short while, and I'd like you to come with me."

She sighed, too tired to resist. "No talks tonight, though, okay, Dad?"

His jaw tightened, but he kept silent, fixing his gaze ahead as they walked down the corridor. If he wanted to talk about Mark, she would refuse. It could wait until she'd at least had some sleep.

They drove to the house, mostly in silence. When they stepped into the front room, her father gestured toward the sofa, his face contorted with emotion. "Kaia, please sit down. I do have something I need to tell you."

She hesitated, but something in his grave expression made her do as she was told. He seated himself next to her on the sofa and took one of her hands in his. His palms were hot and moist.

He looked into Kaia's eyes. "It's your Aunt Elisa," he said gently. "She died last night."

Kaia gasped. "Oh, God," she choked out.

"She took a lot of pills," he continued. "She was on some new medication, your mother said, and she apparently became unstable. That's all we know."

"But Nico was just at the cabin—"

"Yes, I know. It happened while he was in Beaulieu. When he got back, he found her and called an ambulance, but she died at the hospital. I didn't want to tell you at the airport."

Kaia's tears sprang up and she covered her face with her hands. Her father put his arm around her.

After a few seconds she peered up at him. "Have they told Mark?"

"The sheriff informed him, and Mark was in Bangor when I spoke to your mother this afternoon."

"Oh, no. Not Elisa." Kaia started sobbing at first silently, then noisily, and her father hugged her tightly to his chest.

"I'm sorry I had to give you the news like this."

"Why didn't you tell me at the airport?" she asked, taking in deep breaths between sobs. "I could have taken the next flight back."

"This wouldn't be a good time to go back, Kaia."

"Why not?"

"They need to make arrangements, and deal with this themselves."

"I have to be there with Mark and Nico. We'll be going to the funeral, anyway." She stared at him through her tears. "You don't want me to go back. That's why you didn't tell me at the airport."

"I couldn't tell you there, Kaia. I had to bring you home."

She tried to rise, wanting to call Mark, but her father took hold of her shoulders and eased her back down onto the couch.

"Just sit here, Kaia. I'll get you some tea. You look awful. You just need to rest for a while. I know this is hard for you, and how fond you were of Elisa."

"When is the funeral?" She knew she sounded edgy and fierce, but she had to know everything.

"They don't know yet, and I don't think we should go. Your mother can represent our side of the family."

"What?" Dumbfounded, Kaia gawked at her father, at his deeply furrowed forehead. She was starting to feel frantic, and tried to focus. She focused for some reason on the coffee stains on his tan polo shirt. In his rush to get to the airport, he probably hadn't bothered to change, so that he would be there when she stepped off the plane. She clearly pictured him dashing off like that, and was convinced this was the way it happened, this exact scenario.

"Of course I'll go to Maine," she said, her mouth dry. "She's my aunt. She's Mark's mother. I have to call Mark right now." She knew she was jabbering, but couldn't stop herself.

"It's past midnight back there, Kaia. They need their sleep. It would be inconsiderate to call now."

She shook her head vigorously, tears pouring down her face. Mark would want to talk to her. She knew he would.

"I'll make some tea," her father said. "Just stay here. You're in shock, Kaia."

He returned a couple of minutes later, carrying a cup of steaming peppermint tea, and placed it in her hands. The hot porcelain warmed her fingers as she took a sip, absently inhaling the tea's fragrance. Her father sat down next to her.

"I'm flying back, Dad."

He frowned slightly. "You just need to get some sleep. Then we can talk this over."

She started crying again, and her hands were shaking so badly she had to set the cup down. Shivering, she clutched at her father's shirt, and he wrapped his arms around her as if she were a small child and he could somehow shield her from everything.

*

After her father went to bed, Kaia dialed Nico's number in Bangor. Mark answered after a couple of rings and sounded wide awake, but somber. He told her Jean was there and that she and Nico were going out in the morning to make arrangements for the funeral.

"Why is Mom there already?" Kaia asked.

"She was here when I got here. I don't like having her around, but Dad's leaning on her a lot."

"I wish I could be with you right now. If we'd only known, I wouldn't have left."

"You mean you would have delayed leaving."

The bitterness in his tone chilled her. "She's my aunt, Mark. I loved her. Of course I would have stayed on."

He didn't respond.

"I'll get a flight tomorrow," she said.

"No. Don't come, Kaia."

"Why not?"

"I know you loved my mother, but it would be too hard for me if you came. I can't go through your leaving again, on top of all of this." His voice was strained.

"You know why I left. But this is different. I'll come and stay for as long as I can."

"How long is that?"

"Please, Mark. I want to be there with you."

"No, Kaia. Not unless you'll stay with me this time." Mark was choking up he spoke. "After all the time we spent together this summer, I started to believe you were going to live with me permanently. I let myself hope that. I still don't know how you could have left. And now my mother's gone, too."

Kaia was silent for a moment, then asked quietly, "Why did she do it?"

"She found out about your mother and my dad."

"Oh, no. How did she find out?"

"I don't know, Kaia. But she knew."

They talked a few more minutes, and she continued to plead with him to let her come, but he was adamant. It was hard for her to believe he actually didn't want her there with him. She could only hope he would become less upset and would change his mind in the next few days.

But later that night, lying in bed, she told herself she had to listen to him, had to believe he knew what he wanted, even though it was not at all what she wanted or needed.

A few days later, Kaia called Mark again in Bangor, and he told her in a dull voice about the memorial service, and how his father was doing—barely functioning, he said.

"I wish I'd been there," she said.

"Now I wish you could have been here, too. This hurts like hell."

"I can still come."

"No, it's too late, Kaia. I'm going back to the cabin soon."

She absorbed this in silence, her throat tightening.

"I asked your mother to leave," he said. "There was no need for her to be here once the memorial service was over. She left yesterday."

"I knew it would be difficult, having her there."

"Difficult? That doesn't begin to describe it. Anyway, she's gone now. She and Dad both talked to Mom that night on the phone, and apparently one of them told her about their affair. I heard them arguing about who said what to Mom."

Kaia gasped. "I can't believe they would tell her."

"It was idiotic," Mark said. "I guess Dad was drunk when he called my mother. According to him, Jean had been drinking, too, that night. They could have said anything."

"Oh, God, how terrible."

Mark blew out a long breath. "Anyway, after I help Dad take care of some things, I'll be gone." There was a long pause. "And Kaia? Please don't contact me until you've made up your mind about us. It's too painful for me."

"Mark, I love you. I have made up my mind. I've told you, I do want us to be together, just not in Maine right now. Don't do this."

"I just can't take it, Kaia. I want you here with me. Not years from now." His voice shaky, he said good-bye and hung up.

She couldn't bear it, leaving things like that. She pictured him driving northward, miserable and alone in his grief. She had to be there with him.

Two days later, when she called the house in Bangor, Nico answered and said Mark had driven back to Beaulieu.

"He wouldn't let me fly out for the funeral," she said.

"I know. He's in bad shape, Kaia. We both are. Mark needs to be alone now, I think. He loved his mother so much."

"I loved her, too."

"I know that, Kaia, and she loved you very much."

How could they banish her like this, exclude her from their grief?

Her mother called once and left a message to call her, but Kaia didn't return the call; she couldn't bear to talk to her about Elisa or Mark or anything else. Her mother would never admit to anything, Kaia felt sure. Still, it was agonizing, not having a clue about what had actually happened that night, and not being able to be there with Mark.

11

Kaia stayed on at her father's, retreating upstairs every night to sleep in Mark's old bed. It was comforting to lie there with Elisa's silky quilt resting on her shoulder like her aunt's gentle hand. Her father said nothing about her spending her nights in the loft, but he kept a close watch on her during the day, probably out of concern that she would contact Mark. Kaia barely spoke to her father during their dinners together, feeling too listless and sad to bother with conversation. She felt she was now in a world with much different attributes than the one she'd inhabited with Mark at his cabin for the past two months.

She started going into the law office late in the morning, and making herself work on her new case. Inevitably, though, she would start ruminating about Elisa, and about Mark, and would have to leave the office early, too depressed to work. Chandi knew what had happened, and insisted that work was good for Kaia, to get her mind off of "unproductive things." Kaia met Sig a few times for lunch, but couldn't muster the energy to look for her own apartment. A certain inertia, a near-physical queasiness about dealing with practical matters, had settled in, and it was easier to stay with her father. Although she often prepared their dinner, it was always a slight offering of meat and vegetables, and she ate very little, having no appetite. Law school would start in a few weeks in San Francisco, and she knew she would soon have to find a place to live near Hastings.

In late August, she had a dizzy spell while working at the office and had to lie down in the lounge for a while before getting on the bus. As she rode the bus home over the Bay Bridge, the startling thought occurred to her that she could be pregnant. She tried to recall specific occasions when she had actually used her diaphragm during the summer—she always hated using it and had only done so when she wasn't "safe." She couldn't remember having a period since she'd left San Francisco in early June. How could she have been such an idiot?

That evening she bought an early pregnancy test, but then decided to wait a week to use it. That way, she told herself, it was more likely to be accurate. No false alarms that way—and no false hopes. But how could she possibly hope for something she wasn't at all sure she wanted?

During the following week at dinner, she didn't have any wine, just in case. Her normally vigilant father barely raised an eyebrow. He hardly seemed to notice, either, when she started munching saltines in the morning to stave off her frequent bouts of nausea. And she had acquired a sudden aversion to the smell or sight of fish or even the mention of her favorite seafood restaurant. She burrowed into Mark's bed by nine p.m. every night, too tired and queasy to think about anything serious.

She already knew the answer, but finally braved the home pregnancy test one morning after her father had gone to his office. Still in her pajamas, she went into the bathroom and followed the directions on the box. She left for two minutes, too anxious to stay and watch for the result. When she returned, the tester was a bright, unequivocal blue. She gasped in shock. *God. Pregnant. A baby.* She wanted to call Mark, but she couldn't do that. He had no phone. And how would he react? What would they do?

Mark's child—this was what she had always wanted but thought she couldn't have, and here it was, inside of her. She shouldn't be thinking of it as a child already, but she seemed to be letting her imagination run wild. What did she really want, anyway? She would have to be sure, for Mark's sake and her own. He had made it clear it was all or nothing—marry him and live in his cabin, or be apart. Was giving up law school even a possibility? And she might have an early miscarriage—so why risk telling anyone now? Everyone would try to pressure her one way or the other, and she didn't need that. She could almost hear her mother telling her she was about to ruin her chances for a stellar career if she kept the baby. Kaia decided she wouldn't tell anyone—she had to figure out exactly how she felt about this first, on her own. How could she go to law school and continue working if she was having a baby next spring? And what was Mark's role in this?

Then she thought of something else—it wasn't only Mark's and her child; it was also Elisa's grandchild. Kaia thought of the beautiful month she'd spent with Mark in Maine, followed by the tragedy of Elisa's suicide. How could she even consider destroying something that was part of Mark and herself, and also part of Elisa? In her more optimistic moments, she thought that something miraculous could still come of the summer.

She grabbed the Yellow Pages and searched for genetic specialists, running her eyes over the doctors' names. What would she be asking a geneticist to determine, exactly? Could they test for every conceivable birth defect? What would they be looking for, exactly? She shuddered to think what it would mean if something turned out to be drastically wrong with the baby. She could never tell Mark if she decided to have an abortion; it sickened her to think of it, and it would disturb him deeply.

She dressed and drove to the county medical library. With a librarian's help, she found some studies that put the risk of birth defects at a mere four percent or less when cousins had a child together versus two-and-a-half percent for those couples who were not related. Ninety-six percent chance of everything being normal. Pretty unlikely that anything would be wrong.

She hadn't heard from Mark since their last conversation when he was in Bangor, over a month ago. He seemed to be shutting her out, but he was undoubtedly still grieving. And of course there was his ultimatum—not to contact him unless she intended to stay with him.

At times when she was at the office, feeling too woozy to read the papers on her desk, Kaia couldn't prevent herself from daydreaming about the baby, imagining its tiny hands and feet and rotund little body. One morning she had to rush into the restroom at work to throw up. Afterwards, she washed her face and gaped at her gray face in the mirror, but when she went out into the office, no one seemed to notice how sick she looked. Her father clearly hadn't heard her vomiting in the mornings at home, since she was still sleeping in the loft and using the upstairs bathroom. He merely seemed content to have her at home with him.

Law classes were starting soon, and she knew she should start looking for an apartment in San Francisco. But how would law school fit in with the pregnancy? And there was that lassitude that made it hard to do anything that required any degree of purposefulness.

✳

Kaia paused in front of The Orchid restaurant, turning to view the brilliant sunset over the San Francisco Bay. Layers of orange and lavender at the horizon faded upward into a diluted sea-green, blending into a vast cerulean ceiling of sky. The entire panorama appeared glowing, auspicious. She turned and climbed the steps winding through the terraced garden of the restaurant, each level lit with diamonds of white lights and set with pots of burning, spice-scented incense.

Entering, she took in the familiar mirrored walls, cherry-red tablecloths and the mingled scent of chilies, coconut and lemon grass, and was glad that she'd asked Chandi to meet her here. It was one of Kaia's favorite Thai restaurants; she sometimes dined here with her father. She was wearing a new flowing, blue dress, hoping to disguise her thickening waist. She spotted Chandi, seated at a corner table, sipping from a cup. As Kaia approached, Chandi greeted her with a luminescent smile.

"What a lovely dress, Kaia."

"Thanks, Chandi."

Kaia was ravenous and wanted to try everything on the menu. They decided to share the lemon grass soup, green papaya salad, and two vegetarian entrées. The young waiter suggested a bottle of wine with dinner, but Kaia declined, ordering Thai iced tea instead. She glanced across the table to find Chandi grinning at her. Kaia lifted her eyebrows inquiringly.

Chandi winked and ordered a glass of Chardonnay. "I'll have some for both of us," she said, once the waiter had left. "So. Off wine for the duration, but your appetite's back, I see."

Kaia laughed. "So you've guessed? But how did you know?"

"For one thing, when we went out for drinks last week, you ordered Perrier—not like you at all. Then yesterday I heard you getting sick in the office restroom. It wasn't so hard to figure out, really."

"Okay, okay. Obviously you're so clever and observant."

"So is that why you asked me to meet you for dinner, to talk about it?"

"I asked because you're a good friend, Chandi, and the only person I feel I can talk with about this. But I wasn't even sure, to be honest, whether I would actually tell you about it. In any event, you don't have any preconceived ideas about what's best for me, and I trust your judgment."

"Thank you, Kaia. I do consider you a very good friend, too. First of all I must say, though, that you're absolutely aglow—rosy cheeks and all."

"Sometimes I feel more like a pale greenish blob, and the nausea can last for hours."

"My sisters started feeling better in the fourth month."

"I'm not quite there yet, unfortunately. At least I feel better in the evenings—that's when I get really hungry."

"So you've told Mark, I assume?"

"No. I haven't even decided what to do."

Chandi frowned, looking perplexed. "You mean whether you'll have the baby?"

Kaia shook her head. "It's not that, exactly. It's just that I may decide to do this on my own, if Mark doesn't want to be part of this. He may not want to come out here to live with me, and I'm not sure I'd want to have my baby in Maine and live in a cabin in the country."

"Oh, I see." Chandi sat back in her seat, just as the waiter brought their drinks.

Kaia drank some of the sweet, creamy iced tea.

"You haven't told your father?" Chandi said. "Surely he's noticed something, since you're living at home."

"That I'm pregnant with Mark's baby? No, I haven't told him. I just hope you're the only one who's figured it out."

"It will become obvious to everyone soon enough. You can't wait forever."

Kaia dropped her eyes, sighing, then looked at her friend. "I'm *not* absolutely sure, actually, if it's the best thing for me to go through with this."

"Oh, Kaia."

"There's a higher risk of birth defects when cousins have a child."

"I don't think it's that significant, Kaia. All over the world cousins get married and have children. You and Mark are both healthy."

"That's my biggest concern, having a healthy baby."

Chandi leaned forward, squeezing her hand. "Yes, I do understand that, Kaia."

"Dad would be furious if I went through with this, and Mom would, too. Not that I have the best relationship in the world with either of them. But they're the only parents I've got."

"Yes, I'm sure your father would be angry. He doesn't think too highly of Mark."

"That's quite an understatement," Kaia said, smiling.

The steaming, fragrant soup and papaya salad arrived, along with their entrées. Kaia had some of the soup, but she barely tasted it, thinking about all of the uncertainties in her life. They were both silent for a couple of minutes as they ate.

Finally Chandi said, "So assuming you go ahead with this, would you still go to law school full-time? And work, too? You may be rather tired as the pregnancy progresses."

"I don't think it's possible to attend Hastings part-time."

"You could talk to the dean about it, maybe just take one class this semester, then take the spring semester off. And only work as many hours as you can."

"It wouldn't be that easy."

"The main thing is, do you want this child? And what about Mark?"

"Mark would want me to drop everything and move to his cabin in Maine. But I want to get started toward a law career here in California. I want to do children's rights. I want the baby, and I want Mark to be here with me."

"Good. You do know exactly what you want. You can have everything, Kaia, I'm pretty sure about that. Just make one decision at a time. I'll help you in any way that I can."

"Thanks, Chandi."

"Since you do want to have this child, Kaia, that's all that matters. Everything else will fit in. Your parents will just have to deal with it. Mark will have to make some compromises if he wants to be with you and the baby."

Kaia nodded, taking another taste of the salad. "You make it sound so simple. But as far as law school goes, I suppose I could get a loan for the tuition if Dad won't pay."

"Nothing about it is all that simple, I realize that. But I also know you'll make a wonderful mother, Kaia."

"I'll certainly do things differently than my mother did. I would never leave my child, for any reason." Kaia took a drink before going on. "When Mom moved to New York, I kept telling myself it was an ordeal I had to go through for just a short time until she realized how much she missed me. But even on Pine Tree, during our vacation, she was pretty distant. I had the sense I would always love her more than she would ever love me."

"How very sad, Kaia."

"I guess that has something to do with why I've been afraid to get married—making a commitment to love someone and then having it not work out. And my parents' marriage was such a failure."

Chandi caught Kaia's gaze and held it. "You'll always have your child to love, and to love you back." She sat back in her chair, smiling. "And of course I get to be the auntie."

"You'll be a pretty classy auntie, Chandi." Even with the few strands of gray in her black hair and the lines radiating outward from her eyes when she smiled, Chandi somehow managed to appear even more vivacious and youthful than a few years ago.

"I'm so thrilled for you," Chandi said.

"I'm thrilled, too, Chandi," Kaia said, smiling broadly.

If only her own mother would feel that way, she thought. But with Chandi here, she'd have the support she needed from someone who cared about her—someone who believed in the importance of being a mother, even though she'd never been one herself. Chandi had a wonderful maternal side Kaia appreciated now more than ever.

12

A few mornings later, lying in bed, Kaia felt a heavy fatigue that seemed to have settled into the marrow of her bones. Tiredness was supposed to be normal in the first trimester, she'd read, but it didn't feel normal to her. It felt debilitating. What could be wrong?

When she finally dragged herself out of bed and dressed, she called the dean and told him she had to work full-time now, and got permission to take only one class in the fall semester. But she knew that even if she couldn't keep up with everything, the child was hers, not to be tampered with. That was the important thing. And Chandi had said she would help her figure out what to do each step of the way. On a purely instinctual level, and despite her leaden feeling, she had faith in this pregnancy as if it were a newfound religion.

In the afternoon, she was feeling better, and drove into the city to buy her Contracts textbook and to check rental listings at the housing office. She found a card on the bulletin board that read: "Cottage Available in Marin County." Professor Graham was seeking a law student who could take care of his cottage in

San Rafael during the school year while he was on sabbatical in Australia. "Light gardening; rent negotiable."

She grabbed the card and found him in his office, and they quickly reached an agreement. He was leaving in two days, so she could move in this weekend. For a nominal rent, she could have the place until next July. She was more than willing to take the cottage sight unseen, even though it was miles outside of the city. The commute shouldn't be too bad if she left early to avoid rush hour over the Golden Gate Bridge. She couldn't believe her luck.

On Friday she drove to San Rafael and found the vacant white stucco cottage with its red-tiled roof, the front yard overgrown with tall weeds and unmown grass. Letting herself in, she took a tour of the house, admiring the stone fireplace and built-in bookshelves in the living room and the Mexican-tile floor that needed only a colorful rug to warm it. The worn parquet floor in the dining room could be polished to bring out its natural sheen, and the old furniture was usable. Through the French doors, she surveyed the garden, where rose bushes and other plants grew wild; a gravel path led to an old, ramshackle shed. Mark would love this place, she thought. She checked out the bedroom with its old plaster walls and a room next to it that was barely the size of a walk-in closet, and then the kitchen with its old-fashioned refrigerator.

Feeling a new, soaring happiness, she was certain now that this was the place for her and her baby. She realized, then, that she had already decided she wanted this child when she'd first seen the pregnancy test strip turn a vibrant blue.

When she told her father about the cottage that evening, he frowned and said, predictably, "Why not stay here with me in Berkeley? It's much closer to Hastings than San Rafael, and the commute would be so much easier for you."

"No thanks. I really need to be on my own, Dad."

"I just thought—"

"I'm moving into the cottage this weekend."

On Sunday, her grim-faced father and his friend Paul moved Kaia's few boxes and pieces of furniture into the cottage, using Paul's pickup. Kaia wouldn't allow the two men to help her unpack or take her out to dinner. "I'm fine, I'm fine," she kept telling them. This was her own place, at least for the present, and she wanted to ease into possession of it as if she were trying out an old pair of boots she'd found at a flea market, testing them to see how they would feel to walk around in.

After they left, Kaia searched through boxes until she found her kettle and a tin of jasmine tea. She made herself a cup, then retreated to the antique rocking chair she'd just bought at a garage sale. She figured she was about two months pregnant, and couldn't quite imagine what it would feel like to have a baby moving inside her belly. She thought of the bassinet and baby blankets she would need to buy, and the colors she might paint the tiny office, to convert it to a nursery—if Professor Graham didn't mind. Mint green, robin's-egg blue, peach? She would write him to make sure it was all right. He'd already said that anything she did would be an improvement, so it shouldn't be a problem.

She hadn't done any stained-glass work for a couple of months, but she wanted to start designing a new piece when she had time during the winter break; she thought she might be able to use the shed as a studio. Gazing into the garden, she thought of planting pomegranate bushes and a scattering of wildflowers. Already, this house had a quality of yielding to her, even though it was hers only temporarily.

The following week she finally saw an obstetrician, a young doctor who was accepting new patients at a clinic in San Rafael. Kaia would have preferred a woman physician, but the referral service had told her that Dr. Wisecki was excellent and that there were no female obstetricians at the clinic. Kaia was still covered by her dad's medical insurance, but hopefully he wouldn't get any notification of her visits.

"You're approximately eight weeks pregnant," Dr. Wisecki informed her in a neutral tone. He prescribed prenatal vitamins and told her to eat well, take it easy and come back in a month for an ultrasound. Kaia left his office in a state of stunned elation, allowing herself to savor the steady comfort of Mark's baby growing inside of her.

The following Saturday morning, Kaia awoke feeling more energetic than she had in weeks, and decided it was time to tell Mark. She wished, as she had many times, that he had a phone at his cabin, so that she could hear his voice when she told him. It seemed there was so much to explain, but when she took pen to paper it came out rather simply:

> Dear Mark,
>
> I've missed you so much since I left Maine. I know you're grieving for your mother, and unhappy about the way we left things. I've been grieving, too. I wish that I'd stayed with you longer, and that we'd made more definite plans to be together.
>
> You said you didn't want me to contact you until I was sure about our future, but I had to write to tell you something important. I'm pregnant with your baby, Mark. I would have told you sooner, but I thought I might lose it early on. I'm in my third month now and am taking only one law class. I'm working full-time for now, to save up for the baby.
>
> I love you more than anything, and I want you to be here with me. Please call me.
>
> All my love, Kaia

It normally took several days for her letters to reach Beaulieu, and Mark didn't go into town to get his mail very often. The wait was agonizing. A week went by and she still hadn't heard from him, but she was sure she would get a call or letter any day.

She decided to tell her father, just to get it over with, and chose to give him the news over the phone one evening in order to allow for a quick escape.

When he answered, she said, "Dad, I have something to tell you, and I don't want you to argue or get upset, okay?"

There was a moment of silence, then he said, "Well?" He already sounded angry.

"This is going to be hard for you to accept, Dad, but—" She hesitated for a moment, taking a breath.

"Come on, Kaia, out with it."

"Well, the thing is, Dad, I'm going to have a baby."

He groaned sharply, as if in great pain. "Jesus! Is this some kind of joke, Kaia?"

She said nothing.

"How long have you known?" he demanded.

"A while."

"So that's why you moved into that cottage?" He was shouting into the phone now. "You're actually going to go through with this?"

"Yes, I am. But I had been planning to find my own place anyway."

"What about law school? And your job?"

"I'll keep working as long as I can, and I'm only taking one class for now."

"My God, Kaia. If you think I'm going to bail you out of this one, forget it. I won't be any part of this mess."

"I don't need anyone to bail me out. Anyway, this is what I expected from you."

"What in the hell does that mean?"

"You've never paid attention to what I wanted, only what you wanted from me, and what you wanted me to be. Anyway, I'll manage. It's your grandchild, but it's your choice about how to deal with this."

"My grandchild via your goddamned cousin, I assume," he growled. "You can't do this, Kaia."

"Don't ever speak of Mark that way again. And you have no choice in this."

"Yes, I do, and that's to have no part of this."

"What, no part in my life?"

He was silent for several seconds, then said gruffly, "I can't stomach this, I just cannot."

She felt tears brimming up, but said nothing.

"Don't do this, Kaia. Think about your future. What could be worse than being a single mother with no viable means of support, trying to raise a kid? And Mark is your cousin, for Christ's sake—a hermit living in the wilds of Maine—"

"Actually, that's all I have to say about this now, except don't tell anyone yet, especially Mom. I have to tell her myself, when I'm ready."

"I wouldn't want that task," he said, his voice weighted with sarcasm.

"Don't tell anyone, Dad. I'll do it myself." She slammed down the phone.

Her heart was pounding away—which was probably bad for the baby, she thought. All that adrenaline. She took several deep breaths, then got up from the kitchen table and walked slowly around the cottage, trying to slow down her heartbeat. Finally she stood at the French doors, staring into the garden, trying to visualize living alone here with a baby, struggling to survive, isolated from her family and friends, except for Chandi, and maybe Sig. If only Mark would call.

She gave a long sigh, placing her hands on her slightly rounded belly. Maybe it wasn't the perfect way to have a child. But her child was a fact, a small being she already loved, and everything else would have to work around that ineluctable fact.

*

Later in the evening, after she'd had a cup of peppermint tea, she dialed Sig's number and gave her the news.

"God, Kaia. Is that why you haven't called recently?"

"I haven't been avoiding you, if that's what you mean."

"Yes, you have."

"I've just been busy with work." Kaia paused for a few seconds in guilt-ridden silence. "Okay, so I was afraid to tell you. And you don't sound exactly thrilled."

"I'm just trying to understand, that's all. I bet you told Mark right away."

"I've written him, but he probably hasn't picked up his mail yet. He doesn't get into town very often."

"So it's his," Sig said resentfully.

"Of course it's Mark's."

Sig grunted. "Didn't you even consider not having it?"

"I did think about it, a little, but I didn't want to hear anyone utter the word termination in my presence until I was sure what I wanted to do. What it comes down to is that I want this baby, no matter what. I'm only taking one law class for now, and I'll keep working for as long as I can."

"What about your dad? What's he going to say?"

"I told him. He was furious. He said he doesn't want any part of this."

There was a long moment of silence. Then, in a hushed voice Sig said, "So there's an actual little person growing inside of you."

"Yes." Kaia wiped away the tears that had sprouted from her eyes. "Damned hormones," was all she could manage to choke out. "Making me cry at the drop of a hat." She sniffled. "I love you, Sig. You know that, don't you?"

There was a pause before Sig said in a grudging tone, "I guess so, Kaia. I love you, too. No matter what, I'll always be there for you."

"I know that, Sig."

13

David pulled into the long dirt driveway leading up to Kaia's cottage and was relieved to see her faded red Volkswagen parked out in front. He hadn't called her before driving over; he was afraid she would tell him not to come. He was worried about her, living alone in a semi-rural area outside of San Rafael—and pregnant, for Christ's sake. What a disastrous situation, especially since Mark was the father. David also felt uneasy about this idea of a woman having a child on her own. Her plans seemed so makeshift, irresponsible even, and she seemed so cavalier about disrupting her studies and her career.

He wasn't sure how he'd missed the signs, although now that he reflected on it, there had been something unusual about her when they'd last had dinner together at the house, when she hadn't drunk any wine or eaten much. He had assumed that her abstemiousness was related to the recent upheavals in her life—the months spent in Maine with Mark, Elisa's suicide, and then the prospect of starting law school.

But during the past few days, his dread about Kaia's plans had begun to surpass his outrage. It seemed possible, too, that she would distance herself from him permanently if he didn't attempt to rectify things between them. And how would she manage by herself? He had to see her and talk things over, so he'd thought of driving to the cottage to install some extra locks on her windows.

He rang the doorbell and heard muffled steps inside the house; a moment later the door swung open. His lovely daughter stood before him with a look of astonishment on her face.

Kaia hesitated a moment, then exclaimed, "Oh, Dad!" She stepped forward carefully, into his arms. He felt the slight swell of her abdomen in her otherwise lithe frame. She pulled back, scrutinizing his face.

"I hope you don't mind me coming over like this," he said. "It's just that I've been worried about you being here alone, so I've brought some locks so I can make sure your windows are secure." He tried to make his speech smooth and casual, though he felt like a bumbling suitor.

"That's good of you, Dad. I'm sure Carl won't mind."

"Carl?"

"Yes, the professor who owns the cottage. He wrote and said I can fix up the cottage pretty much any way I want."

For one ridiculous moment, David had hoped there might be a man in Kaia's life other than Mark. He held Kaia at arm's length, looking her up and down. She was wearing a soft, gray tunic and burgundy tights, her dark hair hanging loose over her shoulders. At last he fully comprehended that his daughter, standing flushed and bright eyed before him, was bearing his grandchild.

Kaia brought ginger tea and bran muffins from the kitchen and sat down on the rug next to the fire, which she'd lit earlier. She watched as her father, seated in the rocker, surveyed the room, his eyes passing over the ferns she'd hung in front of the French doors, Mark's photo of the nude woman reaching for her infant, and the built-in bookshelves with all of her own books neatly arranged.

There were deeper lines in her father's face these days, and his hair was going gray, his receding hairline accentuating his widow's peak. Now it wasn't so difficult to picture him as a grandfather. The sunlight fell across his face, making one of his eyes appear to be a darker blue than the other one—but then his right eye was in fact a shade darker than the left. She recalled pointing it out when she was nine or ten, the moment she had discovered the difference.

"So how are you, Kaia?" he asked. "You're looking good. How have you been feeling?"

"A little tired these days. I'm working full-time now for Chandi and taking Contracts."

He nodded, staring into her face as she looked up at him. "So what's the deal?" he asked, a hint of gruffness entering his voice. "What are you going to do?"

"Just what I'm doing now, I guess." She took a bite of her muffin, thinking about how to encapsulate her plans. "I'm really happy now, Dad. It's a simple, uncomplicated happiness."

He frowned slightly. "Simple? Well, that brings us to the obvious question of how you're going to live."

She shrugged. "The rent's low, I have some savings, and I have some income. I'll just have to be frugal."

"For now. And what about later?"

"I'll see how things are once the baby's born in April."

He heaved a deep sigh. "I certainly hope you've gone to see a geneticist."

"I've done some research. It's not nearly as high a risk as everyone seems to think."

"But still—"

"I wouldn't consider termination, Dad. No matter what."

"What about adoption?"

"It's out of the question. Please don't mention anything like that again. I'm not abandoning my child to some stranger."

Her father glowered at her. "Since you seem to be intent on going through with this, I want you to know that you can always live with me. And if you do, I'll support you and the child for as long as you want." He rocked slowly in the chair, watching her face with a keen expression.

That was something, his offer of support, except that it was clearly conditioned on her living with him. That was why he'd come, to make this suggestion, she was sure. This was his solution. To have her to himself, under his control again. "Can't you see I belong here, Dad, in my own place?"

"Kaia, have you actually thought this through?"

"Yes, I have. I'm not without skills, you know. We'll be fine."

He gave her a sharp look. "You mean you and the baby, I assume."

"Yes. And Mark, at some point." She could hear the quiet wistfulness in her own voice. She felt it profoundly now, this longing, as an ache in her throat and chest, her yearning to have Mark living with her, sharing her pregnancy and the birth and raising of their child. But she wasn't going to admit to her father that she hadn't heard from Mark, and that she was worried he might not be willing to move back to California.

Her father's face had gone slack at the mention of Mark's name, and he stopped rocking in his chair. "So that's your choice," he said in a somber voice.

"What choice?"

"To have him involved."

Her father couldn't even say Mark's name. It wasn't as if she were choosing Mark over her father. She shouldn't have to make such a choice. "I want Mark in my life, Dad. But I want you to be involved, too. You're the grandfather, you know."

He merely shook his head, his face impassive. She slowly rose to her feet and stood over him with her hands on her hips. "Remember not to tell Mom yet. I'll tell her myself."

"I rarely talk to her anymore."

He stood up in a stiff motion, leaving the rocker to squeak back and forth on the tile floor. "Well, I'm going to start on those locks. I'll get my tools from the car."

He pinched the bridge of his nose, then faced her squarely and took her by the shoulders, standing there for several long seconds just staring into her face. Then he kissed her on the forehead and turned toward the door.

She could see that from his viewpoint, nothing had really been resolved. But she couldn't help feeling that something had shifted, something between her father and her. It seemed to her, at least, like a small step forward.

14

Surely Mark would pick up his mail soon in Beaulieu; it had been eleven days since she'd written him. She had been checking her mail box every day, not sure whether he would write or call. She woke more frequently during the night now and often found she'd been dreaming about Mark—confusing dreams in which she couldn't understand what he was saying, his voice and face indistinct. Then she would lie awake for a long while afterwards, wondering why he hadn't responded, and how she could possibly contact him. She became more and more uncertain about their future each day.

One rainy October afternoon she tramped up the muddy driveway to place a brief letter to her mother in the mailbox. Kaia hadn't mentioned in the letter that Mark was the father, although her mother would of course assume that. Her mother merely had to be informed; how she reacted was her problem.

Returning to the cottage, Kaia lowered herself onto the rug in front of the fireplace, lying down carefully on her side. The fire she'd started earlier felt good, warding off the penetrating chill of the wet afternoon. Sometimes she felt faint from lying on her back; Dr. Wisecki had said it was probably due to abrupt blood pressure changes—a bit early in the pregnancy for that to occur, but otherwise normal.

Kaia kept telling herself the baby would be healthy, since she had always taken good care of herself and was eating plenty of tofu, organic produce, nuts, salmon, fruits, whole grains, and yogurt. But there was still the chance of a genetic mishap, which she hadn't discussed with the doctor since he didn't know Mark was her cousin; she'd been afraid to go into it, fearful of scary news and being unable or unwilling to do anything about it.

At the office, she and Chandi had finished all of the work in Roberta's second appeal, so there wasn't any more they could do on her case at the moment, and Kaia started working on a child abuse case involving an alcoholic mother whose kids had been taken away by the county. It seemed like a test for Kaia, to see if she could be an advocate for the mother, when she felt the father probably should be the one raising the children. Lawyers couldn't choose their clients, at least when the court appointed them as counsel on the case.

But one afternoon while Kaia was reading the transcript in the case, she decided she simply couldn't stomach representing abusive or neglectful parents in termination of parental rights cases. She asked Chandi if she could do some work on adoptions instead, saying she wanted to learn something new. Chandi gave her a questioning look but said sure, and handed her a case file along with a hornbook on adoption proceedings in California.

Kaia was now putting in thirty or forty hours a week, but she stopped in the late afternoon if she got tired, knowing she needed to take it easy. The law class took a lot of time, too, but it was helping her understand the law better, and she found it stimulating.

Occasionally she spent an evening with Sig or Chandi, dining at ethnic restaurants in the City, going to foreign films or folk ballet performances, or just having tea or coffee somewhere. Kaia had already gained seven pounds, and it had filled out her face a bit, but her arms and legs were as strong as they were when she'd been jogging every day. She took walks on Mount

Tamalpais and gardened on the weekends; she was in a more settled routine, ready to deal with practicalities, now that her pregnancy seemed to be progressing well.

One night she found herself standing in the living room in front of the bookshelf, her law dictionary open to where she'd inserted Mark's list of states where cousins could marry—the list he'd given her when he was in law school. After perusing it, she decided she would have to do some research to make sure Maine and California were still on the list.

The next afternoon the phone rang while Kaia was in the kitchen stirring some vegetable barley soup on the stove, her hand resting on the taut curve of her belly. She went to the phone and pressed the receiver to her ear.

"I got your letter, Kaia." Mark sounded breathless. There was traffic noise in the background. "How are you doing?"

"I'm fine!" She was practically shouting, ecstatic to hear his voice, and had to sit down at the kitchen table to calm herself.

"So you're a few months along already?"

"Yes. The doctor says it's due in April. I want you to be happy about this, Mark."

"Of course I am. It was just a big surprise, that's all, and I don't understand why you didn't tell me before."

"I just wanted to make sure I didn't miscarry early on."

Mark was silent for several seconds, and then he said slowly, "Things have been so complicated with us, Kaia."

"Complicated?" She made herself take a deep breath. "Why do you say that?"

"You say you want me to be with you. I guess that means you don't want to come to Maine. And you've always said we couldn't have a baby because we're cousins—"

"I've done some research," she interrupted, "and it's not a very big risk."

He was silent for a moment. "I wish I could see you right now."

"Then come."

During another long pause she could hear him breathing.

"Why now?" he asked quietly.

She felt a tremor of anxiety. "This just feels like the right time. We can't postpone the pregnancy. I want you to share all of this with me."

Mark gave a long sigh. "It's such a big change for you. What about your independence and all that?"

"I'm going to keep working as a paralegal, full time for now, and I'm taking a law class. I don't even care how long it takes to become a lawyer, it's what I want to do. But I never wanted to be independent from you." Her hand on the receiver was trembling. "I haven't changed, Mark, I've loved you since I was sixteen. And I want you to be with me and the baby now."

"A sort of package deal, hey?"

She laughed softly. "It does sort of sweeten the deal, doesn't it? The baby's part of you."

"Kaia, I've been through hell lately, with my mother gone and you leaving. This is just a shock."

"I know, Mark."

"And I've got a life out here. I love it here."

"Yes, but we'll need my income, too. I'm earning good money now, and I'll be able to work part-time a few months after the baby's born."

Mark sighed. "So you've rented a house."

"A cottage. Wait until you see it. It's perfect."

"Are you sure about this, Kaia?"

"Of course I'm sure, Mark." Her throat tightened.

"Okay. I can't come right away, though. I have some furniture orders to finish up. It may be a few weeks."

She groaned at the thought of more days or weeks away from him. "Just come as fast as you can," she managed to choke out. "I'm almost four months along."

"I'll see what I can do. I love you, Kaia. I always have."

"I love you, too, Mark."

15

Jean arrived at the condo late one evening and found Kaia's letter waiting for her. Kaia never wrote letters, and Jean was baffled as to what this could be about. She took off her coat, poured herself a Scotch and sat down. She opened the envelope and started reading:

> Dear Mom,
>
> I know this will come as a complete shock to you, but I might just as well just say it.
>
> I'm pregnant, and the baby is due in April. I'm sure you're going to disapprove, but I want this child more than anything. Please don't call or write if you're going to be upset about this or if you think you can influence my decision in any way.
>
> I'm feeling fine, and everything's progressing on schedule. The ultrasound was normal.
>
> Just try to accept this, please.
>
> Love, Kaia

"Oh, my God—what a disaster," Jean said out loud.

Her first impulse was to call her daughter, but she knew Kaia wouldn't listen to anything she had to say. Frantic, Jean dialed Nico's number. She hadn't seen him since the memorial service, but the few times she'd talked to him recently he'd sounded a bit better—less depressed—than he had a couple of months ago. She'd been hoping he would be ready to see her soon, and think about going forward with their relationship. But now this.

As soon as he answered, she asked, "Do you know what's happened with Kaia?"

"Mark told me. He phoned yesterday and seemed quite happy." Nico's voice was astonishingly upbeat.

Jean took a quick, sharp breath. "So it *is* Mark's, then?"

"Who else's would it be?" Nico said rather curtly.

"It could be another man's."

"No way."

"What are they going to do?" Jean could hear her own pitch rising.

"Mark just said he plans to be a part of it, and I didn't ask for details. I'm just trying to absorb the news myself."

"They're way too close to be having a baby together. It makes me sick to think about it."

"Jesus, not that again. I never actually believed that story about Kaia—"

"It's only a possibility, I've always said that."

"You didn't suggest it was a possibility until the two kids started seeing each other. You'd better not say anything to either of them about it. You would destroy their lives by even bringing it up. You can't do that, Jean."

"You would say that. You don't worry about anything, do you, Nico?"

"Look, it's not ideal, the two of them being cousins, but they've obviously decided they want to do this."

"But what about us? It would be awkward, to say the least, for us to be together, if our children have a baby together. And if they get married, God forbid, it would be that much worse."

"After everything that's happened, and Elisa dead for only three months, how can you even think about that?"

"I'm just looking ahead. I know it's a little too soon, and we both need to get through this. But we've survived everything else together—"

"To be frank, Jean, this news from Mark has made me think about things. I want my son to be happy, and of course I want Kaia to be happy." He hesitated before he went on. "This is the first time Mark hasn't sounded miserable since his mother died. Maybe this is a good turning point for all of us."

"What do you mean?"

"Let's just leave it at that. I'm going to pour myself a nice stiff drink now and go to bed. Good-bye, Jean."

After she hung up, Jean tried to think rationally. This was not what she'd anticipated at all, Nico being on their side. Didn't he see how indecent this was, cousins being together in that way, even if they were only cousins and no closer than that? Especially given the situation with Nico and herself—how could they marry if their children married each other and raised a child together? Talk about an incestuous, or at least an improper situation. And what would their colleagues and friends think about the whole situation?

But maybe Kaia would change her mind and decide not go through with the pregnancy after all. That was still a possibility, Jean told herself, though she scarcely believed it. Or perhaps the baby could be adopted by some young married couple—that would be so much better for all of them. She would have to think of a way to broach the subject with her obstinate daughter. Very soon.

"Kaia, I just can't believe it." Jean leaned back in her swivel chair, aiming to keep her tone reasonable, which was extremely difficult under the circumstances. She was the only person at the office on this icy Sunday morning, and she felt edgy from the three cups of coffee she'd drunk before picking up the phone to call her daughter. "Why did you keep this from everyone for so long?"

"You sound angry, Mother."

"No, just incredulous—that you would allow such a thing to happen."

"You probably didn't plan me, either."

Jean had to think for a moment before responding. "That was different. I was married, and your father was not a blood relative of mine."

They were both silent for a few tense moments. Jean now recalled how morose and bitter David had become when she'd told him, a year or so after their wedding, that she didn't want to have children. "You should have told me that before," he'd said tersely, his mouth an ugly sneer. Then, when she'd accidentally gotten pregnant, he'd been thrilled, and had insisted on opening a bottle of champagne to celebrate.

"Anyway," Kaia said, "I'm four months along now. I think it's a boy."

Jean pressed her fingers to her lips, hearing the tenderness and awe in her daughter's voice. She tried to remember how she felt when she'd learned she was pregnant—amazed, certainly, but also panicky. Eventually she'd allowed herself to feel some excitement about it, too.

"Could they tell anything from the ultrasound?" she asked.

"I didn't want to know the baby's sex for sure, so I tried not to look too carefully."

"Is this really what you want?" Jean asked, trying without success to keep the despairing tone out of her voice.

"I'm sure about this, Mom. I've never been happier in my entire life."

Jean hesitated, then said, "Kaia, I would like to ask you something. Is it Mark's? Please tell me it's someone else's."

"Of course it's Mark's, Mother. How could you even ask that? You've never understood how Mark and I felt about each other, have you?"

Jean forced herself to say nothing; actually, she never *had* understood.

"And everything's going to be fine," her daughter added in a sharp tone.

"Oh, no," Jean moaned, unable to stop herself. "You can't go through with this, Kaia."

"Don't say that."

"You can't have Mark's baby."

"There's nothing that will ever take my baby away from me, Mother. You'll just have to live with that."

"But, Kaia—" Jean drew in a long breath and blew it out. She thought back to the moment the doctor had informed her she was three months pregnant with Kaia. It was all rather hazy now, but she had counted back and had concluded it was unlikely that Nico was the father. Throughout Kaia's childhood, Jean had assumed that Kaia was David's—the two of them were alike in their intelligence and in so many other ways. Maybe it was only in recent years that she'd fantasized that Nico could be Kaia's father—something that would be a stronger bond between Nico and herself. Yet the possibility was so remote, she realized, that she had never felt compelled to spell it out to Kaia.

"We should discuss this another time," Jean said. "Soon. Just not now." She had to think this over.

"Let's not. Not if you're going to upset me like this. It's bad for the baby."

After Kaia hung up, Jean pressed her hands to the sides of her face. Kaia would never believe her if she told her that Nico might be her father; and she would never have an abortion this far into the pregnancy. Jean hadn't even had a chance to bring up the adoption alternative. She threw herself back in her chair and in the process knocked over her coffee mug with her elbow.

"Damn!" she shouted as the coffee spilled onto her lap, soaking her white wool pants. Some of it pooled onto the escrow papers on her desk. She stood and grabbed some tissues and wiped off what she could from her pants, and then blotted the mess of wet, stained paperwork. It would all have to be redone. But that was the least of her problems, especially since Nico seemed to be pulling away from her, and she had to figure out what to do about that.

Not wanting to be alone in the cold, empty office any longer, she put on her coat and rushed out onto the slick New York sidewalk, braving the frigid sleet sluicing down on her as she rushed toward her car.

16

While she waited for Mark to arrive, Kaia worked at the office during the week and spent evenings studying, finding time now and then to work on her new stained-glass piece which she'd designed herself in an art-nouveau style. She loved cutting out the pieces of glass, wrapping the edges in copper foil, and laying them on the dining room table over the graph-paper pattern, watching the brilliant colors knit together into the design. She planned to postpone the actual construction until after later, to avoid lead exposure from the solder during her pregnancy and while nursing. There was always so much lead-filled smoke during the process that it was hard to avoid inhaling it, even with the window open and a fan blowing. She wasn't going to take any risks from toxic elements.

On an unusually warm Saturday in late October, Kaia planted daffodil bulbs in the backyard and herbs in terracotta pots on the patio, then hung chimes made of iridescent metal outside the bedroom window. That night the chimes rang in the breeze and became part of her sleep. When she awoke from a pleasant dream, she imagined the baby could hear them and had been dreaming along with her.

Then, reading in the backyard one afternoon, she was elated to feel a fluttering—her baby moving and making himself known. She had a stronger sense now that it was a boy, and she decided without any reference that his name was Peter. It was as if her child had come forth to greet her jubilantly with his name on his lips. The only thing that would have made her more joyful was to have Mark here with her to share moments like this.

One afternoon a letter came from him. Why had he sent a letter? She'd been expecting a call with his flight date. Standing in the kitchen, her heartbeat pulsing in her throat, Kaia ripped it open.

> Dear Kaia,
>
> I'm glad you're having our baby, but I just want to make sure that we do what's best. I'd still like you to consider coming to Maine to live. I need to finish up some projects here before I make any moves, and I'd have to start my carpentry business all over again if I came to California right now. We'll need the carpentry income once the baby arrives, since you won't be able to work full-time then.
>
> Also, there's something else I need to know. Are you thinking we would get married? That's what I've always wanted. After all we've been through, I want you to be sure about everything.
>
> Write me.
>
> Love, Mark

She clamped her hand over her mouth and sat down at the table, rereading the letter several times, trying to understand his hesitancy. Frustrated that she couldn't call him, she found a pen and paper and wrote back:

> Dear Mark,
>
> You sound so unsure, it scares me. Of course I want to marry you. I was just waiting until I finished law school, but now seems like the perfect time. And it's so clear to me what I want—to be with you and our baby.

> I have a good job, and even part-time it will be enough to live on until your business is established here, since we both have some savings. I'll continue to take one or two law classes at a time, and get my law degree eventually. It will take longer that way, but you know how important it is to me to become a lawyer and defend children's legal rights.
>
> Please come soon. We'll work everything out. Maybe we could move to Maine later on, or spend part of the summer there. I'll take the bar exams in both states.
>
> I miss you and want you here with me.
>
> All my love, Kaia
>
> P.S. I just felt our baby move inside of me. I wish you could be here to feel it.

Two long weeks after she sent her letter, a note came from Mark:

> All right, Kaia. I'll work like crazy to finish up my projects and will be there before Thanksgiving. Find a wedding dress that fits.
>
> Love as always, Mark

When Kaia saw Mark striding down the ramp at the San Francisco airport on a rainy Friday night in November, she rushed to greet him in her jogging shoes, stretchy pants and oversized sweatshirt—not very elegant, but he wouldn't care.

"Kaia—" Mark wrapped his arms around her and drew her towards him, resting his hand on the side of her belly as he kissed her repeatedly on the lips.

"We're going to get married in Mendocino," she said, tears running down her cheeks.

"When? This weekend?"

Kaia took his hand as they strolled toward the baggage claim area. "Just as soon as we can. But I can't exactly fit into a slinky dress."

"You don't need a slinky dress." He kissed her again. "I love you the way you are right now."

Sighing, she imagined herself with her little black knit dress stretched over the bump, but then laughed. "I'm not sure I have enough energy to buy a dress right now, or to plan a wedding. Most of the time, I'm in bed by nine o'clock."

As they rode down the escalator, he turned to her. "You can leave everything to me. It's a simple thing, you know. We'll get a justice of the peace, and you can pick any spot you'd like. Just the two of us and a witness or two."

Once they'd stepped off the escalator, she squeezed Mark's hand and stopped to face him. "I guess we could have a party afterwards to celebrate."

"Just so we find a way to get married very soon. I think I've waited long enough." He gently drew her lips into a pout with his fingertips and kissed her again.

"I know you have, Mark, and I can't wait to marry you."

The rain came down heavily as Kaia drove them from the airport, intense gusts of wind batting her VW bug around on the freeway. They finally headed up the driveway and then stepped into her living room, which was toasty and glowing with the soft light from several lamps. After a tour of the cottage, they sat in the kitchen, eating turkey sandwiches and drinking orange juice. Then, when they stood up to clear away the dishes, Mark turned to her and squeezed her shoulders.

"I should have come here sooner," he said. "I'm sorry, Kaia. I just wanted to finish up some things."

She smiled at him. "That's okay. I'm just so happy you're here now."

Even though the cottage was comfortable, Mark knew he would miss the Beaulieu cabin and the sweet-smelling fields around it, the forest-green lushness of northern Maine, and his simple lifestyle. Maybe they could talk seriously about living there part of the year, or having Kaia go to law school in Maine so he could do his organic farming and carpentry there. Later they would have to talk about all of that. First things first.

After they'd finished putting the food away, he kissed her, and they went into the bedroom. As they both undressed, he saw that she was blushing—maybe she was embarrassed to show her curved belly as she pulled her sweatshirt over her head. She took off her bra, releasing her full breasts, and smiled shyly at him. He wondered if sex was going to be different for them now. But all he saw was Kaia with their baby inside—a beautiful sight—and he grinned at her. She spun her bra around on her finger and flipped it into the air, as if she could tell how pleased he was just to look at her. He went over and peeled off her stretchy pants, her hips smooth and familiar under his hands.

She stepped into his arms. "I love you so much, Mark."

"I love you, too, Kaia."

Once they'd climbed under the covers, he pressed his lips against her chest, inhaling a new scent that reminded him of wild sage, and she gently touched the side of his face. He propped himself over her on his outstretched arms, gazing down at her. She reached out, grasping him by the neck to kiss him, and he felt the firmness that was their baby. She drew him in closer with her legs.

Afterwards they lay together sideways, her bottom pressed against him. A few minutes later, when he'd started to doze off, Kaia got out of bed, put on a robe and went into the kitchen to get them something to drink. When she returned, he sat up and took the wine glass from her, then held her arm to steady her as she climbed into bed. She leaned back against the headboard, clasping her mug of tea.

He was thirsty and the cold wine tasted great. They sat quietly for a minute, but then he couldn't help asking, "Does your dad know I'm here?"

"Not yet."

Mark grunted, and then took another drink. What would he expect, after all—that she would rush to tell her father, and that David would welcome him with open arms?

"When will you tell him?" he asked casually. He didn't want any more confrontations with her father. And he wondered, too, if David was going to be much a part of their life.

"Tomorrow. I'll phone him tomorrow and tell him."

Mark drank more of his wine. "I'm sure he'll be thrilled."

"I wouldn't exactly say that." Kaia grinned. "You know my dad. He won't accept anything he doesn't like unless he's forced to."

"I guess I fall into that category—something he doesn't like."

"He'll just have to get used to you as his son-in-law. But I did tell him I wanted you to be with me." She turned to him. "Let's forget about him, okay?"

"I can make you forget." He kissed her gently on the mouth. "Nothing's going to spoil this, Kaia."

She smiled, tears brimming up in her eyes. It made him so goddamned happy to see her like that.

"I guess I'm on emotional overdrive from having you here," she said.

"So when are we getting married?"

"How about this coming week?" she suggested. "We could drive up to Mendocino in the middle of the week, get married, and spend the weekend at an inn. I've wanted to go back ever since we went camping there."

"That'll be great, Kaia. But don't tell your father about that yet. I don't want him barging in and trying to stop us. Okay?"

She reached over, curling her arms around his neck, and kissed him. "Sure, let's wait and surprise everyone."

Mark and Kaia stood close together on the bluff as a frosty December wind blew in from the ocean. The sky stretched out, shimmering a translucent blue. Mark had driven Kaia up and down the Mendocino coast the previous afternoon while she searched for a good spot to get married; he wanted to make it perfect for her. She had chosen this one with its tall pine trees edging the cliff like sentinels.

The justice of the peace, shivering in her long winter coat, stood in front of them, reading the words of the ceremony from an open book, with her clerk beside her to act as a witness. Coming to the end of the ritual, the magistrate told Mark he could kiss his wife. *Wife*. That sounded so great to Mark, and he was thinking that no one would ever again need to tell him to kiss Kaia—he would do it every day of his life.

A blast of wind whipped Kaia's long, red-flowered dress around as dry pine needles showered down on them. Mark stepped closer to her, feeling the rough pine cones underfoot. And then she turned to him with the most incredible, joyful look on her face and gently took his face in her hands. When she glided into his arms, he placed his hand on the side of her taut round belly, as he'd already become accustomed to doing, and kissed her, knowing that now they had everything.

17

The wreath of pine needles on David's front door made Mark remember the black wreath Jean had placed on the door of the Bangor house before his mother's funeral. Something about the wreath had disturbed Mark at the time—Jean's gesture seemed so falsely proprietary. The obvious fact that his father needed Jean with him then, to help with all of the arrangements and for emotional support, hadn't fully penetrated through Mark's misery and grief.

Now it was Christmas Eve, and Mark was acutely aware that this was the first time he had been to the house since he'd left Berkeley over five years ago. He and Kaia hadn't seen her father since Mark had arrived in California. Kaia knocked lightly on the door, then smiled up at Mark, and he blew out a long breath. He laid his hand on her upper back and stroked her long wavy hair. Her blue coat hung open—she'd laughed when she'd put it on, showing him that she couldn't close it over her belly.

She knocked again, harder this time, then pushed open the door. As they stepped into the foyer, footsteps came from the back of the house. A Christmas tree lit with white lights stood in one corner of the living room.

David entered the room and, without a word of greeting, strode over to Kaia and kissed her on the forehead, then drew her into his arms. "Thanks for coming, sweetheart," he said.

Mark tried to intercept David's gaze, but his uncle's face was a blank screen, as if he were willfully blocking out Mark's presence. It was a mistake, coming here. Even though Mark had mentally rehearsed various pleasantries to use for this incredibly awkward situation, he wasn't even going to have a chance to try. Things would never change, but they still had to pretend that things could be peaceable in the family.

David drew back from Kaia, his hands resting on her slender shoulders, and his eyes fell to her belly, prominent under her white blouse; then he peered back into her eyes.

"Hello, David," Mark said, reaching out his hand. His uncle turned, hesitating a second or two before he stuck out a hand for a loose, quick shake.

David cleared his throat. "Hello. It's a little late to say this, but I'm very sorry about your mother. We all miss her."

"Thanks," Mark said.

David nodded, then offered to get Kaia some apple juice.

"That'd be great, Dad."

"Cognac?" David asked Mark.

"Sounds good." At least the man was trying, Mark thought, although David still hadn't cracked a smile.

Mark helped Kaia out of her coat, and they sat on the sofa. It seemed kind of strange to see her as a guest in her father's house, although Mark had always felt that way himself when he was renting the room upstairs.

David came back with their drinks and sat down in his armchair, rotating his glass with his fingertips, his brow furrowed.

Mark raised his glass. "Merry Christmas."

"Yes. The same to you both." David raised his glass in a perfunctory gesture.

Kaia joined in the toast and they sipped at their drinks in silence.

After a minute, David got up and retrieved a box wrapped in white paper from under the tree and handed it to Kaia, his face flushed. "For you."

"Thanks, Dad. I was going to give you yours tomorrow."

"Open it. It's not a Christmas present."

Kaia unwrapped the package and took out a hand-knit baby blanket, then held it to her cheek. "Coral-pink." She met her dad's gaze. "So you want it to be a girl?" she asked.

David shook his head in a quick, self-conscious gesture, and started to say something, but stopped. He took a deep breath. "It's your baby blanket," he said hoarsely. "Your grandmother—my mother—made it for you just before you were born."

"Really?" Kaia said. "I didn't know that."

"I've kept it all these years. I didn't think you'd remember it, even though you dragged it around with you until you were three." David looked a bit sheepish.

"Oh, Dad, I'm sorry I didn't recognize what it was. Thank you so much." She stroked it and turned to Mark. "Grandma died when I was ten. I wish she could be here now."

"Yes, that *is* too bad." Mark glanced at David. "That's something, that you kept it all those years."

David nodded, looking embarrassed, and took a drink of his cognac. "So what's the due date?"

"April 17," Kaia said. "Give or take a week. The first one is usually late, they say."

"First one?" her father said, a bit gruffly.

"Well, this *is* our first, Dad."

"It sounded as if you might be planning to overpopulate the planet."

She turned and smiled at Mark. "We're starting Lamaze classes in February." She squeezed his hand, then turned to her father again. "You could be there for the birth if you want, Dad."

Mark felt his face heating up. He couldn't believe Kaia would ask David to be at the birth; having his grim-faced father-in-law there would ruin it in so many ways.

Kaia glanced at Mark, and must have caught his frown. She looked back at her dad. "You could be pacing outside, anyway, as I'm sure you were while Mom was in labor."

"I certainly was—for hours, in fact. This time I'll be on call, anyway." He gestured toward Kaia with his glass, then took a long drink.

Mark felt relieved. It seemed as if Kaia had just blurted out her offer without thinking, probably because she was touched by David's gift. Mark knew Chandi had volunteered to come for the birth—apparently Chandi had helped her sisters during childbirth in India. Sig had begged off, saying she couldn't stand the sight of blood.

David poured more cognac for Mark and himself and seemed to relax a little as they all talked. Mark wondered if most fathers had a subconscious urge to keep their daughters for themselves and to fend off all claimants. Kaia seemed more sure of herself with her father now, no longer bullied by him, merely keeping a polite, safe distance. That, at least, was a good sign, Mark supposed. And the ridiculous rivalry between David and himself would probably fade with time.

Jean called Kaia on Christmas, but Kaia didn't have much time to talk; she said she was fixing dinner for her father and Mark. That should be an interesting interaction, Jean thought, the two men trying to put up with each other after what had happened in the past. Jean barely had time to wish them all a happy holiday before Kaia ended the call. She and Kaia had only talked once since the wedding, and Jean had been unable to hide her dismay about the marriage. David had been the one to break the news to her initially, the day after the ceremony.

Strolling over to her broad picture window, a glass of wine in her hand, Jean surveyed the snowy Manhattan scene. The *Times* had reported it was going to be well below freezing all day. She felt weary, a rare state for her, and she had no desire to go anywhere; she merely stood there for several minutes, finishing her drink.

Returning to the kitchen, she poured herself another glass, then impulsively picked up the phone and dialed Nico's number. He answered after several rings.

"Nico, it's me. I hope you're having a nice Christmas."

"Oh," he said. "Jean."

She registered the disappointment in his voice. "Are you busy?"

"Not especially, but I was just about to phone the kids. When they called me right after the ceremony, they sounded so thrilled."

It hurt that they'd called both Nico and David, but not her, right after the wedding. Everything was so damned painful lately, but it was Nico's distance that was the most devastating. He'd made no effort to contact her since Elisa's death; Jean had always been the one to call him.

"I just talked to Kaia," she said, trying to sound upbeat. "They're having David over to their place for dinner. She told me the pregnancy is progressing on schedule; she said she just had an ultrasound."

"Another one?"

"I suppose it's routine nowadays. But I have to admit I've been a little worried about the baby. There are so many things that could still go wrong—"

"As I've mentioned before, I don't want to talk about that." He sounded as if he were dealing with an unwanted phone call from a bothersome salesperson.

But he was right, they shouldn't be talking about this on Christmas. Jean made herself take a deep breath. "And how have you been, Nico?"

"To tell you the truth, I'm finding it very difficult, being in the house without Elisa at Christmas. I miss her every day." He sounded choked up, then, after a few moments, said, "And on the other hand, I don't feel like going out and doing anything."

Jean let out a long sigh. "I know what you mean. I've been missing her, too."

Nico was silent—it was a long, hard silence that seemed to indicate his disbelief, or lack of sympathy, at any rate.

Jean closed her eyes, recalling the previous Christmas, which she'd spent with Nico and Elisa at their home, just the three of them. Mark hadn't come, probably because he'd known she was going to be there.

"Nico?" Jean knew she shouldn't bring this up, but she had to take the gamble. "Do you think it's time for us to get together? Possibly for New Year's?"

"I don't think so."

Jean's stomach tightened. It was so damned humiliating, to have to plead like this. "It sounds as if you're not quite ready."

"You're right," he said sharply. "I'm not."

"You sound irritated." She detested the frantic whine in her own voice.

"*Irritated*? That doesn't begin to describe it. I'm furious at both of us. Outraged is more like it." His voice was getting louder and more agitated. "Those idiotic, drunken phone calls to Elisa that night—" He paused, breathing heavily. "We killed her, Jean. Don't you see that?"

Jean gasped. "That's absurd. It was her illness that killed her."

"We should never have done what we did, any of it, the whole affair. And I can't even imagine going on with it after what's happened."

"I know you're still upset, Nico, and I understand that you can't talk about this in a realistic way quite yet. Let's just wait a while—"

"No, let's get it over with now. I'd feel a lot better if I got this off my chest. From now on, our only relationship will be as the parents of children who happen to be married to each other. Nothing more. And that's all it's ever going to be."

"What? You can't mean that, Nico." Jean stifled a sob. "I've given up everything for you—my marriage, those years I could have spent with Kaia when she was a teenager—just to be near you, and to be able to plan a future together, especially after what we'd agreed to in Santa Fe."

"I do mean it," he said in a gruff tone. "And I never made any promises. I'm sorry, Jean."

"Jesus, Nico, after twenty-odd years, you say you're *sorry*?"

"I have many, many regrets. And I've had plenty of time to think about everything during these past few months. I haven't wanted to get together, so that should have been some indication to you—"

"I can't believe you would say something like that, Nico." Jean's voice had ratcheted up, and she was trembling.

"Jesus Christ, Jean. This is the worst Christmas I've ever had, without Elisa. I loved her so much. And I just need to be alone now, that's all I want."

"Please don't make any rash decisions in the state you're in, Nico. It isn't fair to either of us."

She could hear him expel a forceful breath.

"Jean?" he said after a moment in a low, deadly tone. "I need to hang up now. I'm going to call Mark now and wish Kaia and him a Merry Christmas. Good-bye."

Jean hung up and took long, gasping breaths, but stifled any tears. What had she done to deserve this from him? She couldn't grasp why this was happening—Nico's sudden rejection and his blaming her for Elisa's death. He was acting so self-righteous, when he was the one who was drunk the night he'd phoned Elisa and said God knows what to her. She'd only had a few drinks herself, not to the point of intoxication. He was more at fault, too, for starting their affair while he was married; he had betrayed Elisa while she was in the hospital giving birth to their son. Jean's own betrayal of David had come later, after they were married, when she and Nico were so much in love that it was impossible to stop seeing each other.

But then there was her sister to remember, her only sister, whom she had also betrayed. Jean sat hunched, trembling with the effort to contain her fury and pain, her eyes squeezed tight, and grateful only that no one was here to witness her grief and humiliation, and her shame.

18

"You have to remember to take deep breaths, Kaia," Mark said.

The contractions had started at midnight, at first just mild cramping, but by the time Mark had driven her to Marin General at 1:00 A.M., her contractions were more severe and more frequent. Now Mark looked as pale as egg white, especially in the forehead, as if the blood were slowly draining downward in his face. He was usually so stoic, and always knew how to handle every situation—but not this one, clearly. With a stricken look, he bent over and kissed the top of her head, then sat back down in the chair next to the bed.

Chandi sat on the other side of the bed, patting Kaia's arm and smiling sympathetically. Chandi had arrived around 6:00 a.m., and had been here for several hours; she looked a bit wan herself.

Kaia asked Mark to play another cassette on the portable stereo. During the night they'd been playing Brahms, Mozart and Satie, with occasional gaps when Mark had forgotten to change the music. Now he selected Chopin's *Prelude in A Major*, with its bright, languid notes, and it changed the atmosphere in the room, allowing Kaia to breathe with more concentration when the contractions came. Then Debussy's floating *Afternoon of a Faun* came on, surreal and beautiful. Labor, that's all this was, she thought: the hard work of trying to relax in the midst of pain.

Perhaps an hour later, the phone rang and Chandi picked it up, then covered the receiver and turned to Kaia. "It's your dad." Kaia shook her head. Chandi got back on the phone and told him that the contractions were coming more rapidly now, but that Kaia was doing all right.

After she hung up, Chandi said, "He says he'll come as soon as the baby's born."

Kaia nodded.

In the midst of her next painful contraction she felt a flash of anger that her mother hadn't flown out to be here for the birth, and that she wasn't the kind of mother who would want to be present. They'd left messages for her this morning, but she hadn't called back. After the contraction subsided, Kaia turned to look into Chandi's concerned face and grasped her hand.

Soon the waves of pain were coming every few minutes—prolonged twisting bands of pain that blazed through Kaia's body—with insufficient time to recover between contractions. After a particularly acute contraction, Kaia blew out a long breath and, gasping, turned to Mark. He was standing by the side of the bed, squeezing her hand too hard, his face glistening with perspiration.

"Let's get you some pain relief," he said. "I can't take any more of this."

Kaia shook her head, adamant that she did not want to subject their baby to drugs. There was already enough to worry about—the possibility of birth defects, trauma from the birth—so many things that she was trying to push to the back of her mind.

During the next contraction, she became aware of Chandi pressing a cool, wet washcloth against her forehead and Mark stroking her arm until the pain faded. Another powerful contraction seized her and she screamed as its full force slammed down on her. She tried to imagine riding a wave in a sailboat, but it did nothing to ease the pain. Something was wrong, terribly wrong—it shouldn't hurt this much. Mark had a look of near horror on his face.

When the middle-aged nurse came in, she told Kaia, "Breathe through the pain, dear."

"What in the hell does that mean?" Kaia gasped, squeezing her eyes shut. Even taking a breath during a contraction felt excruciating. Kaia began thrashing about, sweating, imagining horrifying things about the baby, and when she opened her eyes, the people around her seemed like dark figures floating around her, their expressions so stricken that she had to shut her eyes again.

Suddenly she could feel her muscles involuntarily pushing downward, and she screamed for help. Dr. Wisecki had only checked on her once, hours ago, and now Kaia was gripped with panic—what if something went wrong and the doctor wasn't here?

After another twenty minutes she felt the baby's head press downward, and finally Dr. Wisecki appeared and mumbled something to the nurse. The nurse ordered her to "Push! Push harder!" Kaia kept squeezing and pressing hard, grunting, and gasping for breath. She kept at it for what seemed like an hour.

Finally, after a viselike contraction that convulsed her whole body, the baby's slippery body ejected into the doctor's hands.

Kaia could see, her heart pounding, that it was a boy, with a bluish head, his little body covered with blood, hanging limply from Dr. Wisecki's hands.

"Oh my God, oh my God," Mark mumbled. He sounded scared, and it terrified Kaia.

What was wrong? The doctor placed the baby's inert body on Kaia's belly while he quickly cut the cord. Utterly spent, Kaia put her hand on her baby's wet hair and touched his slick back. Why wasn't he moving?

A moment later the doctor scooped him up and handed him to the nurse.

"Suction," he ordered, "Oxygen."

The nurse scurried off to the side of the room with the baby.

"Why isn't he breathing?" Kaia demanded. She watched, shaking all over, as the nurse took the baby over to a table and carefully laid him under a lamp. He still wasn't moving. He was dead, Kaia was sure of it.

"There's meconium in the baby's lungs," the doctor said. "The nurse will apply suction. Now I'm going to have to go in and get the placenta out." Over his shoulder he told another nurse to clear the room. "She's bleeding heavily," he added in a low voice.

"I'm staying," Mark said loudly.

"No, you're not," the doctor said. "Everyone out. Now."

Frightened by the grim urgency in the doctor's voice, Kaia desperately wanted Mark to be there with her, but he slowly left the room, his head turned to watch her. She gripped the side railings, then squeezed her eyes shut, moaning as the doctor worked. This couldn't be normal, all this bleeding—she felt lightheaded and was still cramping painfully. She was faint and weak. And still no sound from her baby. She and the baby were both going to die.

A minute later there was a lusty squall and she turned to see if it could possibly be her tiny infant squealing so loudly. His face was scrunched up as he wailed, finally able to show his outrage at the cold hospital air and glaring lights.

"Oh, thank God!" she cried.

After several minutes, the doctor finished, and Mark strode into the room, his face pale as he stared across the room at her. He went over and peered at their baby. Peter was moving his arms and legs as he cried, and Kaia wanted desperately to hold him and comfort him.

Mark came over to Kaia and took her clammy hand.

"I want to hold Peter," she said.

Just then her father came in through the doorway, heading toward her, but Mark held up his hand. "Just give us a minute, okay?"

Her father frowned, but then turned and walked over to the table where the nurse was sponging off Peter. The baby was still crying loudly, pitifully.

Chandi came into the room and took a look at Peter. "Your baby is going to be fine," she called to Mark and Kaia. "He just doesn't like being on the outside."

The doctor washed up and then went over to examine Peter. Kaia pushed herself up carefully and sank against the pillows. Mark took her hand and kissed it.

After examining their baby, the doctor called out, "Your son is in good shape. Everything looks normal."

Kaia sighed, smiling with relief and joy. The nurse wrapped Peter in a white blanket, and called to Mark, "Papa? Would you like to hold your son?"

Mark went over and cautiously took Peter in his arms, then carried him slowly over to Kaia. Their son was still crying fitfully.

"Oh, look at you," Mark whispered to Peter, then gently laid their baby in her arms.

Kaia gazed into Peter's splotchy pink face and stroked his silky forehead with her finger, and his cries subsided. He was so light, a compact bundle with a cap of dark hair. His clear blue eyes seemed to be staring intently into hers, and she felt her tears flowing in a rush of astonishment. This small, new human being was their son, and part of them.

Mark smiled. "You've done it. You're such a genius." The color had come back into Mark's face, and she'd never seen him looking quite so ecstatic, as he gazed at her holding their child.

"You're a genius, too, Mark. Making a baby without even trying."

Her father came over and stood by the bed with his hands in his pockets. "Good job, Kaia. And a boy, just like you've been saying."

Kaia nodded, too choked up to say anything. She handed Peter to Mark so that she could try phoning her mother. When she didn't answer at home or at the office, Kaia left a message, asking her to call. Then she called Sig, who promised to come over right after work and said she couldn't wait to see Peter. She seemed to assume without asking that their child was healthy, and that in itself was a gift. Kaia watched as Mark handed Peter to Chandi, who broke into a delighted smile as she gazed into Peter's face.

A short while later, the nurse came in to help Kaia start nursing Peter, while Mark sat in an armchair next to the bed. Chandi gently steered David out of the room.

Twenty minutes later, after Kaia had finished nursing her baby, her father and Chandi returned.

"Congratulations," her father said rather stiffly to Mark, as he came over to the bed.

Mark nodded, looking tired. "Thanks."

Her father peered at his grandson, who lay quietly in Kaia's arms. "What a cute little fellow," he said. Peter blinked, then closed his eyes, his diminutive fists relaxing.

Kaia handed her baby to her father, and he sat down in a chair next to the bed. She imagined herself that small, being held in her father's arms. She wanted to feel her son's warmth and lightness in her arms again and inhale his lovely scent, but she made herself wait. She laid her head back on the pillow and turned to Mark at the side of the bed.

He leaned forward and took her hand, pressing it once again to his lips.

It was several hours later when Kaia's mother finally called.

"Is everything all right?" she asked immediately. The anxiety in her voice was jarring to Kaia, who had dozed off with Peter asleep in the crib next to her. The others had gone to the hospital cafeteria so that she could rest.

"Yes, Mom. It's a boy."

"So you're fine and the baby's fine?"

"We're doing great, now that it's all over. Chandi and Mark were here during the entire labor. I couldn't have done it without them."

"What? Why was Chandi there? She's your boss, isn't she?" Her mother sounded resentful.

"We've become good friends, and she was so helpful and calm during the birth. I wish you could have been here, too, Mom." She'd invited her mother to be here, but her mother just couldn't take the time off to "wait around for labor to start."

There was silence for a moment, then her mother said, "I wish I could have been there, Kaia. So anyway, what's next?"

"I'll have plenty to do once I'm home with Peter."

"I'll fly out to see him as soon as I can."

"Sure, Mom. You do that. Whenever you can make it."

19

Kaia watched as Sig perused the wedding and baby snapshots displayed on Chandi's dining room table. Kaia was grateful that Chandi had arranged a celebration of Peter's "fifth month in the world," as she'd put it, especially since Kaia and Mark hadn't managed to organize a wedding celebration for themselves. Any free time they had, they spent taking naps, since Peter was still demanding to be fed around the clock and Mark and Kaia were always sleep deprived; organizing even the smallest get-together seemed like a daunting task.

As Sig bent over the table again to examine a photo of the wedding on the Mendocino bluff, Kaia realized that this was the first time her friend's short hair had grown in completely blonde since Kaia had known her; it lay sleek and fine along the curves of her cheeks, and she looked quite different. Her small earrings were geometric designs in cyan and silver metal—no longer the large hoops and painfully thick studs she'd worn in high school. These earrings reminded Kaia of a Frank Stella sculpture she'd once seen.

Sig pointed to one of the wedding shots with her long fuchsia fingernail. "I like this one best—the way you're turning toward Mark, just as the picture's being taken."

In the photo, Mark faced the camera with a solemn smile, his arm around Kaia's shoulders as she lifted her face to him, her flowing, floral-print dress a blur in the stiff gust of wind that had just come up.

"The clerk took the photos, right after we took our vows."

Kaia glanced across the room at Mark, who was jiggling Peter in his arms as he talked to Chandi. Kaia's father stood a few feet away from them, his arms folded tightly across his chest. After a moment, her dad dropped his arms and slipped his hands into and out of his pockets, and then crossed his arms again. He was staring at the floor now, shifting from one foot to the other. Kaia felt sorry for him. Maybe it was Chandi's presence that had him flustered. As far as Kaia knew, they hadn't been seeing each other since their break-up five years ago, although they'd been cordial enough in the hospital after Peter's birth.

"I would never have believed it when we were sixteen," Sig said to Kaia.

"Believed what?"

"That Mark could turn into someone like this." Sig had an odd smile on her face. "But then I was rather biased."

"Really. How so?"

Sig examined Kaia's face. "Once Mark was around, we didn't get to hang out much."

"I'm sorry, Sig. I really am. And I wish I'd been able to see you more often in the past few months, too. We've just been so busy with Peter."

The last time Kaia had seen Sig, over a month ago, was at an art opening in Oakland, where Sig's colorful, abstract paintings were displayed along with the work of other recent art graduates from Cal State Hayward. Kaia didn't have much chance to chat with Sig, with so many people milling around, talking about art and drinking wine, and she had left after an hour, wanting to get home to Peter and Mark.

Now Peter started crying, and Kaia automatically turned to look. Mark stood swaying back and forth, patting their son's back, while still talking to Chandi. Soon their son's cries became mere whimpers, and he laid his head against Mark's chest. Kaia's father stood there silently, a serious expression on his face; he still hadn't found a way to relate to Mark, and his way of dealing with it was to interact with him as little as possible. Kaia was glad, though, that at least he'd come to the party. Would he ever get over losing Chandi? If he would only take a look around, there were other women he could have in his life. But Kaia had the feeling he wasn't so inclined.

Despite a strong urge to comfort her son, Kaia waited to nurse him, since Mark loved holding Peter and taking care of him. Their baby was a robust, huggable little guy, but sometimes Kaia feared some health problem would crop up later, possibly some inherited condition. She tried not to think about it, telling herself that they would just deal with anything that arose.

"Have you talked to your mom recently?" Sig asked.

"She called last week. She wants me to fly with Peter to New York. She's only seen pictures of him."

"I thought she was coming out here for a visit."

"She keeps saying that, but she hasn't found the time. We're saving up for a trip back to Maine. I guess we'll try to see her then."

"If the mountain won't come to Mohammed . . . "

"She's immovable, all right."

Chandi came over, carrying her champagne glass, and bent to look at the photos on the table. "So, wedding pictures?" She picked one up, examining it, then looked at the other snapshots.

"I'm going to visit with your little son," Sig said. She smiled, squeezing Kaia's shoulder, and strolled over to Mark and Peter.

Chandi turned to Kaia. "I don't know if this is the best time to tell you, but I'm sure you'll want to know."

"What?"

"It's about the *Barrett* case." Chandi took a sip of her champagne. "We lost again in the Court of Appeal. And Roberta doesn't want to go on with any more appeals."

"You've got to convince her to keep trying. Maybe the Cal Supreme will give it a full hearing this time instead of just sending it back for retrial."

"Roberta won't even meet with me to talk it over. She's planning to go to up north to pick cherries again with Miguel."

Kaia sighed. "I don't want her to give up without fighting all the way."

Chandi laid her hand on Kaia's arm. "It's her life, Kaia. She may realize she's not such a great mother for those kids. I think you have to put aside what you think she wants and look at what she's actually saying she wants."

"I hate the idea of leaving the kids in foster care. If I do this kind of work in the future, I'll only represent the children. They're the ones who really need help."

Kaia turned and saw Sig sitting on the sofa with Peter perched on her lap. Kaia's breasts were aching, and she needed to feed him, though he had stopped crying now and was reaching for one of Sig's earrings. Mark had settled into an armchair near them, and he turned toward Kaia and smiled.

She returned his smile, then called to Sig, "Shall we have some of your cake now?"

"I'll go get it," Kaia's father said immediately, heading for the kitchen, obviously relieved to have something to do.

Kaia turned back to Chandi. "I'm thinking of coming back to work soon, but only part-time."

"Well, that's good news. There's plenty you can do. What about law school?"

"I'm taking a Torts class now, so I'll only be able to work a few hours a week."

Chandi frowned slightly. "What are you and Mark going to live on, if I may ask?"

Kaia chuckled. "You sound like Dad. Mark is doing some carpentry and restoring antiques. We have some savings, too.

And I've been designing some stained-glass pieces, so who knows, I might be able to sell some of them later on. I mainly want to focus on Peter for now."

"Sounds pretty reactionary."

Kaia laughed. "We may eventually live at the cabin year round, at least for a few years. Mark's not exactly thrilled about living in Marin County. Our friend Monty started a poverty law practice in Beaulieu, so I might be able to work with him later on. He's fighting for land rights for the Native American tribes in Maine."

"But you'd be giving up a lot, moving back there. And I'd miss you so much. Don't forget, I'm Peter's unofficial auntie."

"I'd miss you, too, Chandi. But Mark would be so much happier living in the country and doing his carpentry and farming out there. I'd like it, too, I think, if we modernized the cabin. And we'd come back to visit often."

"I would certainly hope so. Anyway, you're not thinking of leaving any time soon, are you?"

"Not for a while. Carl is letting us rent the cottage long-term." She glanced across the room, her eyes lighting on Peter, still on Sig's lap. "But it would be much cheaper to live in Maine, and it would be worth it to spend time with Peter when he's young."

"Anyway, I'm glad to hear you'll be coming back to work. Shall I find some office space for you next week?"

"That would be great," Kaia said, and gave her friend a hug before heading over to Mark and Peter.

Mark looked up as David entered the room carrying the chocolate cake, which was ablaze with five candles—one for each month of Peter's life. Sig had made the cake in the shape of a log cabin. David was smiling broadly, Mark noticed, rather than wearing the glum, disapproving expression that often appeared on his face, at least when Mark was around. David set the cake on the dining room table, and Sig carried Peter over to take a look. Mark took Kaia's hand and they joined the others at the table.

Peter's eyes were wide, taking in the dazzling candles, his hands flapping with excitement. Chandi, who was standing next to Sig, peered into Peter's face, then bent more closely toward him. She stared intently for another long moment. "They're like David's!" She glanced across the table at David. "Peter's eyes! They're slightly different shades. The right one is darker, more gray than blue, exactly like David's. Isn't that lovely?"

Mark went over to Sig and reached for Peter, then held him up. "Let's see about that." Kaia and Mark both studied their son's eyes.

"You're right, Chandi," Kaia said. "And I thought I was imagining things, but it's more distinct now."

"One *is* a little darker," Mark said, then glanced at David. His father-in-law's eyes were in fact different shades of blue, just like Peter's, the right one a little darker than the left. David raised his eyebrows, as if in surprise. Why wouldn't David expect some likeness?

But something about it made Mark a bit uncomfortable; he had the fleeting thought that he would now be seeing David's eye color in Peter forever.

David smiled at Kaia. "Well, at least I can say I've had some influence."

"I wonder when your widow's peak will show up," she said, and everyone laughed.

"Someone had better blow out the candles for Peter," Chandi said. "They're melting on the frosting. David?"

He took a deep breath and leaned forward, blowing out all of the candles.

As Chandi cut and served the cake, Mark recalled what his mother had written in her journal about Kaia's turquoise eyes, and about Nico's love being vested in Kaia. He had puzzled over it each time he'd read it. Mark still hadn't shown anyone the journal, although Kaia knew he had it. He should probably burn it, as his mother had asked, but it had proven impossible so far;

he had read and re-read parts of it in the months after her death, wanting to remember her, and hoping to understand what she had gone through.

It came to him now that his mother, in her flights of delusion, might have thought Nico could be Kaia's father. God, what a terrible thing for her to imagine. Had his mother actually thought that? Maybe something Jean or Nico had said on the phone that night had made her believe that. Had Elisa been tortured with that possibility, harboring that awful idea in her mind when she died? Mark fervently hoped not.

Kaia was searching Mark's face, as if trying to read his thoughts. He put his arm around her, kissing the top of her head while holding Peter in his other arm.

Then Kaia began to laugh quietly, and buried her face in Mark's shirt as she laughed harder, something between sobs and laughter, as the others watched her. Mark wondered if, in the past, something had put the same idea about Nico in Kaia's head as well.

Kaia wiped her eyes, and Mark whispered softly in her ear, "Are you happy now?"

"Perfectly," she whispered back.

Then Kaia took Peter into her arms, kissing each cheek, and their son broke into a jubilant smile as he reached up to touch her face with both of his small hands.

20

Kaia held a sheet of clear, textured glass up to the window and inspected it for flaws. Her mother stood a few feet away in the light-filled garden studio in the backyard. Kaia tried to visualize how the glass would look as a frame for the intricate leaf design with its background of indigo glass. She turned back to the table, still holding the large sheet of glass upright in front of her and running her eyes over it. Through the glass she could see the blurred features of her mother's face—the downturned mouth, the eyes like gray rain.

Her mother had arrived two days ago, flying out from New York to see Peter for the first time. He was over seven months old now. The few times she'd called Kaia since the birth, her mother had promised to visit, and Kaia had begun to think she would never make it to California to see her grandson. Nico hadn't been out to see him yet, and Kaia and Mark had been forced to postpone their trip back East for lack of funds.

Kaia set the glass on the table over the full-scale, three-by-five-foot design she had drawn on graph paper. "If I finish cutting the pieces out today, I can start soldering tomorrow," she said.

"What's the rush?"

"I can only work when Peter's napping, or when Mark can watch him for a while."

"I thought we could go into Sausalito for lunch, or do a little shopping, just the two of us."

"Sure. But I'll take Peter along. I should be finished working in an hour or so." Kaia wanted to spend as much time with her son as possible, especially now that she was taking a law class and working as a paralegal two mornings a week. She thought of her young son asleep in his crib now, with Mark close by, watching over him; Mark sometimes liked to lie down on the sofa next to the crib while Peter napped.

Kaia leaned over the table, lining up her steel ruler on the smooth side of the glass. Positioning the glass cutter next to the ruler, she made a long swipe, producing the high-pitched, scraping sound that meant she'd cut deeply enough.

Straightening up from the table, she said, "I'm installing this piece in place of that bottle-glass window in front."

"A stained-glass piece like that would certainly add value to the house. But you're still renting, aren't you?"

"Yes, but Carl said it was fine to install any stained glass we wanted, since he's not coming back to California for another year at least. We can remove it later, as long as we install regular glass when we leave. Anyway, Carl says he may be retiring in Australia, so we might be able to stay here even longer."

Glancing up, Kaia took in her mother's dyed brown hair, and her makeup that appeared masklike in the November light filtering through the studio window. Somehow, despite the web of wrinkles across her mother's face, there was a slightly softer, chastened aspect to her expression now. She probably still missed Nico, although she talked about making a new start for herself. Since she'd arrived, Mark had stayed out of her mother's way, trying his best to be neutral, but he'd seemed a bit churned up since her arrival.

Kaia snapped off the scored piece of glass on the edge of the table and set it aside. She lined up the ruler for another cut, then looked up at her mother, who had picked up the small color sketch of the project and was studying it.

"Your design is quite stunning," her mother said. "I like the leaves, the organic motif. I'm thinking of going into the hotel business and might be able to use some stained glass. There's an inn for sale in Seacrest, on the Oregon coast."

Kaia made another squeaking cut in the surface of the glass. "Really? An inn?" She envisioned something elegant and expensive. Kaia preferred funky old houses transformed into bed-and-breakfast places, or cabins overlooking a river, or campgrounds where you could reach your site only by foot—no cars within miles, no amenities, no radios playing. She and Mark had gone camping in September, taking Peter along; the three of them had slept in a tent in a state park set back in the coastal hills. They couldn't afford to stay at a fancy inn even if they wanted to.

"It's a great opportunity, at an incredible price," her mother added.

Kaia examined the line she'd scored in the glass, then slid the glass to the edge of the table and snapped off the new piece. "Would you move to Oregon, then?" she asked.

"I'm not sure. Somewhere on the West Coast, I suppose, so I could manage the property. Anyway, I'm planning to rent a car and drive up to Oregon to take a look at the inn. I'll leave on Friday."

"Are you serious?"

"Of course I'm serious. Why wouldn't I be?"

"So you actually have an appointment to see the inn?"

"I've talked to the realtor. I can go any time."

Kaia looked down at the glass and lined up her ruler for the next cut. "You should take your time, enjoy the scenery on the drive. That is, if you don't have to get back to work right away." So that was why her mother had flown out here. It had taken a business opportunity for her to come to see her grandson. And the thought of her mother re-locating to the West Coast made Kaia nervous; she wasn't sure if it would work to see her more often. There were still things they had never talked about, never resolved, if they ever could be resolved.

She finished cutting the last clear piece and set the sheet of glass aside, then laid a piece of hunter-green glass over the graph-paper design. She began cutting out leaf shapes, trying to concentrate on the delicate work, but found herself distracted by her mother's presence, and the cuts weren't as precise as she would have liked.

Her mother watched her for a few minutes, then picked up the sketch again. "I'd really like you to make one of these for me. Maybe I'll buy the inn, and then you could make a stained-glass window for it. I wish you could drive up there with me and take a look."

"I'm kind of busy these days, Mom. I really can't take any time off right now."

Kaia caught the disappointment that was a frequent aspect to her mother's face since she'd arrived—it clung to her like flimsy nylon cloth, giving off static electricity.

"Maybe we can do something like that when Peter's older," Kaia said.

But she wasn't sure that was something she would ever do with her mother.

That evening, Mark sat with Peter on the kitchen floor, handing him wooden blocks, while Kaia prepared dinner. Peter could sit up now and was starting to crawl. He liked to take a block, examine it intently, and then drop it when Mark offered him a different one. Mark had made the twenty-six blocks from scraps of oakwood and painted each one with a letter, and it pleased him to watch Peter play with them. Jean was sitting at the kitchen table, drinking Chianti and telling them about her recent trip to Sedona, Arizona, where there was reasonably priced real estate and a low crime rate. She said she wanted to go back there soon to see about buying a duplex as an investment.

"I thought you were looking at an inn up in Oregon," Kaia said, turning away from the stove to glance at her mother.

"I may just buy property here and there. I may move back to the West Coast eventually."

Peter reached for Mark's glass of Chianti, which sat on the floor, and Mark quickly grabbed it and drank what was left of the wine. His son let out a sharp cry of protest, and Mark began stacking blocks between them, getting Peter's attention back to his play. Mark hadn't anticipated Jean moving back to the area. He wasn't sure he liked the sound of it. Kaia seemed uneasy since her mother's arrival, and he still found Jean hard to take, given the past history.

He glanced at Kaia, who was humming while she cooked. He loved the way she often sang or hummed as she went about the house, smiling to herself. Even though she was busy these days, he'd never seen her happier, and she always had plenty of time for him and Peter. Mark got up and sauntered over to the counter, and she smiled up at him. He kissed her, then took a deep breath, inhaling her warm scent mixed with the aroma of the sautéed greens with garlic. He went over to the sink to wash the wild mushrooms he'd picked earlier in the woods when he'd gone hiking with Peter on his back. Mark had needed to get out of the house, away from his overbearing mother-in-law, and he'd been missing the lush, dark-green countryside of Maine, with its moist summer heat that baked him like a hothouse tomato. But it would be cold now in Beaulieu, the snow piling up on the cabin roof and covering the surrounding fields and hills. He missed that, too.

Kaia went over to Peter and picked him up, kissing him on the neck and face and twirling around as he laughed and flexed his legs against her stomach. He was getting to be such a sturdy little guy, Mark thought, and he wondered how long it would be before he would be walking.

Jean stood and took Peter from Kaia, hoisting him into the air. Peter chortled, his cheeks flushed, and she lowered him into her arms. Elisa would have been thrilled with her grandson,

Mark thought, and Peter would have adored her. But he tried not to dwell on the fact that Jean was the only grandmother his son would ever have.

After their dinner of vegetables, tofu and brown rice, Kaia put Peter to bed, and they all sat in the living room talking and drinking some of the Spanish sherry Jean had brought. As Jean went on about her various plans, Mark told himself he had to try to accept his mother-in-law, in spite of the past; it would be better for Peter and for everyone in the family in the long run.

"You sure have a lot of lotions and potions, Mom," Kaia said, late that evening, as they stood facing the wide mirror in the bathroom. It really was amazing—at least a dozen of her mother's miniature jars lined the counter.

Her mother leaned forward and wiped off her eye makeup with a practiced motion of her hand, then glanced at Kaia in the mirror. "I've somehow collected a lot of them, and I figure I might as well use them."

Kaia offered a tired grin. "Sometimes I use Oil of Olay and Preparation H." It was late, and Mark was in already in bed, waiting for her. Peter had been asleep for hours.

Her mother laughed. "My friend Darla keeps telling me that androgyny is the key to happiness for women. Not aspiring to femininity."

"It's not something anyone aspires to, really. Anyway, the main thing is to find passion in your life."

Her mother sighed. "Passion, shmassion."

"It's all that matters." Surely her mother hadn't forgotten what passion felt like, how it made everything else worthwhile.

"What, sex?" Her mother sounded tired. "I don't know if that's so important, at my age."

"You can have passion for—"

"Family? Your children, your work, your friends? Of course that's true." Her mother regarded herself sadly in the mirror, pulling with her fingertips at the bunchy skin under her eyes.

"Mom, there's something I've wondered about. I hope you don't mind me asking this." Kaia held her breath as she thought about how to phrase this.

"Sure, what is it?" Her mother turned around to hang up a hand towel, taking a few moments to smooth it out. Then she turned back to meet Kaia's gaze in the mirror.

Kaia exhaled. "Did you ever think that Dad might not be my actual father?"

Her mother took a sharp breath, her expression transforming into a pained frown.

Kaia found it hard to believe she had actually uttered such a thing; it seemed blasphemous. But the idea kept cropping up in her mind, ever since her mother had told her with such insistence, when Kaia was pregnant, that she couldn't have Mark's baby. And years ago, her mother had tried so desperately to keep her away from Mark. "I'm sorry to ask, Mom, and I know it's probably ridiculous, but I've been wondering." She turned to face her.

Her mother crossed her arms. She looked down, shaking her head, before meeting Kaia's eyes. "I told myself there was a very remote possibility of that. I hadn't thought it possible when I was pregnant with you."

Kaia gasped. "Why didn't you tell me?"

Her mother's brow was furrowed, her lips pursed. "I thought you understood, that time I went to Berkeley and told you about the affair. You seemed so horrified, and then you wouldn't talk to me for a long time after that. And I assumed you had stopped seeing Mark because of it."

"You didn't guess that we were still seeing each other while I was in college?"

"I had no idea. You were on opposite coasts, and I thought it was over. Even when you went to Elisa's that one time at Thanksgiving and Mark was there, Nico told me nothing was going on between you two. And there didn't seem to be, until you flew back to stay with Mark at the cabin. Even then, I thought Nico had told you of the possibility, although he never really believed it was possible. Then you went back to California, and there was Elisa's suicide to contend with, and we were in shock and couldn't deal with anything else. When I found out you were pregnant, you were already four months along. I couldn't say anything then. And in retrospect, it was extremely unlikely."

"We could have had a paternity test. Anyway, we never would have fallen in love if we were . . ."

"Who knows?"

"Why didn't you tell Mark?"

"Nico warned me not to tell Mark. He was afraid Mark would hate him to even suggest anything like that. Anyway, it's clear all that worry was for nothing. Peter has David's eyes. So that's that."

"So I wasn't completely crazy to think of that."

Her mother shook her head. "I'm so sorry, Kaia. I know I did everything wrong. I was so in love with Nico I couldn't think straight—you know what that's like." She took a Kleenex and blew her nose, and then stood there, her eyes a bit red, staring at Kaia.

After a few seconds, Kaia stepped forward and put her arms around her mother, wondering if things would ever truly be all right between them.

In any case, this was the mother Kaia had been given, and she was her mother's only child. But there were other people in the world who would love her the way she wanted, and whom she could love unreservedly.

When Kaia went into the living room the next morning, Mark was standing on a ladder outside the window, knocking the old bottle glass out of the frame. Chunks of glass flew onto the tarp that covered the floor. Rays of sunshine shot through the space instead of the former dim light diffused through the old bottle glass window.

"That's great!" she shouted. "Just leave it like that!"

Mark bent his head down, grinning at her through the broken window.

Her mother entered the room wearing an aqua pantsuit, her cropped hair hanging damp around her neck. Kaia had heard her showering earlier while Mark and she were drinking their coffee and feeding Peter his cream of rice in the kitchen.

Her mother gingerly picked her way through the rubble in her white sandals, her lacquered toenails like Bing cherries. Kaia got Peter from his playpen and carried him outside; her mother followed her and together they watched Mark work. Once he'd finished knocking out the old glass, Kaia gave Peter to her mom to hold, and helped Mark carry the new stained-glass window from the studio. The window wasn't as rigid as Kaia would have liked, since she'd had to dispense with the usual side supports in order to fit it into the metal frame embedded in the wall.

Her mother went to get Peter's stroller and set him in it, a safe distance from the house. Mark climbed the ladder, holding the new window from the top with his gloved hands, while Kaia and her mother held it from either side, walking it upward with their bare hands. Her mother placed one foot on the bottom rung of the ladder, bracing herself.

"Take a grip lower down," Mark told them in a calm voice. He lifted the window higher, nearly into place.

"Watch out, Mom," Kaia said, "the edge is sharp."

"Wait, I have to get a better grip," her mother said.

The glass began to slip downward in Kaia's hands. "Don't let go, Mom!" she shouted.

"Just help me raise it into the frame now," Mark said.

Kaia's side of the window slipped down another inch or two, and she felt a searing pain in her right hand. For a few seconds she strained to keep the glass from sliding further down. Finally, with a joint effort, the three of them managed to lift the window into place.

Kaia let a chestful of air escape. "For a moment there, I thought it was going to break—it was starting to bend." She was aware of the pain in her hand and saw that her hand was rapidly dripping blood onto the ground. "Damn. I should have found some work gloves for Mom and me."

Mark climbed quickly down the ladder, frowning, and took a close look her hand. "That's a bad cut. Let's go inside."

"I'll take care of it," her mother said. "You can finish up out here, Mark. We don't want that window to fall out."

Mark peered anxiously into Kaia's face, but her mother took her by the wrist and raised her bleeding hand high into the air. Mark rushed ahead and opened the front door for them. Kaia and her mother stepped inside, just as Peter began to cry.

It was nearly dusk when Mark and Kaia took a hike through the woods near the cottage, leaving Peter with his grandmother. They walked uphill for close to an hour before reaching the level part of the trail where it widened and led to a lookout deck. Kaia sprinted ahead and ran up the steps to the deck. She was scanning the lavender hills and silvery edge of ocean when Mark came up behind her and laid his hand on her upper back. They stood taking in the view for a while, then climbed down from the deck and wandered over to a grassy area, where they sat under a redwood tree. Mark leaned back against the massive trunk, with Kaia next to him.

"Is your hand hurting very much?" he asked.

"Not too bad. Mom did a good job cleaning it up and made me take some Tylenol."

"I heard you and your mom talking in the bathroom last night."

"We were clearing up a few things." Kaia let out a long sigh. "Being with my mother has always been difficult."

He took her bandaged hand and held it carefully on his palm.

She tried to recall what her mother was like when Kaia was small. Even then, affection and praise from her mother had been scarce, but her father had always been there for her, ready to hold her on his lap or take her places—to the park to feed the ducks, or for ice cream or a movie. Just the two of them. Why had it been that way? Why had her mother let that happen? Kaia thought about how bereft her mother had to feel this past year, with Elisa and Nico both absent from her life—short on affection, undoubtedly, and struggling to glean whatever happiness or pleasure she could for herself. It must have been a lonely, painful time for her.

"I wish I knew how to love my mother the right way," Kaia said.

"I think you know how to love very well." Mark smiled, then leaned over and placed his hand on her cheek and kissed her. After a moment, he drew back, studying her face.

"So do you, Mark." She bent to kiss his hand, then looked up at him again.

Her injured hand was beginning to throb, and she rested it on her lap. For years there would be a scar to remind her of this day—it would become part of the texture of her past. Leaning her head back against the tree trunk, she closed her eyes and envisioned the new window the three of them had managed to put into place. She was happy she had salvaged several of her favorite pieces—an iridescent piece and a few pieces of curved, beveled glass—from a failed lamp project, and incorporated them into the new window design. In the same way, she realized, she was beginning to gather up the shards of her past and put them together in new, unexpected ways. And she saw, too, in her mind's eye, the swirling indigo background that gave a certain cohesiveness to the design and caused the dazzling, luminescent colors to leap out from the new, solid, stained-glass window.

ACKNOWLEDGMENTS

I would like to thank all of those who so generously offered their feedback and advice regarding this book, with special thanks to Bharti Kirchner, Gail Kretchmer, Leslie Patheal, Jo Ann Heydron, Josephine Kendra Ellis, Susan Samuels Drake, Sandy Raney, Barbara Fuller, Kim Mortimer, Lee Holt, Emily Risberg, Vicky Mylniec, Margaret Kinstler, Karen Ackland, Kirby Wilkins, Jerry Kay, Cathy Warner, Doreen Devorah, Carol Foote, Stephanie Howard, Cyndie Weber, Linden McNeilly, Erica Scheidt, Alexa Hammer, Asia Kang, Evan Mason and Phyllis Lichtenstein; and all of my other colleagues, friends and family members for all of their help and encouragement, and especially my husband, Geoffrey for his constant love and support.

CPSIA information can be obtained at www.ICGtesting.com
Printed in the USA
LVOW06s1206280514

387570LV00001BA/20/P